THE FALL OF LINDA WATERS

THE
FALL OF
LINDA
WATERS

R.E. KURZ

SONCATA PRESS
NEW YORK, NEW YORK

This edition first published in 2025 by Soncata Press LLC.
With offices at:
340 West 57 Street, Suite 2C
New York, NY 10019
www.soncatapress.com

Hardback ISBN: 979-8-990851-06-1
Paperback ISBN: 979-8-992645-29-3
eBook ISBN: 979-8-218461-90-4
Audiobook ISBN: 979-8-990851-09-2

Library of Congress Control Number: 2025933650
Cover Design: Howard Grossman
Author Photo by R.E. Kurz 2024

TABLE OF CONTENTS

For everyone who's felt the same way.

And Michael N. ;)

ONE

THE BEST DAY EVER

Linda's lungs stung from the brisk air that filled her nostrils and coated her tongue. It had been a while since she felt any semblance of motivation to run outside, especially in the morning. But avoiding being late to school and therefore drawing unwanted attention to herself was a strong motivator for her crying leg muscles. She attempted to take deep breaths as she ran down the aging street (well, running was a strong word—perhaps walking with intention) toward her small town's public high school, Larch Academy. Linda had spent way too long trying to clear her head in the forest after what happened at breakfast.

When she had walked into the kitchen earlier that morning, the local *Daily Bugle* newspaper was strewn onto the laminate counter. "ONE YEAR ANNIVERSARY OF TOWN TRAGEDY" emblazoned the front page above two photos of smiling teenage girls. Linda's stomach had lurched like she was about to puke. She turned away, but their faces still burned in her mind. One of the girls used to be her best friend. Her name was Kelsie Robertson, and she was dead.

"Good morning, sweetie!" Linda's mom said as she walked back into the kitchen. "How are you doing? Did you sleep well?"

"Fine," Linda mustered, walking over to the fridge. She was thankful that she couldn't see her own expression. *Everything will be fine*, she lied as she forced herself to open the fridge door. It's not like it would bring her friend back to think that way. *Just get the orange juice*, Linda ordered herself, but her body wasn't responding. She stared vacantly at the crowded shelves.

"Oh, shit," Linda heard her mom mutter behind her. "I'm so sorry, Linda, I didn't even think about the newspaper. Your dad dropped it on the counter right before he got in the shower, he was in a hurry," she yammered apologetically.

"It's fine, Mom," Linda answered as she absently reached for sliced ham and closed the fridge. She heard the newspaper rustling, likely as her mom took it away.

"Mike!" her mom yelled, walking out toward the living room, which was uncharacteristically gloomy from the overcast weather outside. *Always a good omen for a Monday*, Linda thought.

It wasn't until Linda sat at the worn kitchen table that she groaned. She finally realized that she had ham instead of orange juice. If her siblings were still at home instead of away for their college semester, probably already suffering through midterms or hangovers or something given that it was early October, they would've ribbed the crap out of her. At the thought of her annoying older sister, Emily, Linda mustered up enough spite to return to the fridge for her traditional breakfast.

"Why is there ham on the table?" Linda's mom asked, evidently reappearing after reaming out her father.

Linda sighed. "I was thinking of mixing it up," she lied.

❦

A blaring car horn tore Linda from the memory. She looked up to see the grille of a silver SUV and a very peeved driver staring down at her as he slammed the horn again.

"Hey kid, watch it! I could've killed you!" the red-faced man yelled before ducking his head back into the car and driving away.

Linda's heart raced. Images of Kelsie flashed through her mind. She still remembered what her coffin looked like, the handles gleaming with silver that would tarnish. The smell of the funeral home. The lilies of innocence way too pungent and clashing with old perfume. Linda felt sick.

She needed something to ground her, a small part of her brain re-minded her. Before it was too late. Linda surveyed her surroundings as her mind swirled, struggling between the past and present. It felt like her brain would split in two. Then a few pieces of paper caught her eye, just a couple paces in front of her. Linda dove for them, vaguely aware that she probably looked possessed. To her horror, as she stood back up, a neighbor stared at her from the perch on his deck. "You alright over there?" he called.

Linda flushed violently. "Yeah," she sheepishly called back as she quickly resumed walking toward her school. She turned her attention down to the looseleaf paper gathered in a paper clip. Thankfully, they had writing on them, so her loss of dignity wasn't entirely fruitless.

In a time long, long ago, there was a fight for power between nature's Queen and her lowly servant, an elf. The elf's only companion was a boy who had powers over frost and snow....

Linda rolled her eyes. It looked like it was written by a twelve-year-old. *What is that description?* But she folded the papers and crammed them into her coat pocket anyway as she raced toward the looming brick edifice of Larch Academy. Linda groaned as the metallic bell resonated through the still, chilly air. She wouldn't be able to stop at her locker if she wanted to make it on time for homeroom attendance, meaning she would be sweating in her down coat. It was going to be the worst day ever.

Linda landed in her painfully unyielding desk chair. Ms. Nory, their dark-haired and mild-mannered homeroom teacher, inhaled deeply to begin treading through the letter "J," which held the multitudinous rendi-tions of "Johnson." After Linda felt herself relax, sure that she blended in with the other morning stragglers, she quickly turned her attention to the now-wrinkled but still-intact papers. She began to read:

The elf put their trust in the boy, shared their plot against their mistress with him, and invited him to aid them, for he was close with the Queen.

"All of my mistress' power lies in her Amber. If we take possession of it, we can rule the world," the elf told the boy.

"Give me time to think about it," he said. "It's a big decision." For many days, he considered the price of power, and the price of saving the Queen, who acted as his sister. He had even attempted to convince the elf to change their mind about the whole matter, but his attempts were futile.

Finally, he requested to speak with the Queen, privately. When she agreed, he informed her of his conversation with the elf, and he asked her what should be done.

"We must set a trap," the Queen decided. "And you will have to say yes."

"John Mason?" Ms. Nory asked, breaking Linda's focus.

"Here," John said quietly. He sat at the back of the room, in the corner by the old wooden bookcases nestled under the large aging windows. He was new to the school, having appeared only a week or two prior at the tail end of September. Linda glanced back at him. John looked the same as usual, sitting quietly and looking out the window into the Maine autumn morning. The bright morning light emphasized the contrast between his pale skin and pastel blue hair and his perpetually dark blue apparel. Every day, he wore dark denim jeans, an unzipped navy hoodie with a blue-grey t-shirt underneath, and his black high-tops.

His hard, blue eyes suddenly looked at her. Linda's face grew warm from being caught spacing out and she turned back toward the front of the yellow room. She refocused on her morning treasure to distract herself.

The boy did as he was told, and anxiously agreed with the elf, telling them where he would place the Amber for them to retrieve. The elf had been too thirsty for power to question his plan. The trap was set, and the boy wished it had never happened.

As planned, the elf left their mistress's palace. They traveled to the world of mortals, to a small clearing of moss in the center of a deep forest uninhabited by any humans. In the center of the bed of moss sat a wooden stool, where the

Amber waited. Suddenly, before the elf could reach it, the boy came out of the shadows of the surrounding trees.

"This is a trap. Please do not try to steal the Amber, I do not want to hurt you," the boy said, his voice shaking.

The elf's small body began to fill with rage. "You betrayed me?" they demanded, only to be answered with silence. "I don't care, the Amber is mine." They strode over to the stool.

Beings came out of the shadows, and the moonlight exposed the Queen of Nature and two more elves: one clad in pink, the other clad in green.

"Mona, be careful," the boy called to the Queen, but she ignored him. Vines had sprung up out of the ground and wrapped themselves around the rogue elf at the stool, immobilizing them.

"Now!" the Queen ordered the boy, and the boy swiftly went over to the elf wrapped in vines.

"I'm sorry," the boy said quietly, "I tried to warn you, but you would not listen."

"We can still rule the world, you just need to take the Amber. You have one last chance at power."

The boy hesitated, glancing at the gemstone. It was not but a foot away from him. "I do not want that power."

The elf struggled against the vines and tried to reach for the Amber one last time, but their limbs began to freeze in place.

"I'm sorry," the boy whispered. He looked away.

"Saying 'sorry' cannot mend the damage," the elf said, watching a tear escape from the boy's eye, the last thing they saw before they were completely frozen in ice.

Linda was suddenly aware that the room had quieted down, and she looked up. "No Arnold Raymann?" Ms. Nory inquired, peering around through her deep brown horn-rimmed glasses. "No Arnold Raymann. Nina Rodriguez?"

"Here!" Nina said too enthusiastically, raising her hand. She was a sweet brunette who was outspoken about wanting to be on Broadway someday. The blind optimism always made Linda bristle. Life was not that kind. Linda looked back down at the story. But nothing was left on the page, and the last paper in the packet was blank. She groaned at its limitations.

"Linda Waters?" Ms. Nory asked.

"Here," Linda answered. She raised her hand just enough to help the teacher find her, then she brought her hand back down so quickly that she hit her funny bone on the edge of the desk. She winced, struggling to hold back lots of curses directed at the desk's maker. Electricity shot through her nerves. She hated attendance and the whispers, the feeling of eyes on her. She hated that everyone in her 400-person school knew what happened. She hated seeing all the people that were spared by the hand of Death while she was alone, her desolate future stretching out before her. She could see the pity on their faces when they glanced at her. Being at school was always a challenging reminder that her best friend Kelsie was... elsewhere... that she wouldn't see her in between classes or at lunch... her eyes began to sting. Linda shook her head. The windows lit up slightly as the sun peeked through the hoary clouds. She looked outside, wishing she was closer to the window so she could lose herself while she watched the autumn leaves rustle.

"Sylvia Wong?" Ms. Nory asked.

"Here," Sylvia answered from somewhere in the back of the room.

Ms. Nory smiled at her, looking as annoyingly cheery as her pastel yellow and purple patchwork cardigan before checking off the last name and shuffling the papers in her attendance packet. The bell rang with its tinny resonance. Homeroom was dismissed and the morning itinerary had begun. *It's Friday*, Linda reminded herself. *You can do this.* She hoped she could lose herself in the routine. Just a few more hours and she would be free to return to the forest.

Everyone stood up and started to exit through the chipping wooden doorway, shouldering their backpacks. Linda suddenly realized that John materialized right next to her in the push of boisterous kids enjoying their three minutes of freedom before their first classes. She found herself staring at him. An impulsive part of her wanted to reach out and touch his hair, which was such an icy shade of blue that part of her wondered what the tousled spikes would feel like. Someone pushed past her, almost knocking her into John. Her face burned as he looked down at her.

"You okay?" he asked quietly.

"I'm fine," she said back as she pulled her coat close around herself. The air was suddenly brisk, almost like someone had just opened a window in front of her. They walked into the windowless hallway, filled with rowdy teenagers and tired teachers bustling in every direction. He walked past her, and she continued to her locker to deposit her coat. The draft disappeared quickly in the body heat of the student mass. The hall was loud with voices, slamming locker doors, and running feet. A few papers flew comically and at least two annoyingly kissy upperclassman couples got in the way. Linda pushed through friends that clumped together like blood clots before finally turning into the art room at the end of the long hall.

"Good morning!" Mrs. Greene, the ancient art teacher, said cheerfully. Her wrinkles and smile lines were deep, her Maine accent thick, and, as always, she stood right inside the door of her classroom to greet each of her students. The perpetual smell of paint and clay met Linda at the entrance while her teacher looked out from her gold-rimmed elliptical glasses. Linda sometimes wondered if Mrs. Greene might be even older than the school. She was long past her retirement but with the energy of a thirty-year-old.

"Hi," Linda replied as she walked past the teacher and went to her seat, which was next to two unpleasant excuses for people: Beatrice and Heather. While they let Linda sit with them in class and at lunch after her best friend died (their one act of charity), it sometimes felt like Linda spoke a different language. It was as if the three of them tried to build the Tower of Babel themselves.

"Do you know what we're doing today?" Linda asked, sitting down at the wide black melamine art table next to Beatrice.

"Maybe still life or something like that. I hope it's free choice," Beatrice answered. She twisted her brown wavy hair around her finger, looking toward the front of the room. The blackboard, streaked with prehistoric white chalk, was otherwise blank and stood out against the hemlock green walls. (Mrs. Greene was integral to the Larch Academy establishment and was therefore allowed to paint her room whatever color she wanted.) Heather, seated on the other side of Beatrice, ignored them while she tapped away angrily on her sparkly purple smartphone.

"I'll take that, Miss Madison," Mrs. Greene said nonchalantly, snatching the phone as she walked by. Heather started to protest in a huff, but Mrs. Greene cut her off, scolding her: "No cell phones in school. Deal with it. See me at the end of the day." She dropped the phone into her old wooden desk and slammed the drawer closed, locking it.

"Yeah, no cell phones!" their friend, Dan Ross, jeered from the next table over from them. Heather turned up her hooked nose at him while Beatrice made a face. He stuck out his tongue.

"No mocking, either!" Mrs. Greene snarled. Even at her age, she was sharper than some of the younger teachers.

The intercom crackled. "We'd like to have a moment of silence this morning for the one-year anniversary of the loss of two beloved members of Larch Academy: Kelsie Robertson and Jane Clari."

Not enough kids were quiet, even though Mrs. Greene looked like she was about to murder those who didn't obey. Linda felt eyes on her, which made her face grow hot. She wanted to be swallowed by darkness. The last thing that she wanted was the anniversary of her best friend's death. Or for people to pity her. A charitable act which didn't change anything.

After what felt like an eternity of hell, the intercom crackled again with the dean's voice. "Rest in peace, Kelsie Robertson. And we would like to remind everyone that the search for Jane Clari is ongoing. Faculty and the police welcome any information, no matter how small. If you would like to talk to a guidance counselor for support, appointments are available. Thank you."

Then the room uncomfortably came to life again. The students chattered around Linda, but it sounded more like a hum as she stared at her hands under the desk. She heard Heather and Beatrice gossip with the other popular kids next to her as they worked on their drawings. No one said anything to Linda. Tears beaded in her eyes, but she forced herself to pick up the pencil and sketch.

Art went by quickly afterward; almost faster than the amount of time it took Mrs. Greene to notice Heather typing away on Beatrice's phone. But not quite. Although the resulting scene was mildly interesting, Linda felt her eyes glaze over. She was glad to move on to Earth Science.

Her teacher, Mr. London, directed everyone to stand along the wall. The Korean American man waited, stone-faced, while the students filed into the room, but a small smile turned up the corner of his lips when he and Linda locked eyes. She managed a slight smile in return before he returned to surveying the class and demanding that everyone quiet down, his tone making up for his small stature. "We won't be changing seats until next year, so if you don't like your partner, you'd better talk to me after class," Mr. London said, pausing a moment to see if anyone noticed his joke. A few students, like Linda, cracked polite grins. Mr. London cleared his throat before moving to the far corner of the room. "Linda Waters." He pointed to one of the paired desks. "John Mason." He pointed to the one directly next to it, before looking around the room expectantly for their faces and movement in his general direction. John and Linda walked forward at the same time and sat quietly while their teacher continued.

Mr. London subsequently droned on for the whole period about atomic theory and the scientific method's involvement in its discovery one last time before they had to turn in their project about it on Monday. Linda paid a perfunctory amount of attention to the familiar lesson, which she had already taught herself from reading her family's aging encyclopedia. She felt the same chill from earlier, despite the many overheating bodies dressed against the near-boreal chill of Maine in the fall. She looked around and saw that the windows were closed. One of the girls sitting in front of her wrapped her dark purple sweater more tightly around herself, although many other students sat in simple long sleeves. The buffer of the aging heating system in the school didn't seem to apply near John. *How is that even possible?* she wondered as she looked over at him, watching him write down notes… in cursive. He paused and looked up at her. *Caught again.*

"What?" John asked.

"Nothing," she said, turning her head to the front of the room. *Who writes in cursive?* It seemed so old-fashioned. They hadn't learned it since elementary school, and her own handwriting was definitely a testament to that.

She thought he muttered something. "Hm?" she asked quietly, but he didn't answer. She thought he had said, "Mortals."

TWO QUIET KIDS

Linda opened her eyes. Saturday morning sunlight streamed in through the blinds. She jumped out of bed and immediately raised the white metallic slats to look out the window. It was beautiful outside. Golden light spilled through the trees and over the blanket of snow that nestled in the spruce and maple boughs, and in the yew shrubs around her house. At the bottom edges of her window, blossoming fractals of frost extended up from the single pane like wildflowers in a meadow. The cold glass kissed her fingertips as she traced the frost. A snowstorm had passed through the night before, which was early even for Maine. October had just arrived.

She heard the faint clinks of dishes and the sound of the rumbling coffee maker from the kitchen, the air tinged with the familiar aroma. Her parents were awake. "Mom? Can I go for a walk?"

"Sure. But be careful! It snowed last night!"

"I know!" Linda called back.

"We'll have breakfast at 10!"

Linda glanced at her alarm clock. It was 8:58. More than enough time. "Okay!" she called back. She quickly slipped on jeans and a navy and cream Fair Isle sweater and then threw her pajamas on her sister Emily's vacant bed (Linda loved the University of Maine for taking her sister a few hours away). Before leaving her room, Linda grabbed her phone from the charger. No messages, as always. She wasn't sure why she even bothered checking; it was like that hope for her friend to come back never died with her. She grimaced but pocketed her phone anyway— this was her parents' compromise for letting her wander alone, but always only in the neighborhood. Linda looked at her wrist to make sure she was wearing her late best friend's last gift to her: a simple beaded bracelet. Reassured by its presence, Linda exhaled and hurried out of her room, eager to be outside. She passed the bathroom that she had all to herself and walked past her brother Kris's room, his door closed as always while he was away at Bowdoin College.

"I'm going!" Linda yelled into the house as she pulled her knit ultra-marine hat on over her shoulder-length brown curly hair, followed by her sky-blue down coat and snow boots at the front door.

"See you later!" her parents called back, and she went out the door.

Linda walked through the fresh, frosty air and the snow-covered sidewalks in her neighborhood for nearly an hour as she admired the bedecked foliage. At the edge sat the neighborhood playground. It was called Penobscot Park, as if that was enough recognition in return for stealing land and turning it into a space for juvenile delinquency. The playground had a metal dome for climbing, swings, and other jungle gym equipment that Linda grew up on. Three inches of snow blanketed the space wherever the wind or some confused creature didn't disturb it.

Linda walked past some little kids who were engaged in a snowball fight toward the aging white wooden picket fence that bordered most of the park's perimeter. As she rested against the fence and watched, she noticed that there was an older boy in the mix who towered over the rest. She took a closer look and realized it was John from school.

Then her attention turned to one little kid who looked like he was seven years old. He grabbed a bunch of snow, clumped it together in his red mittens, and threw it at another boy who wore a blue hat with a pom-pom on top. Pom-Pom Boy dodged it and knocked into another little boy who wore a huge highlighter-yellow coat, and they collapsed into the snow, laughing. John threw a snowball at Mr. Red Mittens, who pretended it was a bullet and dramatically fell over and "died." Linda smiled, but the scene began to tug at her memories. As the children and John pelted each other with snowballs, Linda watched as one girl snuck up behind another and stuffed a snowball down the back of her coat, causing her to scream and chase after her friend. Linda's thoughts drifted. She remembered the last time she had been in a snowball fight, almost two years ago... she sighed, her breath escaping her like a small plume of smoke, like the exhaust of a car—

Snow came in contact with her face, obliterating her train of thought. It froze her skin almost to the point of burning. She brushed it off as some of the ice crystals began to melt and bleed down her face.

"Are you alright?" someone who didn't sound very child-like asked. She looked up as she wiped the snowmelt from her eyelashes and saw John jogging over.

"Yeah, I'm fine," she replied simply, shaking the water and snow off her hands. "I don't mind becoming a popsicle."

"I'm sorry about that, my trajectory was way off, and I didn't see you over here until it was too late," John apologized, rubbing the back of his head with his hand, his normally pale cheeks rosy.

"It's fine, it's really not the end of the world or anything."

"Hey, um, aren't you my science partner?"

"Yeah. John Mason, right?" Linda leaned back against the fence.

"Yeah." He smiled.

After a moment of silence spent watching the snowball fight resume, Linda ventured, "Are these your siblings?"

"What?" he asked, pulling his attention away from the flying snow. "Oh, no, they're just... uh, some kids from my neighborhood."

Linda nodded in response. Silence again crashed the party. She turned to him again. "Where did you move from? People normally leave Larch."

"Larch?"

She stared at him. "Yeah... the town where we go to school?"

His eyes widened. "Oh!" he giggled. "Right, I totally knew that. Yeah, um, I'm from up north. Your town is a lot bigger than my old one." Another pause. "I like your coat. It's a really nice shade of blue."

"Thank you," she said. "Blue is my favorite color."

"It's my favorite color, too."

"Gee, I wouldn't have guessed," she said wryly, making him laugh. It was a nice and deep sound that made her feel surprisingly warm. "That was a bold choice to even make your hair blue," she commented.

"Teenagers dye their hair," he said matter-of-factly.

She smiled at the weird phrasing. "Normally only the alternative kids. I'm not trying to be that way; I like your hair. I just meant that you usually see it in bigger towns or cities, or at least not here." She internally cringed at herself. She felt socially out of practice.

"Um, I didn't have as much control over it."

"Over your hair color?" Linda asked, making a face despite her best intentions to remain polite.

"Yeah, I mean, no, I mean, of course I did, but how could I not?" he stumbled over his words.

"It looks nice, so I don't blame you," she smiled. "It reminds me of deep snow or ice."

"That's what I like about it," he chuckled. "Is that why you like the color, too?"

"Oh, I've never thought about it like that," Linda said thoughtfully, looking up at the cyan sky. It was so bright that it felt like pinpricks in her eyes as blue field entoptic phenomena chased across her vision. "A lot of my favorite things are blue."

"Like what?" he asked. He sounded so earnest that she decided to indulge him a bit.

"Oh, you know, I think it's interesting that there's not much in nature that's blue. Kind of like the sky, blue jays, how ice and snow can sometimes have shades of blue. It's not even a word in some cultures and parts of history, like the *Odyssey* talks about the sea as being the color of wine..." she trailed off. She began to blush. "Sorry for rambling."

"No, it's a good list. I love nature, too," John tittered. "I'd rather be outside on any day, which tends to happen anyway."

"Me too," she grinned. "By the way, aren't you cold, John?" she asked.

He looked down at his outfit: a hoodie and jeans, same as always.

"Oh, no, I'm not. I'm usually fine in the cold." He shrugged. "Anyway, when is the science project due? I, uh, forgot to write it down."

"The atomic theory poster?" she asked.

"Yeah, that one. Is it due Monday?"

Linda nodded.

"Shoot. I forgot to start it," John said, running his hands through his hair.

"It's really easy. You only have to explain the different concepts of atoms on construction paper and write your name on it," she explained, "it didn't take me very long, only a couple hours."

John tried to appear concerned, but at the same time, he seemed calm on the inside. His eyes reflected the stillness of the snow-covered morning, as if the project didn't really matter to him. Linda couldn't find any reason to justify the odd juxtaposition. *Why pretend to care?* Plenty of their classmates were outspoken about not caring at all. Her phone buzzed. She looked back up at John, who she realized was watching her with interest. "Sorry, my mom just texted me. I have to go. See you at school?"

"Yeah, see you!" He watched her until she was out of sight before rejoining the game.

THREE

THE HUNGRY TITAN

The harsh, buzzing sound of the bell broke through the homeroom chatter on Monday morning. As Linda followed the teenage horde out of the classroom, she bumped into John. "Hey," Linda said. She realized she couldn't really politely ignore him anymore.

"Hey," he answered. "Did you have a good weekend?"

"It was fine. You?"

"It was okay. Nothing exciting after the snowball fight." He sounded considerably less alive than on Saturday, but he still smiled when he saw her. That day he was wore a heather blue t-shirt under his navy hoodie. "My mom kept me quite busy with chores, so I had difficulty finding time to squeeze in homework."

"But you had time to play in the snow?"

John smirked as he held the heavy wooden door open for her. "I'm allowed to have fun, you know."

"Okay, true," Linda tittered as they approached her locker.

"See you later, my class is on the other side of the building," he explained as he split off.

"What class?"

"Mathematics!" he said, beaming in an aggressively sarcastic way.

"Have fun with that," she said. "Missing" posters for Jane Clari fluttered on bulletin boards as she walked past them in the hall. The blue-eyed and blonde-haired young woman smiled out at her. That photo always irked Linda—the one they chose was Jane's school photo that was taken at the beginning of last year, right before she disappeared. Linda tried not to think about what happened to Jane. She was just a year older than Linda as a senior... Linda never knew her well beyond seeing her in the hall or organizing for school events, and a guilty part of her almost felt thankful to not have one more person to mourn. She wondered if the young woman would ever be found. Jane was popular, but one of the nicer popular girls... unlike Beatrice, Linda thought sourly as she laid eyes on the brunette in the art room.

"Hey," Beatrice said as Linda sat next to her, smoothing down her wavy hair, the color of dying oak leaves.

"Hi," Linda quietly replied.

"Just a heads up," Beatrice said, leaning over conspiratorially as if she had something important to share, "Heather's been really bitchy. That chunky—I mean plus-size—girl Nina started dating Cole, even though everyone knows that Heather's been talking to him for a while." Beatrice leaned back. "I mean, just because Nina is pretty and nice to everyone and the president of Chorus as a junior, that doesn't mean that she can date whoever she wants. She's not better than us. She's such a slut."

The word vomit wasn't new for Linda. Heather usually did something like that, blowing things out of proportion even though she'd been hooking up with someone or other and somehow finding new drama to be involved in. Then again, so did Beatrice, with her... *colorful* worldview. Linda sighed internally. "Oh," she said. *How did I end up here?* Linda wanted to say something to point out how messed up Beatrice was being, but she learned the hard way that it wouldn't go well. And the idea of sitting alone with her thoughts was painful. *But was this better?*

"Yeah. I also got new nail polish." Beatrice displayed her neon yellow nails. "This color will be *so* in."

Linda nodded with a polite smile. "It'll make you stand out," she commented dryly.

"Right?" Beatrice exclaimed as her bestie Heather came in with a huff, pushing over the classroom threshold along with other students just before the late bell.

"I can't believe Nina! What a sordid bitch!" Heather hissed, throwing her bag on the floor. Linda was surprised that she knew the word "sordid."

Linda and Beatrice didn't need to bother asking Heather about what was going on; Heather was going to rant away without an off button anyway. Linda often felt like she had floated into their problems like splintered wood after a wreckage, stranded on a beach by a tide that dried up.

Heather raised her voice to a shrill extent. "I should have known when Cole started talking to me less. You said he was probably busy, but I didn't know he'd be busy doing her. UGH!" she exclaimed with disgust.

"I thought you guys were close?" Linda asked, wondering what made her feel the need to dignify Heather with a response.

"Apparently not close enough for her to think twice before stabbing me in the back."

"Everyone, quiet down!" Mrs. Greene yelled above the chatter. Her authoritarian tone contrasted her grandmotherly appearance with her natural wool sweater and large purple and green glass beads hanging around her neck.

"Well, Nina's older brother is a senior, isn't he? What's his name? Miguel?" Beatrice whispered while Mrs. Greene explained the agenda for the period.

"No, Beatrice, it's Carlos. And anyway, he's good friends with Cole, which is how Nina probably got an in. He probably wouldn't want to violate bro code since I was so close with Cole. James is pretty cute, though."

The names floated over Linda's head. She knew who they were, but they were as interesting and nice as the plastic fruit sitting at the front of the room.

"Isn't James her ex? That would be perfect," Beatrice said. Linda rolled her eyes.

"Miss Madison and Miss Colton, you're asking for detention. Shut it," Mrs. Greene snapped, causing some snickers in the room while Beatrice and Heather scowled. Dan looked back at them and made a silly face.

Mrs. Greene then moved to the side of her decorated chalkboard behind the long table at the front of the room. Brandishing bright red chalk, she announced, "My colleague, Mr. London, the Earth Science teacher here, and I decided to collaborate on a unit to introduce you to the Solar System. Now, I'm no scientist, but I did go to art school, and I have a penchant for art history. Does anyone know how many of the planets got their names?"

Linda looked down even though she knew the answer.

"Some of the planets were named after ancient Roman gods and myths," a student said. In her periphery, Linda saw Beatrice and Heather roll their eyes at each other, silently communicating how lame that person was. Linda knew this because sometimes at lunch they picked on Linda for her good grades when they weren't bullying her into sharing homework answers with the clique. God, she missed the days when she and Kelsie were able to turn their backs on stuff like that together.

"Yes, exactly," Mrs. Greene said, pulling Linda back to the present. "There's Venus, Mars, Mercury, Jupiter, Saturn, and Neptune, who you might recognize from either astrology or know better from their Ancient Greek equivalents: Venus as Aphrodite the goddess of love, Mars as Ares the god of war, and Jupiter as Zeus. But let's turn our attention to Saturn, a.k.a. Kronos. Does anyone know how Kronos was different?"

Linda remembered the answer from the entry in the encyclopedia at home. Even though she felt more comfortable while reading nonfiction, the encyclopedia glossed over the myth.

"Wasn't he a titan?" someone called out. Dan turned in his seat to roll his eyes at Beatrice and Heather.

"Right. Kronos, king of the titans, ate his children to try to circumvent a prophecy that one of his kids would overthrow him. Talk about eating your problems. Anyway, the myth teaches us that you can't avoid the inevitability of prophecy and of life, the insanity of which I believe the Spanish painter Francisco Goya captures in his well-named painting, *Saturn Devouring His Son*." Linda's teacher taped a large poster of the disturbing painting on her board, which depicted the titan consuming the bloody remains of a person. Linda grimaced with disgust at the graphic image, wishing she could erase her memory.

"Ew!" a boy exclaimed from the middle of the room, earning some laughs. Mrs. Greene ignored him as she hung up a poster of the contrastingly serene and beautiful *The Birth of Venus*, followed by the *Statue of Jupiter*.

"Does anyone know who painted this iconic Renaissance painting?" she asked, gesturing toward the very naked Venus standing in the shell. Linda knew the answer was Sandro Botticelli, but she focused her attention on writing down notes even though the art teacher rarely gave out exams or papers.

Eventually the lesson was over, and Mrs. Greene ordered, "Raise your hand if you have to finish your still-life." Half of the kids, including Linda, raised their hands. "Those of you who are finished, you can get started making your own symbolic and space-themed collage of one of these three works of art. Those of you who have yet to finish, meet me over at the drying racks!"

Linda followed a cluster of students to their oil pastel still life drawings of the cliché fruits in a bowl. She could objectively say that hers was horrible. She was never as artistic as Kelsie.

Mrs. Greene stopped Linda as she passed by to pick up her still-life. "Miss Waters, I can see your eyes light up whenever I ask questions. If you know the answer, don't be afraid to yell it out. I don't bite and it'll help your participation grade," she said with a smile, looking out at Linda through her gold-rimmed glasses. "Here's your still-life. Don't forget to finish it today, even if it means it's more interpretive. I don't want you to be behind while we study the classics of the West." Linda smiled politely as she grabbed her set of materials and walked back to her table.

"Hey, Linda!" a guy named Josh said as she passed him. She'd known him since about kindergarten, but they were only acquaintances, as she was with just about every other person at her school. "How's life?"

"Good," Linda answered with her usual response, even though it was hardly ever true. Distance was easier after last year. Getting close was too difficult. "You?"

"Good."

They all knew what happened.

Linda walked toward her table and wished she hadn't.

"London is definitely a homo. Have you heard his voice?" Dan laughed to Beatrice, leaning forward so that Mrs. Greene wouldn't hear him. "Ugh, why did Greene partner up with him? What a way to make this even more boring." Linda hated that he had taken up residence at her table while one of the group's friends was absent.

"No wonder his wife divorced him. Maybe she couldn't take any more of the gay hair products," Heather sneered.

"How did he marry a woman in the first place? It's just so obvious," Dan said. "It's like that new girl who keeps drawing girls all the time. I saw her sketchbook; it's filled with them." Heather and Beatrice shared a knowing look.

A stone sat in Linda's stomach. *So what if he's gay?* she thought as she sat down in her seat. Mr. London could be really caring. He gave Linda the most extensions after... She sighed. Linda didn't know how to feel as she shaded in the background of her still life with blue and white pastels. She tuned out the crappy conversation and thought about Josh. Part of her wished that people would stop asking her how she felt, as if she was supposed to tell them and know the answers. *How would they feel?* It was like some big charade. Linda tried to smear the thoughts into the drawing. She felt that a monster like Saturn from Goya's painting nibbled away at what was left of her happiness. *Not that I had much to begin with today,* she thought as she watched the oil pastels cause her hands to change colors like a broken chameleon. She looked back up at the bloody painting on the board.

"Why do you keep looking at that, you freak?" Heather asked her, earning some laughs from the popular kids within earshot. Linda's face burned as she looked back down at her pointless art.

Linda finished just as the period ended. After she sat her work on the drying rack, she realized she finally had Science. She hurried out of Art and smeared any remaining traces of oil pastels on her jeans. She stopped by her locker, the only one with a bright blue combination lock. It was the only way she could find her own amidst the long row of the grey metal ones. The inside of her locker was spartan aside from her coat, hat, and books. She gracefully crammed the materials for her next few classes into her bag before speed-walking down the hall.

She was the first one to Earth Science, other than Mr. London, of course. They exchanged greetings, during which Linda glimpsed one of his rare smiles. She accidentally knocked the Korean and American flags out of his pen mug with her open cardigan as she brushed past his desk.

"Sorry!" she exclaimed as she grabbed the mini flags.

"Don't sweat it," he reassured her as he replaced them in his mug. She noticed that in large black letters it said, "I hate mornings."

Linda hurried over to her seat in the back of the room. While she waited for her partner, she meticulously pulled out and arranged her homework, notebook, and mechanical pencil on her desk. It was very rare that Linda could know so little about someone in her small school, and she kept battling between interest and measured indifference over John. Soon other kids spilled into the room, chattering excitedly, bringing the silence to a roar. Among the throng of students was John.

"Hey," Linda said, looking up at him as he sat down next to her.

"Hi," he responded, pulling out his blue notebook and a typical yellow number two pencil that looked like it had seen better days.

"Did you finish the project?" Linda asked.

"Yes, but it sucks."

"It can't be worse than mine."

As he pulled out his project, she noticed that the construction paper he had used was surprisingly fancy, like the soft pressed paper made of plant fibers she would find in journals at Barnes & Noble. The edges of the paper were all a little frayed as if he used a knife to cut them out, or incredibly dull scissors that couldn't even pop a balloon. Before she could say anything, Mr. London started tapping the small bell on his desk. When the class didn't look up, he yelled, "HEY!" That time the students went quiet. His patience was stellar.

"Thank you. Now, pass your projects to the front," Mr. London ordered as he walked in front of the first row of tables, crossing his arms and frowning expectantly. His black hair was shiny with gel. Linda wondered how long it took him to style it just so, combed to one side, while completely gunking it up in the process.

Then Mr. London began an introduction similar to that of Mrs. Greene, although with considerably less flair. He showed the same paintings as he explained the importance of the solar system to humans throughout time. Somehow, toward the end of the class, he made an interesting topic irreparably boring by turning it into another painful lesson about paraphrasing. Linda thought that Mr. London might be losing steam when it came to teaching. He'd never been the most riveting teacher (although it's hard to surpass Mrs. Greene), but his lessons and syllabus had become increasingly bare bones, like he didn't care anymore. It kind of made Linda sad. His interdisciplinary project with Mrs. Greene seemed to bring back some of the spark in his eyes before it flickered out again.

Right before the end of the period, Mr. London handed out work-sheets for homework. John looked at his paper disdainfully as the bell rang.

"Does paraphrasing not give you goosebumps?" Linda asked sarcastically, thankful for once for the blanket of noise to hide her comment from Mr. London's ears.

"It does, just the wrong kind," John said as he stood up next to her, zipping up his backpack.

"Are there kinds that you would want, then?" Linda asked as they left the room.

"I want to not have to do this homework," he answered sardonically as he held open the door for her. "What class do you have next?"

"English. You?" Linda said to John, leaving behind the classroom and its hideous pastel yellow walls. She wondered why schools always seemed to choose that color. Nothing makes teens more angsty than authority figures saying, "Chin up, buttercup! Your future is as bright as these putrid walls!"

"History with Dr. Schoenbecker."

"That sounds fun."

"Not very."

"Do you like any of your classes?" Linda asked.

"Ehhh... I dislike some less than others."

Linda chuckled. "Okay, well bye." She left John behind at the stairs as she walked more slowly to her next class. As she pushed through other students, the feeling of being a fragment of celestial rubble hurtling past loyal orbiting moons returned again. She passed the most basic bulletin board ever, showcasing the importance of the comma! and essays that received A's. Even though Linda wasn't a huge fan of English, the teacher, Ms. McGeady, made it sort of worth it. She was one of the youngest teachers and she always followed the same comforting formula for her riveting grammar and book report lessons.

Unlike Linda's other classes, all the students silently went to their seats immediately upon entering the room. Each of the desks were separated in traditional rows and columns that faced the white board and teacher's desk at the front of the room. The few papers on Ms. McGeady's metal desk were in straight, neat piles parallel to the edges.

"Take out last night's homework, and turn to Chapter 5 in your textbooks," Ms. McGeady commanded. Her hazel eyes watched as the students did as they were told. The class proceeded as usual. They checked their homework under the guidance of Ms. McGeady and a few kids asked questions, so Ms. McGeady called on other kids who knew the answer. She assigned their homework before the lesson. Finally, they had independent work time, which was when Ms. McGeady turned on jazz music as usual. It was the only part of English that Linda actually enjoyed.

The sound of saxophones, trumpets, and trombones soon poured into the room like a smooth-flowing fountain from the lone silver CD player in the back. Linda relaxed as the beautiful sounds washed over her, transporting her away from her reality. She glanced around and saw some kids reading books in their laps while most of the other kids did their class work. Linda just stared down at her paper, forgetting about Saturn and his orbiting moon children. She focused on the flourish of brassy trumpets and the beats of subdued drums. She closed her eyes and exhaled while students wrote in their notebooks and turned the pages. Her teacher typed quietly on her laptop.

Then the bell rang, shattering her peace. Linda opened her eyes. Her peers packed up and began chattering as they filed out of the haven. She followed suit, wishing that she could be one of them. But Saturn lumbered along behind her.

FOUR

CRATERS

"Linda!" her dad yelled, running into her room, startling Linda and her sister. Linda's heart pounded. Her father never yelled. "Kelsie and her family are in the hospital."

The world tilted off its axis. *Kelsie was in a car accident.* Linda leapt off her bed and stumbled as she crammed her feet into her slippers. She ran to the car through the darkness and piled in with her family. Her parents fought about her dad speeding on the way to the local Memorial Hospital. Emily held Linda's hand in a rare moment of support.

Kelsie was in a car accident.

Linda looked out the window and saw Saturn's face reflected back at her, blood dripping down his maw and like tears from his eyes. Linda tried to get away from Saturn, but she was trapped in her seat. Her seatbelt buckle wouldn't open as Saturn pressed his face closer and closer to the window. Suddenly, the bloody titan appeared in front of the car. Linda shut her eyes as their car careened into darkness. She opened them.

Saturn and the crowded car were gone. Kelsie was before her, lying in a hospital bed, bandaged, yet... somehow still bleeding, a nightmarish quality to the way the dried dark red blood stood out against her skin. She was perforated with tubes. Lacerations and bruises blossomed across her flesh. A light flickered overhead. Everything was wrong.

"Kelsie!" Linda cried, rushing to her side, grabbing her hand.

Kelsie's skin was already as cold as ice. Linda held Kelsie's hand against her chest to try to warm her up, but it didn't work.

"Linda?" Kelsie whispered, her voice raspy. Her fingers tightened and curled around Linda's hand, but too weakly. Tears poured from Linda's eyes. She watched Kelsie strain to turn her head toward her, but she soon gave up.

"It's okay," Linda said, praying to God that she wasn't lying. "Don't push yourself."

Kelsie took a deep breath, but it rattled in her chest. Blood spilled from the corners of her lips. Linda cried out for help, but the hospital was silent around them.

"It'll be okay," Kelsie said.

Linda tried wiping away the blood, but it got all over her hands. "I'm sorry," she wept.

"It'll be okay..." Kelsie said again. Then she whispered, "Thanks for making my life beautiful."

"Please stay with me," Linda begged. She called for help again before turning back to Kelsie, whose eyes suddenly looked sunken. "We need to go on our adventure."

"We will, someday..."

"Kelsie, please!" Linda couldn't control her sobs anymore. She looked up and saw Saturn watching them, his feral eyes hungry.

"I'll be okay, don't worry. God said so..." Kelsie whispered, her voice fading as the rattling in her chest grew louder and she began to aspirate blood.

"No! Don't say that!" Linda exclaimed. Saturn moved closer.

"I love you."

Linda looked back down at Kelsie. "I love you, too." But her friend's hand was limp. The machine next to them began to blare like an alarm. Linda screamed and wailed. Kelsie was gone. The light flickered again, and Saturn appeared next to them, sinking his teeth into Linda's neck.

"No!" she screamed.

Her mom shook her awake. "Linda, it's me! It's your mom."

Linda opened her eyes. Her face was wet with tears. "I'm sorry," she whimpered, burying her face in her mom's shoulder.

"It's okay," her mom whispered.

"Don't apologize, sweetheart," she heard her dad say as he sat on the bed next to her, sandwiching Linda between them. Her dad rubbed her back with his large, warm hand while her mom held her.

"It was just a nightmare, sweetie," her mom reassured Linda as her breathing slowed.

Linda wished she was right. No matter how much she had prayed, Kelsie was dead. And that was a nightmare from which she would never wake up.

🌿

After Linda calmed down and stopped crying, her parents went back to their bedroom. But Linda still lay awake, haunted. She craned her head to glance at the clock on her desk behind her bed. It was four in the morning. She dragged her hands down her face. She knew she was going to be totally wrecked getting up for school later that morning, and she felt guilty for waking both of her parents up as they shuffled through the door in their disheveled matching robes.

Linda stared out at her room, which was empty and dark. Emily's bed was as vacant as the bookshelves that sat across the room from her, sitting white like ghosts in the darkness. Linda had torn out all the books because they were filled with too many memories of reading them with her friend. Filled with emotions that she didn't want. The shelves sat there, chipped from use and age. *Something that Kelsie would never grow to see.* Tears threatened to spill again. Faint moonlight crept in through the blinds, but she knew that even the stars and planets couldn't chase away her dreams. She thought of the frozen moons surrounding the planets, some of them marred by asteroids. Scientists still debated whether life existed on them despite their desolation. It felt as improbable as a life without Kelsie, but, *oh look*, she thought. *That happened.*

Linda exhaled in exasperation, staring at the ceiling. She eventually gave up on sleep and decided to read, grabbing the dictionary from beneath her bed. Ever since Kelsie… left, the only things that Linda was able to read were dictionaries, thesauri, and the encyclopedia collection that lived in the basement. The facts were typed plainly across the thin, textured paper with their serifs, the black letters standing out against the yellowing ivory pages. No murky feelings to remind her of the gaping hole in her chest. Her brain felt like a broken record of facts and information. Like the aftermath of the Cretaceous Period, when the asteroids came and killed all of the dinosaurs and their friends. But she was the only one left. And the only one who could jabber off these random facts that she memorized.

Linda easily opened the paperback dictionary as the spine bent along one of its many creases, forcing back the images of Kelsie. Her blood was streaked across the canvas of her mind, like strokes of paint that can never be taken back. The art of the reaper's destruction.

Linda tried to concentrate on the black and white leaves. *Focus*, she reminded herself. *Just black and white, nothing else.* Linda turned the page, straining her eyes as she tried to look for new words to memorize. But Saturn's face played in her mind, his deranged eyes seared into her neurons, mirroring the horror that sat like a rock in her stomach.

FIVE

THE IDES OF OCTOBER

Despite Linda's attempts to just be normal, the next day John asked her why she looked like she felt terrible. "I couldn't sleep," Linda said. Mr. London asked her if she was okay, and she reassured him that she was fine before hurrying off to English. She wished that she could crawl out of her skin when Ms. McGeady didn't leave time for listening to jazz.

The following day, after steadfastly ignoring John's concern about her well-being again ("Linda, are you sure? You look like you've seen a spirit." "I'm fine, John, really."), he distracted her by drawing exquisite snowflakes in the margins of her notebook. She would've been more annoyed if they didn't come out so beautifully. Then the next day, instead of commenting on Linda's eyebags, he folded a sort of paper football and accidentally flicked it into Mr. London's coffee mug as their teacher walked past.

"Sorry, sir!" John exclaimed, even though Linda could tell that he was trying not to laugh.

Mr. London frowned almost comically as he fished out the football and plopped it back on John's desk. It landed with a small splat. "Thin ice, John."

After Mr. London left, John flicked the football at Linda.

"Hey!" she said, flicking it back. "That was your blunder."

"My blunder? What an astute observation," he said, flicking it back.

She nudged it back to his desk.

"You're not supposed to give back gifts."

She snorted. "How is coffee-drenched paper a gift?"

He nudged it back. "The coffee just makes it extra special. One of a kind. No takebacks."

She rolled her eyes. "You're impossible." But she couldn't help but smile anyway.

By Friday, Linda found herself looking forward to Science, at least because of John's antics. But Mr. London also chose that day for patrolling the classroom to accept students' homework before the lesson, and he stopped at John and Linda's desks. Linda immediately handed over her stapled looseleaf packet, but John simply looked up at their teacher.

"Missing homework again, John?" Mr. London asked.

"Evidently, Mr. London."

"That's bad for your grade," Mr. London said.

John shrugged. Mr. London tapped the stack of homework against his desk before walking away.

Linda turned to her partner. "Did you forget it?"

John shrugged again. "I just didn't do it."

"Why?"

"Not enough time," he answered. "It's no big deal, honestly. I can do it tomorrow."

"Tomorrow is Saturday."

"Oh, right, I forgot you observe weekends."

She smiled at his unique word choice. "Do you need help with it?"

"Maybe," he said. "Let's just call it a work in progress for now."

"I usually work on mine during lunch," she said. "It gets it out of the way."

"Do you and your friends always work on your homework during lunch?"

Linda grimaced without meaning to.

"Sorry, I didn't mean that in a bad way."

"No, it's not that," Linda said. "Lunch is just really… I don't like it that much. I don't sit with friends."

"Oh, I'm sorry. Do your schedules not work out?"

"Something like that," Linda looked away.

Mr. London cleared his throat from the front of the room. "Quiet down, please."

"Do you have lunch fourth period?" John asked her as the chattering stopped.

"John Mason, do you have something to say?" Mr. London asked.

"No, sir."

"You can call me Mr. London."

"Sorry, sir."

There were a few snickers. Mr. London took a deep breath as he pointed to the Smartboard and began lecturing.

Linda wrote in the margin of her notebook: *I have lunch 4th period.* She slid it over to John. He pointed to her pen, and she conceded it to his fingertips. She pulled out another from her pencil case when she realized that he didn't have his own. When she sat back up, he slid her notebook back to her. *Mind if I join you?*

She thought about it for a moment before writing back: *Sure.*

In the cafeteria, Linda typically sat at the edge of one of the long rectangular tables that the self-prescribed popular kids dominated, next to Beatrice and Heather. Heather was naturally queen bee, and somehow despite Linda's apparent "dorkiness" (their words), they accepted Linda into their clique on the technicality that she wouldn't bother them. *It's better than being alone,* Linda had reminded herself day after day. Regardless of how she was treated or ignored, they always left a seat open.

But that day was different. Jack caught Linda's eye in the cafeteria and smiled as he began to walk over, carrying his lunch tray. Linda scooted over to make room for him to sit down next to her, and the moment his tray touched the table, the atmosphere at the table shifted. You could hear a plastic eating utensil drop.

"Who said you could sit here?" a girl, Clara, asked John with a sneer.

His expression was indiscernible, but he looked at Linda from the corner of his eye.

"I did," Linda said, the words slipping out of her mouth. Her voice sounded surprisingly steady despite how much her heart was racing out of her chest and into her throat.

"You dork, you can't invite guys like him," Beatrice said.

Linda didn't know what to do with all of the attention she drew to herself. "Well, he's my friend," she answered before he could say anything.

"Really?" Heather added, looking… disgusted, in that way she and the other girls had of looking at a guy who they didn't think was "hot" or "cool" enough. *John is actually really handsome, though,* Linda thought. The difference was that he actually had an incredible thing called substance.

"Yeah, Heather," Linda responded sharply. She stood up and extricated herself from the bench and John followed suit. The two of them walked away from the table and sat down at a half-empty one on the other side of the cafeteria.

"You didn't have to do that," John said, the expression on his face genuinely astonished.

"We're friends, right?" Linda asked him, sipping some water from one of the disposable cups. Her hand was shaking. She could tell that John was trying his best to not notice.

"Well, yeah…" he said.

"Then why wouldn't I? They weren't nice, anyway," she said truthfully. Her face burned, though. She was surprised she didn't puke from the excitement.

"I'm sorry," John said quietly, picking at his mashed potatoes.

"Why?"

"They called you a dork. But you're not. I should've said something back."

"Don't worry. They always talk to me like that. I really didn't like them that much."

"Really?"

"I hope I don't seem like a person who would genuinely enjoy their company. Have you heard half the things they say?" Linda said, admitting it to herself for the first time. What did John think of her? Was she just a placeholder for him like the chronically crummy clique was for her?

"Well, this is the first time I've sat with someone at lunch," John admitted.

"Really? Where do you usually sit? I've never seen you in the cafeteria."

"Exactly."

"Oh."

"Yeah."

"Well, if it makes you feel any better, it's fun to sit with you."

"Are you serious?" John chuckled. "You need to raise that bar."

"I mean it's fun to talk to you," Linda said, toying with her mashed potatoes and sad-looking chicken. If there was more shape to the meat and less crumble to the mashed potatoes, she would have made them into a frowning face.

"It's fun to talk to you too," John admitted quietly, a faint blush playing across his cheeks.

They chatted until the bell rang, signaling the continuation of the day. John and Linda got up and dumped their trays before leaving the cafeteria with the usual craziness.

"See you later!" John called as she went to her locker.

"Bye!" she called back with a wave, before grabbing her textbooks and hurrying down the hall. But a small lump of mystery mashed potatoes sat in her stomach.

SIX

THE HEART OF A SNOWMAN

After a small heatwave that lingered in the fifties, the glorious snow melted away. As much as autumn was her favorite season in Maine, Linda could always count on its inconsistency. She was glad to at least be able to spend more time in her forest. She hadn't been back in almost three weeks—she didn't want her pants would be soaked from snowmelt. Linda realized with a start that she was last there the day she found that lame written story—the anniversary. She grimaced so noticeably while she sat in Earth Science that John asked her if something was wrong. But, anyway, nature decided to loan out the forest to her again, and she was excited.

Later that day she waited for John at their usual meeting place outside the hellhole—she meant school—underneath the large maple tree across the street. While Linda waited for her friend, she reminisced about how their after-school ritual started almost two weeks before when she decided to ask if he wanted to walk home together. The execution, however, did not go to plan: she stumbled over her words while the two of them walked down the hall after Homeroom.

"John, um, do you, um… well… I forgot," Linda had stammered before clamming up. She began to blush furiously. Maybe it wasn't worth the trouble.

"Let me know when you remember," he said, cracking a smile (John secretly liked it when Linda got flustered, although he never dared to admit it to her). He continued, "By the way, would you like to meet me after school? We could walk home together."

And it became an unspoken agreement ever since.

Breaking out of her reverie, Linda stared up at the maple tree again. She realized that she had been waiting for over five minutes at that point, so she decided to call her mom.

"Hi sweetie, what's up?" her mom's voice floated through the phone, the connection crackling slightly. She was probably out running some last-minute errands.

"I'm going to be home a little later today because I'm showing John my forest," Linda explained quickly before she could change her mind.

"Okay, that sounds like fun! Just be home before dark, as usual," her mom responded.

"Okay, thanks! Bye! Love you!" Linda said before shoving her phone back into her bag. She looked up and saw some more students trickle out of the building, but not any tall guys with faded pale blue hair. *Where's John?* she wondered. She couldn't text him since he didn't even own a cell phone, which she didn't understand. He lived even farther away than her. Even still, she never had to wait longer than five minutes, but this time it had been ten minutes. Which was strange, even for him—the boy who wore nothing more than a hoodie in rain, snow, or shine, and even during a dip into ten degrees. If she ever offered her mittens on an especially cold day, he politely and sometimes firmly declined, even though he was the same guy who was all too ready to borrow a pencil or accept homework help. Linda realized that she didn't know where he lived, either.

Linda looked up at the beautifully shaped scarlet and amber leaves rustling overhead in the delicate zephyr. Some of the veins were still green, piercing through the warmer anthocyanin and carotenoid pigments. She thought about how people in the past justified these processes—as elves, fairies, or Jack Frost painting and frosting each leaf. The idea still pleasantly tickled a speck of her imagination. Nature's canvas never disappointed her, and it was better than waiting in the missing poster-plastered lobby. The bright blue sky, dotted with puffy white clouds whose underbellies were shades of cornflower, peeked through the spaces in the foliage. The sunlight illuminated the leaves and made them look like a stained-glass window.

Someone tapped her shoulder, and she nearly jumped out of her skin. "What the hell, John?" she exclaimed, swatting his upper arm as he snickered. "Why were you out so late, anyway?"

"I had to withstand some peer mediation," John explained, waving the issue away with his hand. According to the school, peer mediation was a cutting-edge tactic to decrease detention times. In other words, the incident happened too late in the day for lunch detention and wasn't serious enough to prevent faculty from going home at a decent hour.

"What did you do?" she asked.

"Gee, I appreciate your faith in me, Linda," he said sarcastically. "I almost 'instigated a physical altercation,'" he said with air quotes.

She looked up at him, surprised. She had never pegged him as the type since he was usually so quiet. "Why?"

"A guy was being an asshole in gym, so I told him to shut up, but he wouldn't stop so I grabbed him by the front of his shirt," John explained. "I didn't hit him or anything like that. But, of course, the teacher started paying attention by that time, so I got a ticket to talk about my feelings. The jerk never showed up to peer mediation."

"Why did you pick a fight with him over him being an asshole? It's not that necessary," Linda said as they started to walk down the street.

"He was saying stupid things about people to his morons, and I wanted him to stop."

"So, you almost beat up a guy just because of his ignorance?" Linda asked. She didn't get it. If she had a nickel for every time one of her peers said something worthy of a slap, she'd be rich.

"It was more than that. He was talking about... inappropriate activities and certain people. Just never mind, forget I said anything," John half-explained.

Linda noted that he didn't deny trying to start a fight. "Who were the certain people?" she pressed.

"Just don't worry about it, Linda," he said in a tone that strongly implied he wasn't going to change his mind. Despite her burning curiosity, she resisted the urge to bring it up again. As they neared Cherry Lane, which intersected Lexington and was across from Chickadee Street, she found herself satisfied with his vigilante attitude. Reaffirmed in her friendship with him, she asked John, "Can I show you something?"

"I guess?"

"Great! Follow me!" she said. She suddenly felt quite anxious, which translated into her running down the street. But he quickly caught up without any commentary.

Cherry Lane was a very quaint dead-end. On all sides, except for its mouth to Lexington Street, it was thickly bordered by various kinds of trees. Linda, in her copious free time, had identified them as oak, maple, birch, aspen, hemlock, and pine. Leaves littered the yards, cracked sidewalks, and the old grey fractured street. Everything the leaves touched was ablaze with color.

There were a few houses on each side of the road. One of the residents was outside, raking the leaves in her yard. Her house was a small pastel yellow two-story, one of the closest to Lexington Street. Linda recognized her—it was Mrs. Pierre. Her family had just moved there within the past couple of weeks, but Linda hadn't met her children yet, even though the younger one went to her school. The older one went to St. John's, a private school the next town over.

"Hello, Mrs. Pierre!" Linda called as they ran past.

"*Bonjour, sorcière!*" Mrs. Pierre called back in her Québécois accent. Linda was by no means close with her, but Mrs. Pierre was amused by Linda's frequent visits to the forest and began jokingly calling her a witch in French.

"Where are we going?" John asked as they approached the end of the street. Ahead of them sat a pint-sized basketball court decorated with an old hoop. Adjacent was the last house on the street: a small lilac-colored cottage that a recluse author inhabited. Behind it stood trees that led into the woods.

"Just follow me," Linda answered, dashing across the cracking court. She used to play there with Kelsie and some Cherry Lane kids. Normally, she was able to ignore the thoughts, but her breath caught in her throat as they broke the barrier of the trees, passing through a crumbled section of an old stone wall left by White settlers a few hundred years prior. She nearly tripped, finding her balance just in time, and she slowed to a walk.

John matched her pace. "Are you okay?"

Linda nodded. "Yeah, I'm fine." She held back tears. *I can't fall apart now*, she thought. She took a deep breath as she led him down an ever-so-slightly worn path for a few minutes until a lichen-spattered rock, where she turned left. At a forked oak tree, she turned right and kept walking until the trees opened onto a clearing. Many of the tall, ancient boughs stretched over it, creating a botanic canopy. The afternoon sun lit the changing trees on fire, brightening up the lush green bed of moss that stretched out before them.

"This is it," Linda said, taking off her backpack and sitting cross-legged. The trees hid some of the sky. Some leaves floated down in the breeze, gently landing on the ground. Much of the moss was sprinkled with the autumn-kissed leaves.

"Wow," John breathed, sitting down next to her.

"Yeah," Linda whispered. "It's my favorite place on earth."

"Do many people know about it?"

"No, and I intend to keep it that way," she responded, firmly but quietly.

"I understand," John replied, offering a reassuring smile.

They were silent for a while as they watched the branches sway gently from the occasional zephyr above them, the only origin of sound aside from the occasional birdsong or chittering squirrel scampering across the branches. Eventually, Linda pulled out her textbooks and began working on her homework. John lay down with his eyes closed, his arms crossed behind his head.

"You okay?" Linda asked after a period, looking up from Mr. London's generous contribution to her afternoon. John looked peaceful and relaxed, his chest slowly rising and falling with each breath.

"Yeah, I'm just resting," he responded calmly, not opening his eyes. Linda had never seen him so... at ease.

Silence entered again, but it was filled with serenity and color. She then opened her math textbook, and when she was on the fifth problem, a leaf landed right on top of what she was reading. The large crimson sugar maple leaf was tinged with orange and yellow and... blue.

"Hey, John," Linda said.

"Yeah?" he asked, sitting up.

"There's this strange leaf... it has the color—"

"Blue?" John finished for her.

"Yeah—wait, how did you know that?" she asked, looking up at him, searching his face in an attempt to find any answers.

John took a breath. "Because I did it."

"What—how—that's not possible," Linda said, turning over the leaf to look at the back. The blue wasn't paint; it was a part of the leaf, but only at the base, its color just barely entering the veins. His favorite color... blue like his clothes, like his hair. It didn't make any sense. It didn't even make sense if he somehow premeditatively injected it with blue ink.

John took the leaf and held it by the stem, in between his thumb and index finger. "My real name isn't John Mason," he said as he twirled the leaf.

"What is it? James Bond?" she joked.

"Jack Frost," he said seriously. He watched her face.

"Are you screwing with me?" Linda asked, smiling out of confusion. His expression remained serious, his eyes like a still winter night.

"Are you crazy?" she asked tentatively, standing up. *Probably not the best question to ask a crazy person*, she noted.

"No, I'm perfectly sane," John said, standing up before her. He was at least four inches taller, which she had never noticed before. He held up the leaf from her textbook and gently touched the tip. Frost slowly began to envelop it, starting from the tip and the edges all the way down to the petiole.

Linda couldn't believe her eyes. "Wow," she said, reaching out to touch the leaf. It was genuinely cold, and the frost began to melt slightly from the warmth of her hands. "Oh my god." She looked up into his blue eyes, which reminded her of the depths of glacier ice. He was dead serious. "Are you fucking with me?" she asked.

"Why would I do that?"

"Why would I believe that you're some magical snow pixie?"

"Nature spirit," he corrected her.

She rolled her eyes. "Same difference."

He took her hand in his so that the frosted leaf sat in her palm. He placed his other hand over it, and she watched with widening eyes as the ice crystals grew into a fuzzy white hoarfrost before they bled together and became a block of clear ice. It sat with a freezing weight in her palm. "I can also make it snow," he said. Immediately clouds formed and snowflakes began to fall from the sky, softly landing on the moss and their hair and shoulders.

"Okay, but that could be a coincidence," she said. But she still held the ice in her hand, and it began to melt from her body heat, water dripping down through her fingers.

"I, uh, could make a snowman," he blurted.

"There's not enough snow," she retorted.

He gestured his hand to himself. "Look who you're talking to. Okay, so what do you want it to look like?"

"Fine," she said, "I'll play along." He already began constructing the base of the snowman out of thin air. "Give it a diamond-shaped torso and put antlers on its head." After a minute, she stared dumbfounded at a snowman that defied the laws of physics with its realistically shaped diamond torso and snowy moose antlers. "Make it say, 'Linda Waters' in ice across the chest," she ordered.

"Finally, something more interesting," he said as he tinkered with the snow until it turned shiny and blue, spelling out her name in Times New Roman font. After he stood back, she punched her hand through the snowman's chest. The ice splintered against her knuckles and the chill of the snow began to burn her skin. She pulled her fist out with a handful of snow and stared at it as some of it began to melt in her palm.

He gasped. "You just killed him! Heathen."

She stared up at him. "This must be some sort of vivid hallucination."

"Linda, I don't know how else to prove it to you," he said, and began counting on his fingers, "I frosted a leaf, froze it in a block of ice, I made it snow, I created a snowman in front of you following your instructions, and then you *took out its heart*, which is slightly more violent than I was expecting."

"So, you were expecting some violence," she smirked despite herself. "Still, this is all just hard to believe, John."

"Jack."

"Sure."

"Look, if you'd rather us not be friends because you think I'm insane, we never have to talk again. I won't tell anyone about your special hideout, and I appreciate you showing it to me. We can just leave it here," John said.

Linda stared at him. Then she sat down and rubbed her face. "It's just a lot to… absorb. But…" she began, then took a deep breath. "I don't want you to leave."

"Are you sure?" he asked.

"Yes, I think so," she answered. "This must be why the air around you is always kind of cold."

He sat down next to her. "It is?"

"I mean, yeah, it is," she said. "Although you probably don't notice since you don't need to wear a coat even when it's ten degrees."

John—no, Jack—chuckled. "That makes sense."

She leaned back into the moss until she was lying down. She stared up at the sky. "Can you make it snow again?"

"Yes," he said. And delicate snowflakes floated down from the sky, landing on her eyes, nose, cheeks and forehead. Their chill kissed her face before melting away.

"Why did you tell me?" she asked.

He was silent for a moment. She watched his face. He fidgeted with a small sphere of ice that he manipulated into different shapes with his fingertips. "Well," he said finally. "You're my best friend. And you showed me something special to you. So… I wanted to share the only special thing I had with you. Apparently for better or for worse." He chuckled softly.

"Are you lonely?"

He laughed again. "That's such a burn!"

"Sorry." She blushed.

"I mean, I told you, a human mortal, about my real identity despite your analytical and jaded approach to things. So yes, I guess you could say I'm lonely."

"I'm lonely, too," she admitted, picking a sprig of moss and twirling it between her fingers. She couldn't admit that he was currently her best friend, at least by process of elimination. *Is he?* The question made her chest tighten. "Thank you for telling me." The heavy snow clouds began to drift away, allowing in the orange sunlight.

"Please don't tell anyone," Jack said earnestly.

"Who would I tell?" she laughed. "No one would believe me. I barely believe you."

He smiled briefly before saying, "No one can know that I'm anyone other than John Mason. There are more… beings out there than you know exist."

"Should I be concerned?" Linda asked, feeling a little disconcerted at the expanding world. She suddenly became more conscious of the leaves of moss and trees around her and the sky bending above her, the thin cataracts of cirrostratus clouds tinged with the periwinkle of dusk.

"I would let you know if you should be. As of now, hopefully that's never the case," Jack answered. "I'm… uh, technically not supposed to be here."

"Interesting," she commented. After he didn't elaborate, she asked, "Why?"

"Mother Nature doesn't think I should be interacting with humans," he said quietly.

"Mother Nature is real?"

"Yes," he answered.

"Why can't you interact with humans?"

He shrugged. "Keeping the worlds separate and all that."

"So, why now?" she asked.

"Why any time?" he asked. "I've never done it before, and I was tired of my life as it was."

"Fair enough," she answered. Then she became aware of the darkening scenery and remembered her mom's warning, so she suggested they get going. After a few moments of silently walking, she asked, "How do you give the world autumn?"

He smiled. "Very carefully."

"You know what I mean," Linda said, and she pushed him playfully while he chuckled.

The recluse bobbed her bag of green tea in the hot water, the faint chlorophyll color sinking and staining it, standing out against the white glazed ceramic mug. She looked out of her kitchen window that was wreathed in ivy at the two children walking by, chattering about nature. She had watched them disappear into the forest earlier. The girl rarely looked so happy—the girl whose friend was on the news last year. The recluse used to hear the girl and her friend, Kelsie Robertson, laughing and playing as they grew up. They were inseparable. Until it stopped. A tear rolled down her cheek.

SEVEN

A HAUNTING

A few days later, Halloween came, on a Friday. It was Linda's second Halloween without Kelsie but her first with Jack. The whole day Linda felt a peculiar sensation, and she couldn't explain it until she walked over to Jack's locker after school, when he turned to look at her with a smile on his face saying that he was looking forward to going over to her house. She realized she was excited. She felt like a traitor. To be fair, her mom had suggested the hangout because she wanted to meet John. So maybe Linda wasn't a total traitor, but she was certainly aiding and abetting.

As Linda waited for Jack to finish up taking his borrowed textbooks and single notebook out of his locker, she noticed the stormy look in his eyes. Unsure of how else to broach the subject, she asked, "How was your day?"

"It was okay," Jack said.

"Just okay?"

He sighed, taking a painstaking amount of time to zip his backpack. Or she was just impatient. She pulled up her shoulder-length hair into a ponytail.

"Your hair looks nice like that," he commented, looking up briefly.

"Um, thanks," Linda said. She smoothed her left hand over her ponytail and adjusted her backpack strap with her right. "What happened today?"

"Are you guys going on a date?" a girl called to them. Linda looked behind them and saw Nina Rodriguez and her "stolen" boyfriend, Cole Huffman, who was considered one of the hottest and most popular guys in the grade. Linda believed that most of that collective opinion was due to the fact that Cole was mysterious, and he hid most of his substance deep down inside his being.

"We're not together," Jack said flatly, pushing his locker shut.

"It's nothing to be ashamed of," Nina added cheerfully. "Just like me and Cole." She batted her eyes at the dark-haired wonder boy, who smiled smugly.

Linda was instantly irritated. "We're just friends."

"Ookay," Nina replied, in a slight sing-songy voice that really said, *I don't believe you but I'm a half-decent person and will leave you two alone.* Nina clutched Cole's arm and continued, "See you two tomorrow!" Then the couple walked away.

"That's why my day was only okay," Jack grumbled as he turned to his friend.

"Oh… Nina and Cole were bothering you?"

"No—that's the problem. Other people were bugging me, too. People are starting to think we're dating," Jack said, holding open one of the double doors for Linda as they walked out of the building.

"Oh," Linda said, the realization hitting her. "That's… not great."

"Exactly," Jack said, gesticulating as they crossed the street.

Linda rolled her eyes. "You don't have to be *that* bent out of shape about it, geez."

"Are you saying you want us to be together?" Jack turned around, an impish but also slightly concerned look on his face.

"No!" Linda exclaimed, only for him to cackle in response. "You just don't have to make it sound like I'm the worst possible option to be stuck with out of your *two* universes. Anyway, no one bugged me about it yet."

"Yet," Jack said, raising his index finger. "You know, I never thought I would have this problem."

"Welcome to the mortal world, where despite our comparatively short lifespans, we care about who dates who. I think Beatrice and Heather might have said something." Linda frowned. Honestly, part of her was surprised that the gossip wasn't more immediate.

"Those were the girls whose group you kicked yourself out of?" Jack asked.

"You didn't even know their names?" Linda asked.

"Are you kidding me? I'm 'the new kid,' and I frankly don't really care about assholes."

"You curse a lot."

"Is that bad?"

"No, I'm just surprised that you know so many curse words."

"Please, I'm not five, and high school is very... educational."

Linda laughed out loud. Jack realized he liked the sound whenever she genuinely laughed. There was weight to it, like thunder. *Thunder?* he asked himself. *Whatever.*

"I wish more people called Cole a cabbagehead," Linda admitted after a little bit.

"Why? His hairstyle? Most guys have that," Jack said.

"Well, 'cole' also means cabbage, or other forms of brassica vegetables like kale."

"I think you're the only one nerdy enough to make that connection."

"Jack, shut up."

"Well, you are nerdier than me... and him."

"That isn't much of a challenge," Linda muttered.

"Oooh ouch," Jack laughed.

"I'm joking! About you anyway."

"Please, my grades speak for themselves."

"You just don't like to do your homework. You're plenty intelligent."

"Anyway, calling someone a cabbage doesn't really increase leverage."

"Fair enough," Linda agreed as they walked down Chickadee Street toward her house. Pumpkins sat on doorsteps, some of which were glowing jack-o'-lanterns, along with witches, skeletons or ghosts. In one yard, Linda noticed some startlingly realistic tombstones, and as they passed by, Linda thought she saw Kelsie's name on it. The memory of Kelsie's casket being lowered into the ground filled her mind. Linda tripped, but Jack caught her before she face-planted and helped her to stand upright. She would've been more surprised by his reflexes if not for her pounding heart. She put a hand on her chest and took a deep breath. And then another.

"Are you okay?" Jack asked, gingerly letting go of her as if he was scared that she would fall over again.

"Yeah, I just…" Linda said, her voice trailing off as she glanced back at the tombstones. Kelsie's name was gone. The one in the front just said "John Doe" and had X's where the dates would be. *They're fake,* Linda reminded herself. *They're only spurious, not real, false, made of foam.*

Jack glanced at the tombstones. "Just… what?"

"My best friend died last year," Linda said quickly. She looked away from him. She never actually intended to tell him that. She wished she didn't say it. She felt sick. *God, what a mess.*

"Oh. I'm sorry," he said quietly. "What happened? I mean, you don't have to tell me. That sounds terrible."

"It was a car accident," she whispered, her voice breaking. Her throat tightened. If she said anything more, she felt like she would choke.

"I'm really sorry. I can't imagine how horrible that felt. Or still feels," Jack said gently. Then they just stood there. He reached out as if to hug her, and then the two of them paused and began to laugh nervously.

"It's fine, Jack, I appreciate the sentiment," Linda giggled. "Those girls suck."

"Yeah, rumors ruin everything," he groaned.

She cleared her throat. "Well, um, my home is just over there." She pointed to a small yellow house the next yard over.

"Oh cool!"

Linda made a face. "Cool? It's not like it's a historic mansion or something."

His eyes panned over the autumnal trees and the lone blue spruce that ringed the yard. "I've never been in a house before." He took a deep breath as they walked up the small stone path installed by her dad and brother over the summer. "Somehow, this makes sense. I like it."

"Why?" She loved her home, but she never thought about it being similar to her in any way.

"There's nature everywhere."

"Sometimes I forget that you're actually Jack Frost until you say stuff like this," Linda commented. She noticed he was smiling as he examined the borderline unkempt yew shrubs against the house. "You've definitely seen shrubs before. They're pretty standard."

He saw the amused and perplexed expression inhabiting her round freckled face. "Sorry! I just think it's interesting."

"Do you not live in a house?" she asked as she pulled out her keys. The green front door opened, causing the miniature pumpkins on the autumnal wreath to bounce slightly. "Hi, Mom!" Linda greeted. "You beat me to it."

Her mother, Angela, looked up at Jack. He towered over her like Linda's brother Kris.

"Oh, right. Mom, this is… John. John, meet my mom," Linda said, taking a millisecond to not accidentally call him Jack.

The greying woman plastered a smile on her face. "It's nice to finally meet you, John!" her mom said, shaking Jack's hand while looking at his blue hair. *This is going all too well*, Linda thought with a sigh.

"It's nice to meet you too, Mrs. Waters," Jack said politely. He smiled nervously.

"I'll give you a quick tour of the house," Linda announced, leading Jack inside. After leaving their shoes and backpacks at the door, Linda took off her coat and tucked her hat and mittens into its pockets before hanging it on the oaken coat rack that they got from their cousins in Ontario.

"John, where's your coat?" Angela asked, closing the door.

"Oh—I don't get cold," Jack explained.

Her mother looked over at Linda questioningly, one of her brown eyebrows subtly raised. Linda shot her a look to let her know to drop it, for now. She couldn't tell her that "John" didn't really have parents. *Wow, not even his real name.* They already shared a secret. Her mom put up her hands in one of her "just being a mom" gestures.

"Let me show you around while Mom gets a snack," Linda announced. She grabbed Jack's wrist, carefully avoiding his hand, and led him out of the foyer. "This is the hall, obviously," she said, letting go of him, "and if you go left you end up in the kitchen, but if you go right, you go to everyone's bedrooms, and the bathroom." She showed him the cramped yellow and white bathroom that was specifically hers, except for when Kris and Emily were home from college, a detail which her friend found amusing. Linda pointed out her eldest sibling's room and then the room that she shared with Emily's stuff down at the end of the hall. Her orange cat jumped off her bed and padded over to them, his tail curling upward.

"Hi, Nicholas," Linda said as he brushed against her legs, then Jack's. He bent down to scratch behind the cat's ears.

"He doesn't normally like new people," Linda commented.

"That's interesting," Jack said. "I have nothing against cats, but I don't interact with them very much. We don't actually have pets at home."

"Speaking of homes, where do you live if, well, you know," she asked him as she led him through the living room.

"I live with Mother Nature and Father Time."

"Really?" Linda whispered in shock. "There's a Father Time?"

"Um yeah, of course," he said like it was common knowledge.

"Where do you guys live?"

"Well, Mother Nature has a palace, and I live there with both of them," he explained, as if that was completely normal.

"Really?"

"Yeah."

"Is Mother Nature, like, a tree or something?"

Jack snorted. "No, she's a person, like me."

"Oh, sorry," Linda tittered.

"It's okay," Jack laughed.

"Wait what about Father..." Linda began to ask, but they had already made it back to the kitchen, and therefore, her mom. Linda and Jack exchanged looks. "I mean, what's your father like?" she asked quickly as her mom looked up at them.

"He likes to keep to himself, and he's old," Jack explained, although Linda wasn't sure whether he meant Father Time or his imaginary dad.

"Oh," Linda said.

"So, you've seen our place, John?" her mom asked, directing them to the dining room.

"Yes." He nodded. Apparently, her mom made their backpacks magically gravitate over to the table. *Way to send a hint*, Linda thought, rolling her eyes.

"By the way, John, what time do you need to go home?" her mom asked politely.

"I think about 5:30?" Jack guessed, as if a supernatural being had a curfew. It was about as likely as him needing to do his homework.

"Will someone pick you up or do you want us to take you home?" Mom asked, putting a plate of veggies and ranch dip on the table in front of them along with two glasses of water.

"I can walk home."

"Do you live near here?"

"Sort of. I always walk home from school. It's okay with my parents."

"I don't want you to walk home alone after dark, when it gets even colder."

"I'll be fine."

"I mean, it is Halloween, Mom," Linda ventured. "There's going to be people out. He's not going to get abducted."

Her mom shot her a look. "Are you sure? We'll drive you home," her mom insisted in a rigid but pleasant tone.

"Okay, sure," Jack said finally. Linda could tell he wasn't particularly pleased with the arrangements. His small smile looked super fake, almost frozen on his face, like he was hiding a dark and stormy look. She tried not to laugh.

"I'll do the laundry while you two hang out and do your homework," her mom said as she left the room. "Let me know if you need anything! We also have cookies."

After they started their assignments, her mother flitted between the living room and the basement while carrying a large plastic basket heaping with clothes. Jack opted to pass Linda a note. In blue ink (one of her pens, of course), it said: *What do I do now?*

Linda wrote back: *Idk.*

He looked down at her note and sighed before scribbling on it. *Seriously? Not helping.*

She took back the paper and wrote while he annoyingly looked over her shoulder. *Maybe just have my mom go to Longfellow Rd. or something & make her stop at a house w/ no lights on. It's not too close but not too far.*

He reached his arm over hers to write back: *Will she want to meet parents?*

She pondered for a moment before adding: *If there are no lights on...*

"I hope you're right," Jack said.

"Me too," Linda answered, ripping up the paper and hiding the evidence in the trash.

At 5:30 p.m., Angela, Jack, and Linda sat in the white minivan as it backed out of the driveway. Angela looked mystified when Linda had to help Jack use the seatbelt, and despite their best efforts, the friends dissolved into giggles. The rest of the ride was relatively quiet, except for when her mom asked Jack a probing question. Linda was internally dying. That evening hadn't gone at all as she hoped.

"I can get out here," Jack suggested as they made it to the corner of Longfellow Road.

"Okay, fine. There are beginning to be more trick-or-treaters, anyway," her mom agreed. "Be safe! Have a good night, sweetie!"

"Okay, thanks! You, too!" Jack said as he climbed out of the car.

"Bye, John!" Linda called to him.

"Bye!" he called back, turning and waving before he walked quickly down the street. Linda scooted over to the vacant seat and slid the door closed as they pulled away from the corner.

"*Blue hair?*" her mom finally demanded.

"Yeah…" Linda responded, looking out the window.

"Isn't he cold in just that hoodie? It's like twenty degrees outside."

"He's used to it," Linda said. She knew immediately that she chose the wrong words as her mom peppered her with more questions.

"What's he like at school? Does he have many friends?"

"He's pretty quiet," Linda said, but then remembered his stint in peer mediation. She decided not to mention that.

"He actually walks around town alone?"

"Yeah?"

"Longfellow Road is so far away to walk, though."

"Not really, Mom."

"Pray for that kid."

"Okay."

EIGHT

THE ANCIENT ONE

After school, Jack and Linda quickly picked up the routine of either spending time in the forest or at her house, depending on the weather. They tried and failed at hanging out together in the school library because they kept making each other laugh. Linda was pretty sure that the librarian hated them. Realistically, they spent half of their time wandering around the neighborhood before going to her house, especially when it was too cold for her to sit in one place in the forest, and she was not about to huddle up with Jack for warmth. Whenever they were outside, Linda asked Jack the most about his life as they were in less danger of her mom overhearing them.

On one of those early November days when it was still just warm enough for Linda to be outside, the pair wandered down another street in the neighborhood. Linda balanced herself on the concrete curb, holding her arms out like she used to do when she was younger. For some reason, Jack always brought out the playful side in her that she thought died a year ago. Threads of darkness began to pull at her mind at this thought, but she tried to push them away and asked him, "How did you come to life?"

Jack attempted to follow her lead and balance on the curb behind her. He was not nearly as graceful. "I just... existed," he answered, taking a few tentative steps. "I have no mom, unlike you."

"Mother Nature and Father Time aren't your parents?" she asked, stopping and turning to face him.

"Wait—Linda, why did you stop—oh my god," Jack laughed, trying not to lose balance.

She grabbed his wrists as he wobbled. "Oh my god, you're starting to sound like me," Linda laughed.

"I give up, I'm too distracted," Jack said, stepping off the curb. As she laughed at him, she suddenly slipped on ice and fell on her butt into the yard behind her.

"Hey! That's not fair!" she exclaimed as he tried hard to stifle his laughter.

Jack feigned surprise. "What's not fair?"

"That ice wasn't there before, you imp."

He shrugged. "Maybe you weren't looking carefully enough."

She rolled her eyes as he helped her up.

"You know, I could do it again if you're not nice to me."

"Can you not?" she answered. He grinned.

As they began to walk back towards her home, she stepped on a tiny, perfectly placed patch of ice. She grabbed onto him to prevent herself from fully slipping. "Jack, you goose, stop it!" she shrieked.

"Did you just call me a goose?" he snickered.

"Yes, yes I did," she said, swatting playfully at him.

"Anyway, going back to your earlier question, despite their names, Mother Nature and Father Time aren't actually my parents. Their titles have nothing to do with me. We're not really that related. The only spirit that I would actually consider myself related to is Old Man Winter—why do you look so confused?"

"Who's Old Man Winter?" she asked.

"Are you being serious right now?" Jack asked, stopping in his tracks.

"Please enlighten me, O Ancient One."

"Okay, one, don't call me that," Jack said, giving her a dark look. "Being a smartass is not becoming."

"At least I don't make people constantly slip on ice," Linda retorted. "Twelve-year-olds laugh at that."

"Linda, you have only four years of seniority."

"You called me a smartass," she huffed.

"Okay, I'm sorry," Jack said. "But you were."

"Don't make me—"

"Okay, okay," he snickered. "But in all seriousness, Old Man Winter is another, older snow spirit, but that's all that really relates us. His age would probably signify a closer connection to someone like Father Time."

"What do you mean?"

"Well, there's a reason why I'm not called That Old Geezer Jack. In *relative* time, I'm considered a relatively young spirit, as opposed to people like Old Man Winter and Father Time, who are considered ancient. So, they've been around much longer than me, but other than for Father Time, we have no scope of time in our realm. We don't grow or age. We just exist forever."

"Okay... so does that mean Mother Nature is middle-aged?" Linda asked slowly. Her head was beginning to hurt.

"Um, yes, I guess you could say that," Jack said, pausing thoughtfully for a moment, some of the late afternoon light illuminating the tips of his icy tousled hair like fire. "You sound so human right now," he laughed.

"What does that even mean?"

"Just the way that you talk about age as if it's a definition of someone. Then again, I'm not exactly human, but I'm closer to human than the elves or the crazy ocean spirits that cause hurricanes."

"But hurricanes come from winds off the Sahara Desert in Africa—"

"Okay, so the crazy wind spirits, I don't keep track."

"Jack, you're from that realm, whatever it is, you should know this," Linda snickered. "What's your world called, anyway?"

"We call it Pryddia," Jack said. "It's a big, scary place full of lots of chaos, like the wind and the earth spirits constantly fighting the water spirits for a domain. I generally prefer to spend most of my time in the mortal world."

"I really did not expect that," Linda admitted as they rounded the corner of Chickadee Street.

"Well, you did know that nature is crazy."

"Just not that crazy," she said. She stopped again. "Am I safe?"

"You're fine, Linda," Jack said, putting a hand on her shoulder. "And even if you're ever not, I will protect you. I promise."

She looked into his eyes for a moment. "Thanks, Jack."

🌿

After Jack left her on the porch that evening, Linda settled at the dining room table to do her homework. Her parents watched the news, which Linda was normally able to ignore. But then she heard the last name: Clari. The surname of the missing girl. She froze in the middle of her history homework.

"Mr. Everett Clari, why didn't you represent your brother?" a reporter asked. Linda realized the reporter was asking about Tim Clari, the drunk driver who crashed into Kelsie's car. Her hands began to tremble.

"It's hard to represent the person who brought shame upon the Clari name," Everett said solemnly. "What he did to that girl and her family…"

"It must've been hard to report Jane missing shortly after. Do you know if there's a connection between the two tragic events?"

"It's hard to say what goes on in Tim's mind. I didn't just lose Jane, my beloved niece; I also lost my only brother," Everett said.

"I'm very sorry to hear that, Mr. Clari," the reporter responded in a sympathetic tone. "And remember folks, if you learn any information, please report it to the police."

"Anything helps," Everett added weakly but earnestly.

Linda stood up slowly and walked to her room, almost stumbling over her cat as he lounged in the darkling hallway. She didn't want to tell her parents that she heard the TV. And hear them tell her how sorry they were, and how much her feelings mattered to them. She inhaled and exhaled. But her body was shaking.

NINE

THE MORTAL WORLD

"Why do you look so tired today, Jack?" Linda asked as they sat across from each other at lunch later that week. She didn't notice it as much during Homeroom or Science because he never seemed particularly excited to sit through a lecture, but he usually perked up in the cafeteria.

He looked at her wide-eyed. *Shit.*

"Oops, sorry, I can't believe I just called you the wrong name," Linda said, feigning having more air than grey matter. "I was just daydreaming about my... crush." She cringed. *That was the first word you could think of?* she chided herself.

He gave her a weird look. "You have a *crush* named Jack?"

Linda rolled her eyes. "Whatever, John," she insisted. "Seriously, you look super tired."

"I could say the same about you," he commented. He noticed that she bristled, and he decided to drop it. "My mom put me to work last night with a lot of errands for the family business and we got in a small fight. It wasn't very fun," he explained, rubbing his face. They had gotten used to talking in code at school.

"Do you have more to do today, too?"

"Unfortunately, yes, fall is always a busy time of year for us," he said. Then he reached over and touched the bracelet that poked out from the sleeve of her flannel shirt, turning one of the beads. "I like your bracelet. Where did you get it?"

"Do you want a copy or something?"

"No, I'm just curious. I see you wearing it a lot," Jack said.

"Awww! Don't they make a cute couple?" Beatrice asked one of her cronies as she passed by their table, giving Linda a venomous grin.

"Jealous?" Linda smirked. Beatrice's friend stifled a snicker.

"Don't be revolting," Beatrice hissed, looking her up and down before walking away in a huff.

"Damn," Jack said as he pulled his hand away from Linda. "That was great."

Linda blushed fiercely. "It honestly just slipped out." She took a big swig of her water even though her hand shook slightly. "Kelsie made this bracelet for me."

"It's really pretty," he said as the bell rang.

"Thank you," Linda smiled. As they walked out of the cafeteria, Linda saw a flash of red hair pass them: it was Jasmine, one of the prettiest girls in the school. There was a sort of alluring charm about her, and it drew in many of the guys (and some girls). Linda looked up and saw Jack's eyes follow her. *Apparently*, she thought, *not even Jack Frost was immune.*

As Linda walked over to Jack's locker at the end of the day, she heard someone call, "Hey, John!"

Linda turned to see Jasmine walking over to him with some pep in her step while Jack stood emptying out his locker in his typical slow and enthusiastic manner.

"I like the ice blue hair. It suits you," Jasmine said with a smile.

Jack's cheeks took on an unusual hue of... pink? *Oh my God*, Linda thought from her perch at the other end of the hall, where she pretended to be busy so she could watch the unfolding scene, *he's blushing.*

"Thanks, Jasmine. Your red hair suits you, too," Jack said, almost stumbling over his words. Linda tried not to laugh. But Jasmine just smiled without skipping a beat.

"How did you do it? Did you get it professionally done? I know you weren't born with it," Jasmine babbled—*if only she knew*, Linda thought—as she twirled some of her shining red curly hair around her fingers, clutching two of her notebooks to her chest. She wore a flowing black square-neck blouse that tastefully showed off her chest. A little gold charm sparkled on her clavicle.

"Well, no, I just do it at home. I've gotten used to the process," Jack replied.

"That's some dedication—I'm sorry if that was weird," Jasmine said with a laugh. "I always notice you… I mean your hair, in history. Sorry, I've had a very busy day today," she said, waving at the air.

Jack smiled. "No need to apologize."

"Well, um, I've got to go to fashion club now. See you in history, John," Jasmine said, smiling one last time before walking away down the hall.

"Bye, Jasmine," Jack said, turning and watching her.

Linda took that moment to approach from her post. "Someone's blushing," she said slyly, leaning against the locker next to his.

"Shut up, Linda," Jack said. He rolled his eyes but grinned anyway.

"Is that the first time you've talked to her?"

"Outside of class, yes. She picked me out as her partner for classwork once before now, though," Jack smiled.

"You're blushing more," Linda teased.

He sighed and then closed his locker to see the big, toothy grin on her face. He rolled his eyes again. "Don't you like anyone, for real?"

"Nope," she smirked. "So, I get to make fun of you all I want."

"That's just great," he groaned as they started walking to the doors.

A rush of freezing cold air hit Linda after she stepped outside, making her shiver. "Was that on purpose?" she demanded.

He looked at her. "Was what on purpose?"

"John, I swear," Linda snapped, folding her arms to conserve warmth. "That blast of cold air seems like your handiwork."

"I didn't do that."

She scowled at him in response.

"No, I'm serious. I wouldn't do anything to make you cold. That wouldn't be fair," Jack insisted. "Would you rather go to your house to warm up instead of going to the forest?"

"So, you'll make me slip on ice but not make me cold?"

"Yes, exactly. Nature spirits have standards, you know. We're not uncivilized."

Linda stepped forward with her right foot and it suddenly slid forward. She grabbed onto him for balance. "You're getting on my nerves. Go bother your girlfriend instead," she snapped.

He laughed out loud. "I like your optimism."

Suddenly, from a few feet behind them, they heard a disgruntled yell followed by cursing. They looked back to see Mr. London regaining his balance. Jack turned back around, visibly trying not to burst into laughter.

"You have problems," Linda stated. He started giggling. She shook her head. "Are you okay, Mr. London?" she called to her vexed science teacher.

"What? Oh, yes, Linda, thank you for asking," Mr. London said, glancing up before looking around at the snowy ground, which bordered the shoveled concrete walkway and sparkled slightly in the dull sunlight. "They need to do a better job laying down salt," he grumbled darkly.

"Are you missing something?" Linda asked.

"When I slipped on the ice, I dropped my keys in the snow, I think," Mr. London said. "I'm already late for my ex-wife's birthday party."

"Oh, I think I've found them," Jack said, bending over to pick up something in the snow.

"Over there? Really?" Mr. London asked incredulously. The keys somehow traveled almost eight feet, but Linda figured that Jack had something to do with it.

Jack shrugged. "Aerodynamics can be surprising," he commented while he handed over the car keys. Linda rolled her eyes.

Mr. London gave him a weird look before saying, "Thanks, John. I didn't even see you there, but I suppose I should've expected it," he sighed, as if regretting sharing too much in front of him. "Take care, Linda. And John." Mr. London added Jack's pseudonym as a polite afterthought before waving and walking away to the parking lot.

"You too," they said in unison.

After Mr. London drove away, Linda abruptly turned to Jack and raised an eyebrow. "How did the keys end up by us?"

"I control snow, what do you think?" Jack retorted.

"Even fallen snow?"

"Does its spatial location change its essence?" Jack smirked. "Come on, Linda, you should know more chemistry than me."

"Dude, I just never thought about it," she said as they continued walking.

"Why is Mr. London always so nice to you? I didn't even know he could be like that. Or open," Jack commented. "It's not some sordid history, is it?"

"Oh my God, Jack. You're being such a teenage boy," she scowled. "That's disgusting."

"Relax! I'm just kidding."

"It's just that he was there when... everything happened," she said quietly.

"What do you mean? He knew her, too?" Jack asked.

Linda nodded. "Can we not talk about this?" she asked. Her throat tightened.

"Yeah, no, I mean we don't have to. I'm sorry," Jack said gently.

"It's fine," she replied. "What were you and Mother Nature arguing about half the night?"

"It wasn't that bad, but she was basically nagging me for not getting enough nature stuff done or that there's been too much snow in some regions," Jack said with a sigh as they crossed Lexington Street. Linda remembered that there were reports of heavy snow across the Midwest and Canada in the news. "It's hard to keep up with school sometimes with all of these new responsibilities she's been adding to my plate."

"What responsibilities?"

Jack inhaled sharply as if he said something he shouldn't have. Linda was surprised—well, shocked. She never considered that there might be more to his presence than... *what exactly?* She didn't know.

"Oh, you know, just watching out for anything suspicious, well, unnatural. Things that shouldn't be happening at this time of year."

"Is that just... seasonal protocol?"

"You could say that," Jack said, not looking at her. She followed his gaze to the matted clouds above them. They walked in silence for a few moments as they neared Chickadee Street, the sound of their footsteps echoing ever so slightly against the white paneled house next to them despite the surrounding bulbous bushes. Linda noted that they practically swallowed up the sound.

"Is that why you're at my school?" Linda asked. She didn't know how to feel about it, but the knowledge sat like a stone in her stomach.

"Oh, no, Mother Nature is not pleased that I'm a student right now. She thinks it's pointless and a distraction."

"Well... what do you think?" Linda ventured.

"I mean, I don't like a majority of the subjects, but I was curious, and now I'm glad that I met you," he said, smiling a big, genuine smile. "I was serious when I said that you're my best friend."

"By the way, what do you like about Jasmine?" Linda asked, changing the subject.

"Um, I'm not sure. There's something about her that I can't put my finger on, but she's intriguing. What do you know about her?" Jack answered.

"She's the niece or goddaughter of a lawyer named Everett Clari, the uncle of the missing girl. She came last year to live with him."

"Trouble?"

"Maybe. She's always seemed pretty fine to me, but she's one of those popular kids that Beatrice and Heather try to keep up with."

"Ooh, do I hear some poison?"

"You don't like them, either."

"I know, you've just said so many zingers against them today."

"Two is not that many. And what do you mean, 'do I hear some poison?' What kind of phrase is that?"

"Don't judge me," Jack laughed.

TEN

THE BITTER PITH

I n Visual Art the following morning, Linda sat through another
enthusiastic lecture by Mrs. Greene about the history of charcoal
use in art, a common practice in the Renaissance. Naturally, this meant
they had to create their own charcoal versions of pre-approved Renaissance paintings or sculptures. As Linda walked back to her seat after
picking up materials from the front of the room, she found herself
talking to Josh for the first time in a while. She had complimented him
on his charcoal sketch, in which he somehow made it about a head of
garlic instead of the statue David by Donatello. Even though he tried
to deny that the lines actually formed reasonably shaped garlic. Josh
had looked pleasantly surprised that she was talking to him, and in her
peripheral vision, Linda noticed Mrs. Greene smiling at her, which
soured her mood. She didn't want to be the little charity case recovering
from the town tragedy. She quickly extricated herself from the
conversation.

As Linda walked past another table, she looked down by chance to
see a gorgeous charcoal sketch of a half-nude woman sitting on a planet.
"Is that Venus?" she asked in spite of herself. She was not in the mood
to engage in a yet another conversation, but it was too late. Her stupid
curiosity killed the cat.

"Um, yes," the girl stammered shyly.

Linda realized that it was the new girl who she hadn't met yet—

Lavender Johnson-Pierre, one of Mrs. Pierre's kids, Linda remembered. "I love it," Linda said with a smile. She continued before Lavender could quietly thank her and finally retreated to her seat where she could peacefully be ignored by Beatrice and Heather. When Linda looked up at the board, she noticed that Dan was standing over Lavender and laughing as he held up her sketch. He showed it to his friends. Lavender yanked it back from him. Linda frowned.

During the next period, Linda secretly enjoyed watching Jack suffer through the quiz that he blew off studying for while Mr. London militantly paced throughout the classroom to catch any cheaters. Linda had to try to hide her chuckle. Mr. London always took quiz questions directly from the textbook chapter for that week. They were not challenging.

In English class, Ms. McGeady announced the new unit: poetry. Linda groaned internally. She didn't hate poetry, but the way that English classes usually had to painstakingly analyze poems about inane topics like a vase of flowers was pushing it. However, Ms. McGeady chose a poem about grieving...

"I search for you," the first student read aloud. Linda closed her eyes.

"Sinking my hands into the snow..." another student read. She tried to keep the familiar feelings from swallowing her up, to keep the memory of seeing her best friend die at bay.

"I hit the ground."

Linda desiderated that she could perish. She tried to think of entries from her dictionary, but the verses were so simple. It was a futile endeavor.

"You're so far away."

She wiped away tears as she quickly got up from her chair without permission, breaking the cardinal rule. But the teacher said nothing as Linda fled the room. She hurried to the stairs in search of Jack, who she knew would be on the other side of the school in his history class.

Linda appeared at the door of his classroom after sufficiently wiping away any stray tears to avoid capturing extra attention. She saw him sitting in the room, looking almost comically bored out of his mind, occasionally glancing over at Jasmine. Then his gaze traveled to Linda, and they locked eyes. He looked away and waited a moment before standing up to leave class. Linda walked to the side of the door to avoid being seen by the other students. She didn't need any more embarrassment for the day.

"Are you okay?" Jack asked once he had closed the door behind him. Linda shook her head. She was unable to look up at him as she fought to hold back hot tears from flowing down her face.

"Can I?" Jack asked, holding out his arms. Linda nodded and moved closer to him, burrowing her face in his soft chest as he wrapped his arms around her. He didn't say anything as he held her, rubbing her back lightly. Kelsie's absence sat like a cavernous pit in her stomach. The world felt vacant around her, despite Jack's surprising warmth, but it somehow didn't matter. Nothing really mattered.

"Are you feeling better?" he asked quietly, his deep voice slightly comforting.

She shook her head against his shirt.

"Okay," he said.

"Aren't you two supposed to be in class?" a kid asked as they walked past the two of them.

"Fuck off, it's a free period," Jack shot back, his tone snarky. Linda almost laughed.

"We don't have a free period until senior year," she said, her voice shaky and half-muffled by his shirt.

"Oh, I see how it is, not saying anything until you have something to correct me about," Jack teased. "I thought all high schoolers had free periods and that I was just unlucky."

"Your limited immortal knowledge is showing through," Linda smirked into his shirt. "And the idea of you having a free period probably terrifies Mr. London."

"Oh, come on, I don't get into that much mischief," Jack said as he let go of her. "More importantly, how are you feeling, Linda?" His eyes were tender with concern, and she felt some color trickle into her cheeks.

"I'm okay."

"Do you want to go home or something?"

"Would they even let me?"

"I mean, you've already missed at least half of class. It doesn't bother me," he added once he saw her about to apologize for getting in the way of the education he didn't want.

"I'm fine, I think," Linda said. "I might as well go back."

"Okay," Jack said. "I'll walk you over."

"Are you sure you're not just using this as an excuse to get out of class?" Linda joked as they walked past bulletin boards plastered with classwork, "Missing" posters for Jane Clari, and reminders about the dangers of strangers, underage drinking, and drug use.

"Oh, please," Jack said, rolling his eyes. "Everyone knows I would do anything to go on a rendezvous with my girlfriend."

"Oh my God, shut up," Linda laughed, lightly pushing him.

"In all seriousness, Jasmine's in my class right now, so that should tell you something."

"How could I forget," Linda answered sarcastically.

Once they were on the first floor, they saw Mr. London walking out of his classroom in the otherwise empty hallway. "What are you doing out of class, you two?" he asked, looking... somewhat amused. *Oh God,* Linda thought with a sinking feeling, *has he heard the rumors?*

"Linda was upset," Jack stated.

"Why?" Mr. London asked.

Linda looked up to meet Mr. London's softened eyes and slightly furrowed brows, his face steeped with concern, before she looked away. "My teacher had us read a poem... about death," she said quietly. "So, I went to get John."

"Who?" Mr. London demanded.

"Ms. McGeady."

"So you don't get in trouble with her, I'll write a note for you," Mr. London said in a tone that allowed no space for disagreement. Linda and Jack followed him to his room and stood at the door while he attacked a piece of paper with a ballpoint pen. He then pulled out a sticky note and scribbled on it as well before returning to them, crossing his arms to deliver the note to Jack and the folded paper to Linda.

"Give that to your teacher if they give you trouble, John," Mr. London instructed. "Linda, you *must* give my letter to Ms. McGeady. I will know if you don't."

Linda nodded. Then Mr. London locked his classroom door behind him before walking back down the hall, calling, "Don't dally, John!"

Jack and Linda exchanged looks before they resumed walking back to her classroom.

"I'll see you later, Linda," Jack said, putting a hand on her shoulder before looking down at Mr. London's note and crumpling it into his pocket.

"See you, Jack," Linda said, disappearing into the classroom.

At the end of the period, Linda followed her science teacher's instructions and gave the paper to Ms. McGeady. She saw the teacher distinctly flinch as she read it. Mr. London could apparently be scathing, and if Linda didn't feel so terrible she would've laughed.

"Don't worry about today, Linda," Ms. McGeady said softly, and Linda slipped out of the room.

Linda kicked some stones into the grassy lawns as she and Jack quietly walked home after school. Before they reached her street, he suddenly asked, "Can I show you something?"

"I guess?"

"Great. Follow me!" he said, taking off running down the street.

Linda bolted after him, taking almost a whole minute to catch up to him. "What are you showing me?" she asked as she finally jogged alongside him.

"A secret," Jack said mischievously. "There's also a limited amount of time before any kids run onto the soccer field at the park."

Eventually, they made it to Penobscot Park, which was unusually empty, as Jack had promised. He stopped abruptly and Linda crashed into him, almost knocking him over. "Linda!" he giggled in surprise as they regained their balance.

"I'm sorry, I didn't expect you to stop so suddenly," Linda exclaimed, catching her breath. That was about the closest they'd ever been. Aside from him hugging her earlier. Which didn't count because they weren't squished together. There was still room for Jesus.

He gestured for Linda to follow him. They walked quickly past the jungle gym, and, at the edge of the huge and empty soccer field, he knelt and touched the grass. Gradually, she noticed that the otherwise fading green field began to turn white around the perimeter. The frost slowly moved inward from the edges, creating a constantly shrinking and intricate snowflake of green in the center of the field. Eventually, the ground in front of them was covered in a blanket of scintillating hoarfrost.

"Wow... that's... that's amazing," Linda breathed.

"You think so?"

"Of course!" Linda exclaimed. "I'm your best friend, so naturally I have to appreciate you anyway," she teased, grinning up at him.

"Gee, thanks, Linda," he replied sarcastically, playfully rolling his eyes and smiling back.

"For the record... Kelsie's and my favorite season was always autumn." The mention of her name hung in the frosty air between them. It reminded Linda of the distinct lack of her late best friend that she felt earlier, and it hurt to see her breath hanging in the freezing air: the air that filled and exited her functioning lungs, the warm breath of life. She looked over to see Jack's breath hanging in the air slightly as well, although not nearly as distinct.

"What?" Jack asked, noticing her looking over at him. "Are you thinking about her?"

"It was difficult... to watch her leave," Linda said quietly. She took a deep breath.

"You were there?"

"At the hospital with her. I had to say goodbye."

"I can't imagine how that felt to experience."

"I still get nightmares. It's a strange way of remembering her, to see her die," Linda admitted, staring at the frost around her feet.

"I'm so sorry, Linda," Jack said, moving closer to her.

"I wish your saying 'sorry' could help," she said, accepting another hug from him. For a second, she saw the look on his face, but she couldn't tell what it meant. The emotion hung right under the surface. "I'm sorry if what I said came off as mean."

"No, it's okay, I understood what you meant," Jack responded, rubbing her back.

"I appreciate you showing me the frost," Linda said as they separated. "It's really one of the coolest things I've ever seen. I didn't even know that was possible."

"Really?" Jack's face lit up. "I've never heard someone be so excited about frost. Except for me."

"What do you mean? I can't imagine anyone who hates it. Well, except for gardeners or farmers."

Jack chuckled. "Yeah, I suppose they don't like me that much. Mother Nature and Father Time are usually pissed at me for it, though. They always think my timing is off, and Father Time is nagging me about accidentally starting another 'great freeze,'" he said, making air quotes with his fingers. "It's not like each year is my first time doing it."

"You know, you curse a lot for someone who's new to the mortal world," Linda commented. "That sounds frustrating, though."

"It is, but at least it's a lot of fun being able to make people slip on ice," he said, making Linda chuckle. "And, I mean, some immortals do curse, but it's not usually English curse words. The wind spirits have especially dirty mouths. Although I love what the Germans have done for the English language."

"You mean the *Germanic* peoples?"

"Yeah, them. You know what I mean. History is not my strong suit."

"It's technically linguistics."

"Okay, I get it," Jack said, holding up his hands, "I curse a lot. At least I'm getting something right."

"You're fine, Jack," Linda laughed. "We should also start heading home so Mom doesn't flip out about us missing in the cold."

"Why would she flip out about *me* missing?"

"She cares about you."

"She doesn't seem to like my hair, since she's always staring at it."

"She's just not used to people who supposedly dye their hair. And, you know, she doesn't know you're Jack Frost."

"Oh. Right."

"Yeah. Race you!" Linda said, running past him.

"Hey!" Jack exclaimed, laughing. He quickly caught up to her, and they ran side by side the whole way home.

"Hi, Mr. and Mrs. Waters, come in!" the science teacher greeted the two parents as they were let into his classroom by a frazzled student helper. Mr. London had seen the boy a few times around the school before this, notably roaming the halls for unspecified reasons. He figured that this was probably some sort of dean-mediated penance. But Mr. London also didn't care to learn the student's name despite the hour he had been there.

"Hi, Mr. London, good to see you again," Mrs. Waters said. She never quite liked his personality aside from how kind he had been to her daughter.

"How's the wife?" Mr. Waters asked, making Mr. London's face grow unbearably hot. *Was this man really that much of a twit, or did he keep his head in the sand?* Mr. London wondered sourly. The teacher cleared his throat before answering, noting the wife's pursed lips and exasperated sigh. *This sort of thing must happen often*, Mr. London thought. If not for the sore subject, he would've chuckled.

"Oh, um, she's not my wife anymore, Mr. Waters. I thought everyone knew," he said.

"Oh, I'm so sorry! I didn't realize!" Mr. Waters gasped, covering his mouth in what seemed to be genuine shock.

"Please forgive my husband, he keeps his nose hidden in the newspaper whenever he's not at work," Mrs. Waters explained, sighing again. "We hope you're well, George."

Mr. London cleared his throat again, mildly surprised that she used his first name, but he didn't mind. "I am, thank you," he said. "So... your daughter, Linda."

"Yes," her mother said, peering at Mr. London over her maple syrup-colored metal frames. The teacher realized that Linda had gotten her serious brown eyes and round face from her mom, but her button nose, freckles, and borderline sardonic smile were from her dad. "How is she performing?"

"Splendidly, actually. She is easily the brightest student in her class, despite everything," he explained, taking great pain to exclude a mention of John's terrible classroom habits that somehow seemed to neither help nor hurt Linda.

"Oh, that's wonderful news!" Mrs. and Mr. Waters said in sync, beaming.

"Yes, I agree. However, I am concerned for her emotional well-being. I won't say too much of my own thoughts as I don't want to overstep, but I think it would be helpful if she spoke to a mental health professional."

"I was afraid you'd say that," Mrs. Waters admitted. "She hasn't ever brought it up after the school offered sessions with the guidance counselor, so we never pressed the issue one way or the other."

"That's fair enough. Again, I don't want to impose—"

"Relax, George, we've known you for almost two years and one tragedy now," Mrs. Waters interrupted, waving her hand. Mr. Waters nodded in agreement.

"Right. Well, um, but even with her friend John, who I'm sure you've probably met by now, she isn't anywhere close to how she used to be. Her demeanor is completely different. I hate to see her suffer."

"We appreciate your concern, Mr. London," Mr. Waters said. "We're taking it one day at a time. But we're glad that she has you for a teacher. We've only ever heard good things about you through the grapevine."

"Oh, um, thank you, sir," Mr. London stammered, pulling at the collar of his button-down shirt. He wasn't used to compliments. He knew that many teachers had a similar experience.

"Yes, we're very thankful for your kindness. It's definitely helped Linda," Mrs. Waters said before glancing at her watch. "Oh, I'm afraid we'll have to go to our next appointment soon. Is there anything else you'd like to discuss?"

"Well, that's a question I should be asking you," Mr. London chuckled warmly. "Unless there's anything else, I think we're all set. If something comes up, feel free to shoot me an email, and I'll be happy to meet with you."

"Well, thank you, Mr. London. Have a good night!" Mrs. Waters said, standing up alongside her husband, who reached out to shake the teacher's hand. Mr. London stood to return the favor.

"Goodnight and get home safe!" Mr. London said as they left. Mr. Waters wished him good luck as the frazzled student reappeared at the door. A very stout woman and a red-faced, red-necked gentleman pushed past the kid. They were dressed to the nines—at least in terms of their small Maine town—and reeked of perfume, cologne, and cigarette smoke, with the faintest underlying trace of marijuana.

Mr. London wanted to scream as the father greeted him, "So you're the effeminate hardass who's failing my son, aren't you?" The wife smiled at Mr. London maliciously.

Just a year and a half more of this crap, Mr. London grimaced, forcing a saccharine smile.

"Angela, what do you think about what London said?" Mr. Waters asked his wife as they walked home, linking arms and bracing against the familiar chill of their hometown.

"I don't want to push Linda into anything. You know she avoids talking about her feelings like the plague," Angela said, smiling sadly.

"I know," he answered. After walking for a bit, he asked, "How is she doing with John? He seems like an odd choice for a friend, but they seem inseparable."

"She seems to be happy with him, I just hope it's able to last, Michael," she answered.

"Me too," he agreed.

"Have you heard from Colin recently?" Angela asked. She saw her breath hang in the air, illuminated by light pouring from one of the houses on their street.

"No, but I tried reaching out. He hasn't been the same since Kelsie passed, either," Michael answered. "I'll try again. I miss our nights out."

"I can't imagine what it's like to lose a child," Angela said softly.

"I don't want to know," Michael said as they reached their front door. "Let's take a deep breath, Ange."

"Okay," she said, nodding. "You're right, Linda and John will still be doing their homework like when we left."

"Right," he said, giving her a kiss. Then he opened the door.

After Linda and Jack finished the bulk of their homework, they had a surprising amount of time to play one of her family's favorite card games: Slap. Linda's mom joined in while her dad disappeared into his post-work lair in the basement, and Jack picked up the game surprisingly quickly despite simultaneously gobbling a large quantity of her mom's freshly baked cookies. Then 7:00 p.m. rolled around, and it was time for him to leave.

"Goodbye, John," her mom said at the front door. She offered a hug, which he accepted, although he was slightly reluctant at first.

"You're welcome here whenever," she said with a smile.

"Gee, thanks, Mrs. Waters," Jack said with the faintest hint of a blush, rubbing the back of his head.

"Will you be able to get home fine in the dark?" her mom asked.

"I'll be fine—my folks are going to be worried, though, if I leave much later than now," Jack explained.

"Let us know if you change your mind at any point and want a ride home, okay?"

"Thank you," Jack smiled warmly. "It means a lot."

He turned and unlocked the front door, the boreal night air tumbling in softly, like a whisper. The streetlights sprinkled along the road had already flickered on, life in the embers of their metallic filaments.

"Bye," Jack said, "See you tomorrow."

Linda wanted to tell him not to leave, but her voice caught in her throat. She wrapped her arms around him instead. He held her back.

And then he was gone.

ELEVEN

BEAUTIFUL

The next morning, Linda woke to another glittering snow-covered utopia outside her window. Late-morning sunlight filtered into her room through the blinds that she forgot to close the night before. She nearly had a heart attack, wondering why her alarm didn't go off and let her sleep in until 10 a.m., until she remembered that it was Saturday. An hour later, Jack showed up on the doorstep, and she happily agreed to go for a walk with him.

"I figured that Maine was getting a little overdue," he grinned, gesturing to the snow that glittered everywhere outside.

"It's absolutely wonderful," she beamed, before saying, "woah, you're wearing something different. What's the special occasion?"

"Nothing, I just figured it would be fun to mix it up and blend in with the mortals. I'm assuming it would be too cold to just wear a t-shirt and hoodie today for people like you," he explained as she closed the front door behind her. He still wore his Converse—Linda was jealous of how his shoes never got soaked or caked in snow—but instead of his hoodie and t-shirt, he wore a beautiful cream-colored Fair Isle sweater with a blue pattern like the stellar dendrites on snowflakes. Her eyes nearly popped out of her head at the distinct change in his appearance. *When did he get so handsome?* She immediately pushed the insipid, hormone-fueled thought out of her mind.

"Am I not allowed to dress for the cold?" he asked with his stupid mischievous grin.

"Jack, you always *emanate* the cold."

"That doesn't mean I have to act like it."

"Okay, true. You look nice though."

"Thank you. You look very warm."

Linda made a face. "Thank you?" she said as they descended the stairs.

"What? Your coat looks nice and warm, a perfect combination," Jack said as they began their walk toward Cherry Lane. Linda felt extremely thankful for the tread on her snow boots as only partial constituents of the sidewalk were shoveled. The small walkways were covered in a few inches of sparkling snow that practically blinded her while her eyes adjusted.

He suddenly stopped and pointed to a tree branch on the other side of Cherry Lane, putting a hand on her shoulder. "Isn't that a chickadee?"

"Ummm... no, I think that's a nuthatch," she said, squinting to see the bird. "There isn't as much black around its head as a black-capped chickadee."

"Oh, okay. I always mix those up. And lots of other birds, which infuriates Mona."

"Mona?"

"Oh, sorry. That's what Father Time and I call Mother Nature."

"Do you have a nickname for Father Time?"

"Just Time," Jack replied, then quickly asked, "Do you have a nickname?"

"Yes, but you can't use it."

"Why not?"

"My siblings came up with it when we were little. They called me 'Lindy.'"

He smiled. "That's cute."

"Do you have a nickname?" she asked.

"Me? No," Jack said, a little too quickly to be believable.

"If you did, would you tell me?"

"Definitely not."

"Oh, come on, that's not fair!"

"I never liked my nickname, and I prefer 'Jack.' And the being that gave it to me… isn't around anymore," Jack confided quietly, clearing his throat. "It translates to 'Snowflake.'"

"Jack, come on, that's a cute name," Linda said. "I'm sorry about your loss, though." After seeing the dark look on his face, she quickly added, "I promise I won't use it."

"Thank you. Can you imagine if people overheard you call me Snowflake at school? I would never live it down."

Linda grinned. "Even better if Mr. London heard it."

"Don't you dare!" Jack exclaimed, turning toward her while she cackled.

Soon, they were in the forest. The snow was beautiful, and it covered just about everything, making the trees, saplings, and rocks dazzle like diamonds. Jack and Linda talked as they walked through the trees, whose branches held up small perfect piles of snow like what Linda would expect in wintry landscape paintings.

Jack tripped on a hidden root and Linda caught his hand.

"Are you okay?" she asked as he regained his balance.

"Yeah, thanks," he said.

Linda looked at his somewhat large hand. "Your hands are so warm," she said.

"Did you expect them to be cold?" he asked, his tone amused.

"I mean, yeah, especially out here," Linda tittered as she began to compare their hand sizes.

"Wow, your hands are small," he laughed.

"Shut up, yours are just really large. Why are your fingers so long?"

"They're not that much longer than yours! It's only by one segment or whatever it's called," he said.

"Jack Frost? What are you doing here?" a voice booming with superiority asked from behind them.

Jack immediately dropped Linda's hands, and his shoulders tensed.

She saw his expression before he turned to face them—he clearly recognized the voice and was *not* happy about it. "I'm here on your assignment. What are *you* doing here?" he demanded. The ire in his voice startled Linda. She looked past him to the woman he addressed.

The slender woman towered over them at nearly seven feet. Her deep brown skin had a warm, golden radiance, and her long black hair was dark as a moonless night, the tight curls tumbling down her back to her thighs. In contrast, her eyes were a striking bright green, the color of new leaves in the spring. A tiara of shining emerald leaves on braided gold vines sat on her head, and she wore a flowing pine needle-green silk cloak that moved with an energy all its own despite the windless day. A large amber stone, glowing softly in its ornamented brass bezel setting dotted with aqua patina, held together her cloak on her left shoulder. Her presence was nothing short of regal, and Linda instantly felt the strange urge to throw herself at the woman's feet.

"Rosie and I were alerted of a strange presence in the area, but we did not expect to see you cavorting around with a mortal," the woman said, crossing her arms. It was only then that Linda noticed the short woman next to the queenly figure. She was dressed entirely in cerise garments, which would have made her seem almost like a little girl with her large hazel eyes if not for the maturity in her face. Her skin was almost a light pink that reminded Linda of a delicate rose. Pointed ears poked through her wavy brown bob, which was adorned with small pink rosebuds.

Jack groaned violently out of exasperation before he turned to Linda. "That's Mother Nature," he said to her, pointing to the tall woman.

Linda fainted.

TWELVE

BITE

"Linda, are you okay?"

Linda slowly opened her eyes. Biting cold seeped through her jeans, and she saw Jack kneeling in front of her, cupping her face in one of his hands and rubbing her shoulder with the other.

"Time is valuable, Jack Frost. I am running out of patience," Mother Nature said harshly. Jack helped Linda to sit up before he turned to the Queen. Linda noticed the elf still standing at Mother Nature's side. It was one too many elves for her sanity. And the sunlight was very bright.

"Mona, it's not what you think. I am looking for the book, okay? I was just talking to a friend to learn more information," Jack snapped. Linda froze. *What book? What information?*

"You two looked rather close for my taste. Holding hands? What's next, butterfly kisses and letting the stolen text get destroyed? Jeopardizing something more important than the entire human existence? HAVE YOU LOST YOUR MIND?" Mother Nature roared. "Maybe this is too much responsibility. You might be better suited *guarding the palace,* so I don't have to do damage control!"

Jack stood up. "Linda is just a cover, okay? You want information; I am finding information. I can't blend in if I don't get to know the beings that live here. Get off my case and go focus on your migration patterns."

His words cut through Linda. Her head swam. It was too much to take in. *Linda is just a cover.* The sentence bounced around in her head. She was nothing to him, after all. He was just impersonally curious while he was on some mission that he deliberately hid from her. She should have realized when he was so fascinated with her home, and her mortal way of life. Linda felt sick as her mind raced. Her worst fears had been realized. It really was too good to be true. After everything she had shared with him, things that she never told anyone else. Of course, she was just a dumb human. She wanted to vomit. How could she be so stupid to think that someone really cared about her, especially an immortal? Blood rushed in her ears and her face. Her heart pounded and it felt like it would burst out of her chest.

She hated him.

She precariously stood up, and Jack turned toward her, reaching forward as if to help her. She pushed his hands away. "Don't touch me," she said darkly.

The look of shock on his face was unmistakable. "What?"

"I hate you. I can't believe I thought I could trust you," Linda snapped.

"I thought you would understand," he said, his tone practically begging.

"Fuck off," Linda snapped at him.

"Linda, I didn't mean it—"

"So, you *are* close with your cover?" Mother Nature said, her tone frigid.

"Will you shut up?" Jack growled at the Queen. "Linda!"

But Linda was already running away, pushing through the trees weighed down by frozen water.

"You aren't going anywhere," she heard Mother Nature order Jack as the raised voices faded behind her.

At the edge of the forest, she tripped on a hidden rock and landed in the freezing snow. It was numbing to her exposed hands. She stood up and brushed off the dull melting crystals, tears spilling down her cheeks, and she ran. She stopped at the end of Cherry Lane, where it intersected Lexington and Chickadee. Her chest physically hurt, but she couldn't tell if it was from her bleeding heart or the cold air. She doubled over for a second, putting her hands on her knees, but she didn't like the thoughts that stillness invited into her mind. It was too much. After catching her breath, which was shaky and broken by tears that spilled over and cries that escaped her mouth, she walked down the sidewalk as quickly as possible. Linda passed grey and white houses, a putrid and dreary blue abode, and evergreen vegetation littered with snow.

When she reached her house, her feet felt heavy like lead as she walked up to the porch. She tried to open the front door, but the metal was so cold to her frozen hands that she resorted to ringing the doorbell a million times. Finally, after maybe five minutes, her mom opened the freaking locked door and Linda stumbled inside. She ignored her mom's questions as she threw her coat in the direction of the coat rack after tearing it off her sweating body, yanking off her boots and then carrying her heavy existence to her bedroom where she collapsed face down on her bed. She didn't care if she would suffocate and die.

Apparently, her mom did care, since she sat down next to her and stroked her hair. "Sweetie? What's wrong?" she asked.

Linda began to sob. "Everything," she mumbled.

"What happened? Where's John?"

"John and I aren't friends anymore," Linda cried. "I hate him."

THIRTEEN

SESQUIPEDALIAN AFFAIRS

Linda cried so much that she felt herself slowly desiccate.

That night, she couldn't bring herself to eat dinner. Instead, she had ice cream and watched a desert nature documentary until she grew sad about animal friendships. Then she went to her room and cried until she fell asleep. The next morning felt no better. She couldn't forget what Jack had said. *Just a cover.* Did she even actually know him?

She reached down under her bed—trying not to fall off in the process—and grabbed her dictionary. A thin layer of dust had formed on its cover. She flipped to a dog-eared page and found that it was at the letter "S." She read through the entries: *solar system... sole... solemn... solitary... solo...* she just threw the stupid book somewhere else in the room. Even the dictionary was conspiring against her when all she wanted was to sleep and forget.

Eventually, though, her stomach won out when the hunger pains began to make it feel like her abdomen would implode. Eating nothing but a sugary frozen dairy product in lieu of normal meals was a horrible idea.

She spent the remainder of her day confined to the pool of light from her desk lamp, feeling as if she was stranded in a wasteland. Occasionally, her parents stopped by in attempts to extricate her but to no avail. Her cat even tried to snuggle against her, but she nudged him away. Linda only wanted to be around one person, but that person... She looked down at her bracelet from her best friend—*late best friend*, she corrected herself. The glass beads reflected some of the lamp light. Kelsie had gotten them during a visit to a craft store and made a bracelet with two of Linda's favorite colors one time, just to surprise her. Warm tears fell onto her wrist.

FOURTEEN

SATURN'S MOONS

L inda got to school late that Monday. Because that was exactly what she needed: to oversleep, get ready in a rush, hurry to school, go to the Main Office (and pass by Kelsie's memorial plaque posted directly outside of it, which she could normally avoid just by never going to the office) to be counted for attendance when she would rather be at home crying while the office lady argued with her for not getting up on time like everyone else. In Visual Art, she got to the table after Beatrice and Heather, and both called her a freeloader under their breath after she tried to sit in her usual seat, which they occupied with one of their backpacks. So, Linda had to go sit next to the new girl, Lavender, who wanted to talk and be friendly until Linda told her that she was having the worst day ever and sorry but talking made her headache worse. Linda felt bad for shutting Lavender down. She had seemed so interested in talking. But that combined with seeing Mrs. Greene get excited about dead people who had come up with great new ways to lengthen her lectures was not improving her mood. Or her splitting headache. She wanted to defenestrate.

And then her day got even better when she walked into Earth Science. Mr. London decided it would be a great idea to spend the period teaching them how to discover the density of an irregular object, because that was a skill Linda totally needed to prepare her for the rest of her life. The object he picked out for them happened to be a key.

Linda snarkily wondered if any of the keys that he passed out to each set of partners belonged to his ex-wife.

She tried to talk as little as possible to Jack. He tried to greet her, but she opted to ignore him because she was a young, mature adult and couldn't bring herself to look at his stupid face. Despite that, they somehow managed a silent agreement that if he took whatever measurements were needed, Linda would record them and do the calculations. He didn't even need to be there as an immortal, which just reminded Linda of what he said. It just made her even more angry.

When she was halfway through calculating the total volume of the key, Jack knocked the very full graduated cylinder over onto her open notebook.

"Oh shit, I'm so sorry," Jack gasped, covering his mouth.

Linda was so sick of everything, including his clueless countenance. She looked down. It would be hard to save her notebook. And she just didn't have it in her.

"I swear I didn't mean it, it was an accident," Jack explained earnestly. But she stood up, grabbed her dripping notebook by one of its corners, and walked briskly to the front of the room where she unceremoniously chucked it into the trashcan so hard that she saw Mr. London jump at his desk. Then she turned and left the room, unsure of where to go to gather her thoughts.

"Linda, wait," Jack said as the door to the classroom closed behind him.

"Don't bother me," Linda said, turning away from him and walking down the hall.

"Can we please just talk?" he begged.

She decided she would go to the bathroom. "No," Linda snapped. He flinched at her tone.

The door to the girl's bathroom opened right as Linda began reaching for the handle. It was Lavender. "Hi, Linda!" she said cheerily.

"Hi," Linda said. "Talk to you later."

"Okay," Lavender said without missing a beat.

Linda stood in the bathroom, thankful that the rest of the stalls were empty for once.

"John, why are you loitering outside the girls' restroom?" she heard Mr. London suddenly demand on the other side of the door.

"I'm waiting for Linda," Jack quickly retorted.

"Why? She can come out of the bathroom whenever she's ready just fine on her own," their teacher said. Linda stifled a snort.

"But I need to talk to her."

"You can talk to her later. Come back to class and clean up your mess."

"But you don't understand. What if she doesn't want to talk to me later?" Jack blurted.

She heard Mr. London sigh. "John, give her some space. You can't pressure her to talk when she's not ready, that's not how it works. Come back to class and finish up the work before the period is over, your grade can't afford to suffer much more."

"Fine," Jack grumbled.

Eventually, Linda heard the bell ring—it was the end of the period. She hurried back to the classroom after she was sure that Jack, as well as most of the students, would've been out of the room. Mr. London looked up at her as she walked swiftly to the back to collect her backpack. As she tried to leave the room, Mr. London stopped her.

"You were absent from class for more than half the period. Were you sick?" he asked.

"No, I'm fine."

"I've known you for almost two years. That was pretty out of charac-ter for you."

"I guess so."

"Would you like me to move your seat?"

Linda hesitated. The second bell rang.

Mr. London raised an eyebrow. "You nearly gave me a heart attack in the middle of class from throwing out course materials. I know you probably heard me speaking to John outside of the bathroom. I don't like sticking my nose into business that's not my own, but I would normally give someone detention or a zero for how you acted today."

Linda sighed exasperatedly and looked down at her shoes.

He sighed and leaned back in his desk chair. "Linda, I don't get paid enough to pretend to genuinely care about student conduct. This job is crap. Did he apologize to you?"

"…Yes, he did," she said slowly as he wrote out a late pass. When she reached for it, he pulled his hand back, holding the pass up in the air.

"Sincerely?" he asked firmly. "Don't lie."

"He seems to feel really bad. I'm talking to him at the end of the day," she decided.

"Good. Anything less from him is bullshit. You deserve better," her teacher stated. "I've kept you long enough, enjoy the rest of your day." She grabbed the note from him and headed for the door.

"Aren't you forgetting something?" he called after her.

"What?" she asked, trying to hide her irritation.

"Don't you need your notebook?" he asked, gesturing toward the trashcan next to his desk.

"I know everything in it already," she responded simply.

"I know you know everything," Mr. London said as he fished it out from the otherwise mostly empty receptacle. "There wasn't enough water in those graduated cylinders to totally destroy it, you ought to keep it." He handed it to her.

She reluctantly accepted it. "Okay."

"Keep me updated," Mr. London said, and then she left the room, the door slowly closing behind her. He sighed, looking back down at his desk. A pile of new worksheets sat in the middle, scribbled over in ink and graphite and ready to grade. He picked up his pen. He hoped that John was suffering with guilt. The only way that a devoted student like Linda would act like that would be if something big had happened. If John, the little shit that failed every other assignment, ever hurt Linda again, Mr. London would make his life as much of a living hell as he could legally get away with—the teacher's thoughts were interrupted by a plastic pen clip hitting his face, his thumb scratched from breaking it off. He sighed. He would talk about that with his therapist.

Linda ate her lunch in the library that day, grabbing bites of a PB&J sandwich that she snagged from the cafeteria in between filling out homework questions. She and Kelsie had learned that doing homework was the only way they were allowed in the library at lunch, and that it made it possible for them to spend more time hanging out after school instead of doing tedious math problems. At the memory, a knot settled in Linda's stomach. She put down her sandwich and took a deep breath. She didn't want to cry in front of the librarian.

She looked up at the ceiling, then at the shelves of old books, anything to distract herself. Her eyes settled on a book titled *The Elf Queen*, its purple and silver spine wrapped in a plastic dust cover. Linda normally wasn't interested in fantasy, but her mind drifted to that story she had found the day she and Jack started talking. *Did the person who wrote it get inspired from this, or something else? They wouldn't know that elves are real. Did it even matter?* she wondered. *Does anything matter?*

As Mr. London walked down the hall to the faculty meeting, he took his time as he passed by the high school's prized student trophy case. One of the trophies was his—how else do you think he ended up in this small town? Despite his adolescent athletic achievements, he didn't very much miss being a teenager. Although he didn't very much enjoy being an adult from the favorite millennial generation in his thirties, either.

He looked down at his trophy:

Track & Field Championship
3rd Place 400 Meter Dash
George London

But there was something new underneath it. The wood trim framing the glass case was scarred where someone had crudely scratched in the slur, "FAG," in big, ugly letters. He felt a knot in his stomach. He knew it was meant for him. After the divorce, more eyes had been on all the small details that set him ever-so-slightly apart from the ideal stereotypical heterosexual male. He knew that people thought that his marital relationship was a beard, that people whispered and gossiped and thought he was gay because of his fashion choices, the way he styled his hair and cared about hygiene, and the way his voice was somehow the slightest bit effeminate. He'd had friends who were the most generic, heterosexual cisgender men who, by their own admission, said they were surprised about him being bisexual. Even though it was supposedly just a thirty-odd-year-phase.

Mr. London turned away and began to walk down the hall more quickly. He wished he could leave behind the whispers that told him his identity was a problem even though he loved his wife. *Ex-wife*, he reminded himself. He should be used to it by now, he thought sourly. He'd been the adult that he wanted so desperately to be when he was in high school, or at least he tried to be. He didn't want to blend in, but he didn't want to stand out. George sighed as he pushed the door open for the meeting. From the table filled with faculty, Mrs. Greene the art teacher smiled up at him. He struggled to return one. Not everything would change just because he was older.

His wife still divorced him.

He was still called a fag, just more quietly and with less shoving.

At the end of the day, Linda pushed her locker door shut. She took a deep breath. *Now's the time*, she thought.

"Hey, Linda!" someone called cheerily.

Linda looked up to see Lavender jog over. Linda internally groaned. She didn't mind Lavender at all, but this was the longest day ever, and she had just steeled her resolve to confront her ex. *Ex-friend.* Couldn't she catch a break? "Hi, Lavender," Linda responded, unable to completely keep her frustration out of her voice.

"How was your day?" Lavender asked.

"Long. Yours?" Linda replied.

Lavender's face fell. "Not great," she answered. She began to play with her necklace. Linda noticed that it was a silver cross with a blue topaz heart.

"I'm sorry," Linda said quietly. Was Lavender trying to talk to her about it? *Why? She barely knows me.*

"Some girls teased me about something," Lavender admitted softly, her eyes seeming to moisten.

Linda groaned internally again. As distant as she wanted to be, she couldn't allow herself to be apathetic. "What did they tease you about? Are they bullying you?" she asked.

"I told Beatrice who I like because I was hoping we could become better friends, and then suddenly all of her friends knew in just one weekend, and they all made fun of me. One of them said she talked to him and said he didn't like me back," Lavender explained as her face began to flush.

Oh no, Linda thought. *Tears incoming.* Linda was not prepared for this. "Do you have a friend to talk to about this?"

Lavender turned away, wiping her face.

Oh, Linda realized.

"I'll leave you alone," Lavender said, her voice quavering.

"No, Lavender," Linda said, grabbing her wrist. "I—my best—I'm no good with emotions and I've had a very draining day. Beatrice and her friends suck."

Lavender turned slightly to face her, staying in place. She wasn't leaving. *Lavender's lonely...* Linda realized. *Like me.* So, she stammered, "This...this may be dumb, but when you think about it, her name also spells 'beet-rice.' Who would want to eat beet rice? Or to beat rice? It sounds as dumb as her."

Lavender giggled and took a deep breath. "Maybe I should remember that."

"Her parents messed up at least three times between her name, letting her be a jerk, and by having her," Linda added. She knew she was saying dumb stuff, but it was the only thing she could think of to distract Lavender from her pain.

"That's so mean!" Lavender exclaimed in surprise, but she loosened up, laughing and wiping her eyes.

"You're not disagreeing, though."

"Don't even," Lavender chuckled.

"Hey, Linda," Jack called over to them. "Can I—oh, hi, um, am I interrupting?" he asked when he realized Lavender was there.

The girls exchanged looks. "This is Lavender. Lavender, this is John," Linda said.

"Can I walk home with you guys?" Jack asked.

"Uh… sure," Linda said slowly after Lavender nodded.

As the three of them began leaving, Beatrice and some of her friends crossed their path, heading towards the parking lot. Lavender groaned.

"You live on Cherry Lane, right?" Linda asked.

"You're right! How did you know?"

"I've run into your mom a few times."

After a beat, Lavender said, "It's hard being the new student."

"I can imagine," Linda answered. "I know John had difficulty at first, too."

"You're new, too?" Lavender asked, looking up at John. "You seem to fit in so well."

"Well, I wouldn't if not for Linda," he said. Linda looked away like she'd been slapped across the face, and he flushed when he realized what he said. "I mean, she's my only real friend. I spent a lot of time alone before moving here, too."

"That's really sweet. Most of my friends are at my old school. I really miss them," Lavender said.

"Where's your old school?" Linda asked, clearing her throat.

"In Quebec."

"Oh, that explains why you're so nice," Jack smirked.

"Don't even start with that," Lavender said. "If you met my mom's side of the family, you would know that's not true. They are the most passive-aggressive people known to man."

"Are you sure they're not American?" Linda laughed. "Honestly, I barely noticed your accent."

Lavender rolled her eyes despite a smile playing across her lips. "I think you'll hear it when I say 'about' or start talking about 'loonies and toonies.'"

"Now I can hear it," Jack chuckled.

When Lavender's street came up, Jack and Linda said bye to her, and then they were standing alone on the corner. Linda watched the silent process of John Mason reverting to Jack Frost, the loosening of his shoulders and stance, him standing closer to her. But Linda forced back the feelings of comfort that came from this. "I want you to know that I'm only talking to you because I overheard you whining to Mr. London when you were waiting for me to come out of the bathroom," she said.

"...Right..." Jack said. He sighed, running his hands through his spiky, messy hair. "I was being a piece of shit."

"Yeah."

"It's kind of a long story."

"I'm not waiting any longer. Either I'm your stupid cover, or you're lying to Mother Nature," Linda snapped.

Jack sighed again before continuing. "You're not my cover. Initially, yes, I will admit that you were. But that was when we were barely talking, and I was as close to you as my teachers. But you became much more than that, which is why I decided to share my identity with you."

"Why would you want to do that?"

"Because..." Then he hesitated.

"Because why?"

"Because I was tired of trying to hide myself from you when I wanted to be closer to you. Look, I didn't mention my true mission because I didn't want our friendship to be dominated by some ulterior motive. I just wanted to enjoy it. When I told Lavender that I didn't have many friends before I moved here, I was being honest. You're my first real friend that I've had other than Mother Nature and Father Time. It's hard to be friends with their elves because of the weird power dynamic."

"And you don't think there's a weird power dynamic with you hiding everything from me, a mere mortal?" Linda spat.

"I didn't want you to be in danger."

"Jack, my best friend died. I could die at any moment in the same way as her. I don't care."

"You should care!" Jack snapped at her. "*I* care. I don't want you to get hurt, and there's a reason why Mona doesn't want me to become friends with humans. It's because we're not supposed to impact you guys—"

"Well, it's my choice, too!" Linda raised her voice. "*I* made that choice!" she said, angrily gesturing at herself. "You might be a supernatural being, but you're not God. You're just an idiot who happens to be an immortal snow pixie. I know my life is short and meaningless and just a speck in yours, but you make my shitty life... *better.*" Tears rolled down her face. "And I want you here if you'll actually be my friend." She angrily wiped away her tears. "This is so stupid. I hate crying."

"But your life isn't meaningless. I've lived forever and you're the best friend I've ever had, Linda," Jack responded.

"What does that even mean? You're lying."

"I'm not lying."

"You're mean," Linda said, laughing but still crying.

"Come here," he said, pulling her into a hug.

"I hate you," she said into his chest.

"I hate your verbal abuse," Jack chuckled, rubbing her back. "Calling me a snow pixie. How dare you."

After she calmed down, he asked, "What do you want to know?"

She let go of him and wiped her face again. "What book are you looking for and why is it so important?"

"Okay, so, Father Time records the passage of time in ledgers that he keeps in his library. These books are sacred, and if one of them gets damaged, then that threatens the past, present, and future, and therefore the flow of nature and its processes."

"So, you mean things like evolution and weather patterns?"

"Yes—events could fall out of place, species could change, anything could happen. It could cause total chaos. Basically, the end of the world as we know it. The books are heavily protected, maintained, and accounted for—it's been happening since the beginning of time. Recently, though, one of the mice found a discrepancy in the ledgers—"

"Wait, mice?" Linda asked.

"Yeah, mice. Well, they're large mice because they feed on the sacred sap from Mona's maple tree, but they're still mice. They like hoarding stuff in their nests so they're naturally excellent bookkeepers," Jack explained as if it was completely normal. "Anyway, they realized that one of the books went missing. Mona didn't explain much more beyond that, other than that she knows it went to the mortal world, and seems to be somewhere here specifically, which is why I'm here. I've been trying to keep track of weird weather patterns and any signs of disturbance, and who better to hear from than gossipy teenagers?"

"Why didn't Mona tell you more?" Linda asked. "Isn't that weird to not know everything?"

"I know what I need to know, and I don't care to learn more," Jack shrugged. "I'm a simple guy."

"How do I know I'm not your cover?"

"Well, I'm certainly endangering my duties by spending time with you and also drawing attention to myself, so... you're a hindrance."

"I like that."

Jack laughed. "Don't let it get to your head."

"I wouldn't dream of it," Linda smiled. They began walking down the well-worn path to her house. She kicked a stray stone with her foot. "By the way, did you know that your hair color makes you stand out?"

"I watched this town before I went through that godawful process of enrolling in a school system that only mortals could devise. I knew that there was a status quo, but I didn't want to change my hair color, so I went with it," he explained. "I cannot believe you thought that I did not think this through."

"Jack, you've got to admit that you can be impulsive," Linda returned.

"I'm not *that* impulsive."

"You tried to start a fight."

"At this school, yes," Jack corrected. Before she could protest, he added the codicil, "I knew what I was doing, mostly. It was a split-second judgement."

When they reached her house, passing the yew shrubs that dotted the perimeter of their neighbors' yard, Linda realized that her mom hadn't learned anything about the new developments. "Fair warning," she said to him, "my mom might hate you."

"Why? Is this because—"

"Yes, she was there when you hurt me and I cried my eyes out," Linda clarified matter-of-factly.

"I really am *so* sorry, Linda," Jack said, his voice sad and sincere.

"I know," she answered. She rapped the door with her exposed knuckles. When the door opened, the glare that her mom gave Jack caused him to flinch. The petty part of Linda found it completely satisfying.

FIFTEEN

HISTORY LESSONS

A s Linda walked back into her bedroom from her short stint in the bathroom, she saw Jack standing over her desk, examining something. Without looking up, Jack asked, "Linda, what's this?" He slowly pulled a sheet of paper out of the chaotically organized pile on her desk.

"Why are you looking at my stuff?" she asked, walking over, but he continued reading.

"I was waiting for you, and it caught my eye," he said, holding up a finger. "Hold on."

"What do you mean, 'hold on'?" she demanded, grabbing the paper away from him. "What are you reading?" She examined the page. It was the hand-written piece of fantasy writing that she had found almost a month ago. She hadn't thought about it in a while.

"Where did you get that?" he asked.

"It was on the street one day, before we were even friends, calm down," she said, nudging him out of the way to put it back in the right place. "It's just a story, Jack."

He reached around her to try to get it back. "No, it's not. Someone transcribed it from the book that I've been looking for," Jack answered, his tone steely. "Why didn't you tell me you found this?"

"How am I supposed to know that this was supposed to be real? I'm not some stupid superior immortal, Jack."

"Linda, have you read it? It talks about the people that you've met," he chastised her. "Mother Nature. Elves. *Me*."

Linda put her hands up. "I didn't think that someone else would know you existed. Also, elves? I met my first one a few days ago. Give me a break."

"Okay, fine." He took a deep breath. "This is still really important."

"So, you're telling me this is a serious case of supernatural intellectual property violation? What can you do about this?"

"Well, it means that the book itself is hopefully close and that I've actually been on the right track. I finally have some evidence for Mona before she forces me to stay in the palace. But I don't know who could've been able to transcribe this."

"What do you mean?"

"Whoever wrote this was able to read the original text, which is in an old, sort of runic alphabet that humans have never seen before," Jack said, staring down at the papers as if wishing that they would reveal their secrets. "And whoever could read that could also read and speak human English."

The next day, something weird happened. During lunch, Jasmine Clari went over to Jack and Linda's regular table. At least, it was weird to Linda. She didn't realize that Jack and Jasmine were getting so close.

"Hey, John," Jasmine said, waving as she walked over. When she seemed to notice Linda's existence, she said hi as well. Linda smiled and nodded curtly. Jack shot her a look, and Linda returned the favor.

"Hey, Jasmine," Jack answered. "What's up? I didn't realize you had lunch now."

"Oh, I usually go help a teacher or work on a project. Events don't plan themselves," Jasmine giggled. She had a nice, deep laugh. Linda nearly found it enchanting. Jack certainly thought so from the smile on his face. Linda fought the urge to roll her eyes.

Jasmine pulled out a history textbook from her backpack, plopping it onto the table. "I was wondering if you could help me with the history assignment. I don't have much time to complete it tonight."

Linda excused herself to get more water to keep from laughing. Jack was a horrible person to ask for help. He barely finished his assignments even at Linda's very strongly worded suggestion.

After she finished filling the clear plastic cup that she prayed the school actually bothered to recycle, Linda almost bumped into someone. "Oh, hi, Lavender!" Linda exclaimed, barely saving her cup from losing its contents.

"Hi, Linda!" Lavender said, perky as usual.

"I didn't know you had lunch now," Linda said.

"Oh, I didn't. My academic counselor just swapped me out of a class my old school didn't prepare me for," Lavender explained.

"Oh, okay," Linda answered. After a beat, she asked, "Where are you sitting?"

"Oh, um," Lavender blushed, "over there, alone." She pointed to a rare spare corner of the room.

"Do you want to sit with us?" Linda offered.

"You mean, you and John?"

"Um, yeah, sorry," Linda said, clearing her throat.

"Sure, I'll get my stuff and be right over!" Lavender said, hurrying away as Linda followed her so she could direct her.

"Hey, Lavender!" Jack said as she sat down next to his best friend. Jasmine looked up from the textbook. She had a weird expression on her face as she and Lavender exchanged looks.

"Do you know each other?" Jack asked.

"Um," Lavender said. "Well—"

"I've been assigned to help her acclimate to the Events Committee," Jasmine said quickly. Lavender nodded and smiled, although Linda wondered if it almost seemed forced. Maybe she imagined it.

"Cool!" Jack said. "Now, uh, Jasmine, what were you asking me? Who's... Swamp Fox?" Jack looked over at Linda as if saying, "Help?"

Linda shrugged in response, even though she knew the answer.

After school in Linda's home, Jack finished the exact same homework with some of Linda's help while she finished up a math assignment for the oh-so-lovely Ms. Peters who demanded instant algebraic perfection.

"How was your day overall, Jack?" she asked him as she switched gears to her own history homework.

"It was relatively normal. I guess a bonus was that Jasmine talked to me, but that's about it."

Linda's hot chocolate coursed straight down the wrong pipe and nearly out of her nose.

"Are you okay?" Jack asked as she coughed her lungs out.

"Yeah," she managed a few seconds later. "Wrong pipe. I think your girlfriend is detrimental to my health."

"She's not my girlfriend," he responded, rolling his eyes. But he didn't resume his homework until he was convinced that Linda wasn't going to die on him.

Eventually, after Linda refocused, she leaned back into her chair and let out a long and agonizing groan. Her history textbook's description of the French Revolution became so dry that it would've been hazardous near an open flame.

"Are you for once finding a textbook boring?" Jack asked, feigning shock. An amused smile curled up on his face.

"For a chaotic revolution, they're just about putting me to sleep," Linda said, standing up to stretch. Then she went to look over his shoulder. "What are you working on?"

"...Math theory?"

"That's interesting."

"No, it's not," Jack lamented. Then he whispered in her ear, "I'm a nature spirit. When will this ever be useful for me?"

"I hate to break it to you, but this curriculum wasn't designed with any type of spirit in mind," she whispered back.

"You know, you're not helping," Jack countered.

"Who said that was my goal?" she chuckled. "Also, Jack, you're not good at history. Why was Jasmine asking you for help earlier?"

"I'm offended," he joked as he scribbled out an answer for a math problem. "Also, why do you keep bringing her up?"

"I'm not, you literally did first earlier," she said, heading to the kitchen to retrieve more of her mom's specialty chocolate chip cookies, with a touch of peanut butter for protein. Whether that was actually enough protein to be worth it was beside the point.

"Oh, yeah, you're right," he answered. "Okay, well, either Jasmine is really bad at history, or she just wants to talk to me." Linda reappeared through the kitchen's archway with a handful of cookies and began to munch on one.

"Ooh, can I have one?" he asked.

She nodded and walked over. She looked out over the oaken table. Between the two of them, they managed to take over half of it. "What do you like about her, anyway?" Linda asked, leaning on his chair.

"Well, from the very little that I know about her, she seems nice and she's very pretty," he replied thoughtfully. "She's also weirdly comforting. She sort of reminds me of someone, but I can't remember who or when I knew them," Jack said. The look on Linda's face accidentally betrayed her. He continued, "I don't mean that she's more comforting than you, it's almost more like a weird déjà vu feeling? It's nothing serious. But her hair is gorgeous, though."

"She does have nice titian hair," Linda conceded.

"What?"

"I said—"

"I know what you said, but 'titian'?" Jack asked, turning in his seat to look up at her.

"It's a shade of golden or reddish brown. Although it's technically closer to an auburn. It's from the Italian Renaissance painter, Titian."

"How do you know words and things like that?"

"What do you mean?" she asked. It felt like a small lump of coal settled in her stomach.

"You know some of the most unusual or in-depth things off the top of your head, and you know what they all mean."

"I'm a nerd, like you said," Linda answered quietly, trying to smile. She apparently wasn't convincing.

"I didn't mean to upset you," Jack said, his tone softening.

"No, no, it's fine," she responded, looking away and breathing deeply. Her throat constricted. She didn't expect for this topic to come up. She kept her books under her bed or in the basement for a reason.

"I didn't realize I hurt your feelings when I call you a nerd. I was just messing around. You're incredibly smart and it's really cool."

"You're fine, Jack," Linda breathed. "This isn't about that." Her eyes smarted and she blinked really hard. She took a deep breath. "I'm fine."

He looked up at her for a moment longer as if he didn't believe her, but he chose not to press the issue. "Is this your favorite type of cookie?" he asked, holding up Exhibit A.

"Actually, snickerdoodles are my favorite, but those chocolate chip cookies are a close second. Mom's recipe has never failed."

"Oh, that's what they're called?"

"Jack, you didn't know this whole time?"

"No…" he admitted sheepishly, ducking his head.

"What if they were grasshopper cookies? And you would just eat them without asking what they were?"

"Okay, first of all, I trusted you guys with what I'm eating. Second of all, grasshoppers don't taste like chocolate," Jack said.

"Gross!" Linda exclaimed. "You would eat bugs?"

"What? Does that offend your sensibilities?"

"What are you guys talking about? What's gross?" Her mom poked her head out from the kitchen, some flour streaked across her grey sweater.

"John's eaten grasshoppers before, Mom," Linda announced, gesturing toward him.

"Ew! Why?" my mom demanded.

"My parents are nature enthusiasts, relax," Jack asserted defensively. Linda shook her head.

"What?" he asked. "They were cooked! I didn't just eat one off the ground!"

SIXTEEN

SYMBIOSIS

Lavender looked into the girl's hazel eyes, which sparkled in the warm light of the lamp in her bedroom. They were facing each other, lying side by side on the lavender quilt that Lavender's grandma made for her, although she was unsure if her grandma would approve of its current company. The girl interrupted her straying thoughts by tucking a lock of Lavender's shiny dark brown hair back behind her ear.

"What are you thinking about?" she asked, moving closer.

Lavender's heart soared. "I love your eyes," she answered. "They're so beautiful." Sometimes she wondered how one of the most enchanting girls in the school ended up there, with her. It felt like a dream.

"Thanks," the girl said, but there was a small downward tug on her smile.

"What's wrong?" Lavender asked.

"I'm wearing colored contacts," she admitted quietly. She hesitated before continuing, "I don't like my natural eye color." She looked away as if studying something else that just caught her eye, although her distraction didn't seem genuine.

"I'm sure it's beautiful, too," Lavender said, noticing a greenish tinge around her inner irises, encircling her dark pupils very closely. They had become less dilated. It almost seemed like that was where the contacts ended and her eyes began since the color seemed deeper and more organic, but it was hard to tell for sure.

"You're never going to see it," she said.

Lavender couldn't discern the emotions in her tone. *Great going*, she thought to herself. The moment was ruined. The girl sat up.

"I'm sorry, Jasmine," Lavender said, earnestly but more quietly than she expected it to sound.

"It's okay, Lavender," Jasmine smiled, although it was small and delicate as if it could be blown away. She leaned forward and kissed Lavender lightly. "I enjoyed spending time with you today, but I might have to go soon. The sun will be going down."

"Curfew?" Lavender asked knowingly, sitting up so that her shoulder touched hers. It was warm. Lavender's upper arm tingled. So did her stomach.

"You know how my godfather is," Jasmine said. *It's always the same*, Lavender thought. Jasmine's godfather was *never* flexible. Even Lavender's parents could let things slide sometimes. And the days were getting shorter as the Maine autumn inched toward winter, meaning less time to be with Jasmine. Lavender couldn't wait for the spring.

Jasmine interrupted her thoughts by resting her head on Lavender's shoulder, almost nuzzling her. Lavender felt like she would melt. Then the moment ended. "I have to go now, sorry," Jasmine said, sliding off the bed.

"It's okay," Lavender said, getting up as Jasmine fixed her backpack and checked to make sure she had everything, as usual. Jasmine was always so particular. Lavender hurried into her bathroom (her own bathroom, what a luxury compared to their old house) to check her hair and sheer lip gloss while she waited on Jasmine to finish up. When she got out, she thought she saw Jasmine standing up from zipping Lavender's backpack, not her own. Before she had a second to think about it, Jasmine said, "I was preoccupied when I was opening my bag and confused ours. I was still thinking about when we were lying together." The way Jasmine said it made Lavender blush.

"No problem," Lavender said, walking forward and wrapping her arms around Jasmine. "I wish you didn't have to leave." She kissed her.

"I wish I could stay, but you know how strict Everett is." Jasmine returned the favor.

Lavender nodded. Everett was Jasmine's estranged godfather—they were never close. Lavender's parents would kill her if she called them by their first names, though. She didn't know how White kids got away with that stuff.

Lavender led the way to the hall, where she paused in front of a framed photo of her late little brother, Cody. Jasmine hugged her waist reassuringly, offering Lavender a knowing smile. Lavender smiled back. They continued downstairs to the entryway between living room and the kitchen, which smelled richly of simmering stew. As she went to open the front door, Jasmine glanced outside and picked up the pace as she threw her gigantic coat over her shoulders.

"*Au revoir, Jasmin!*" Lavender's mom called over in French.

Lavender felt herself stiffen. Sometimes she was so focused on Jasmine whenever she was over that she forgot their relationship was a secret. Lavender was too scared to tell her parents that she wasn't straight. It was hard enough with the rumors about her at school and the constant homophobic digs, much less having to live with her own family after they knew the truth. At least Jasmine understood and felt the same way. No one knew about their relationship, and some people didn't even realize that they hung out sometimes. Jasmine took care of that with her own friend group, although Lavender wished Jasmine didn't make her sound so lame, including that time with Linda and John at lunch. She kind of hated it, but she couldn't see any other way to handle it.

"Bye, Mrs. Pierre! Have a good night," Jasmine responded, pulling Lavender back to Earth. Her coat was on, and she was stuffing her feet into her boots. Lavender bent down to help her. Her head accidentally brushed against Jasmine's legs, and she felt her face grow molten hot. *Why is this happening to me?* Lavender thought as she straightened up. She didn't want her mom or her annoying nosy brother to notice. They wouldn't think twice if it was with a nice Christian boy, especially someone from their Penobscot Nation (it would be the answer to her grandma's prayers), but a White girl with bright ginger hair? Forget it.

"Let's go," Lavender said, opening the door for Jasmine, who pulled her hood up after wrapping her head in her wool scarf. Jasmine was so sensitive to the cold it was as if it was already winter. *She would never survive Canada*, Lavender thought.

Lavender looked up to see two people walking down the street toward them, although thankfully they were still at the end over by the recluse's house. "Bye," Lavender said quickly, beginning to sweat despite the chilled air.

"Bye," Jasmine said without looking back, hurrying down the concrete stairs and away down the block as quickly as could appear normal. She was enshrouded in her long black puffy winter coat, which incidentally also concealed her identity. Lavender turned and went back inside before the pair got any closer. In her periphery, she realized they were John and Linda—his blue hair and height was an unmistakable combination. She just dodged a bullet.

"Who do you think Lavender was with?" Jack asked Linda as they got closer to Lavender's house, the front door's autumnal wreath still slightly bobbing. The very bundled-up person that had left had already disappeared down the street, turning in the direction of their school on Lexington.

"Could be her secret lover," Jack mused.

"Only if she's gay," Linda responded, kicking a stray stone. The coat's silhouette was pulled in some at the waist, she had noticed. "But that seems unlikely because of her crush on that guy Jake."

"Could be. Or could be a nanny. Or tutor."

"Why wouldn't a nanny have her own car?"

"Dunno. Secret lover sounds more fun."

"Aren't we too young to have secret lovers?" Linda asked, craning her head to look up at him.

He looked down at her. "Are we?"

She felt... weird when he said that. She looked away and focused on trying to crunch a leaf underfoot. "Dunno," she answered.

"It was strange that the person seemed to leave so quickly. It's also not that cold out. She looked prepared for the Arctic tundra."

"Jack, you never think it's that cold out. You literally only wear a single layer in Maine."

He laughed. "Guilty as charged."

SEVENTEEN

LOSING SLEEP

"Hey, Jack, I have a question," Linda asked the next day as they walked down the street.

"What's up?"

"So, if that story thing is real, like the one that I found from the book, does that mean you froze someone in ice?"

"Um, yeah," he said, shifting uncomfortably.

"What does that mean? Did you, like, imprison them?"

"Ummm…" he said.

Linda waited. After he said nothing, she replied, "Ummm… what? What happened after the story cuts off?"

"The elf was frozen… in a block of ice… for centuries."

"Wouldn't that freeze them to death?"

"Theoretically," he said weakly. He cleared his throat.

"So…" Linda said, her voice trailing off. "You killed someone?" Her heart skipped multiple beats in her chest. He didn't say anything, but he nodded.

"My best friend is dead. Someone killed her. And you… did the same thing. To someone else."

"Yeah," he sighed sadly. "That's not a part of my life that I like to revisit."

"Yeah. Because it's beyond disturbing," Linda said angrily. "Just when I think we're fine again, I learn something else about you."

"Ouch."

Linda's eyes burned with tears. "You murdered them. How am I supposed to be okay with that?" she demanded.

"I didn't expect you to be okay with it, I just hoped you would be more understanding about why I felt like I had to. I wish I could go back and change it now as much as I did in the moment, but that can't change anything. It's over. It happened. I killed them." He threw his hands up in the air. "I don't know what else I can say. I'm being honest with you and I'm not hiding anything from you anymore and I've kept to that promise."

Linda sighed in defeat. She felt terrible. It was just supposed to be a normal walk home from school with her new normal life as she coped with losing Kelsie, but it was ruined. Her best friend made her want to vomit, thinking about how he made someone go cold like Kelsie did when she died.

"I need a break, Jack," she said quietly, turning and walking away from him. She realized they had stopped in front of Ms. Leeds's house. She hoped the reclusive author wasn't listening.

"Okay," he said even more softly. Linda wondered if she heard him sniffling, but that didn't matter. It *almost* didn't matter. *Haven't I suffered enough?* she thought. *Why can't things go back to normal?* Why can't her life just be... *normal.*

Ruth Leeds peered out her front window at the boy. He wiped his eyes despondently after watching his friend leave. She wondered if she should do anything. Before she could make up her mind, they locked eyes. His tears almost seemed to harden, and he turned to walk into the forest. There was a flash of bluish light from just inside the trees, and Ruth unbolted her door and ran out to see what had happened. But everything at the edge of the wood looked normal, except there was no boy. She shrugged, determined to keep her wits about her, and she walked to her car as calmly as possible. As she sat in the frigid seat, waiting for the humming engine to slowly wake and warm her up, she wondered what had happened. Would she have even done anything? Did she imagine the light? What would her "man of science" brother think? She scoffed at the thought. Her brother wouldn't answer the phone.

Linda woke up that night, gasping for air, her heart racing. She felt the mattress push against her back underneath her, and the hot sheets' static clung to her pajama pants and shirt. Sweaty strands of hair stuck to her face and neck. She had another nightmare, and Kelsie's dead face hung in her mind. Linda's hands felt chilled from Kelsie's hands in the dream, where they cooled down too quickly. It didn't make sense. Linda grasped the warm blanket and comforter in a futile effort to forget the sensation. Her room was dark aside from some faint moonlight streaming around the edges of her blinds. She tried to think of anything, anyone, else. The emptiness of her room pressed in on her. She wondered if pain kept up anyone else at night.

George London, on the other half of their very small town, fell out of sleep again. He sat up, rubbing his face roughly, before collapsing back down into his pillows, which hurt his neck. His hand and arm automatically stretched to the smaller empty space beside him, a reminder of his different bed. The sheets were cold, and the mattress was puffy, as if no one ever slept there. Because it was only him. It was only him who purchased the bed; it was only him who lived in the dumb and stupid apartment, his desk overflowing with exams to grade and papers to write for class. He stared up at the ceiling. Yellow light from the streetlamp outside pierced the dark void of his room through the blinds. It was more persistent than his wife. *Ex-wife*, he reminded himself automatically, which made him feel somehow worse.

He looked over at the telescope sitting by the far window in his room. It was a gift, his ex-wife lovingly reminded him when he had expected her to keep it. It was very expensive, and even though it was well-used, it was in fabulous condition, and she could've sold it for good money. She never cared quite so much about the stars, just their constellations and what they meant. Or what she thought they meant. It went against every fiber of his anal and analytical being, but he always found it endearing. It was her story, her belief, one that was no longer his to share. The stars depressed him, especially when they were too close. The flickering lights just reminded him of her. His hand closed around the empty air, chilly with the faint heating in his shitty apartment.

Linda wondered how she would ever fall back asleep. Memories kept flooding her mind. She would occasionally share the bed with Kelsie during sleepovers, especially when it got really cold at night, and for some reason Linda desperately missed Kelsie's warmth next to her. All she could think about was how cold Kelsie was. It was different than Jack's snow and ice, which was cold and bright; Kelsie was cold and dull, she was dying, she once had warm skin, she once held her hand, she was once sad and she was once happy, and she once told Linda stupid stories when they couldn't fall asleep, stupid stories that Linda could never remember even when she had time to write them down. And now they were all gone with that wonderful brain of hers, that wonderful mind, that wonderful friend.

She wondered if Mr. London had ever felt that way about his wife. She couldn't imagine his ex-wife being a very good one if she let him feel so alone. Did Mr. London ever sleep at night anymore?

No, Linda, no he did not.

🌿

Jack slammed his chisel into the wall of ice in his room. Usually if something was on his mind and he wasn't busy enough to find ways to procrastinate his homework assignments, he would turn to carving the ice. But his best friend left him there outside a random human's house earlier that day, leaving him crying and for someone else to notice him. He leaned forward and rested his forehead against the cool, forgiving ice. If he had known Linda would react that way, he probably wouldn't have told her about killing the elf. He shook his head against the wall. He was always going to tell her, even if he didn't really want to. But the way she looked at him after she found out... it killed him. It didn't matter to Linda that his past actions used to eat away at him and haunt him at every corner for literally hundreds of years. It didn't matter that a part of him died that day along with the elf. It didn't matter that he couldn't look at Mother Nature for a decade, much less speak to her. It didn't matter how much he loathed his existence. Linda knew that he was a monster parading among the rest.

His eyes burned with tears. He stood up straight again, willing—or attempting, whatever you like to think—to suck back in his tears as he took a deep breath. "Nope, I'm not crying," he said out loud. "I've reached my daily quota." As usual, the marble and ice walls didn't answer him. They never did when he was alone. He chuckled absently at his absurd internal joke. It was a nightmare whenever Mona or one of the elves caught him talking to himself. They usually responded to whatever he said, no matter how embarrassing the situation. They sucked at knocking.

He left the room, walking through the marble halls and columns until he was downstairs. The perimeter of the main floor was sustained by arching marble columns slathered in branches and vines. There were no walls or glass windows like in the overly sheltered human world, so he easily jumped out one of the open spaces onto a patch of pillowy moss three to four feet below. An owl hooted overhead in its nighttime rounds in the lush, wild landscape that stretched in front of him. He walked through the impossibly diverse trees that he occasionally etched with frost whenever he felt like pissing off Mother Nature. Dead leaves crunched underfoot. Soon, the chlorophyll overdose gave way to autumnal fare. There were different regions of the island, one for each of the seasons with a blend of different climates and ecosystems radiating across the land. Linda would have a field day exploring everything, from the stones to the birds that flew in the air. Jack smiled sadly as he walked, passing a late-working elf every once in a while.

Soon, he reached the wintry part of the island, the area which his room overlooked. He walked away from the palace, heading through a wooded region that was blanketed in snow. Jack took a deep breath of the revitalizing air and jumped across a small frozen-over stream, followed by a roaring and freezing river. He hopped across the stones but slipped on the last one—it had been ages since he came to this part of the island, and his feet decided to be forgetful traitors. He plunged into the water. A human would have frozen (pun intended) in shock at the temperature, but the only thing that bothered Jack was that he was soaking wet.

He grabbed hold of the rock before the powerful current swept him away, his fingers crying out to him as he eventually managed to climb onto the frozen shore. It was strangely exhilarating, but he took a moment to sit in the snow and catch his breath. He shuddered, but not from the hypothermic temperatures. He was returning to his crime. Twenty feet away sat the guarded entrance to the cave that held the block of ice containing his prisoner. The thought of it made him want to vomit. He wrapped his arms around his legs. It would probably bother Linda that he was basically returning to his victim's sarcophagus, but he did it occasionally to remind himself of her memory and what he did. He wasn't sure if it meant that he had issues, but he knew that humans would visit the dead to honor them or to remind themselves of different things. Maybe he wasn't so weird.

The moon glowed softly overhead as Jack plodded over to the cave. It was presently unguarded, which was common. There usually wasn't much reason to hide the elf, but no one really visited. It was irrepressibly sad. As Jack walked inside, his heart plummeted. The cave walls were hard and grey, arching overhead, glittering faintly from torchlight. The frozen prison finally lay ahead of him. He looked up.

His heart felt like it plummeted to the core of the earth.

The elf was gone.

EIGHTEEN

PIROUETTING

Linda's science partner was absent the next day. He didn't show up for Homeroom and she assumed he was late, even though he rarely was, but then his seat was vacant in class. *That's fine*, she thought to herself. She wouldn't have to share air with a murderer. But it didn't really sit right with her, although she couldn't begin to explain why.

She looked up and watched Mr. London as he taught the class about the different states of matter. He looked like he hadn't slept in a week. It made her heart twinge, and she looked away, out the window. She wished she could bury herself in her dictionary, but she knew she wouldn't find solutions there. None of this would be happening if she could talk to Kelsie... Linda took a deep breath.

At lunch, Linda found Lavender sitting at their side of the table. When Linda approached, Lavender looked up and smiled and waved. Linda felt like she could almost feel Kelsie there, but just barely, like she was losing her grasp.

"Are you okay?" Lavender asked. "You don't look so well."

"I'm..." Linda started. "I don't know." She took another deep breath. Tears had started to prick her eyes. *Damn it.*

"That's okay, you don't have to talk about it," Lavender said. "I'll be here if you do want to, though."

Linda nodded. "How has your day been?" She poked at the food on her plate and swirled around the weird green beans.

"Linda's taken, you know!" someone jeered.

Linda looked up to see Dan walking past with some of his friends. He looked back and smirked at her before continuing while his friends laughed. "What the hell?" Linda said. "That's so random?" She turned back to Lavender. "Hey, are you okay?"

Lavender's tan skin reddened and she looked down while she fiddled with the pendant on her necklace.

"Hey, um, I like your necklace. What is it?" Linda asked.

"It's braided sweetgrass," Lavender answered, lifting it to show her. The dried sweetgrass was woven in a circle, almost like the top of a tiny basket. "It's important to the Penobscot Nation. I'm part of it."

"It's beautiful," Linda smiled.

Lavender looked up at her and smiled weakly back. "Thanks."

"Linda! Linda!" Jack called as he raced down the street after her.

"I thought we agreed that I wasn't talking to you yet," Linda said, rolling her eyes. "You weren't even at school, what are you doing here?"

"I know we said that, but I found out that the ice block is empty. The elf is gone."

"Wow, congrats, now you just have to find their corpse!" Linda answered without missing a beat. But her heart nearly stopped at his news. Not that she would admit it to him.

"That's the thing, it looks like they might be alive," Jack urged, ignoring Linda's dig.

"That doesn't erase the fact that you tried to kill them," she retorted.

"I know, it doesn't. But it also means that—"

"You have a potential manipulative usurper running around plotting your destruction?" Linda interrupted. "I have an appointment, and I need to meet my mom," she added as they reached her driveway. "No murderers allowed."

"Linda, can you *stop* poking fun at something traumatic?" Jack shot back angrily. "I hated myself for eons, and I still do. I don't need you to be a jerk to me, too."

"My best friend dying was traumatic. Her loss can't be reversed. I'm not friends with someone omnipotent like your 'father,'" Linda snapped as they reached her car.

"I can't ask him to throw around time and reverse anything, either. That's not how it works."

"Good to know, John," Linda said as she climbed into the car and closed the door in his face.

"Sorry, John, we're in a hurry, come by later!" Mrs. Waters called out as she walked down the porch steps to the car, appearing oblivious to Jack's talk of time alteration. He wasn't sure what Linda's mom would think if she overheard even a quarter of their conversations.

"No worries, Mrs. Waters, I'll see you guys around," Jack said tightly through a fake smile. He glanced in through Linda's window and turned to walk away, jamming his fists into his hoodie pockets. Linda hadn't failed to notice his non-mortal apparel: it was way too cold for that outfit, and he would normally dress halfway accordingly.

"Everything okay, Linda?" her mom asked as she started the car.

"Yes," Linda said, watching her friend walk down the street. He walked further and further away.

"You sure?"

"Yes."

"Okay," her mom sighed. "Next stop: the dentist."

"My favorite place," Linda answered sarcastically. She leaned her head against the cold window.

❧

"John?" Ms. Nory called during Homeroom. Quiet chatter answered her. She looked over the edge of her clipboard. "John Mason?"

Linda tried not to look up. She didn't want people to snicker at her looking for her "secret boyfriend."

"Absent again," Ms. Nory frowned, marking her paper. "Emma?"

"Here," the girl said clearly.

"Good," Ms. Nory answered. "Anwar?"

Linda proceeded to zone out. She couldn't stop thinking about what Jack said yesterday even though she hated to admit it. *How could the elf be alive? Who would even want to move their body?* Linda wondered. That seemed rather grisly. The bell rang and she filed out of the room. *Why didn't he ever refer to the elf by their name?* she realized. Even the transcription neglected their name. *If he really felt so bad about it, why wouldn't he bother to use the elf's proper name?* She was so deep in thought that she didn't realize that she just about bumped into him as she walked down the hall.

"Woah, Linda," he said, stopping her gently with his hands on her shoulders. He smelled like freshly fallen snow and vaguely of pine needles as always, and she felt herself soften at the comforting familiarity before steeling herself. She brushed his hands off of her and pushed past him through the crowd before he could say anything else. To her surprise, she didn't hear him begin to speak.

After distracting herself with her classes, and not talking to him while Mr. London taught, Linda finally reached lunch. She let out a sigh of relief as she entered the cafeteria, sitting down to find only Lavender at the table. Following their chattering about their art class's first-ever assigned homework, Linda looked up to see Jack walking over... with Jasmine. The thought of having to suffer through whatever that meant made her stomach lurch, and she began to stand up. But Lavender did the same.

"I have to go," Linda said, grabbing her tray.

"Me, too," Lavender answered as they walked toward the tray collection area and dumped the remainder of their lunches before Jack and Jasmine reached the table. All smiling and bullcrap like that.

"Why don't you want to sit at the table?" Linda queried.

"Why don't you want to sit there?" Lavender returned.

Linda went silent for a moment as they walked out of the cafeteria. "I need to help out Mr. London with something."

"Oh, okay," Lavender answered nonchalantly. "I thought you and John would be inseparable after he was absent yesterday."

"I'm not talking to him right now," Linda answered. Their footsteps echoed down the hallways. "What about you?"

Lavender made a noise in her throat. "I need to look up stuff in the library."

"For what?"

"Oh, this is Mr. London's room. I'll see you later," Lavender said quickly before heading down the hall in an inefficient path towards the library, past a bulletin board dedicated to resources about abduction and Jane Clari. Linda stood outside her teacher's door and watched Lavender walk away. When she turned to look in the window of Mr. London's door, she saw him looking at her with an annoyingly amused and curious expression.

"What can I do for you?" he asked as she opened the door.

"Is there anything I can help you with?" Linda asked.

"Why?" he asked.

"Why not?" she countered.

"You've never offered to help me," he said, looking smug. "Are you... avoiding someone?"

She scowled and he smirked. "Did you notice John and I weren't talking in class?"

"Scientists are observant," he said. "I hope that you're not offering aid purely for personal gain."

Linda wanted to be mad; but she felt he had a point.

"If your offer is genuine, I have a long-term proposal," Mr. London continued.

She looked at him hesitantly. "What is it?"

He picked up a very large rubber-banded stack of papers and dropped it on his desk in front of her. "You're easily my best student, Linda. Would you be willing to help me grade assignments so I can get more work done for my graduate courses?"

"You're in grad school?" Linda asked.

"Yes, I am. Do you want to help me?"

"Uh, sure," Linda responded. "How do you know that I'll grade everything correctly?"

"Follow my answer key and use good judgment," he said, splitting the stack in half. "And be bad cop."

"You've never graded my assignments harshly," Linda answered, accepting the stack.

"Have you looked at your friend's returned assignments?" Mr. London asked incredulously.

"He *might* throw them away," she said with a shrug.

"Wow, you are really throwing him under the bus, Miss Waters," Mr. London said as he handed her the answer key and a red pen. "Also, don't write anything other than a check mark, if there's a problem just set the homework aside," he instructed.

"Sounds good," Linda said, her eyes already skimming the first page.

NINETEEN

SANGUINARIA

At the end of the day, Linda hurried out of the building before Jack or Lavender could meet her. She needed to be alone. Sure, talking to Jack could help answer her questions, but she didn't want to talk to him yet. It also felt weird realizing that Lavender was hiding something from her, but Linda didn't know what. *Did she have a crush on Jack?* Linda wondered. That seemed unlikely, but she felt herself bristle at the thought for some reason. She didn't like the idea of sharing—wait, she thought, stopping herself as she reached the corner by Lavender's house. Why would she be upset about sharing a friend that murdered someone?

"Why is this even an issue I have to deal with?" Linda angrily asked out loud. Naturally, the air didn't respond aside from lightly blowing against her face. Linda sighed and trudged toward the forest. Even though it was cold out, she hoped that it would ground her like it usually did. *Would she even be friends with Jack if Kelsie was alive?*

She took her time walking through the trees, challenging herself to identify them based off their bark patterns, even though she wasn't sure if she was right. Eventually, she made it to the clearing, which was covered in a blanket of snow. She took a deep breath of the pleasant, wintry air, even though it stung her lungs a little bit, before she exhaled and watched her breath hang in the air. The tips of the evergreens were a deep green in the afternoon light, although many of them were still crowned with snow.

She looked down and noticed something green sitting in the snow ten feet beyond her, which seemed odd. *Were those leaves?* As she walked closer, it became apparent that they were flowers, but specifically bloodroot flowers—suddenly, in the silent winter air, she heard a twig snap. Her head whirled around to identify the source, hoping it was a squirrel or a deer, but saw Jack instead.

She groaned. "You're terrible at taking hints."

"You weren't at lunch—"

"I was, and then I left," Linda said, turning away from him to investigate the flowers. She walked up to them and was hit with an unnaturally intoxicating fragrance. She immediately bent down and gazed at one of the blooms, which looked strikingly beautiful and alive despite the inanimate snow surrounding it.

"What is that?" Jack asked as he walked towards her more quickly.

An overpowering urge compelled her to reach forward.

"Wait! Don't!" he yelled as Linda touched the delicate, soft petals. The moment her fingers grasped the stem and the curled leaves, her mind went blank. She picked the flower.

The ground in front of her exploded. Linda screamed in shock and fell back. As the snow and soil rained down, a seven-foot-tall orange humanoid rhizome caked in dirt rose before her, brandishing a disturbingly large and gnarled cudgel made of roots. The little flower that she picked bobbed slightly on top of its head, and if not for the sense of impending doom, Linda would have laughed.

"LINDA, LOOK OUT!" Jack shouted.

Linda didn't even realize that she had remained rooted in place, but a massive weapon coming down on her reminded her that it was time to move. She immediately rolled to the side as the bloodroot spirit roared. She looked up to realize she wasn't smashed to bits. Instead, what looked to be a spear made of ice impaled the creature's shoulder. Red sap oozed out of the wound. A strong hand yanked Linda to her feet. "OW!" she cried as her left arm was nearly pulled out of its socket.

"Run—" Jack exclaimed, pushing her away, but he was cut off. Before she realized what was happening, she heard a loud "OOF" and saw Jack fly back a few feet. She was not envious of that experience. He had just begun to sit up when the monster advanced upon him in just a few steps. Linda's heart leapt to her throat. She ran to his side and helped pull him up.

"Making friends with the mortals, I see, Frost? You should stick to the elves," the monster laughed, before bellowing in pain. Jack had picked up a fistful of snow from the ground and hurled it at the spirit. This snow transformed into many glimmering ice shards that the spirit failed to deflect with its cudgel. Suddenly, a longsword appeared in Jack's hands, and he pushed Linda behind him as the spirit quickly re-gained composure after the distraction. As the bloodroot spirit advanced upon him, Jack raised his sword to meet the monster's falling blow, and the cudgel splintered on impact. Fragments flew everywhere. As Linda fled to the line of trees, she felt some splinters land in her hair and bounce off her backpack. Once she felt like she had reached a safe distance, she finally turned to face the battle.

A cut bled on Jack's cheek, the red blood pronounced against his pale skin and hair. The spirit's face contorted as it roared in rage. Its serrated red teeth gleamed in the afternoon light and its vermilion eyes glowed. Then, the spirit extended its arm and sprouted a nightmarishly large crimson cleaver that shone in the sunlight. To Linda, it looked like solidified and sharpened bloodroot sap. Jack took the opportunity to swipe his sword through the air and sent a sheet of ice flying at the spirit, who slammed its sparkling cleaver down through the ice. The sheet burst with the sound of an immense glass plane shattering as thousands of fragments flew everywhere. Some fragments were large enough to cut into the monster's arms and legs, causing it to bleed more red sap, which looked uncomfortably like real blood. A lot of blood. One large chunk of ice sank deeply into its abdomen so that it stuck out sickeningly and painfully. Linda was glad that she had run away before she became collateral damage. Even Jack had to shield his head and face from the ice shards. The spirit bellowed in pain as it fell to its knees. Birds flew away from their perches at its screams.

"Stop fighting! I want to spare you!" Jack shouted at the bloodroot spirit as it slowly pushed itself off the ground, using its cleaver as support.

"You're going to perish, right along with your mortal friend!" the monster thundered, and it swung its cleaver at Jack. As it was about to smite him, the shining blade coming near his light blue hair, Jack raised his longsword to meet it. He somehow managed to push back up against the weight of the monster's arm, which was easily as thick as two of him tied together. Then, Jack conjured a small snowbank and ran onto it before jumping off onto the spirit. He plunged his sword deep into the monster's sternum. More red sap flowed. The monster roared as all its wounds, including where Jack hung from the hilt of his sword, began to glow a bright azure until its presence was replaced with an explosive flurry. Jack fell through the air and crumpled into the snow.

TWENTY

HYACINTHUS

"JACK!" Linda screamed as she ran and stumbled through the snow back over to him.

"I'm fine, I'm fine," Jack called as he very slowly pushed himself up off the ground. As she got closer, she could hear his very colorful language. "Are you okay?" he asked with a grimace as he stood up and brushed off the snow and ice. He looked up at Linda. She didn't respond. He repeated more gently, "Are you okay?"

"I don't know," she answered as she stopped in the snow. Her voice trembled. "That was so scary."

"I know," he said, quickly closing the distance between them since he was evidently able to walk lightly over the surface of the snow instead of sinking into it with each step like her. Linda wasn't sure if she had ever noticed that before, but it was a little too much to absorb in that moment. She fell forward into his arms.

"Hey—Linda—are you okay?" Jack asked, trying not to lose his balance.

"It looked at me," Linda recounted weakly, remembering the spirit's terrifying stare.

"Sometimes nature spirits do that," he said as an attempt at a joke, before continuing, "woah, don't pass out." Linda leaned very heavily into him.

Suddenly, they were enveloped in a strong gust of wind that whirled around them, and Linda felt her feet leave the ground. A bright burst of light almost blinded her. Jack instinctively held Linda more tightly, which was unnecessary as she tightly squeezed his abdomen between her arms. Then, just as suddenly as the wind and light started, they stopped. Linda looked down to see a white marble floor streaked with charcoal. "I think I'm going to be sick," Linda blurted, pushing away from him. Her stomach promptly emptied itself with a splatter.

"Jack Frost, what is *she* doing here?" a familiar voice demanded, filling the entire space. Mother Nature walked around a massive half-globe sitting in an ancient bronze metal basin. Her finger left a fading blue light on the sculpted bronze landmass, which seemed to be Northern America. Some realistic and miniature clouds hovered and swirled over the northeastern coast, including over Maine. The surrounding teal ocean had actual miniscule waves that rolled across the surface, the occasional sea creature rising for air. Linda could smell the faint salt of the ocean.

"I don't know, why did you summon me suddenly?" Jack retorted as he helped Linda stand upright while she apologized.

A nearby elf snapped her fingers, and the vomit melted away into the floor. Linda wondered if she was losing her mind. She sagged against Jack and was too out of it to properly acknowledge his arm around her waist.

"We caught Bluet stealing angel's trumpet from my garden," Mona said.

"Okay… and…" Jack said, gesturing impatiently at the queen to elaborate.

"It's a poisonous plant that can be brewed into a powerful memory loss potion," she explained. "That's why we can't remember what the elf looks like or what their name is."

"Okay, great, we were all drugged," Jack said. "I just had to kill a plant spirit that sprouted out of the earth from a *flower.*"

"You *what?*" Mother Nature demanded. "How did it break through?"

"I don't know!" Jack retorted. He looked down at his unwell friend and asked more gently, "Do you need to sit down, Linda?"

She shook her head. She was not sitting down on the floor that was capable of absorption. But a sinking feeling settled into Linda's already upset stomach, which was not a fun combination. *She* plucked the flower that caused the spirit to enter the mortal world, and endangered herself, Jack, and potentially other mortals. She was too scared to bring this up in front of Mother Nature, who glared at her like she was one piece of information away from turning Linda into a mold spore.

"Are you okay?" Jack gently asked, bending down slightly so that he was eye-level with Linda, holding her face with his surprisingly warm right hand. She felt her cheeks grow hot with blood. Mother Nature made an impatient and slightly disgusted noise.

"Sure," Linda said weakly, pulling away from him. Then she continued even more quietly, "It's not like we escaped death and then I puked in front of the Queen of Nature or something embarrassing like that."

Mother Nature looked amused as she went to sit in her throne, which was a large chair—well, a chair-shaped tree—growing out of the marble, its roots acting as the steps leading up to the wide seat-like trunk. Lush branches extended like verdant rays behind her. "You are the first mortal to make it this far and experience the grace of Jack Frost," the queen said. Linda blushed again despite her own wishes. "I do not normally take it upon myself to address your kind," she continued in her regal tone, her voice melodious and deep. She turned to Jack. "And I would not have to if you did your job *properly*."

"What's *that* supposed to mean?" Jack demanded. Linda prayed that she wouldn't have to witness two supernatural fights in the span of five minutes.

"If you had properly killed that elf all that time ago, we would not have to deal with this chaos now!" Mother Nature snapped. Her words visibly sliced through Jack, the look of pain clouding his face as if she had just stabbed him.

"Well, if all you're going to do is complain, then I see no point in my presence, your Highness," Jack responded coldly, his voice even and unwavering. He turned to his friend. "Let's go, Linda."

Linda nodded silently. A rush of air enveloped them, and their surroundings disappeared again behind the lights. When they faded,

Linda realized they were in a bedroom. In *her* bedroom. The wind had disturbed anything that was loose: papers were scattered across the room, along with a couple shirts, and her sheets were pushed back. "Jack!" she exclaimed.

"Oh, shit. I'm sorry, I didn't even think about where I was going," Jack said sullenly. "Oh my god, I'm so stupid."

"It's fine, it's fine," she said quickly as she began to pick up the papers that had flown off her desk. Linda looked up when Jack collapsed on her bed. It bounced and creaked as he lay down on top of her unmade sheets.

She suppressed an annoyed sigh before pausing in alarm. "Jack, you have a cut on your face!"

"What?" he asked, sitting up with a start and then groaning. Followed by more colorful language.

It didn't occur to Linda that he had hidden the side effects of fighting the snow spirit to the death. "Are you okay?"

"Yeah, I'm fine, just sore," he sighed, leaning back. "Wait, sorry, I should've asked if it's fine to lie down." He started to stand back up.

"It's fine," Linda said, putting a hand out to stop him. "You just saved my life, relax."

He chuckled. He reached out and delicately touched his hand against hers. She pulled her hand back.

"If you don't want to be friends with me anymore because you know I'm a monster, please just tell me instead of letting me hold onto false hope," Jack said after a few minutes of silence. He was unable to keep the sadness out of his voice.

"What?" Linda asked, her tone surprised. "I don't think you're a monster."

"Well, I am. I shouldn't have just blindly listened to Mother Nature and killed the elf, I should've figured it out on my own and found another way. You don't have to make excuses for me," Jack said, running his hand through his hair and tugging slightly at the ends.

"You did what you thought you had to do to keep your family safe," Linda answered. "You're not a monster."

"I killed someone."

"No, you didn't."

He chuckled. "Evidently because I'm terrible at it. But at the end of the day, intention and deed are the same thing. And now this elf, who I can't even remember what they look like, has suffered for centuries." He covered his face. "This is such a mess and it's all my fault."

"I think you're being too hard on yourself," Linda said. "You're not terrible because you made a mistake. And... you're not a murderer."

He looked away from her. "What made you change your mind?"

"Well..." Linda started. "After thinking about it, and almost dying, I realized I was making an unfair comparison between you trying to prevent some insane magical coup and a careless drunk driver committing manslaughter. And... I think I was angry for my life not being normal anymore. Which isn't about you. I was projecting my issues onto you. I'm sorry."

"I was careless enough to listen to Mona. I just wish... I don't know what I wish. But now we're in even more danger."

"It sounds like you keep looking for reasons to be angry at yourself," Linda observed, poking his hand. "Why?"

"I just... remember the look on her face when she realized she was going to die. That I, her friend, betrayed her."

"Jack, what are you talking about? She betrayed you. She shouldn't have made you choose between your family and herself. You trusted her to be your friend and not to manipulate you into a tool for her own personal gain."

He was silent.

"What would you have done differently?" Linda pressed. "At the time, in that moment. Not now."

"I'm not sure if I would've known what to do. I was so scared of what would happen if the elf took the Amber because they never told me more of their plan. What if they did bad things and endangered everyone? Mona wasn't perfect but she tried her best to be fair to all life forms, even slime molds."

"You did what you thought you had to do. It doesn't mean you're evil. I'm sorry if I made you feel like that."

Jack wiped some tears away. Linda had never seen him cry before. She reached her arms out for a hug, and he leaned into her, his warm tears wetting her shoulder as she held him. He cried quietly.

"I'm sorry, Jack," Linda whispered.

"Don't be sorry," he sniffled. It sounded surprisingly cute to her. Her cheeks felt warm suddenly despite the serious situation. She became acutely aware of how his head rested in the crook of her neck. *He's trying to move past attempting to murder someone eons ago*, she reminded herself, trying not to laugh at the absurdity of the situation because that would have *absolutely* made everything better.

"I should have tried to listen to you sooner," she said.

"I understand why you weren't able to," he said, leaning back against her pillow again. Then a smile played across his lips. "Although I could've gone without having you introduced to a real-life example of how nuts Pryddia—my world—is."

"Me too," Linda giggled.

The door burst open. They looked up to see her miffed mother. "Linda? John? I didn't know you two were here!" she exclaimed. "Linda, I tried reaching you, but the messages wouldn't deliver."

"Oh, sorry, my phone must've died," Linda lied sheepishly. She realized that she was in Pryddia when her mom texted her. "John was... having family issues and I was distracted."

"You know you need to keep me updated with everything that's going on in this town," her mom scolded. Then she saw Jack's face. "John, oh my god you're bleeding!"

"I'm fine, it's nothing," he quickly reassured her.

"Come to the bathroom, we need to clean it off," her mom urged. Jack sat up slowly. Angela Waters shot her daughter a worried look.

"He's fine, he just had to do some heavy lifting at home last night," Linda lied. "Since his parents are old and all."

There was no stopping her mother, however, and she whisked Jack off to the bathroom for first aid while Linda carried out orders to make tea.

Later, Linda and Jack worked on some homework on the sofa, and Angela eventually found them passed out together. Linda's head rested on his shoulder as he turned toward her. Angela remembered the last time when Linda and Kelsie napped together on the same couch after a long day out. She smiled sadly as she draped a knit blanket over her daughter and her new friend.

TWENTY-ONE

STIGMATA

"**A**re you bringing anyone to the dance?" Lavender asked at lunch the next day.

Linda blinked. "What dance?"

"You know... the Fall Hop? They've been talking about it every morning on the intercom this past week," Lavender said.

This brought up some vague memories for Linda, like blurs of words and images on posters. "Oh, no, I'm not going," she said, feeling a pang in her chest. She used to go to them all the time with Kelsie. It still felt too soon. She picked at the brown plastic seam that ran along the edge of the table. The cafeteria was loud with teenage howling and chatter as usual.

"I'm not sure," Jack answered, breaking through the din. "I've never been to a school dance before. I'm not sure if I'm ready to break tradition."

Lavender giggled.

"What about you, Miss Curious?" he asked.

"I'm not sure. I was thinking of going if you guys were going. I'm surprised you're not Linda's date."

"What gave you that impression?" Linda asked Lavender, making a face. "He's probably a terrible dancer."

"Hey," Jack said, shooting Linda a *what-the-frick* look. "I dance. Sometimes."

"When? I've never seen it," Linda said.

"You've only known me for a month and a half," Jack shot back.

"Wait, you guys have only been friends for a month and a half?" Lavender exclaimed. "I thought you've been friends for years. You guys already argue like an old married couple."

"She rags on me like an old partner," Jack said, earning a playful swat from Linda.

"It's only because you don't do your homework."

"I'm going to tell my parents to ditch their Blockbuster membership so we can watch you guys instead," Lavender said. Linda and Jack laughed with her.

"Where's your girlfriend?" Linda asked Jack.

"How am I supposed to know what Jasmine does?" Jack retorted.

Lavender's head popped up from her lunch so quickly that Linda almost worried she'd see her friend break her own neck.

"Lavender, are you okay?" Linda turned to find that Lavender's normally warm tan skin was ashen. "What's wrong?" she asked, rubbing Lavender's shoulder.

"N-nothing," Lavender stammered.

"Is there anything we can do to help?" Jack asked.

"No," Lavender said quietly. "My stomach hurts. I think I'll go take a walk." She started to stand up.

"Do you want me to come with you?" Linda offered.

"No, it's okay. Thanks, though," Lavender said, picking up her tray and leaving.

Linda and Jack watched her walk away. "What do you think is going on?" Linda asked.

"I don't know, I thought you would know," Jack said.

"Something's been on her mind lately, but she hasn't told me," Linda sighed. "Have you noticed that?"

"It sometimes seems that way, but it's never seemed to affect her this much," Jack said. "I hope she's okay."

"Me too," Linda responded.

That afternoon, after the last bell rang, Linda met Jack at his locker. Of course, Jasmine was chatting him up and touching his arm. Linda rolled her eyes as she walked over. "Hey, John, and Jasmine," she greeted them.

"Hey, Linda," Jack smiled.

Jasmine waved. "Best friend time I see," she commented. "I'll see you later, John!"

"Bye," they said as she walked away.

Linda turned to John. "Before we go, I have to make a quick stop at Mr. London's room."

Jack made a face. "Why?"

"I'm his informal TA, remember? I have to drop off some papers," Linda reminded him as they walked down the hall. When she handed Mr. London the graded homework, the door opened behind them. Linda and Jack turned around, and their eyes nearly popped out of their heads.

"Ruth? What are *you* doing here?" Mr. London asked.

"How do you know Ms. Leeds?" Linda asked, whirling back around to face her teacher.

"Hi Linda, I didn't expect to see you here, otherwise I would've waited in the lobby," Ruth replied.

"Classrooms usually contain students," Mr. London said flatly. "How do you know Linda?"

"She's one of my neighbors," Linda answered.

"Linda and Ja—I mean John—walk past my house frequently on their way to the woods," Ruth explained simply, waving her hand as if to signal the information as inconsequential. Jack bristled. He remembered catching Ruth watching them through their window. *How much did she actually listen?*

Mr. London turned to Linda with mild concern traced in the lines on his face. "Why do you go to the forest with him?"

Linda felt herself blush. "We spend a lot of time outdoors talking, Mr. London," she answered tersely. "It's no big deal, I'm used to being out there."

"How do you know Ms. Leeds?" Jack asked from behind Linda. "You don't live near the school, Mr. London."

Mr. London opened his mouth as if to answer before stopping and giving Jack a weird look. "You're right, John, I don't," Mr. London answered. "I don't know if I even want to know why you know the general vicinity of where I live, but Ruth is—"

"George London is my brother dearest," Ruth cut him off.

"Oh, I can see the resemblance now, very clearly," Jack said, and Linda caught that Mr. London shot Jack a dirty look. Jack knew that he just entered negative levels of brownie points, but he really didn't care.

Linda began to notice the subtle similarities between the siblings' appearances: the shape of their eyes, their small noses, and even the curves of their lips. Although Ruth's long black hair was untidily held back in a clip as always, unlike Mr. London's that always stayed neatly in place. "I didn't know you had a sister," she blurted, and immediately regretted it. Dangerous looks passed between the siblings.

"She made a pass at my ex-wife when we were still together," Mr. London said, his dark eyes momentarily burning like the coals in a train engine. Linda and Jack exchanged looks.

"I was drunk, and you've never forgiven me for it, as if I've never seen you act like an imbecile," Ruth replied, her sharp tone slicing through the air between them. "I see we are airing out all the dirty laundry in front of minors. That's rather low, isn't it?"

"Why are you here, Ruth? I don't remember us speaking for some years," Mr. London demanded.

Linda felt a hand grasp her own, and she looked down to see it was Jack's. "John and I need to head home now, Mr. London... and Ms. Leeds. See you later," Linda said politely, backing away into her friend.

Mr. London sighed. A pained expression was very clearly painted across his tired face. "I'm sorry you were here, you two. Get home safely."

"Bye," Jack said as he and Linda quickly left the room, walked down the witch-hazel-colored hall, and out of the building.

"Holy shit," Jack breathed as they walked down the street.

"Holy shit is right," Linda answered. After a moment, she continued, "they have a worse dynamic than you and Mother Nature."

"Hey!" Jack exclaimed, giving her a light push as she cackled. "I mean, you're not entirely wrong though. Although I hope Ruth didn't drive Mr. London to killing someone."

"I don't know if he would be able to teach teenagers with a record like that," Linda said. "I didn't expect Mr. London to tear into her like that. Jeez."

"Don't you have siblings?" Jack asked.

"Well, yeah, but in front of two kids? Well, a kid and a nature spirit," Linda said. "Oh shit."

"What?"

"I didn't get the new assignments that Mr. London wanted me to grade," she groaned.

"You're complaining about... less work. Are you feeling okay? Did you catch whatever was ailing Lavender?" he asked, feeling her forehead.

She swatted him away. "I'm fine! I just want to help him out... and grade harshly."

"Are you the reason I almost failed the last quiz?"

"I don't grade stuff for our class. That was all you."

"Jasmine, can you help me study for my math test tomorrow?" Lavender asked her girlfriend after school. Jasmine was on her way toward her own locker, which would be surrounded by the other popular girls, but Lavender didn't care. "It's urgent, I'm totally lost."

"Um, sure, I'll meet you at the entrance in five," Jasmine said, barely glancing at her. Sometimes it killed Lavender.

So, Lavender left Jasmine to wander to her locker while she waited on one of the benches in the lobby. Time passed slowly. Unfortunately, the benches faced the bulletin board that reminded everyone about the missing student, Jane Clari, and to always tell others about your location and to stick together. She tried to ignore it, but the bright garish letters from the poster clung to her mind. *Stick together*. Lavender shifted uncomfortably. As groups of friends walked past her, she stared down at her boots and pretended to be busy.

Occasionally, a straight couple with raging straight people hormones passed her, locking lips or holding hands or engaging in other forms of snuggly PDA. It was a common sight in a high school, even at her old one in Canada. But she and Jasmine always had to hide it, almost entirely in Lavender's bedroom since that was the only place where they had an ounce of privacy. She heard the familiar voices of the only two people who didn't make gay jokes about her and quickly turned towards the wall, praying they didn't notice her. And when they left the building without addressing her, she breathed a sigh of relief that quickly turned to an ache. Lavender had to hide so much.

Finally, Jasmine appeared. The sunlight filtering in through the windows above the front doors of the school illuminated Jasmine's hair, making it seem as if it was glowing like a brilliant red fire. Lavender almost swooned. Soon, they were back at Lavender's house, climbing the carpeted beige stairs and eventually finding their oasis behind the closed door. Jasmine cupped Lavender's face in her hands and kissed her. Lavender sighed as they parted and rested her forehead against her girlfriend's.

"I've been waiting to do that all day," Jasmine smiled.

"I've been waiting *for* that all day," Lavender answered. Jasmine leaned away and sat on the edge of Lavender's bed, taking Lavender's hand and pulling her over. Lavender felt warmth flood her stomach, but she tried to focus. The warmth turned to a stone. "There's something I need to talk to you about."

"What is it?" Jasmine asked.

Lavender couldn't tell what she was thinking from her expression. She almost never could, which could be both annoying and attractive to her. Lavender took a deep breath and plunged ahead anyway. "Why do you keep flirting with John Mason?" she asked, her voice wavering.

There, she thought. *I did it.*

"You want to stay in the closet, right?" Jasmine asked Lavender.

"Yeah," Lavender answered quietly. She knew this would be Jasmine's argument.

"Then let me pretend to like John," Jasmine said, cupping Lavender's face with her left hand, brushing her thumb gently across her cheek. "I know what I'm doing. Trust me. It's no different than your fake crush on Jake."

"Today at lunch, Linda called you John's girlfriend," Lavender blurted, pushing her hand away. She tried to ignore how sweet Jasmine smelled, like strawberries. "What the hell."

"He's just another boy."

"I want you to stop this."

"It's all fake, I've told you this before."

"I don't care, Jasmine. If this relationship is going to work, I can't keep seeing you string along John," Lavender said as firmly as she could despite the shakiness of her voice. Lunch that day was too much—John and Linda only made her feel worse while they tried to help. She wished she was able to tell them what was going on, but of course it was never that simple. *This wouldn't even be happening if she could tell them about Jasmine.*

A tense silence hung between them. Lavender picked at the edges of her own nails while her hands rested in her lap.

"Fine," Jasmine said, breaking the silence. She let out a sigh and reached for Lavender's hand, grasping it firmly to stop her from destroying her nails.

"Fine?"

"Fine," Jasmine said again. Lavender half-wondered if she really meant that. *Someone's words are only as good as their actions*, her grandma's advice echoed in her brain, back when Lavender was having issues with her Canadian friends. *Wait and see.* Lavender missed when her life was considerably less complicated, but that was when her little brother was still alive. But that was a few years ago. She pushed away the thought as Jasmine leaned against her, hugging her around her waist and nuzzling her. *But why John?* Lavender wondered, but she opted to pull

Jasmine down with her as she collapsed back onto the quilt. The question could wait.

That Friday, the day of the inspired "Fall Hop," Linda saw an almost unsettling eagerness in Jasmine's eyes as her full focus was on Jack during lunch. The whole day, it seemed like everyone buzzed about their dates and what they would wear to the semiformal dance that Friday evening, and Linda just couldn't stand it. Jasmine was the last straw. Lavender wasn't even there that day to help buffer the experience. Linda stood up, strongly gripping her lunch tray as Jack was clearly preoccupied by the redhead's ethereal beauty, a gold trinket twinkling on her clavicle like a stupid little priss because of her lucky little life.

"Bye, I'll see you later, John," Linda said, at her best attempt to be friendly, but she couldn't fully remove the edge from her voice.

"See you later, Linda," Jack said with an annoying and dopey smile.

Jasmine looked up at Linda and grinned as well, forcing Linda to crack a tight smile back at her. "Don't worry, I'll return him as soon as I finish," Jasmine said. She flashed her teeth.

Linda wanted to punch her in the face. Instead, she took the level-headed approach and inhaled and exhaled while remembering that chimpanzees smile with their teeth before they attack. *Of course*, she thought, *humans were different*. Linda suddenly hated everything about what led her to having to share the same chance molecules of air as Jasmine.

"No rush," Linda answered. She felt some eyes on her as she left the cafeteria, trying not to hurl the tray into the dishwasher counter. She quickly exited the site and walked straight to Mr. London's classroom.

"Avoiding a walk in the forest?" Mr. London asked, briefly glancing up from his papers.

"No," Linda snapped sharply, making her teacher perceptibly jump at her tone. *Woops.*

Mr. London cleared his throat. "Is there anything I can do to help you?" he asked.

She took a deep breath and sighed, letting go of the tension from the cafeteria in his quiet classroom. "I don't know."

"You can do something I've been procrastinating while I grade," Mr. London offered, grabbing a book from the edge of his desk.

"Sure," she said, surprisingly perking up.

He wasn't sure what led to her willingness to help out with menial tasks, and he wasn't sure whether he should be happy or concerned. *Could it be some kind of anniversary for her and Kelsie?* he wondered. He couldn't remember the date of her late friend's birthday. "Can you please organize the books in the back of the room and write down all of the titles in this?" he asked, handing her a worn green spiral notebook.

"Why do you need the titles?" Linda asked as she walked toward the sloppy bookshelf.

"In case someone steals one."

"Who would steal your books?"

"I like to pretend that students care about the subject that I teach and are eager to learn more," Mr. London responded.

"You must have a robust imagination," Linda said under her breath.

"I heard that!"

Linda chuckled as she examined the worn-looking shelf. She noticed some words scratched into it so that it looked like it had pale lignin scars where the dark stain was gone. "How old is this bookshelf?" she asked, turning around to look over at him.

"It was in the room already when I got here, so maybe 147 years old give or take a decade," he answered dryly.

Linda returned to surveying the inventory and noticed a word that made her voice catch in her throat so that she made a weird noise. In ugly, fat letters that mangled the wood it said, "FAG." She noticed it in multiple places, and as she started to try to mark it out with her pen, she saw a more direct message: in permanent marker, someone had scrawled, "London is a FAG."

Had Mr. London seen this? Linda frantically wondered. *Is this why he doesn't want to take care of the books?* She suddenly felt horribly sad. And angry. *Who would* do *that?* She looked around the room for a permanent marker. Not seeing any, she pulled her keys out of her pocket and started to scrape away at all of the messages, starting with the marker graffiti.

"What's that scratching sound?" Mr. London asked from across the room.

"I don't know," Linda lied, scratching more quickly. She was determined. On the last slur, her fingers got too close to the raw, splintery wood and snagged. "Ow! Fucking shit."

"Are you okay?" he asked, standing up and pushing back his chair so that it scraped against the waxed vinyl tiles.

Linda gritted her teeth. "I'm fine."

"What happened?" Mr. London demanded as he walked over.

She quickly pocketed her keys. "I scratched my freaking fingers," Linda said, looking down at her throbbing fingertips. They were bleeding and splintered.

Mr. London took her hand in his and examined it. "Wow, you really did a number on them. I would give you Band-Aids, but you'll be better off going to the nurse. Are you scared of blood?"

"No, I'm okay. Thanks, Mr. London," Linda said. *I've seen it before,* she thought with a shudder. She reached forward to put back a book that was on the floor.

"I can manage. Please go to the nurse," he said.

Linda nodded and grabbed her backpack. "Do you have any other papers you want me to grade this weekend?"

"You're not going to the dance?"

"God, no," Linda answered.

"I can't say I blame you. If you come by after school, I'll have a stack ready. Now go to the nurse before you bleed everywhere."

Linda nodded and glanced back at the bookshelf as she walked away and smiled at her shoddy handiwork. It was impossible to read the slurs.

TWENTY-TWO

IT'S BETTER IF HITCHCOCK STAYS
IN FICTION

As per their Friday ritual, Jack and Linda walked toward the forest. It was cold out as always that time of year, but Linda lived for the fresh air, and she was dying for nature. While they walked down the street—and she avoided any unsalted patches of black ice—they noticed that the front door of Ruth's house stood open. They looked at each other before going up her porch steps.

"Hello?" Linda called into the house. "Your door is open!" Then she looked around. Papers had been thrown onto the floor and drawers opened.

"Ruth Leeds?" Jack called, stepping inside.

"Who is it?" Ruth asked, appearing in the kitchen breathlessly. "Oh, it's you two."

"What happened? Is everything okay? Your door was open," Linda inquired.

"I'm okay, but it seems as though someone broke in," Ruth sighed, loosening her hair from the bun and then putting it back up. "Would you like some tea? I need tea."

"Do you want us to call the cops?" Linda asked, closing the door behind her and Jack. "Are you missing anything?"

"I—I don't know," Ruth stammered as she shakily opened a box of tea.

"Here, let me help you," Linda said as she went to fill the electric kettle. Jack started picking up the papers on the floor. While his friend helped the frightened woman, who was still dressed in her plum-colored puffy winter coat, he stole upstairs and set some papers on the desk in her study. Curiosity got the better of him and he tried to surreptitiously peek at some papers while trying to gather others off the floor. Her bookshelf behind the desk was a total wreck.

"You found my humble observatory," a voice said suddenly from behind him.

He jumped and turned around. "You scared me!" he gasped, clutching his chest.

"Sorry, Jack," she said.

Again, the wrong name, he thought, but he didn't correct her.

"Thanks for helping clean up."

"Of course," he said. "Am I putting these papers in the right place? They were scattered everywhere."

"Yeah, anywhere's fine," she answered before she sifted through the items on her desk. Then she swore.

"What's wrong?" Jack asked.

"A book is gone. It was one of a kind," Ruth explained angrily.

Linda appeared at the door, holding a steaming cup of tea. "Is everything okay? You're not missing any valuables, are you?"

"No, just a book I was studying," Ruth sighed. "I found it in the forest. What a fascinating tome…"

Jack looked past her at Linda and raised his eyebrows as the reclusive author sat down.

"Do you want to report it?" Linda asked as she walked over to give Ms. Leeds her tea.

"Over a book? I don't think so. It was unique, but…" Ruth exhaled. She dragged her fingers down her face and then sipped her tea. "Thank you, my dear."

"Do you know who'd want to steal it from you?" Jack asked innocently. Linda rolled her eyes.

"No, no one," Ruth answered.

"This is normally a safe area, I'm shocked this happened," Linda said. "I'm really sorry. My mom and I will make cookies for you."

"Oh, no, that's not necessary," Ruth smiled warmly. "You don't need to worry about that or telling your mom. I'll get it all sorted out. It was just a major shock. It could've been a poltergeist or something, I'm fairly certain there's some restless dead nearby."

"That's... understandable," Linda tittered lightly. She struggled to resist the urge to make a face. *Although,* she thought, *it's hard to judge her while I'm literally friends with Jack Frost. But at least I have a reason to believe he's real.*

Ruth stood up. "Thank you both so much for your help, it's probably time you went home now, though."

"Of course, anytime," Linda and Jack said, leaving the room.

"I can't believe I have to deal with this and a wake tonight," they heard Ruth grumble to herself as they walked down the stairs.

After they made it onto their own street, Linda asked, "How do you know it's *the* book, Jack? And why would Ruth have it?"

"We'd have to look at the other stuff in her office tonight to make sure. You heard her. She won't be there," Jack said simply, shrugging his shoulders.

"So, you mean... commit a crime?" Linda extrapolated.

"What crime?"

"*Breaking and entering,*" Linda whispered emphatically. "You *do* realize that's a crime?"

"Either we break and enter or the world ends, you choose," Jack answered.

Linda groaned. "Don't be unfair."

"So... you're not disagreeing with me."

"If we get caught, I'm going to kill you."

"What's that phrase? Thick as thieves? You wouldn't do that to me," Jack said innocently, batting his eyelashes.

"Unlike you, I can't run away to Pryddia when things go south," Linda said as they reached the porch. She looked for her keys. "Ouch. Shit."

"I mean, you could. And are you okay? What's wrong?"

"Yeah, I just got a really bad scratch earlier," she said, holding up her bandaged fingertips. She neglected to mention that the school nurse had to pluck out large splinters from the wound earlier that day.

He held her hand and looked at her fingers. "I'm sorry. That sucks. What happened?"

Linda pulled her hand away. "It was just a scratch. I was helping Mr. London with something. It's fine."

"Okay," he said. "Anyway, we won't be breaking, just entering." He held up a pair of keys.

"Jack! What the hell?" Linda exclaimed. She pushed his hand against his stomach before anyone could see.

He smirked. "Hey, loose morals for the sake of the world and you. Give me the lecture later," he said as he dropped the keys back in his pocket. "You don't have to come with."

Linda groaned and contemplated her life choices before grumbling, "You know I'm coming with, asshat."

＊

"Hey Mom, John and I are going out for a walk to look at the constellations," Linda said later that night as she stood in the living room. Jack hovered behind her.

"At this hour?" her mom asked, turning in her seat on the sofa. "Why? You know I'm not a fan of you being out after dark."

"It won't be for that long," Linda pleaded. "We just wanted to look at Ursa Major and Orion's Belt."

Her mom stared into her soul for a moment before sighing. "Keep me updated, you two. If you don't get back by 8, I'm putting out a missing persons alert."

"Sounds good," Linda and Jack answered before hurrying to the front door, where Jack waited for Linda to get ready for the cold. Then they walked quietly to the Ms. Leeds's house. They got antsy as they passed Lavender's house since they knew that they would be even more easily recognized there. Linda and Jack were grateful for the sparse streetlights. But finally, they made it. And Ruth's unkempt driveway was vacant.

"Jack, look," Linda whispered, grabbing his sleeve and pointing down. They both turned to look at the small flowering raspberry plant creeping up toward the concrete stairs to Ruth's front door.

"Hm," he said thoughtfully. He grabbed the keys and unlocked the front door quietly.

Before he could do anything else, Linda opened the door and yelled, "Ms. Leeds?"

"What are you doing?" Jack demanded in a whisper.

"Covering our asses," Linda whispered back. "Ms. Leeds!"

Jack covered her mouth. But they heard no response. Her car wasn't in her driveway, and no alarm had gone off. Jack let go. "You and I have fundamentally different perspectives about this process," he whispered.

"Says the guy who wanted to teleport into a house without checking first," Linda shot back. He rolled his eyes and held open the door for her before checking behind them one last time and pulling it shut again.

They stole up the stairs, which were creaky as hell, something that Linda didn't notice earlier that day. She internally scolded herself for her inattention as she followed Jack upward. Eventually, they made it to Ruth's study. While Jack scoured the desk, Linda tentatively followed a trail of loose and crumpled papers to the bedroom. A trashcan overflowing with paper proved to be the culprit. Linda was clearly in an author's house. She rolled her eyes. When she looked up, she saw the shadow of a cord hanging down from the ceiling—leading to a panel for the attic. She reached up and tugged, and the ladder unfolded easily. She looked back at the entrance of the bedroom, lit by a plug-in nightlight, and then at the windows which were steeped in pine bough garlands. Then Linda ascended.

And screamed.

A skeleton sat in a cozy chair next to a desk.

She heard Jack running into the room as her hands slipped and she fell down the ladder into his arms. And then onto the floor, her faithful friend becoming her cushion.

"Ow, shit," he groaned. "Are you okay?"

"There's a skeleton up there!" Linda whispered.

"No offense, Linda, but I'm pretty sure the dead can't hear you," Jack said back.

"Give me a break," Linda said, getting off of him and helping him up. "There's also a desk."

"Were there papers, notebooks, or books on it?"

"Obviously."

"Then let's go," he said, starting up the ladder.

"Seriously?" she demanded.

"It's just a skeleton," he answered. "It's natural."

"*You're* natural," Linda muttered.

He disappeared up into the attic. Then he poked his head down through the entrance. "Linda, it's fake."

"What?"

"The skeleton is made of plastic. And yes, I touched it to make sure. Get up here," he instructed.

Reluctantly, she followed him up. "Why would you touch what might be a cadaver?" Linda asked as she stared down the skeleton.

"Better question: why the fuck would Ruth have a fake skeleton up in her kooky writer's attic where she clearly spends a lot of time?" Jack said, pushing a small collection of used mugs to the side with his arm. The tags of the tea bags fluttered slightly.

Linda shivered. "I don't know if I want to know." Regardless, she went over to the desk and pulled out her flashlight as she helped him scan the various paperclipped papers. Unsatisfied with his preliminary findings, Jack went over to the filing cabinet that sat along the adjacent wall and began to pore over their contents.

"Jack, is this it?" Linda asked, quickly skimming yet another paper.

"Let me see," he said, hurrying over to her. He looked over her shoulder at the text she underlined with her fingertips. "Yes, that's it!" he exclaimed. Then he did something she didn't expect.

He cupped her face in his hands. And he kissed her. "Thank you! You're a literal angel!"

Then he let go. He paused for a moment. Then quickly returned to leafing through the papers in front of them for any more evidence, trying not to disturb too much.

Linda remained frozen in place. In the dark, her friend couldn't see that her face was as red as a raspberry. Finally, she said, "Jack, save it for Jasmine."

"Oh, she turned me down."

"What?" Linda demanded. "When was this? Why didn't you *tell me?*"

"At the end of lunch today I quickly asked her if she'd be interested in going to the dance with me. Since the dance was tonight, I figured I might as well find out what's going on. Then, she was like, 'No, and shouldn't you be going out with your girlfriend?'"

"She said that? But she's the one who started it."

"Exactly! I was shocked. But it's just how it is. I'm fine. Just surprised. There's no way it would've worked, anyway."

"Why?" Linda asked.

"She's a mortal, I'm a snow pixie parading as a mortal. There's no way it would ever work," he explained simply. "I was never that serious about her, anyway."

"Oh," Linda said. She felt a pang in her stomach.

His lips were so soft.

He smelled like the snow that sits on balsam boughs.

His hands were so warm and gentle.

A car door closed outside.

"Oh shit," Jack said.

"Shush!" Linda whispered. "We need to leave the attic. You can't teleport with all this loose paper."

"Dammit," he groaned. He grabbed the papers they needed and followed her out of the room. They tried to move as soundlessly as possible. They heard the front door close. The moment they climbed back down the ladder into Ruth's bedroom, they heard the stairs begin to creak. Jack grabbed Linda around the waist, and they disappeared.

TWENTY-THREE

IS IT PLOTTING AND SCHEMING IF YOU SAVE THE WORLD?

"W e're back!" Linda called into her house as she took off her coat.

"Just 15 minutes left," her mom answered.

Jack took a sprig of spruce needles from Linda's hair once she stood back up after strenuously extracting her feet from her snow boots. "It would be hard to explain that," he chuckled. He had accidentally transported them back under one of the trees next to her home.

Linda's mom walked over from the kitchen. "How were the stars?"

Linda pushed Jack down the hall in the other direction. He still held the papers from their uninvited visit to Ms. Leeds's house.

"Oh, and did you see that bright light when you were walking back? I don't know where it came from," her mom asked after she gave Linda a hug.

"What light?" Linda asked.

"It was a bluish-white color. It was weird, but there's probably some sort of explanation. I saw it only very briefly after I dropped off some clean clothes in your room," her mom explained. She cupped her daughter's face in her hands. "You look a little flushed, are you feeling okay?"

"Yeah, I'm okay, thanks, Mom," Linda smiled.

"Maybe it's just the cold air," Mrs. Waters suggested as Jack came back. "Would you like some hot chocolate, John? I still don't know how you don't wear a coat outside. I'll have a stroke if you ever go out in shorts."

"I'll make sure to wear long pants whenever I'm around you, then," Jack snickered. "And I would love some hot chocolate. Also, where's Mr. Waters? He's usually home by now."

"Oh, he just went out to get drinks with an old friend after work," her mom explained, leading them back to the kitchen.

"That's nice," Jack answered. "Actually, I just remembered I have a homework assignment that I need Linda's help with. Is it okay if I steal her for a bit?"

"Yeah, I'll leave your drinks out on the counter," Mrs. Waters smiled.

Once he was alone with Linda, he handed her the papers. "Linda, I realized that the papers I took have some drawings on them, too. And a taped leaf," he said, handing them to her. "There's also some notes and transcriptions on the back that I need to run by Father Time, but some of the characters that Ruth used were unmistakably from the sacred text."

Linda skimmed the paper again—it was from the stack that led to him kissing her... she blushed again. *God help me*, she thought crossly. *Why is this such a curse?*

"It says that the leaf was from the tree where Ruth found the book," Linda said. "Does that woman not live in the real world? How was she fine with that?"

"We're talking about someone who has a skeleton in her attic and thinks that poltergeists steal her books," Jack answered.

"Fair enough," Linda laughed. "I also know from the leaf that the tree is nearby. Well, that *kind* of tree is nearby. I need to go ask Ruth if she ever forages or something."

"You *want* to spend *more* time with her?" Jack asked, a look of dismay on his face.

"For the case of the stolen book, yes," Linda said. "It's the obvious next step. Even if I cross-referenced the kind of bark patterns that this kind of tree has since all of the leaves are off the trees now, it looks like it's a popple. Although... it's only one of the most common deciduous tree species in Maine..."

"Please don't make me go with you."

Linda raised an eyebrow. "Are you allergic to books *and* authors now?"

"Why don't you bring her the cookies and connect with her over nerdy stuff. I'll ask other nerds to help me learn anything else from this paper," Jack said.

"What if I need you or something?" Linda asks. "Since, you know, you lack cellular service."

"I will think of a solution," he said. "That's a good point. Also, the elf that Rosie caught has been interrogated. She won't give up any information," Jack explained. At Linda's confused look, he explained, "Rosie is one of Mona's righthand elves. Mona wouldn't be able to survive without her. She's the best."

"So, you all don't know who you're looking for?"

"The best mice are on the task in the records," he said.

"You know, that doesn't inspire much confidence for mortals," Linda retorted.

"Well, it should. You guys need to stop killing all the rodents," Jack said.

Linda was about to argue but decided against it.

"Is everything... packaged?" Jack said, a look of awe on his face as he stared out at the grocery store's many aisles. It was the next day. Linda knew that the grocery trip would be a doozy from the moment Jack asked her mom if he could join last night.

"Um, yeah, this is fairly common," Linda said.

"Mrs. Waters, can we get more hot chocolate?" Jack asked with stars in his eyes. "Where does it come from?"

"Of course, John," her mom laughed. "It'll be in the aisle with other instant drinks and things like tea and coffee."

"John, do you get out much?" her dad asked with an amused look.

Linda turned to him and mouthed, "no."

"Linda, what all does your family get here?" Jack asked, his voice low, while they waited for her parents to get carts.

"All of the food we get that's not from the farmer's market," Linda answered.

"Really?" he asked.

"Yes, really."

"What's that?" he asked, making a beeline toward the eggs.

Linda followed quickly after him like a mother following her young child in an antique store. "Look at the packaging," Linda instructed. "There's a reason that it's there."

"Linda, there's no need to be so sassy," her mom chided as she joined them, pushing cart one of two. Jack opened one of the egg cartons.

"Please be careful," Linda warned.

"I know what eggs are," he said, sticking out his tongue. "But why are they in this weird pink plasticky material?" He began to turn it in his hands while he read all the information.

Linda anxiously took it from him before they had to pay for broken eggs. "It's just another kind of carton. Some of them are made out of paper, some are Styrofoam, and some are made out of clear plastic, but those are usually too expensive."

"You have to pay for everything?" he whispered to her.

"Yes, Jack," Linda whispered back.

"Why?"

"We're not growing it ourselves, are we?"

"Ohhhhhh," he said. "Where do you guys get the turkey?"

"It's in the frozen meat aisle, they usually have it on sale a couple weeks before Thanksgiving."

"Wait," he said, his eyes widening as if he had a culinary epiphany. "Is that... something I would want to see?" he asked tentatively.

"Don't worry, dear. It's separate from the butcher section. Don't go over there if it'll bother you. We don't want grocery day to be traumatizing," her mom laughed. She pulled out her list. "Actually, we do need a dozen eggs. Can you check the price on the extra-large ones?"

At one point, Jack split off with Linda's dad after he found out that would lead the way to the hot chocolate, and Linda found herself alone with her mom. "Do we need cream of mushroom soup for the green bean casserole?" she asked.

"Yes," her mom said slowly, perusing the list. "Only two cans, though. I'm not going to use the soup for anything else, ever."

Linda laughed. "I didn't know you hated it that much."

"Some things simply exist to serve a purpose, Linda," her mom answered sagely.

"Like mushroom soup."

"Exactly."

While they looked for canned oysters, her mom said, "Did I tell you that Kris and Emily are staying at school for Thanksgiving?"

"Yes!" Linda exclaimed, pumping her fist.

"Linda," her mom scolded.

"We're going to be seeing them for Christmas," Linda answered sheepishly.

"I was hoping that you'd have a slightly different reaction," her mom said as Linda placed a few cans in the cart.

"Mom, you know Emily and I don't get along very well," Linda reminded her, before muttering, "It would be easier if she had a different personality."

Her mom rolled her eyes. "Kris has always been a good role model for you."

"When he isn't treating me like I'm five," Linda said.

"I'd love for them to meet John," her mom said as they walked to the next aisle.

"Why?" Linda asked, making a face.

"You guys have been getting closer…"

"And…?"

"You know, just in case he becomes part of the family," her mom said.

"What are you insinuating?" Linda asked.

Her mom sometimes felt like her youngest utilized a larger vocabulary than her two other children combined, and she tried her best to stifle a laugh. "Well, I've noticed that you two have been pretty comfortable being touchy—"

"Mom, he's my best friend," Linda groaned, but she felt herself blushing as she remembered the kiss from last night. "Oh, I forgot to get the fried onions. I'll be right back." And then she hurried off in the direction opposite of her mom to keep her from noticing her pink face.

Her mom rolled her eyes as she pulled out her cell phone to call her husband.

"Yeah, I'm in the World Food aisle with Jackie," Linda's dad answered.

"Jackie?" Ange asked. "Michael, who do you know that's named Jackie?"

"Oh, sorry, I meant John. I asked him why sometimes Lindy calls him Jack and he said we can call him that, too, if we want. It's a family nickname. Anyway, they have cricket flour and Jackie recommends it—"

"NO," Ange exclaimed. She heard John snickering in the background. "Mike, absolutely not. We are not having bugs in our kitchen."

"But Ange, they're already processed!"

"Nope!"

TWENTY-FOUR

THE GOOD IS OFT INTERRED WITH THEIR BONES

"You look good, brother," Ruth said as she walked over to him at the funeral reception that Sunday, two days after the wake. George was dressed to the nines in a black suit with a black button-up shirt underneath. He straightened his black bowtie. "Well, I couldn't underdress for our great aunt. You look exquisite yourself," he said.

Ruth wore a black frilly neo-Victorian number with a matching black hat and satin gloves that went up to her elbows. For once, her updo was neat and shiny. "Like you said, it's important to dress up for such an occasion," she answered.

They looked out at the reception. It was nothing like the small, quiet one after Kelsie Robertson's funeral. He had helped some of Robertson's family friends in the outdated kitchen with the food while the surviving family sat shell-shocked on the worn couch. No one was able to reach them, and most people didn't stay very long in their small living room.

His late great aunt's reception was held at her aging stately house. There were a lot of people sitting on plush red couches in the entry hall and the sitting room. They ate deviled quail eggs or drank wine while they talked. All of the large windows, which screamed a massive heating bill in Maine, had black velvet drapes. A large ornate antique vase filled with white lilies sat on the table beside them in the center of the room, next to a gilded framed photo of their late great aunt. People approached his great uncle to give their condolences while he smiled sadly and sipped at his pinot noir. Despite the presentation, the siblings *were* overdressed. Most guests wore somber versions of Sunday clothes. When George had arrived at the cathedral that morning, his *eomma* had given him a disappointed look before tersely whispering, "This isn't a *celebration, adeul.*" He had only smiled in response and glanced up at the elaborate tympanum.

"I can't believe you left the wake early," George said in a low voice. "I had to drive back with both of our parents as they talked about Jennifer," he added, referring to his ex-wife.

"It was a very long day even without the wake," Ruth answered, looking up at the grand chandelier that hung over them.

George studied Ruth's face. He hadn't apologized to her for tactlessly reaming her out in front of Linda and John, but something had changed after the wake. He and his sister finally had something in common again. Confronting death seemed to have that effect. "Isn't it funny how such a beautiful funeral can hide that someone was such a homophobic racist?" George commented.

"They should've imported black dahlias and *Atropa belladonna*," Ruth scoffed, jutting her chin toward at the lilies.

"It would've aligned with all the comments she made about our mother," George answered.

"Don't forget all the comments about how incorrect our eye shapes are for a place like America," Ruth pointed out. "Although you avoided the brunt of it, *namdongsaeng.*"

"I don't think she was capable of realizing that having a monolid doesn't negatively define a person. Or, for that matter, being bisexual."

"I hated her."

George sighed. "Me, too."

"I cannot believe that she requested for you to be a pallbearer."

"She had to remind me that she would still be above me one last time," George said, sucking his teeth. "You wanna get out of here, make up for lost time? We're dressed like a couple of vamps, might as well enjoy it."

"What about our parents?" Ruth asked. They looked across the room where their aging parents sipped espresso and chatted with other relatives and friends, their dad's arm around their mother.

"They'll be okay," George said. "They have their own car." He offered his arm. "Come on, let's go. Portland is only an hour away."

"If we survive the drive," Ruth smiled, hooking her gloved arm through his. "Do you think Purgatory is real?"

"For Aunt Ada's sake, I hope so," George laughed.

TWENTY-FIVE

THE TURKEY RITUAL

Linda sat on the floor of Mr. London's classroom again, cross-referencing the book titles with his notebook. She was supposed to be at lunch, but she wasn't hungry. Jack had asked her why she wanted to leave him and Lavender, but Linda had lied and said her stomach hurt and wanted to see the nurse. For some reason, it was easier than saying she kept seeing Kelsie in everything, and that the looming holiday was just a reminder of how absent her friend would be. He would've understood, but Linda couldn't stand the idea of sitting in a loud cafeteria and being aware that Kelsie wasn't going to walk over and add to the noise.

Sometimes she wanted to just disappear. Not really disappear forever, but the feelings could be too much. Sometimes she was fine, and she felt like time was mending her like everyone said it would, and sometimes the floor fell out from beneath her feet at the smallest reminder, and all she wanted to do was let go of the ledge that she held onto. Her fingers hurt and ached. She wished someone could pull her out, but sometimes all the words of encouragement she heard bounced off of her ears or her scratched up fingers. She never knew when the floor would open up again beneath her feet.

She looked up at Mr. London, a melancholy expression on his face as he stared down at the exams he was supposed to be grading. *Maybe he was sometimes hanging on for dear life, too,* she thought. Maybe the pit was smaller than she realized, or at least he was there with her, and she didn't realize it before. The thought didn't make her happy, but it was a weird relief.

He looked up at her, his sad look fading some. "Do you need help with something?" he asked.

"I think I just figured it out, thank you," Linda said before looking back down at the notebook she was supposed to be writing in. "Actually... Mr. London, one of your books is missing."

"Goddammit, already?"

"It would've been within this past week at the most."

He groaned. He wondered why he bothered buying books for his students on his crap salary when he couldn't even get one of them to respect him enough to ask.

"I'm guessing they didn't ask you first," Linda commented.

"You would be right," he said, pinching the bridge of his nose. "Do you know who it could be?"

"Well, I know it's not Jack because he doesn't like science that much. No offense."

"Jack?" Mr. London asked her, a puzzled look on his face.

Linda was about to have a coronary. "Oh, sorry, I mean John. His nickname is Jack."

"Oookay," Mr. London said, looking as if he could laugh. He knew that it was an old nickname for John, but it always seemed so arbitrary. And Linda seemed stressed about it. But he decided to let it go. "We'll see if the unknown delinquent returns their book before break in the spirit of Thanksgiving."

"They probably won't."

"Let me believe, Linda."

❦

The next day was Wednesday, the day before the yearly turkey ritual, and Linda returned to the cafeteria. Unfortunately, Jack wasn't in school that day—something about Mother Nature freaking out about the turkey population.

"What are you doing for Thanksgiving?" Linda asked Lavender at the lunch table.

"Actually, it's a day of mourning for Native Americans," Lavender explained. "So, we're visiting my grandmother in Penobscot Nation to remember our culture and everyone who has died."

"Oh, I'm sorry. I didn't know," Linda said.

"Yeah, no offense, but not many White people know about it for some reason," Lavender said. "It's not like they made a holiday to celebrate their conquest over my ancestors or anything."

"Oh my God, I never realized that," Linda said, aghast.

"Um, yeah," Lavender answered.

"Is there anything I can do to be more respectful?" Linda asked.

"Of course! I can loan you some books so you can learn more," Lavender offered. "They're kind of heavy, but, you know, so is genocide and stuff. I can give them to you after school if you want."

"That would be really great, thank you," Linda smiled.

"Hey, by the way, where's John?" Lavender asked, glancing around the busy room.

"Oh, um," Linda stalled. "He's... helping with the family business. They're having... turkey issues."

"Does he live on a farm?"

"You could say that."

*

George London was thankful to have a break from school. That is, both kinds: graduate and high school. And it was even better to be able to enjoy his mother's cooking. He sat next to Ruth at the Thanksgiving table, something that hasn't happened in a few years. It was... nice? Even if he had to listen to her kooky supernatural beliefs. What was happening to him?

"We're so happy you two are friends again," his father said, breaking the lull in their family conversations. George looked over at his dad from the other side of their nice dining table laden with Korean

American fusion dishes. The old man's crow's feet deepened as he smiled.

"You know, your father and I won't be here much longer," George's mom added. "You'll need each other."

"*Eomma*, you're only 57!" George exclaimed.

"One foot in the grave," his father echoed solemnly as he ate some more of his wife's famous cranberry *banchan*. Their mom had always loved experimenting with their two cultures' cuisines in the kitchen, much to the dismay of the young George when he brought packed lunches to grade school. His peers gagged at her delicious homemade kimchi until he begged her to pack him PB&J or fluffernutter sandwiches instead.

"Dad!" Ruth exclaimed next to her brother. Their father shrugged. George sighed into his soju.

"When's the last time you've had Korean food, George? You're getting fat," their mom said.

"*Eomma*, we live in Maine, and I was married to a White woman. I usually eat Korean food when I visit you guys."

"Tsk, tsk. You can look up Asian markets, they're not that far," Ruth chided.

"I cannot believe you're not backing me up," George said. "And I do drink soju at home."

"Soju doesn't count as a vegetable when you're drowning your sorrows in it."

"A lot of people get divorced, Ruth. I see people consult me at the firm all the time," their mom interjected. "Just because your brother couldn't maintain a happy marriage doesn't mean you should poke fun."

"Okay, thank you," George said, standing up and pushing back his seat. "I'm going to go watch the game." He downed his drink.

"Good idea, son," his father said, doing the same before giving his wife a peck. "Please don't put away your food, dear, I'm going to come back for more."

"I know, *yeobo*, you always do," she said back as he followed their son to the living room. George heard his *eomma* begin to lovingly grill

Ruth about her new metaphysical novel before he turned on the TV. He rolled his eyes.

Linda walked into her kitchen that evening, which smelled of warm sugar and cinnamon, carrying the heavy book about the Native Americans that had the misfortune of meeting the Pilgrims four hundred years ago. The smell reminded her of when she and Kelsie attempted to make pumpkin pie two years ago, but didn't realize they forgot the sugar until they took their first bites. The memory made something twist in Linda's chest. It was so vivid that she could almost imagine Kelsie standing by her parents, helping them ice the cookies and sticking out her tongue in concentration.

Linda took a deep breath to try to ground herself before approaching the counter. "What are all these extra turkey cookies for?" she asked as she watched her dad struggle to evenly ice the cooled sugar cookies. Last night they already baked a few batches for themselves and for church before they started some Thanksgiving meal prep. Her mom took another full baking sheet out of the oven, laden with golden naked turkeys.

"We're just making a few extra for church," her dad said without looking up. A bead of perspiration collected on his brow. "You're welcome to help if you want."

"Sure," Linda said, washing her hands in their warm kitchen before picking up an orange bag of icing. "I could use a break from learning about how many Native Americans died from colonizer diseases," Linda said.

"Why not read about something happier on a holiday?" her mom asked as she took off her oven mitts.

"I'm sure the Native Americans wish that they could've had a happier holiday," Linda responded.

"Fair enough," her parents answered.

After the cookies were finished and their daughter escaped to eat more gravy-fied sweet potatoes and blueberry pie, Mike and Ange assembled the basket of cookies for Kelsie's surviving family.

"Angela, we can't protect her forever," Mike said in a low voice.

"Michael," Ange said firmly.

"I'm just worried about her being so closed off. She wouldn't have helped us if she knew these cookies were for the Robertsons," he elaborated. "You know I'm far from forcing Linda to do anything. Maybe George was right, and we should take her to a counselor."

"That's a conversation you can have with her," his wife said, putting on her knit hat. She sighed. "This is not an argument I want to have."

"It doesn't need to be, darling. We both want what's best for her and the Robertsons," Mike said earnestly, taking her hands in his.

"I agree," she said, giving him a peck. "Which is why I'm taking these cookies over. Do you have the note?"

He nodded and helped her tape it to the basket.

TWENTY-SIX

A PERIOD OF TIME

The geriatric art teacher, dressed in red and blue New Age fashion, caught everyone's attention the following Monday morning with her announcement of their first group project. Groans filled the room. Their partners were already predetermined as well. More groans. It would be their table partners. If it was a table of four, then they work with the people oblique from them, just for a bit of extra pizazz.

Lavender looked at the empty seat next to her. Linda was almost always on time for Visual Art, but evidently that morning was an exception. Lavender hoped she would eventually show up. Even if Linda could be grumpy in the morning, it always made Lavender's day better to hear her quiet quips.

When Linda woke up that Monday, her stomach hurt. It got worse while she was getting dressed, and worse and worse until she vomited into the toilet.

"Are you okay, sweetie?" her mom asked when she found her daughter hugging the toilet.

"No," Linda groaned.

"Is it a stomach bug?"

"I'm having the worst cramps ever," Linda said. "I think it's my period, but it's been so many months I don't remember."

"It could be a bit of an adjustment period. No pun intended," her mom said, stifling a laugh at her own joke. Linda groaned. "Let's just see what happens or if it gets any worse before we take you to the doctor."

"I'm not going to school," Linda called weakly as her mom left the bathroom for Tylenol.

"I wouldn't do that to you, sweetie," her mom called back.

Lavender approached an almost empty lunch table after being let out early from class. The cafeteria slowly filled with noise after the bell rang, and John walked over slowly, balancing a cup of water on a lunch tray. He really was dressed the same as ever in a navy hoodie and a slate blue t-shirt.

"Hey, John," Lavender said over the din.

"Hey, Lavender," he smiled warmly. "How has your day been?"

"Fine, I guess," she said. "My teachers seemed to have caught the group-work bug all at the same time, it's actually a nightmare."

"What classes?" he asked.

"Math, History, and Art. I don't even know how to do a group art project, I thought it was supposed to be an independent thing," she said. "It's not like it's Theater Arts."

"That actually sounds like hell," John sympathized. "Although isn't Linda in Art with you? Do you get to work with her? She's the best partner you could ask for."

"Yes, and I was going to ask you about her. She wasn't in class. Is she in school today?"

"No, I think she's at home. I didn't see her at Homeroom or Science," he said. "I hope she's okay, she's at school like every day."

"Haven't you texted her or something?"

"Oh, I don't have a phone," he said sheepishly. "My... uh... parents don't believe in it."

"They don't believe in cell phones?" Lavender asked incredulously.

"You'd be surprised."

"So, you and Linda just plan to meet each other—"

"All the time, yes," he finished for her.

"Are you sure you two aren't into each other?" Lavender ventured, watching his expression.

He rested his chin on his hand. "That's a bit heteronormative, isn't it?" he asked, an amused look on his face.

Lavender blushed. "No, you guys just seem in love with each other, that's all."

"I feel like romance isn't exactly on Linda's mind," Jack said, looking away. "She's not very happy."

"Oh," Lavender said, clearing her throat. "So, I suppose that means you don't have her phone number?"

"That would be correct," he laughed. "I can give her yours for your project, though. If you want."

"That would be amazing," Lavender exclaimed, whipping out a notebook and writing it down. "I'm going to have to do so much planning between these projects and midterms."

"Midterms?" John asked.

"You know, those looming exams and essays that determine half our grades?" Lavender said. "John, have you dropped off the face of the earth? I swear it's been all everyone has talked about."

"I prefer chaos. It's inspiring."

"My parents would hang me by my toes if they heard me say that," Lavender laughed.

Later that afternoon, Jack quietly approached the plaid couch in the living room where Linda's mom told him she would be. Schoolwork, pill bottles, cookies, and mugs littered the coffee table in front of her, and the couch itself was covered by blankets, pillows, and, of course, his friend. "Hey, Linda," he said tentatively. Her mom had told him that she wasn't doing well. "I missed you at school today."

"Yeah," Linda groaned. She had watched the sunlight from the windows stretch into long orange panes, counting down the time until he hopefully appeared.

"Are you okay?"

"Noooo," she moaned, leaning forward into a couch pillow. "I think my uterus is trying to kill me." She heard Jack stifle a snicker. "I'll kill you if you laugh at me," she groaned.

"I swear I'm not laughing at you; it was just the way you said it," he explained earnestly. "I really am sorry. Is there anything I can do to make you feel better?"

"You can let me use you as a source of heat," she said, staring blankly at the dark TV while she was literally in fetal position.

"Why not your cat?"

"Nicholas was here earlier but then he left. Traitor."

"Okay," Jack agreed, holding in another giggle. If Linda had it in her right then, she would've rolled her eyes. He sat down next to her, and she proceeded to flop over into his lap.

"I feel like you'd be more comfortable with a pillow," he said, grabbing one from behind him.

"No, Jack, I clearly want my face near your crotch," Linda said sarcastically as she took the pillow and then mashed her face into it. "Everything hurtsssssss."

Jack was wildly thankful that she wasn't able to see his face after her comment because it was incredibly flushed. He tried to ignore it and thought about ice, but somehow it only made him think about her more and he wished he could escape. "I'm sorry," he said, gently rubbing her back, trying his best to shove away his thoughts and focus on comforting her very apparent agony. "It'll be over soon, right?"

"Probably in a week," Linda groaned. "I hate my life."

Jack stroked her curly hair. "That sounds miserable." He heard her sniffle slightly. "Are you okay?" he asked gently.

She nodded. But she wiped her eyes.

"Hey, Linda," he said, rubbing her shoulder. "It'll be okay."

"No, it won't."

"Cramps don't last forever," he said gently. "I remember how bad they can get, like your body is out to get you."

"I know," she said. Her voice sounded strained, like she was holding back tears. "But it's just the icing on the cake, isn't it? My best friend died, and my life is all messed up. Nothing will ever be okay again even if I have people like you," she lamented.

He didn't know what to say, but he leaned forward and did his best to hold her. "Things do get better even if they're not the same," he said. "I promise."

"Make it happen faster. Why does it hurt so bad?" she cried sadly. "I remember when Kelsie got her first period a few years ago, she was over here. To distract her from her cramps, we watched movies together and ate brownies. Even if you and I do the same, it'll be just because she's not here."

"I know," Jack said. He took a deep breath. "I remember feeling that way about the elf. It's like there's a hole in space where they should be."

Linda nodded and sniffled.

"I know that Kelsie wishes she could be here with you, too. She'd want you to know that it'll be okay even if it doesn't feel that way," he said softly. He reached over to the end table for a tissue and found an empty box, so he used his sleeve to help wipe her face. She turned and cried into his stomach and held onto his waist while he stroked her hair. Eventually, she calmed down and her breathing became steadier.

"Uteruses suck," she said.

"They do," he agreed.

Then they went silent, and she fell asleep in his lap. He looked down at her as he gently stroked her hair so as not to wake her up. Even though her cheeks were still moist from tears, she looked peaceful. "I'm really sorry, Linda," he whispered. "You deserve better."

❧

"Well, here goes nothing," Jack said, steeling himself before driving his chisel sharply downward into the enchanted ice on his wall. The chunk broke off cleanly into his waiting left hand. He took a deep breath and let out a sigh of relief. No magical explosions. And the rest of the ice was still intact, despite Father Time's vaguely worded warning. *Damn him*, Jack thought darkly. Time didn't do it often, but sometimes he liked to keep Jack on his toes. Just for fun.

"Jack, why do you keep hoarding books in here? They belong in the library," Mona said at the door to his room, making him nearly jump out of his skin. The ice slipped in his hands, and he juggled it in the air until he was able to recapture it.

"Have you heard of knocking? I've only been asking you to for a couple centuries," he snapped. "And I'm not hoarding, I'm reading."

"Reading?" Mona demanded. "Have you been drugged again? What's wrong with you?"

"I'm fine, Mona," he laughed. "I've just been trying to find ways for Linda to communicate with me when she needs me." He knew it wasn't his fault, but he felt bad when he realized that she couldn't contact him earlier that day about not feeling well. Not that he could do something productive like stopping her period.

"This better not be for coitus," Mona said.

Jack's face grew boiling hot, and his eyes nearly popped out of his head. "What? No!"

"Humans seem to have a bizarrely large desire to populate—"

"Please stop talking," Jack interrupted. "It's just in case she runs into trouble while investigating. Or existing."

"She's *not* supposed to be helping," Mona reminded him sharply. "You're already on thin ice."

"She's the one who helped me find more about that mortal who had the sacred text. Linda's helping. And she knows the risks," he stated matter-of-factly as he manipulated the piece of ice in his hands, stretching and bending it into different shapes.

Mona sighed with resignation. "You give me headaches." She rubbed her shimmery temples.

"If you gave her a chance, you'd like her," Jack said.

"Thin ice." She left the room.

❧

"What's this?" Linda asked as Jack handed her a small wooden box after school the following day.

"Open it," he said. Inside was a pewter ring with a modest blue gem set in the center, although the gem seemed to faintly glow in the afternoon light.

"You didn't have to give me a ring, Jack," Linda said, a confused expression on her face as she looked up at him. "Mortals don't usually do this when someone's on their period. It's usually for the opposite event."

He laughed. "I know. It's how you can communicate with me," he explained. "If you turn the ice three times, you'll basically be sending me an SOS. I have my own ring, I can do the same thing with you," he said, holding up his left hand.

"Oh my god, the gem is ice?" Linda exclaimed excitedly. "That's so cool! Thank you, Jack," she said, giving him a big hug.

"Don't mention it," he said bashfully. "Check to make sure it fits before you get too excited. I don't want you running into danger and have it slip off."

"You worry too much. *You're* the one who will run into danger," she stated, trying on the ring. It fit perfectly.

TWENTY-SEVEN

DEAD END

"I want us to do the project on something Penobscot-related," Lavender said as soon as Linda approached their table. "American History class didn't even bother to examine how Native Americans were affected by the White colonists."

"Good morning to you, too," Linda said as she sat down next to Lavender, who blushed. "I think it's a great idea. Do you have something in mind?"

Lavender began to talk about the Corn Mother and Nokomis, important women in Penobscot lore, but Mrs. Greene began to call for the class's attention.

"Art has significance beyond just paint slapped on a canvas or clay that's been smashed together," Mrs. Greene lectured. "The research portion of your midterm project has to be just as robust as the art."

"How are we supposed to make copies of famous paintings?" Heather demanded from her seat in the back.

"If you were paying attention when I first explained, you need to *emulate* the style of the movement or artist. Do we need to refresh on what 'emulate' means? Miss Waters, can you please explain to your peers?" the teacher cold-called Linda.

"It means to imitate or mirror, Mrs. Greene," she answered.

"Exactly, thank you," Mrs. Greene said as she continued, saying how they would be meeting at the computer lab tomorrow morning for more research.

"Nerd," Dan shot at Linda. It was loud enough for her to hear but not loud enough for Mrs. Greene to yell at him.

"Shut up, Dan," Lavender shot back.

He scowled. "Shut up, dyke. Know your place," he hissed. Lavender paled.

"Leave her alone, asshole," Linda said, turning to face him.

"What are you going to do about it?" he said.

"Is there a problem?" Mrs. Greene asked.

"Yes," Linda said, although Lavender grabbed her arm. Linda's own heart raced.

"I was just asking for help," Dan said. "Problem solved."

"He called me a slur," Lavender blurted.

"No, I didn't!" he exclaimed.

"Yes, you did," Linda said.

"How dare you—"

"Daniel Ross," Mrs. Greene said tightly. "Dean. Now."

"Liberal hippie," he muttered as he grabbed his bag and left, his voice so low that Linda barely heard him.

Lavender's hands shook a bit on the desk. Linda held her hand. Lavender looked like she was going to cry, but she didn't. After they were allowed to have independent work time, Linda asked, "Are you okay?"

"Yeah, sure," Lavender said, taking a deep breath before going and picking up some colored pencils. But she was still pale. Linda felt a stone sit in her stomach.

"That piece of shit!" Jack growled when Linda explained what Dan had said. Initially, he had a blank look on his face and had to ask what the slur meant.

"At least he's in detention," Linda pointed out.

"Yeah, like he's going to learn anything from that," Jack grumbled.

"Hopefully, he'll learn to leave her alone," Linda said, although she knew that likely wouldn't be the case. She listened to the sound of snow crunching under her feet. She had waited to tell Jack until after school when Lavender didn't bring it up. Linda didn't want to upset her by being the first to talk about it, but she also wanted Jack to know. Part of her hoped that Jack would find a way to surreptitiously give Dan Ross frostbite or something. But she also didn't want to encourage Jack's more impulsive behavior.

"He'll be sorry if he doesn't," Jack said as if reading her mind.

"As much as I support this, I don't want you to get in trouble, either."

"I don't care if I get in trouble," he said.

"I care," Linda said.

"I'm not exactly concerned about the mortal school system's 'consequences,'" he said, making air quotes. "What will they do, peer mediate me to death? Put it on my permanent record?"

"You could get expelled," Linda warned.

"He's not worth getting expelled over," Jack said.

"If you have too many marks on your permanent record—"

"I won't be staying long enough for that to matter," he said.

Linda felt her heart twinge. She knew that he was a nature spirit, and he would only go so far with school, but she hadn't taken the time to consider what that might mean. She wasn't in the mood to entertain that thought.

❦

"Ruth, do you believe in nature spirits?" Linda asked, carefully sipping the mugwort tea that the author offered to her the moment she walked through the door. It tasted putrid.

"Yes, I've been trying to commune with them for ages!" Ruth exclaimed. Linda grimaced at the flavor of her tea, but Ruth didn't seem to notice. "I've been studying all of these old texts to see how different cultures have done it." And then she proceeded to prattle on about various forms of animism until Linda's eyes glazed over. And then she finally mentioned it: the book.

"You found it... under a tree?" Linda asked. Her heart was racing, although she found it hard to get over what she was hearing.

"Yeah, can you believe it? I hardly can," Ruth said, as if reading her mind.

"Which tree did you find it at?"

"Oh, it's been hard to remember after I stumbled over a tree root and hit my head. Weirdly enough, that's the only thing that I've forgotten."

A shiver shot down Linda's spine. "Were you alone when that happened?"

"What kind of question is that?" Ruth asked. "Do you think something... else... is going on, young lady?"

"Not at all," Linda lied. "I'm just worried about you getting a concussion."

"Oh, I'm fine. No other symptoms according to WebMD," Ruth said, waving her hand at the insinuation. Linda didn't feel very reassured.

"I was able to go back to that tree one other time to see if nature left me any more surprises, but I fell when I was leaving. I just couldn't remember after that. What a shame," Ruth sighed.

"Yeah," Linda lamented with her.

Not long later, they said their goodbyes and Linda promised to bring Christmas cookies later. While she walked back, she twisted the ring on her finger before activating the ice crystal. Suddenly, Jack appeared directly in front of her, and they almost knocked each other over.

"What happened?" he asked, eyes wildly examining their surroundings as if he was ready to fight someone.

"Ruth doesn't remember," Linda said.

Jack immediately looked unimpressed. "That's what you called me here for?"

"You only gave my ring one function," she retorted.

"Fine, I get it, I'm not the smart one," he said. "It's all I could figure out."

"It's whatever," Linda said. "But Ruth lost her memory, very specifically. Like you did. I think her memory loss was induced. She remembers everything else but the tree, and she even went to it twice." Linda quickly recounted everything that happened, sparing Jack the details of Ruth's animated animism lecture.

"Maybe that's something to work with," Jack said, but there was no hope in his voice.

Linda felt the same way. It was an indicator that they were on the right track, but also a definite dead end.

TWENTY-EIGHT

SNOW GOONS

"Jack, I have a crazy idea," Linda said as she worked on the floor in her room.

He hung upside down off the edge of her bed so that his hair looked like it was standing on end. "Making snow goons in a blizzard?" he asked.

"No," Linda laughed. "Have you noticed that there's been less… supernatural activity lately?"

"That's boring," Jack groaned, pulling himself upright on her bed so that he was lying on his stomach. He swung his legs in the air. "Snow goon plans are better."

"That's not even that crazy. Building snow goons in a snow fortress during a blizzard would be crazy, though."

"It would be amazing," he said. "But now that I think of it, you're right. I haven't had to use my scythe on any new weird bloodroot in the forest in a while. It's almost like the calm before the storm." He shook his head. "I don't like that idea."

"Or a nature spirit that's serious about their education," Linda suggested.

"Okay, *that* is kind of crazy."

"You're a nature spirit at a high school," Linda countered.

"Yeah, but I don't care about midterms," he said.

Linda rolled her eyes.

"I guess it couldn't hurt to keep our eyes peeled in school," he conceded, although he still sounded doubtful.

Linda's phone pinged. She went over to her desk to look at it. She rarely received text messages.

It was Lavender. *Hi! Want to work at my house after school tomorrow?*

"What is it?" Jack asked. "You look... stressed."

"Nothing, I'm fine," Linda said. She typed out her message in agreement and sent it. *It's just a different house*, she reminded herself. Linda had occasionally noticed that sometimes Lavender looked disappointed when she and Jack said bye to her at the end of the day, but the idea of inviting a new girl friend over... it felt like replacement. For some reason, Jack was different. *Maybe because he's so different from Kelsie, unlike...* Linda shook her head. She didn't want to get sucked into those thoughts, not right then.

"Something that would be crazy is causing a blizzard just to have a snow day and a three-day weekend," Jack said with a fiendish smile. His eyes glittered in the lamplight.

"That would be crazy," Linda smiled. "Tomorrow *is* Friday."

"What a coincidence," Jack said. "Eh, I'll think about it."

Linda rolled her eyes. "Keep me updated, Frosty the snow pixie."

"Hey!"

After Jack left that night, Linda and her parents had a calm dinner and sat down in front of the TV to watch the news. A weather warning popped up about a severe blizzard for the next day.

"There's already so much snow outside. We need to salt the driveway again," Linda's dad groaned.

"Mike, I don't think you're going anywhere in that weather," Linda's mom laughed.

"Looks like you might be stuck with us, kiddo," Mike said to his daughter. "Although, I'm surprised that they didn't predict this ahead of time."

Linda tried not to laugh.

🌿

Of course, school was cancelled. The snow didn't let up until nine in the morning. And, of course, Jack came over anyway.

"Time for some snow goons," he announced happily once Linda opened the door.

"I almost think you overdid it," Linda said, looking at the three feet of snow that covered everything, including the first few steps leading up to the porch. "How am I supposed to get to Lavender's later to work on our project?"

He made a face. "It'll be Friday night, why are you doing home-work?" he whined.

"Don't worry, there's plenty of time until then. It's only 9:30 a.m.," Linda said, pulling him inside.

"Jack, how did you get here so quickly?" Linda's mom asked as she walked over in her robe. "Do you want coffee?"

"Good morning, Mrs. Waters! Can I have hot chocolate after Linda and I get back?" he asked.

"Sure," her mom yawned. "I'm getting coffee."

Jack waited semi-patiently (meaning he bounced on the balls of his feet while Linda tied her bootlaces) for her to get ready before they ran outside. She pushed him into the snow-laden yard, but he grabbed her arm and pulled her down with him so that there was a funny-shaped crater in the snow.

"You have slow reflexes," he said as he lay back.

"I do not," Linda said, sitting up and throwing a gloveful of snow into his face. He laughed. Then he chased her into the backyard, pelting her with snowballs. She caught him under a tree and shook it until the snow fell off the boughs on top of him. She ran back to the front yard and onto the porch, hurriedly packing some snowballs. When he didn't appear for a couple minutes, she started down the stairs to check on him, but he teleported behind her.

"Jack! That's so unfair," she exclaimed, throwing her only in-hand snowball at him. He made the snowball just barely graze him, missing his chest entirely.

"Let's make snow goons," he said.

"No magic, it has to be the traditional way," Linda said.

"Well, yeah, that's more fun," he said. "Although I may add antlers to one so it matches your house's Christmas lights."

"Fine," Linda conceded.

They spent the rest of the morning building snowmen and snow goons. Three snow goons sat in the yard, sitting in a circle and facing each other as if they were in a cult, with their twig arms reaching into the air. Each one was slightly different, but they each had non-circular heads and button frowns or smiles under their carrot noses. Linda made one normal snowman with a bright red scarf and beanie, but when she wasn't looking, Jack added cartoonish moose antlers. To Jack's delight, Linda asked him to help her make a gigantic snowman. They started rolling the base in the front yard and pushed it all the way to the back so that it was more than half Linda's height. As he helped her push the middle section onto the base, he looked over at her. Even though her brows were knit in concentration, Linda had the biggest and most carefree smile that he had ever seen on her face.

"Does Mother Nature know that you made a snow day?" Linda asked him with an unexpected giggle. She started packing snow together for the snowman's head.

"Definitely, she just about killed me for it," he admitted. "It's worth it, though."

"I'm so glad," she said, suddenly wrapping her arms around his neck.

An image of her giving him a kiss flashed through his mind. He scolded himself for thinking of something so ridiculous. He felt really warm. He hugged her and patted her back politely. "I'm glad you're enjoying yourself," he managed. He was glad that she couldn't see the blush on his face. He wanted to dive headfirst into the snow before she noticed. What was wrong with him? "Our snowperson is still missing his head. He looks decapitated."

"Oh no, you're right," Linda said as she pulled away from him. "Can you help make his head more circular with your magic?"

"I thought you said you wanted to do this the 'traditional way,'" he said, mimicking her with a falsetto tone.

"I do not sound like that, butthead."

"I guess you don't want him to have a spherical head, after all," Jack shrugged, shaping the snow into a perfect square.

"Don't make him look like a weirdo," Linda said, trying to take the block of snow away from him.

"Take that back, all of my children are beautiful," he said, holding the block just out of her reach.

"You're too tall, that's unfair," she whined. Linda couldn't help it, but she started laughing.

"Jack! Linda!" her mom called through one of the living room windows.

"What?" Linda called back.

"Lunch is ready! Wait, Jack, where are your gloves? Your hands must be freezing!"

"I'm fine, Mrs. Waters! Don't worry about me," he said, hefting a now-spherical head on top of the snowman, which was actually taller than him.

"I always worry about you," she said, closing the window again.

"Did she really just say that?" Jack asked.

"Jack, you gotta admit, if you were a mortal, your hands would be changing colors at this point," Linda pointed out as they walked back around to the front.

After lunch, Jack asked Linda, "Do you know how to ice-skate?"

"Not well," she responded. "If by ice-skating you mean falling on my face, then sure."

"Do you have ice skates?"

"Of course! How can I live this close to Quebec without owning skates?"

"Hey, well what do you know? I have ice skates, too!" he said, pulling a pair of white ice skates from behind his back. The light blue blades looked more like solid ice than steel.

"Did you just pull them out of thin air?" Linda demanded.

"No, I conjured them," he said as if that was completely obvious.

"Oh, pardon me," she said. "Is this your way of saying you want me to conjure a Zamboni or something?"

"I got that covered. Let's go ask your mom if we can go ice skating," Jack insisted, smiling mischievously.

Linda chuckled as she followed him to the living room, where her mom sipped tea while she watched the weather report.

Jack leaned over the back of the couch and said, "Can Linda go ice skating with me?"

"Oh, geez!" she exclaimed as she jumped in her seat. "John Mason!"

"Oooh, she used your full name," Linda said as he apologized.

"Where will you guys be skating?" her mom inquired.

"Washington Pond," Jack answered.

"That's a big one," her mom said. "Are you sure it's safe? Or even cleared off?"

"It's perfect, I already checked it this morning," he said. "The ice is definitely thick enough. I tested it."

"Jack," she sighed. "You stress me out."

"It's fiiiiine," he said. "My folks showed me what to do if ice cracks when I was young, I knew what I was doing."

"Please, can we go?" Linda pleaded.

"Linda, if you don't text me in thirty minutes, I'm going to—"

"You'll come looking for us or call an ambulance, I know," Linda said.

"Go before I change my mind," her mom said, waving them away.

After Linda grabbed her skates and bundled up again, Jack teleported them to Washington Pond, which was still caked in snow. While Linda put on her skates, he stepped forward and snapped his fingers, making the snow explode into a flurry for the entire area. After putting on his skates with disturbing speed (well, disturbing for Linda because of how much she struggled with the laces on her own), he jumped onto the ice and absolutely showed off. Linda's jaw dropped as he skated backward in the flurry, pulling off jumps and even a couple axels. Then, he did a couple gigantic figure eights while his fingertips brushed against the surface.

"Jack!" Linda exclaimed as she looked up from her phone, seeing him land a double axel.

"Yes?" he asked, turning to face her with an annoyingly impish grin.

"Oh my god, you're intentionally showing off," she said. "Please."

"I'm just warming up," he shrugged, skating back over to her. She put her hands on her hips. "What? You have no proof to the contrary. I am Jack Frost; I have to live up to the name."

"But this is a mortal sport."

"Oh, please. Who do you think showed the mortals how to do it? I invented it but patenting didn't exist back then," he said. "Now, come on. I'll help you up."

Linda nearly face-planted the second she was on the ice. She could tell that Jack was trying really hard not to laugh as he helped her steady herself.

"How about you let me hold your hand while I get reacquainted with the skates," Linda suggested. He agreed and he showed her—reminded her—how to bend her knees and how to turn. Eventually, she was able to skate the whole way around the pond without his help. Until she slipped. While she shouted some expletives, he managed to catch her, sort of, but she accidentally knocked him over and landed in his lap.

"Sorry! I didn't mean to make you my cushion," Linda said while he grimaced.

"It's fine," he said. He seemed to quickly recover before helping her back up. When he helped her stand, she realized his hands were on her waist and she felt herself blushing, even though it wasn't even a romantic gesture. That was the most stable way for him to assist her. Why was her face growing hot? *This is stupid*, she thought. She was so consumed by her own thoughts that she barely noticed him ask if she was ready for him to let go.

They resumed skating, and Linda found herself gliding across the entire length of the pond. She felt exhilarated as she watched the space between herself and the snow-covered bank shrink, the cool air brushing against her face as she listened to the quiet sound of their ice skates slicing the surface of the ice. As she came to a stop, she saw something green in the snow. "Jack!" she called. "Is that what I think it is?"

Jack turned to look where Linda pointed. Indeed, through the snow, a plant sprouted from what looked like footprints.

"Let's follow them," they said simultaneously.

"Great minds think alike," she said as they nodded in mutual appreciation. They quickly changed out of their skates, Jack making his disappear while Linda hung hers over one shoulder, and they hurried over to investigate.

◆

The plant was definitely not a hardy tree sapling, although Linda would have been shocked if one had survived on its own that far from other trees' shelter. "Are those actually…"

"Footprints," Jack finished for her. The footprints were surprisingly shallow despite the depth of snow. In some areas where the snow had drifted, it was nearly up to Linda's hips. He quickly made the decision to will the snow to support her weight as she walked, like the snow naturally did for him.

They followed the prints, which Linda noted were definitely made by a featherless biped, all the way into the forest. The leafless trees creaked above them in the wind, occasionally causing small snow flurries. The prints stopped suddenly in front of a tree and didn't continue past that. The only way the person responsible could have left the area would have been by climbing the tree in question, which would mean they were part squirrel because of how high up the limbs were. Or they retraced their steps backward, which seemed unlikely but not impossible.

"When were these steps made? It looks like it was after the snow had already stopped," Linda said.

"I can't tell, but it was likely this morning. They don't look fresh enough to be a few minutes ago," Jack said, crouching to examine them.

Linda looked at the tree trunk more closely. She couldn't tell what kind it was from the bark, although it definitely wasn't an evergreen. She took off her glove and ran her hand along the rough trunk but couldn't find anything. Jack didn't seem to have any better luck. That is, until they dug out the snow to look at the rest of the trunk and found lots of slash marks that were clearly made by a big knife of some kind.

"Uh, okay," Linda laughed nervously. "Let's leave?"

He examined them more closely. "Whoever did this was really mad at the tree, the marks are very deep. Poor tree."

Before they debated any further, they silently agreed to teleport, just to avoid meeting any lingering knife-wielding maniacs.

When they reached her house, they were exhausted from the day and went to sit on the couch. Nicholas padded up and jumped onto Jack's lap, chirping contentedly and making biscuits. Linda rested her head on Jack's shoulder and unknowingly allowed sleep to take her.

When Linda woke up and looked at the time, she nearly had a heart attack. Her sudden start woke up Jack, who groaned in response. She jumped up and ran to check her phone, which she accidentally left on her bed. There were lots of texts from Lavender.

OMG IM SO SORRY, Linda texted.

Bro where r u?? Lavender replied.

Jack & I fell asleep we just woke up. Linda texted back. *Can we meet tomorrow? I'll bring cookies.*

Fine. Are you guys dating yet?? Lavender asked.

No!! It was platonic! Linda texted.

Sureeeeeeeee, Lavender texted. *See you at noon tomorrow! I expect details and cookies.*

Linda rolled her eyes and threw her phone back onto her bed. Of course Lavender ended up on the shipping train.

TWENTY-NINE

LAVENDER

When Lavender opened the door for Linda, Linda's nostrils were flooded with the delightful aroma of a simmering beef stew. The inside of Lavender's home was very calming and almost like it was taken out of an L.L. Bean catalogue, especially with the open concept, which was unusual for their small town's houses. The walls were all a light cream color, and much of the furniture was wooden or a warm brown leather. It wasn't anything like Kelsie's house, but Linda's chest still felt tight for some reason. *Get a grip*, Linda said to herself. She handed the wrapped plate of chocolate chip cookies to Lavender.

"I didn't expect you to bring so many," Lavender said, her eyes wide. "I was mostly joking."

"*Mostly*," Linda teased as she followed Lavender into the kitchen. They ate a couple cookies while they stood at the quartz island because Lavender explained that her mom doesn't like food upstairs. Mrs. Johnson-Pierre stopped by to say hello and stir the stew before disappearing again.

Linda followed Lavender up the staircase, the walls of which were heavily decorated in family photos. Linda's heart swelled with warmth at the obvious attention to detail that went into hanging up each framed photograph, many of which drastically ranged in size. Occasionally, there were black-and-white photos, and a small one was prominently displayed above the top of the stairs under a hanging woven basket with fading colorful designs. The photo looked like it was from the 19th century and depicted a man and a woman wearing traditional Penobscot clothing.

"Are those also family members?" Linda asked, pointing to the photo.

"Yeah, they're my great-great-great grandparents," Lavender explained.

"Oh, cool!" Linda said. "My parents don't have any pictures as old as that."

"Yeah, we were really lucky to have that photo. We had to petition a museum to get it back," Lavender said sourly.

"That's crappy," Linda said, making a face.

They finally made it to the top of the stairs and turned right, past the bathroom, and made it to Lavender's room. Down the hall, Linda could hear angry emo music blasting through a closed door labeled with a plaque that said, *Damien*.

"Don't mind my older brother," Lavender said, nodding at the door. "He's just a pain."

Linda giggled. "I'm very used to siblings being pains."

"You have siblings? You've never mentioned them," Lavender said as she opened her door. It also had a painted plaque of her name, but it had strikingly realistic sprigs of lavender painted around the white cursive letters.

Linda told Lavender about her super annoying older siblings and how they were away at college, although due back later that day for Winter Break.

The inside of Lavender's room was decorated in many striking different colors, from her medicinal pink wall behind her bed to her orange curtains to her lavender comforter. Some of her own art hung on the walls between posters of artwork. A majority of them were images of very beautiful women. One of them looked vaguely familiar, with fiery red-orange hair that was painted with painstaking detail. *Could it be Jasmine?* Linda wondered. It seemed unlikely that Lavender would intentionally paint her likeness, though, since she was just Lavender's tutor, and they didn't seem to like each other that much.

Linda turned away to look at the other wall, in front of which sat an easel and a very organized desk. The easel still had a half-finished painting of a nude woman on it.

"Oh, don't mind that!" Lavender exclaimed, running over to the easel and flipping the worn canvas cover back over it. "I forgot to cover it up."

"You're very talented," Linda said. "I'm genuinely impressed. Do you think you'll go to art school?"

"Well, I want to, but that's different than actually getting a job," Lavender laughed lightly. "We'll have to see. Damien's going to be an engineer, so hopefully that takes some pressure off of me. Or not."

"My sister is at journalism school, which was a compromise after she initially wanted to be a model," Linda said. "My parents were scared that she'd starve herself and take drugs if she went into modeling."

They sat down on Lavender's bed and got started with planning out their project about the Corn Mother. Linda let Lavender take the reins since she knew so much about the topic and the history. She was surprised that she never learned the story of the Corn Mother, and only of the Three Sisters: beans, corn, and squash, although in Linda's education, the Three Sisters were often regarded as just a children's tale taught to kindergarteners instead of something with real ecological and cultural value. The story of the Corn Mother's sacrifice was beautiful yet disturbing, but Linda felt like she couldn't say anything after reading many of the stories in the Bible.

Linda looked over Lavender's shoulder as Lavender started drafting some of their ideas for the actual art for the project in her sketchbook. As Lavender flipped through the pages, Linda caught glimpses of drawings of beautiful women. She decided to not say anything about it after Lavender was so flustered over the unfinished nude painting earlier.

As Lavender explained certain ideas, Linda nodded along and rarely offered any critique because she honestly thought Lavender was full of amazing creativity. Linda said, "You know, you remind me a lot of Mr. London."

"Isn't he gay?" Lavender asked tentatively. Her heart pounded. Linda was sitting so close to her that Lavender worried that she would hear it. *Why do I remind her of him?*

"I've never asked him," Linda responded, thinking of the homophobic slurs that were carved into his classroom bookcase. "Either way, he's really great. Just... more as a person than as a teacher."

"So... it doesn't bother you if someone's gay?" Lavender ventured.

"Nope," Linda said, glancing at the healing wounds on her fingertips. The scab on her middle finger had begun to give way to faint, white scar tissue. "Does it bother you or something?"

"Oh, no, not at all," Lavender said before blurting, "I'm a lesbian." She clapped her hand over her mouth.

"That's fine," Linda said.

"Really?"

"Yeah."

Lavender collapsed back on her bed out of relief. She giggled.

"It explains why you love drawing beautiful women," Linda commented.

"How can I not? They're so much prettier than guys," Lavender said matter-of-factly. "Although, I must admit, John is a pretty boy."

Linda laughed. "I guess you could say that."

"I know you've seen his eyelashes up close and personal. They are very long. My eyelashes could never."

"Really? I never noticed," Linda commented. Lavender stared at her.

"What?" Linda demanded.

"Do you like him? Ooooooh you're blushingggg."

"No, I'm not," Linda said quickly, even though she felt her face grow warm.

Lavender rolled her eyes. "Then why is your face red?"

"I don't know, it's probably because he kissed me one time, but it didn't mean anything—"

"So, you're napping with him, and he kissed you?" Lavender shrieked.

"Don't say it like that!" Linda exclaimed, burying her face in one of Lavender's lavender pillows.

"How recently did you guys kiss?" Lavender demanded.

"It was a couple weeks ago, I don't know," Linda lied. *It was exactly two weeks and one day ago*. It bothered her that she remembered that. "It was just because he was thankful that I helped him with something important."

"Girl."

"It was! It was just a quick thing, that's all."

"What, like a quick smooch or just a peck?" Lavender asked.

"What's the difference?"

"Have you ever kissed someone before?"

"No, that was kind of my first time…"

"Don't hide behind my pillow, I'm not judging you," Lavender laughed. "I'm not sure if that even counts as your first time. It would only count if you, like, kissed him back. Wait. Did you?"

"I don't know, I was surprised. It was quick." Linda neglected to say that they were also in the middle of rifling through her neighbor's possessions.

"Okay, let me model a peck on your cheek," Lavender said, waving Linda closer. "It's barely anything."

Linda thought about it for a moment and moved an inch closer. Then Lavender leaned in and barely kissed her cheek. "Was it like that?"

"It might've been slightly longer?" Linda admitted hesitantly.

Lavender laughed out loud. "It's either a peck or you guys were totally smooching, there's not much in between."

"I don't knowwww," Linda said, covering her face with the pillow again.

"Has he kissed someone before?" Lavender asked.

"We've never talked about it."

"It just means you need to kiss him again to know for sure," Lavender said slyly. Linda swatted Lavender with the pillow. "I'm joking! I'm joking!"

THIRTY

BLOOD IS THICKER BECAUSE OF CHOLESTEROL

That evening, Linda's siblings came home. Her sister, Emily, arrived at six and her brother, Kris, came home at eight. Both wore sweatshirts from their schools: Emily's was a heather grey University of Maine hoodie, while Kris's black one bore Bowdoin College's polar bear. As usual, Kris mussed Linda's hair instead of hugging her. He was too tall for Linda to mess up his in return. Thankfully, they were too tired to bug Linda for the rest of the night, although she knew that the next day would be different.

On Sunday, they went out for dinner at a restaurant in town, something that they rarely did. Linda's siblings were surprisingly well-behaved. Emily saved her crass jokes, and Kris was quiet while he enjoyed the restaurant's unlimited garlic bread. But then Linda's dad asked about where Jack was, since he was usually with them. Emily finally had ammunition. Linda could tell from her sister's little smile.

"So, Linda, who's this Jack guy that Dad mentioned?" Emily asked during the ride home. It was fifteen minutes, but it already felt like it was taking forever to Linda.

"He's just my best friend," Linda said. "He only moved here this year."

"He seems to be over a lot. Are you sure you're not dating?" Emily pressed, turning towards her sister. Linda caught their mom glance at her in the car's rearview mirror. She internally groaned.

"Don't you have a crush on him?" their dad asked.

"DAD!" Linda exclaimed.

"I'll take that as a yes," Emily said.

"Shut up, Emily."

"Linda Estelle!"

"Mooom, I'm joking," Linda sighed.

"So, when's the anniversary?" Emily asked.

"There isn't any anniversary," Linda said through gritted teeth. "He's just my best friend, okay?"

"Emily, how's Arthur?" her mom interjected about Emily's boy-friend.

"Yeah, how is Arthur?" Kris asked, leaning forward from the back and poking Emily's shoulder. Linda exhaled through her nose.

Linda's bed was cold when she climbed into it for the night, but it wasn't comforting like the cold air outside. She shivered, waiting for her body heat to warm up her space under the blankets. Even though Linda shared a room with her sister again, she somehow felt more alone.

Lavender had hugged her when they said bye the day before. Linda remembered being startled by her warmth, and she hadn't planned on hugging Lavender. Linda knew that she was a little too rigid when she hugged her back, and she hoped that Lavender didn't notice. Linda remembered the first time that she hugged Jack, and how she was startled about how warm his embrace was, too. She didn't like to think about why it bothered her... the feeling of Kelsie's cold hands in the coffin flashed across her fingers, like a ghost. The last time Linda hugged her best friend was so long ago.

When her sister opened the door to their room later, Linda closed her eyes and pretended to be asleep. She heard her sister sigh before climbing into her own bed, the well-used bed frame creaking underneath her.

🍃

When Linda walked into class the next morning, she was unprepared for how jarring it would be to see Lavender. Part of Linda felt like she was losing her mind. For some reason, Lavender seemed to have Kelsie's glittering brown eyes, and her braided hair matched Kelsie's favorite hairstyle. Why was it just now affecting her this much?

Linda was quiet that day. And the day after that, and the day after that. It was a huge relief whenever she was with Jack, because the same feelings didn't bother her. She didn't see Lavender's sad expression when she left school talking animatedly to Jack, while Lavender stayed behind.

"Is everything okay?" Lavender asked Linda after school that Thursday, catching up to Linda at her locker.

"Yeah, why?" Linda said nonchalantly, beginning to walk down the hallway.

"You've been... distant since last week," Lavender ventured.

"Have I?" Linda replied.

"Yeah. Did I do something?"

"No, you're fine," Linda said.

Lavender followed her out through the front doors of the school. "Then what is it?"

"I..." Linda's voice trailed off. "It's nothing." Her tone was stiff. She walked away from the school. She didn't want to deal with this within earshot of everyone.

Lavender followed her. "Why don't you want to talk to me? You're fine with being with John all the time, but you shut me down. Why can't I come over? Why not me?" Lavender asked.

"Lavender, that's different."

"Are you sure it's not because *I'm* different?" Lavender demanded as they crossed the street. "Are you not cool with what I told you on Saturday?"

"What? No!"

"Then why are you being so distant? I don't get it." She crossed her arms.

Linda shifted her feet. "It's not about you."

"Then why don't you want to spend time with me specifically anymore?"

"I do!"

"Why do you always keep me in the dark?"

"I'm not trying to," Linda lied.

"You're not trying to? We even sit at the same lunch table, but you're just icing me out," Lavender shot back. "Linda, if you don't want to be friends, just say it."

"I do!"

"Then what?"

"I—" Linda started, sinking her fingers into her hair.

"What?"

"My best friend died, okay?" Linda raised her voice. "She was killed by a drunk driver last year. It was Kelsie Robertson. You should have heard about it by now."

"Why are you taking it out on me?" Lavender demanded. "Just because someone died doesn't mean you get to treat others however you want. And I wouldn't know that Kelsie was *your* friend. Not many people want to talk to me."

Tears pricked at Linda's eyes and nose. "I'm not trying to take it out on you."

"I could help you, Linda," Lavender softened.

"What are you going to do, resurrect her?" Linda demanded.

"We could talk! You're still alive!"

"Sometimes I wish I wasn't!" Linda blurted. Before she could keep fighting it, the tears began to spill over. "I want to be friends with you, but I don't want to continue without her." She sobbed. She covered her face with her hands. "I'm sorry." Linda couldn't stop crying.

Lavender held her.

"I'm really not trying to take it out on you," Linda managed between sobs. "You just remind me of her so much."

Lavender smoothed her friend's hair. "My baby brother, Cody, died a few years ago," Lavender admitted after Linda had calmed down. "He had drowned in an accident during a regular fishing trip. It nearly tore my family apart and I was depressed for so long. We moved back to this town to be closer to our family and our Penobscot community. Meeting you and John... well, I hoped that I would belong somewhere again."

"I'm so sorry," Linda said through her tears. "I'm sorry for being so distant, it's been so hard to feel anything."

"I get it," Lavender said. "Trust me, it gets better."

"Really?" Linda asked. She took a deep, shaky breath against Lavender's shoulder.

"Really," Lavender smiled. "You don't have to understand everything to feel better." Linda nodded as Lavender patted her back.

"You're allowed to heal," Lavender said to her. "She loved you. She wouldn't want you to be miserable."

"I don't want to forget about her."

"What if you visit her sometimes, then?" Lavender suggested.

"I haven't been back since she was buried," Linda said. "I think I'll fall apart."

"That's okay," Lavender said gently. "There are other ways, too, if you're not ready. I wasn't able to visit my brother's grave for months, but I like physical presence more, anyway. That's why I go to church with my family."

"This is hard to talk about," Linda said, sniffling.

"I know," Lavender said, putting an arm around Linda's shoulders.

"Why do you keep trying to be friends with me? I haven't been good to you," Linda said. She wiped her face.

Lavender looked down. "Trust me, you've been nicer than others."

THIRTY-ONE

STICKS AND STONES

"Hey, Linda," a girl said as Linda left Art. Linda spun around to find Beatrice, of all people, behind her.

"Hi?" Linda answered as students rushed past them. "If you need someone to do your homework, ask someone else."

"It wasn't cool what you did to Dan," Beatrice said. She was flanked by Heather, who nodded.

"What did I do to him, exactly? We never talk," Linda responded.

"He was sent to the Dean. Why did you tell on him to Greene? It was nothing," Beatrice said. Heather nodded.

"He called Lavender a slur," Linda said. "He got what he deserved."

"It was just a joke, relax," Heather hissed. "He's going to an Ivy. You can't mess it up for him."

"He'd better watch his mouth then," Linda said, turning and walking away.

"He was just telling the truth," Beatrice called.

Linda slowed for a moment and a student pushed into her shoulder. Linda started to apologize for getting in their way. But as they passed her, she realized it was Dan.

Lavender looked up from the school water fountain with a sinking feeling in her stomach. Dan Ross and his friend were leaving the boys' bathroom. She turned to walk away and pretend that she didn't see them, but Dan yelled, "Hey! Virginia Woolf!"

Without meaning to, she froze.

"Yeah, didn't you hear? Look at me when I'm talking to you. The least you could do after getting me written up."

"I don't see how that's my problem," Lavender shot back at Dan, turning to look into his ugly face, his jaw way too chiseled for someone so putrid.

"You tattled like a baby, it was just a joke," he said back.

"I wasn't being homophobic to myself, you were," Lavender said, her shaking hands balled into fists. Too late, she realized she just outed herself. Panic rose in her throat.

Dan made a step forward. "Watch your mouth," he said. "You know what? You should go drown yourself like Virginia."

The words felt like a slap in the face. Tears rose in her eyes, but she didn't want to give him the satisfaction.

Suddenly, John appeared next to Lavender. "Back off, Ross."

"Aw, you have a bodyguard," Dan sneered. "Better tell Linda that you're cheating. Too bad for you, Lavender is a lesbian."

"Grow up, Dan," Lavender said, turning to walk away. Dan grabbed her by the shoulder and pulled her back, but John seized his hand.

"Don't touch her," John growled.

"John, let's go," Lavender said, tugging on his sweater sleeve.

"Once Danny apologizes," John said coldly, squeezing Dan's hand so hard that Dan's fingertips were turning purple. Dan's angry face was the color of an overripe tomato.

"You can't scare me, Indian giver," Dan laughed maliciously.

Lavender gasped. John punched Dan in the face. A sickening crack was audible. Blood splattered on the floor. Dan cursed loudly. Lavender grabbed John's free hand and pulled him back.

"Go," John urged her.

"This wasn't your fight," she said.

"Too late," he answered as Dan's friend Brian grabbed John by the shirt. John kneed him in the stomach. Lavender backed away.

"Hey! Break it up, you three!" a teacher yelled as she left her classroom. Another teacher came out of his room, barking at the class to stay put, and helped the first teacher pull John and Dan apart. Blood was on John's hands. Lavender fled into the nearest girls' bathroom as the bell rang. It wasn't until she saw herself in the old, scratched mirror that she realized she was crying.

Dan was not in great shape.

Jack knew he might've pushed too hard when he felt Dan's nose break, but he was so angry seeing such a stupid, piece-of-shit excuse of a human treating Lavender like that. He had seen the fear in her eyes when Dan grabbed her shoulder, and saw her crying after he punched Dan. Okay, so maybe he shouldn't have punched Dan, but Jack kind of didn't care. Scratch that. He didn't care at all. He only hoped that he didn't make Lavender cry from shock over the situation.

The teacher that pulled Jack away from Dan looked ready to burst a blood vessel. He didn't listen to Jack when he tried to explain why it was perfectly reasonable that Dan's blood was on the floor or that Dan's crap-nugget friend walked with a hobble. Dan didn't even have a black eye, just a broken nose. Adolescent human bones are *fine* at healing.

But Dan blubbered like a baby about his nose and the other teacher, Ms. McGeady, led him toward the nurse. Jack hated Ms. McGeady, too. He hated everyone at that moment. Part of him wished he could freeze Dan in place, but that would make him a murderer. Human school rules were so stupid. Dan shouldn't have been allowed to talk to Lavender like that and treat her like shit. Mr. Hard Ass gripped Jack's shoulder tightly as he led him and Brian down the hall through the staring group of kids.

"They were defensive wounds!" Brian whined to Mr. Hard Ass. "John started it!"

"Just stay on the sidelines—" Jack started.

"Shut it," Mr. Hard Ass snapped. "You broke that kid's nose. It was swollen like nothing else."

"He deserved it."

Brian stared angrily at Jack, but Jack shot him a daring glare. Brian wimped out and looked away.

As they walked down the hall, past the rows of lockers, Jack spotted Linda on her way to class. She looked over at him with wide eyes as she quickly assessed the situation, with Mr. Hard Ass's grim face and Brian's shuffling. Her gaze dropped down to Jack's right hand, which was bruised and split at the knuckles. He glanced down quickly as he slowly began to register that it ached. Some of Dan's gross blood was on it. He groaned and wiped his hand on his pants before looking back up at her. He mouthed "Lavender" at her, hoping that she understood to check on her. Before he could attempt to communicate anything else, Mr. Hard Ass rigidly steered him through an open door.

"John, again?" the nice secretary, Ms. Lakeisha Jenkins, asked as they walked in.

"We're here to see the dean," Mr. Hard Ass said darkly. He nodded at Jack. "His victim is in the Nurse's office with Ms. McGeady."

"I only broke his nose!" Jack said defensively. "Ms. Lakeisha, he's making it sound worse than it is."

"Address her properly, John," Mr. Hard Ass snapped.

She groaned as she got up from her desk. "Ms. Rocklan!"

❧

Lavender cried into her girlfriend's chest on her bed after school.

"It's okay, it's over," Jasmine said gently, holding Lavender in her arms. They both knew that it wasn't.

THIRTY-TWO

WORDS SHARED

"*Suspended?*" Linda demanded. She had been waiting for him in the lobby to avoid the cold, which was unpleasant given the "Missing" posters everywhere. The sun began to set by the time he left detention.

"Linda, don't," he groaned. "I just listened to Ms. Rocklan yell at me about it for like an hour."

"Jack…"

"Is Lavender okay?" he asked as they pushed through the double doors.

"Not really," Linda admitted. "She wanted to go home right after school. So, what happened? She wasn't in the mood to talk about it."

Jack recounted the whole ordeal, at least what he had seen. He told her about how he saw Dan and his crony intimidating Lavender, and how he overheard Dan tell her to kill herself. He shuddered before relaying the rest, and about how satisfying it was to break that piece-of-shit's nose.

"Did you tell the dean about what they were doing to Lavender?"

"No, I claimed full responsibility. I didn't want Lavender to be more involved," Jack said. "She looked so scared, Linda."

Jack sat down uncomfortably on the living room sofa and Emily sat in a nearby chair while Linda's mom yelled at her in the parents' bedroom—Linda had confessed to her mom when they got home. He could tell that Emily was listening more intently than he was as she slowly munched on a chocolate chip cookie. Even their cat, Nicholas, seemed to be curious about what was going on as he padded in, rubbing against Jack's and Emily's legs while his tail twitched, his eyes on the door. Jack rolled his eyes, but he knew he did the same thing whenever Mona and Father Time had a fight.

"He's *suspended?*" Linda's mom demanded, staring at her youngest daughter. "Linda Estelle Waters!"

"He was defending Lavender!" Linda said quickly, putting her hands up.

"What did he do to get suspended if he was defending her?"

"He might've broken a nose…" Linda admitted slowly.

Her mom ran her hands through her hair. "That is so not okay!"

"A guy named Dan has been horrible to her," Linda interjected. "As far as I know, he deserved it."

"What do you mean by horrible? Is Lavender okay?" her mom asked, tentatively softening.

"He was calling her slurs and harassing her," Linda explained quickly. "We told the teacher that he had called her a slur and then he got in big trouble. He's mad because he wants to go to Dartmouth like his dad, and he seemed to be intimidating Lavender about it."

"Did Dan get suspended, too?"

"No, because he didn't start the fight," Linda said. "Jack punched first, but it was because Dan said another slur and grabbed her."

"Didn't Lavender tell the dean what was going on?"

"No, Jack took responsibility for the fight," Linda said.

"Do you know if she's talked to her parents about this?"

"I don't know, she didn't tell me."

"If she hasn't, please try suggesting it. She shouldn't have to deal with any of this," her mom said, sounding kind of sad. "Let her know that you're there for her."

"Don't worry, I have been," Linda said.

"Good job, sweetie," her mom said, kissing her on the cheek. "I need to go check on the cookies. You can bring some to Lavender if you like."

"Yeah, I think I will," Linda said, following her out of the room.

Of course, Jack and Emily half-pretended to not be listening. Even Nicholas seemed to be interested from his perch on Jack's lap. The cat slow-blinked at Linda as if he wasn't just eavesdropping with the other traitors.

Linda texted Lavender later and asked if she was okay, but she didn't get a response.

◆

The next day, Lavender was late. Linda noticed that something was off—her clothes weren't disheveled, but she looked like she couldn't sleep last night. Her normally silky-smooth dark hair was also up in a messy bun. As consolation, Linda gave her a container filled with snickerdoodle and chocolate chip cookies. For a second, the typical sparkle returned to her friend's eyes.

At the end of Science, Mr. London stopped Linda at his desk. "Linda, do you have time to come at lunch?"

"Um, yeah, sure," Linda agreed before leaving the room.

At the beginning of lunch, she met Lavender at her locker and told her that she'd be late to the cafeteria before hurrying over to Mr. London's classroom.

"Hi, Mr. London," she said as she pushed open the door.

"Hi, Linda," he said.

"What did you want to talk about?"

"I heard that your friend got suspended," her teacher ventured.

"Yes, it seems he did," she replied coolly.

"It doesn't bother you?"

"Not really. I'm not the one who got suspended."

"Linda, he's violent!" Mr. London exclaimed. "How can you keep defending him?"

"He was defending my friend Lavender, Mr. London. Dan and his friends were being assholes."

"He could just walk away with her, he didn't have to make it a fight," Mr. London said. "Trust me, I would know."

"What if they didn't give her a choice?" Linda demanded.

"We're not dealing with hypotheticals, we're dealing with what already happened," Mr. London said rigidly.

"Oh my god, can you relax?" she said. "I thought you said you didn't care so much about discipline."

"Linda, this is different. He broke a student's nose!" Mr. London raised his voice.

"Daniel deserved it!" she shot back.

"Daniel probably deserves many things, but you can't just hang out with people who get suspended. Ms. McGeady was there with Dan. The kid needed to be taken to the hospital. She said it was pretty bad."

"Of course," Linda said bitterly.

"She came afterward to talk about it," he said. "There was a lot of blood."

"You're friends with her?" Linda said. "After what she did earlier this semester?"

"That was a lapse in judgment. She's a newer teacher, she didn't mean to hurt your feelings."

"She still did."

"It's not you against the world. It's childlike to hold a grudge like that," Mr. London said. He knew as soon as he said it that he went too far.

"Maybe *you're* the one who's childlike. The world isn't so black-and-white, and you certainly don't understand everything," Linda shot back, her voice wavering. "John understands. I'd rather spend time with him."

"Linda, I'm sorry—"

"And Lavender, the real victim, gets it. He was there to help her. The teachers haven't been so helpful."

Her teacher didn't respond.

"Bye, Mr. London. Enjoy your lunch," Linda said stiffly, turning on her heel to leave.

THIRTY-THREE

A FLOWER BLOOMS WHEN

IT'S READY

Lavender wanted to do something.

She didn't want to take Jasmine's and Linda's advice to talk to the dean. She didn't want to think about Dan any more than she already had to. John was the only one who didn't advise her to do anything whenever he saw her. He still met her and Linda after school the past two days even though he was suspended. (Linda didn't see it, but Lavender could tell that John seriously had a crush on his best friend.)

Lavender sighed and pressed her feet against her headboard of her bed. Her mom hated it when she did that. Sometimes Lavender felt better doing something weird and gross like wearing her lavender shoes in her bed while she lay on her back, staring at the ceiling. It made her feel more human. Maybe that was weird to think, but she never let it stop her. Her life was weird and uncomfortable as it was. She closed her eyes as she listened to the music blaring from her (lavender) iPod Shuffle. Lavender played "Teenagers" by My Chemical Romance on repeat. Every time the song ended, she started it over. Over and over and over. She was trying to drown out what Dan said to her. *Drown yourself.*

She remembered the sound of Dan's nose breaking. His blood on the floor. The rage in John's eyes that softened when he told her to leave. Honestly, she didn't have a violent bone in her body. The idea of hurting other living things repulsed her. And Dan hadn't been back to class since the Incident, as she thought of it. She heard that it was because of anything from severely expensive surgery to just taking an extra few days off before Winter Break. Her feet, still propped up on her headboard, began to fall asleep and she flopped onto her side. Her gaze drifted over to her paintings and drawings on the wall, all of women. She still felt like she didn't do the feminine figure justice. *Dyke*, Dan's voice floated through her head. She shut her eyes again. What if Lavender did talk to the dean? *What would happen?* The thought of being the center of extra drama made her want to crawl back into her skin and hide. Why couldn't Dan and his friends just *go away*.

Lavender sighed and opened her eyes. She stared up at the ceiling. She could see the faint graphite outlines she had drawn of lavender blooms, stars, and wind on her ceiling, in anticipation of a future mural. Assuming she convinced her parents to let her. Assuming her parents wouldn't kick her out the moment they found out that she was a lesbian and not a nice Christian heterosexual girl. What if the dean told her *parents*? She sat up and experienced a head rush. Lavender couldn't tell her parents what was going on. She plodded over to her easel, which still had the same unfinished painting of Jasmine that Linda saw. Risqué, yes, but Lavender hoped to put it in her portfolio. She stared at it. The oil paint was still drying. Jasmine's face still turned away into the canvas.

Lavender's parents knew that something was bothering her. Even her older brother, Damien, asked her why she seemed out of it, which was shocking coming from him. But she just said that she was stressed about school. Which was technically true. It seemed like her peers received lessons on how to make her wish that she was different, while she somehow missed the classes on how to handle it. How could she tell the people who were supposed to love and support her about her sexuality when they've always condemned gay people? Their preacher talked about how sexuality was a sin, that it goes against nature, and Lavender sat in church watching in horror as her parents nodded along. "It's unnatural," they said. "God didn't build you for that." But God built them to be reproduction machines, instead of humans with souls?

Lavender squeezed out some more paint onto her absolutely soiled paint palette and began to dab at the canvas with a brush, adding a layer of orange fire for Jasmine's mane. It made her heart ache. As a little girl, Lavender heard that God created everyone in His image. *Why was it only acceptable for a man to love a woman if He built* everyone *in His image?* Was Lavender made in the wrong one? Was Lavender the image that would burn in Hell while her parents, Dan, conversion therapists, and the preacher watched by their place with God, because there was something fundamentally wrong with her? Just because Lavender wanted to have a happy family with a beautiful woman, just like her own father? Lavender tore out her earbuds as tears rolled down her face, blurring the canvas until all she saw was the eternal fire. She knew that people believed that she and Jasmine were just rejects from God. The ones that He built wrong just like Eve. The ones who made the wrong "decisions" and everything was blamed on them. Jesus died for their sins, but it seemed that it didn't matter when it was the wrong sin.

Lavender's phone buzzed in her pocket. She glanced at the screen. It was a text from Jasmine, asking how she was doing. Lavender looked back up at the ceiling. She was doing just peachy. Just casually considering whether it was worth it to come forward about homophobic bullying to a school that may or may not do anything about it or tell her parents and get her kicked out. *Kids will be kids*, one teacher told her. *They're just joking*, another said. *Don't take it so seriously*.

Lavender wished she was happier than ever. In some sort of world where rainbows glowed in the sky. Where her little brother, Cody, would still be alive, and she and Jasmine could walk around together, holding hands and kissing whenever one of them said something stupid. Where Lavender wouldn't have to be tormented for being sodomite scum. Her family would love her no matter what, because they gave her life, and they wanted her to be there. Jasmine would be welcome at home as her girlfriend but wouldn't be allowed to stay overnight, just like her older brother wasn't allowed to have his girlfriend overnight. Lavender would be allowed to have a normal teenage life. Where John wouldn't have gotten suspended because of her, because of who she was. Where Lavender wouldn't have to hide. Where people wouldn't want her to kill herself, and the teachers would defend her instead of telling her to grow thicker skin. *Because kids will be kids.* Where she was allowed to exist.

And what if Jasmine was the only other gay kid at school? What if Lavender was going to be the rainbow sheep forever? She wasn't even out, and people gave her shit about it. Dan told her to drown herself while his friend looked on with an approving smile. All it took was someone seeing her sketchbook and she was labeled a homo who didn't deserve to be alive. That she should die, just like Cody, who had liked to draw pictures of "pretty girls" with her, even though it stressed out her parents that he would grow up to be a gay wuss. But he didn't grow up and she became the gay wuss.

Lavender sighed again. She still wanted to do *something*. She wished that she could meet other gays. She knew that something was off between Linda and Mr. London (of course, Linda was doing that minimal explanation thing that she did over emotionally charged topics), but he was the only other gay person that Lavender that Lavender heard about. Well, other than Jasmine, but that didn't help. Lavender still hadn't officially met Mr. London—she only saw his short (well, okay, he was taller than her, but definitely a little below average height for a man) angry stature hurrying through the hallway occasionally, and she heard hilariously concerning anecdotes from John, but she never met him. Maybe that would have to change.

Lavender walked into school feeling relatively confident the next morning. Until she felt the popular kids' eyes on her. Dan definitely told them what happened. Her determination wavered. But when Lavender passed Jasmine in the hall and they made eye contact, Lavender felt a surge of hope. Maybe one day they could make out in the hallway like those other annoying straight upperclassmen who awkwardly blocked the flow of traffic with their unnecessarily heavy PDA. Maybe talking to Mr. London could be the beginning of it all. Or maybe Lavender was obsessing over a fantasy in attempt to ignore more pressing matters, but maybe that was okay. Maybe she could just be a normal teenager, whatever that meant.

At the start of her lunch period, she zipped through the clusters of kids as she looked for the right classroom. Once she finally found it, she took a second to compose herself before she knocked on the door and went in. "Hi, Mr. London," Lavender said, walking over to his desk.

"Hi… your name is Lavender, correct?" Mr. London asked, scratching his chin. She nodded. Mr. London's hair really was as slicked back as John had mentioned. "Linda's mentioned you before," he explained. "So, um… how may I help you?"

"Ummm…" she stalled but decided to steel her nerves. "I heard that you might be gay."

He looked cautiously amused as he looked up at her from his worn desk. "Technically, I'm bisexual, but yeah, sure. I'm assuming that you're not here to bully me, seeing as how you're friends with Linda."

"Yeah, um…" she hesitated. She shifted her weight. All of her confrontational courage had diminished. "Is there some sort of gay pride club here?"

"Unfortunately, no. Most students seem intent on being as homophobic as their parents here," Mr. London said, laughing without warmth. "But would you be interested in a club like that?"

"Um, yeah," she answered. "Is there a way to start that?"

"We can certainly try," he answered. He pulled out a notepad that looked like it was on its last breath. "If you could write down your name and school email, I can get the ball rolling. If you're fine with being one of the club presidents."

She hesitated for a second, then took a pen out of the designated pen mug on his desk.

"Are you an ally, or part of the LGBTQ community yourself?" he asked.

"I… um…" Lavender hesitated.

"You don't need to share anything if you don't want to. I'm just curious."

"I'm... gay," she managed. "Only Linda—well, probably John, too—knows," Lavender admitted. She noticed that Mr. London stiffened at the mention of John's name. *Is that what their fight was about?* Lavender realized. "John is a good guy, by the way. He's suspended... because of me."

"What do you mean?" Mr. London asked, sitting up with alarm. A lump of guilt formed in his stomach as he remembered his... well, fight with Linda. She had mentioned that John was defending Lavender, but he didn't give it much thought beyond that. *Dumbass*, he scolded himself.

Lavender took a breath, then another one, before continuing. She really hadn't intended for the conversation to go this direction. "The guy who John punched, Dan, has been harassing me. He saw my sketchbook and decided that I'm lesbian," Lavender explained. "The other day, Dan found me in the hall and was saying horrible stuff to me again, and John came over and stepped in. Then... Dan grabbed me... and John got really mad." She realized she was shaking. "Dan called him an Indian giver for not letting it go, and John punched him. John said he didn't tell the dean about me. I still haven't told the Ms. Rocklan. I'm... scared."

Mr. London frowned with sympathy. "Thank you for telling me. Has Dan done anything else?" he asked, his voice soft.

"Aside from being an asshole?" Lavender asked before gasping. "Sorry! That slipped."

Mr. London laughed. His real laugh was surprisingly hearty. "You don't have to worry about that in front of me, I've heard Linda say plenty worse."

Lavender smiled briefly. Then she decided to spill her guts. She was already waist deep. "Okay, well, Dan also tells me things like how I'm supposed to respect him and know my place. He blames me for getting him in trouble—he called me a dyke in Art, and Linda and I spoke up in front of the whole class and Mrs. Greene sent him to the dean. And he told me I should... kill myself. He said I ruined his perfect record. That it was all just a joke."

"It's not your fault, Lavender," Mr. London said.

"I know," she answered. But tears rolled down her cheeks. "But I'm not out to my parents. I've been so scared to tell anyone. Dan was already so angry at me the first time. And if it comes up in other classes, other teachers just brush it off. No one takes it seriously, like I'm just supposed to take it."

"That's fucked up," Mr. London said firmly. "I'm not going to stand for that, and I know some other faculty, including Mrs. Greene, who won't tolerate it, either. I can help you report it, Lavender, and we'll make sure that you don't have to be scared of bigoted assholes like Dan. We can do it without your parents being involved."

Lavender looked at him, her eyes wide. "Really?"

"I will not let it slide. It's wrong, and Dan and other kids shouldn't be getting away with it. I'll support you every step of the way, I promise," he said.

"How do you know it'll work?" she asked.

"I'm half Korean and bi. My whole life, even from my own relatives, I've had people make judgments about me and treat me certain ways because of my heritage and my sexuality," Mr. London said. "Bigots are just scared of recognizing their own mediocrity and feel more comfortable in their own hate. They don't deserve to get away with being monsters. You have the right to exist as you are without being scared. I will not let Dan get away with intimidating and harassing you." Mr. London pushed back his chair and stood up. "We're going to Ms. Rocklan right now."

"Okay," Lavender said nervously, toying with a lock of her hair as she watched him grab his keys.

"Ready?" he asked.

"No," she admitted. "But I want to."

"You're being very brave," he said. "I couldn't do this when I was your age. I just tried to hide my entire identity."

"Did it work?" Lavender asked.

"Nope," he chuckled sadly. "It was a nightmare. Now come on, let's go."

THIRTY-FOUR

TIPS FOR HELPING AN IMMORTAL WITH AN EXISTENTIAL CRISIS?

"Linda, I don't know what to do," Jack said dejectedly as he slumped forward on her desk. "It feels like I'll never find that dumb book and the world will implode at any moment."

Linda looked down at him. He wouldn't ever admit it, but he was struggling with being suspended. The sudden lapse in routine left him wandering aimlessly during the day (he admitted) before going to Linda's home, talking with her mom and her cat while he ate cookies until Linda herself got home. It had literally only been two days.

"We just hit a dead end, Jack," Linda said. She didn't tell him that she'd been worrying, too. It was hard to sleep well knowing that you and your best friend, an important nature spirit, had lost the trail of something so literally earth-shatteringly important. But she wasn't a nature spirit. What could she possibly do?

He groaned, pressing his face against the dead wood of her desk. She wondered if it ever bothered him that her furniture was basically painted tree corpses.

"Well, have there been any new clues in Pryddia or at the palace?"

"No," he whined. "Why did Mother Nature entrust this task to me? I'm useless."

"I mean, she kind of gave you one of the hardest tasks ever."

"I really am just the most useless nature spirit."

"Jack."

"The world is going to end and it's all my fault. All I've managed to achieve in your world is getting suspended and being turned down by some mortal girl."

"Take a deep breath. It's only been a fraction of a second in the world of immortals," Linda said.

"Aughhhhhhh," he moaned into her desk.

She tapped her fingers against her face while she thought, and the ring Jack gave her brushed against her cheek.

"I still haven't had to actually use my ring yet," she pointed out. "That's good, right?"

"Yeah, I suppose so."

"Can you please peel your face off my desk?"

"There's no point."

Linda rolled her eyes. "Let's just make a new plan."

"Ruth was just a dead end. She really is just a crazy lady."

She tried nudging him. "I feel like there might be more there."

He turned his head so that he faced her. "All we did was find out that she has slight amnesia. It's not exactly groundbreaking."

"But it was over a specific detail like yours."

"The elf didn't give me head trauma, though, I was drugged."

"I still think it's a sign of some kind."

"Okay," he sighed. "Then what?"

"Well, there was that tree with knife marks."

"All we did was find a suspicious tree."

"Or someone with anger issues," she sighed.

"Liiiindaaaa," Emily sang, waltzing into the room. "Geez, what's with the serious faces?"

Linda looked at her sister and crossed her arms. "Yes? What is it?"

"Mom and Dad just hid the mistletoe!" Emily sang again. "You two have fun with that!"

The two of them watched the older sister leave before Jack spoke again. "The mistletoe spirits are also getting angry this time of year."

"Do all plants have spirits?" Linda asked suddenly.

"What? Yes, of course."

"Are they sentient enough to understand what they might witness?"

"Sometimes, yes. Where are you going with this?"

"Can we talk to them?"

"I don't know how to with most of them, but elves can," he explained. Then he sat up with a start.

"Jack!" Linda exclaimed.

"Oh my god!"

"We need Rosie!"

"She can talk to the tree that had the knife slashes," he said. "But I don't know when she'll be able to."

"Just go ask her now," Linda said.

He disappeared in front of her. Of course, any loose objects were instantly thrown around her room. She groaned, wishing she at least thought of pushing him out of the window first. *Priorities.*

THIRTY-FIVE

THE CHRISTMAS SPIRIT

"How long does your Christmas festival last?" Jack asked. He followed Linda up the stairs that same evening while they each carried a box of Christmas tree decorations. His was labeled "TINSEL," whatever that was.

"It's not really a festival. And people often celebrate for the whole season," Linda explained. "But it's fun to put up the Christmas tree."

"Okay…" he said slowly as he set down his burden next to the unboxing station at the couch.

"Oh, Linda, we're going to the tree farm this evening when Emily and Kris get back from visiting friends," her mom said, looking up from the tree lights she was testing.

"Aw man," Linda whined.

"It's always been a family activity," her mom chided.

"Tree farm… you guys are planting trees…?" Jack asked.

"No, we pick a tree, it gets chopped down, then we bring it home and decorate it," Linda explained.

Jack looked mortified. "So… you're decorating a plant's corpse?"

"I mean, it sounds horrible if you say it like that," Linda said. "You've definitely seen Christmas trees before." She patted his back.

He looked pained. "This isn't an improvement of the situation. They have souls, you know."

"Don't make me feel terrible about this. It's a fun holiday tradition!"

"It's carnage!" he exclaimed.

Linda ignored him and went back to the basement. As she picked up a box of reindeer decorations, she saw another one behind it and groaned, thinking it was yet more Christmas stuff that materialized. But she recognized her own handwriting instead of her mom's or dad's. It was the box of books that used to be on the empty bookshelf in her room. Linda put down the reindeer decorations and opened it. A bunch of different titles jumped out at her, including *The Hobbit*. It was a volume that she and Kelsie shared, passing it back and forth every other week, hoping to share a similar adventure together someday.

Linda's eyes teared up as she held the book in her hands. It felt so... familiar, like an old friend she hadn't seen in many years. The paperback's covers were worn, and the spine was creased, something that used to bother Linda. She was always the more careful one, and she used to complain to Kelsie about the condition of the book whenever she returned it. But now Linda would've loved to be annoyed by any little thing that Kelsie did because at least she would be there. They never got to go on that big adventure. Instead, Linda felt like she was crashing through unknown terrain. Without her. Even though they promised.

"Are there any other boxes?" her mom called down the stairs.

Linda took a deep breath before responding. "Yeah! Just one!" She trudged back up the stairs with the decorations.

Even though Jack's discovery of faux pine garlands and tinsel was hilarious, Linda's thoughts kept being dragged back to her books. After hanging the last pine garland on the mantle, below the TV and above their perpetually empty fireplace, Linda went back down cellar. The box was right where she had left it.

"Do you need help?" Jack asked as he appeared behind her.

"Yes, please," Linda said. He picked up one side while she carried the other. Eventually, after some cursing and teetering on the stairs, they brought the books back into her room.

She unpacked her favorites onto the shelf, even *The Hobbit*. Then she glanced out the window and saw an elf. "Um, Jack?"

"Yeah?" he asked. "Oh, it's Rosie! Come on, it's time to go look at the tree!"

The human, the nature spirit, and the elf found a man with skin the color of manzanilla olives gasping for breath in the snow while the tree burned behind him. Rosie ran forward and began checking his vitals. She talked to him in a strange language that sounded like leaves rustling.

Linda looked up to see the flames catching on the branches of another tree in the wind. "Jack! Do something!" she yelped.

Jack looked up and raised his hands, grimacing in concentration. Freezing rain fell over the area, putting the fires out, but he looked drained, and his hands were blistered. "It's from the warm temperature of the unfrozen snow," he explained to Linda when she reached for his hands. "I'll ask Mona to heal me later."

They turned to Rosie and the spirit, whose body was smoking. Literally. The rain didn't heal him, and his tree was blackened. Linda ran forward and held his hand, which made him flinch before he grasped her fingers tightly. He said one more thing in the rustling language to Rosie. Then the tree spirit crumbled into ashes in front of them.

"No!" Linda cried, reaching into the ashes. They were still warm but were cooling quickly.

"There's nothing we can do," Jack said sadly, pulling her back. "Trust me. Let his ashes scatter in the wind, back into nature."

"Can't we bury him?" Linda wept.

"That's a very human way of doing things," Rosie answered.

Linda looked up at him, tears streaming down her face. "Jack, please," she said.

Rosie stared at him as if waiting to see what he would do.

"Fine, yes," Jack answered. "I can clear the snow, but I need a shovel."

"I can help with that. The fellow ash and the oak are mourning. The tree spirit was their friend. The fire woke them from slumber. Their roots will help us," Rosie said.

Linda watched helplessly as Jack and the elf worked with the other trees, creating a shallow hole in the ground in front of the dead aspen tree. Linda helped gather his ashes and put them in the grave, and then Rosie instructed the trees to refill it with earth. For a moment, Linda thought she heard the trees creaking and groaning with melancholy.

"Mortal, you surprised the Aspen," Rosie commented, breaking the silence as they stared at the grave. "Tree spirits aren't used to touch."

"Oh, I'm sorry," Linda said sheepishly.

"They said they felt warmth," Rosie said.

"Well, yeah. He was set on fire," Jack said.

"Jack Frost!" Linda shouted, hitting his arm.

"Sorry! I'm using humor to cope!" he said, shielding himself from more blows.

Rosie groaned in exasperation, rubbing her temples as if she was used to it by then, before recomposing herself. "From what I could gather, your mortal friend had the right idea, Frost. I believe the Aspen was a victim of the elf. He said he had failed them for not protecting their book or identity. They interrogated him then a man set him on fire."

"That's it?" Linda asked.

"Tree spirits experience the world so differently. You two will have to decipher it since you're in the world of mortals."

Linda looked back at the grave. "I thought nature spirits were supposed to be immortal."

"Most aren't," Jack answered.

"Well, I must be going. I've been apart from my Lady for long enough," Rosie said. "Keep investigating." And then she disappeared with a shower of pink biodegradable glitter.

Jack walked Linda back to her house, and then he said goodbye. She felt like she was looking out at the world through a window. She barely registered that she was at home and lying on her bed with her boots on until Emily walked in and questioned her sanity.

"Oh, I didn't even notice," Linda said, sitting up to see the foot of her comforter, which was wet with melting snow.

"Are you okay?" Emily asked, softening for a moment with what looked like actual concern. Then she added, "did you and Jack break up?"

"What? No," Linda answered tersely. She kicked off her boots. "I'm fine." Then she collapsed back into her bed. She stared up at the ceiling, but her eyes were unfocused. She couldn't see anything.

That evening, they all got into the family car to go to the Christmas tree farm, despite Linda's emotional pleas to get a faux tree.

"We always get a real one," Emily protested.

"Is this Jack's influence?" her dad asked, his eyes glittering mischievously.

"No! It's just... they're alive," she said. She couldn't hide the haunted undertone from her voice.

Her mom looked at her. "Linda, they are trees. They don't have feelings."

Linda felt like she was going to be sick. But she didn't know what to do. She thought about summoning Jack, but the last time that happened, he teleported directly to her, and he couldn't do that in front of her family. *Could he?* she wondered for an impulsive moment. She brushed her thumb over her ring, turning the ice crystal once before they walked to the car.

While they were at the farm, delicate little snowflakes floated through the air.

"What about this one?" Kris asked, pointing to a huge pine tree.

"That's way too big for the living room," their dad said.

"What about this one?" their mom asked, gazing at a pretty spruce tree, its boughs full and bright from the fresh snow.

"No, that one has a crooked trunk," Emily said, looking down.

Linda held out her hand and a snowflake fell onto her glove. While her family chattered away about the trees, she examined the delicate design of the snowflake, which scintillated in the lights. A couple more fell onto her palm and fingers. It almost looked like they had a few tiny hearts in their designs. *Tiny hearts?* she thought. Was she hallucinating? Did Jack do that on purpose?

"Linda?" Emily asked.

"Yeah?" Linda asked, looking up at her. She wiped her glove off on her warm corduroy pants.

"Which tree do you like? We need you to be a tiebreaker." Emily pointed out the ones that they were discussing. Linda pretended to look around, and a tree at the far end of the lot caught her eye. A little balsam fir tree sat alone, barely taller than her five-foot-ten dad. Its needles and branches had a light layer of sparkling snowflakes. Normally, she would've picked it, but all she could think about was how it was alive and had a soul. She thought about the burning tree spirit. "I don't know."

"Awww," her mom said, pointing at the tree Linda was looking at. Emily grudgingly admitted that it was very cute.

"That's puny," Kris complained.

"It's the perfect size," their dad said.

Linda wanted to die. It was three against two. Linda flinched each time the axe hit the trunk. After her parents paid for it, a worker helped them tie the tree corpse to the top of the car.

That night, Linda returned to her room alone while her siblings and her parents talked in the living room. She looked over at her bookcase, and the books on the white shelf felt more like lingering ghosts than old favorites. Linda knocked them back into the open box and shoved the top back on it. Tears leaked down her face as she lay in her bed, dripping annoyingly into her ears instead of serenely down her face like they would in the movies. She wrapped her arms around her legs, the air feeling far too warm and empty around her as she turned to face the wall. She wished Jack was with her. The blanket smelled vaguely of him, just a hint of balsam in the winter air. Which reminded her of their Christmas tree, and then the burning tree spirit.

She tried to distract herself by thinking about how warm she felt when Jack looked down at her while they talked and when she listened to his heart beating in his chest. The kinds of things that Linda and Kelsie would excitedly talk about when they shared the bed during their sleepovers… Linda absentmindedly reached for her bracelet, but it felt startlingly cold against her fingertips as it sat on the nightstand just past her pillow, cold, cold like Kelsie's hands.

THIRTY-SIX

GEORGE IN THE DARK

M r. London retired to being George as he sat down in his secondhand easy chair for the night. He had just gotten back from his night class, and his brain was totally fried. He couldn't even look at the pile of ungraded exams and papers—it caused his head to physically ache.

George pressed the cold bottle of soju against his face, letting the chill bite his skin as it stole his warmth. He probably looked like an alcoholic, but he was too tired to think about cleaning another glass. The TV mumbled in front of him about an ancient tree being a victim of random arson, but he didn't hear it. Even though he tried to disengage from his job the moment he left the school, his mind had drifted to Lavender, Linda, and John. There was a small pang of regret in his heart as he thought about the things he shouted at Linda. He had lost his cool and acted inappropriately, which he wasn't able to admit to his therapist. Dr. Nathan always knew when George was hiding something—George could see it on his face, when the man looked more tired than usual. But Dr. Nathan never pushed him to talk until he was ready. It was both comforting and frustrating. If it was his mom, she would needle him until he fessed up. Dr. Nathan pointed out that he was a therapist, not a mom, and that George should think about why he hesitates to share certain things. In this case, George knew that he felt guilty. He couldn't help but feel responsible for Linda's well-being

(Dr. Nathan suggested that he felt paternal attachment for his student, which irritated George).

"The police say that the investigation continues for Jane Clari," the news anchor said through her unnervingly white teeth. George's eyes refocused on the TV. The local news was again asking for any leads for Jane Clari. It was a last-ditch effort, one of George's friends who worked in the forensics lab told him. The police were all out of leads. George didn't know Jane very well—she had been his student once, yes, but their relationship had started and ended there.

A silent part of him was thankful that he never got the chance to know her. It broke him when he found out that Kelsie Robertson had died, and he was worried about the results of the investigation for Jane. He couldn't imagine coping with even more loss. It broke him seeing Linda become so broken. He wasn't close with either of them before Kelsie died, but they were both his students, and he therefore grudgingly developed feelings of concern. After going to Kelsie's funeral, George realized he couldn't stay a teacher. Granted, he was still on the fence about applying for grad school until his wife divorced him, but he had realized he needed a different life. One where he wouldn't see his students die or have to relive the bullying from when he was a student. Like poor Lavender.

John was a better kid than George gave him credit for, despite his violent streak. George paused and took a sip from his soju, letting the burn sit on his tongue. Ms. Rocklan agreed to lift the two-week suspension, although because John was still out of line, he had to serve detention in the library for a month. But George felt that Ms. Rocklan still let Daniel off too easy, with some "diversity lessons" from the guidance counselor and a week of non-service detention. Both would be continuing their detention in the new year. George couldn't help but wonder if the dean would've been harsher with Daniel if Lavender wasn't an indigenous lesbian. He thought about calling his sister to complain. He looked over at his cellphone sitting on the table, but he took another sip from his soju instead.

THIRTY-SEVEN

SEVERED

"Are you okay, Linda?"
"Hey, Linda! You look so tired. Are you feeling well?"
"Do you want to talk about it?"
"Hi, Linda. I just wanted to check in. Are you okay? You seem out of it."

All day.

Linda wanted to call home sick, but then she would have to talk about it with her parents and her siblings would bug her. She didn't want to talk about it. Any of it. The emptiness was just a crushing weight that she couldn't escape as it sat on top of her chest, making it hard to breathe. She went through all of the motions: she got up, showered, ate not enough breakfast because the eggs felt like too much, and lumbered to school. Her feet felt so heavy in their boots, and she just didn't care.

Jack gave her a hug while they sat together in class, but it didn't change anything.

Nothing mattered.

She couldn't even remember what it looked like to see the tree spirit collapse into ash. She just knew it happened.

And that was too much.

At the end of the day, Lavender walked to the school's library, and when the librarian, Ms. Scarlet, wasn't looking, she slipped into the backroom.

"I'm still working on the same—oh. Hey, Lavender," Jack said as she walked in. He stood at one of the carts that overflowed with disorganized books. Ms. Scarlet had explained that the previous librarian did a terrible job of staying on top of things, and she seemed a little too enthusiastic to have Jack be subjected to it.

"John, what happened? Why is Linda so distant?" Lavender asked.

"It's… hard to explain," he grimaced, his chipper tone changing immediately.

"Did something happen with you two?" Lavender asked.

He looked back down at the book he held. "You could say that."

"Like what?" Lavender asked. "Was it romantic?"

"No," he said.

Lavender just stared at him. John and Linda were blocking her out. Again. Even after all John went through for Lavender, he still wouldn't tell her stuff.

"What?" he asked when he was aware of her silence.

"You guys keep a lot to yourselves," Lavender said.

Jack blinked. "Do we?"

"Yeah."

"Like what?"

"Goddammit John, you and Linda are always so evasive," Lavender snapped.

"You don't exactly tell me everything either," he shot back. "Like what's going on with you and Jasmine?"

"Shut up," Lavender hissed.

"Don't tell me to shut up," Jack said. "If you tell me why you're so weird about Jasmine, I'll tell you why Linda is upset." He regretted it as soon as he bargained, but he couldn't take it back. *Dammit, Linda is always better at this stuff,* he thought grumpily.

Lavender looked taken aback. "That's unfair."

"Is it?" he asked. "Maybe we both have our reasons."

She stared at him for a moment. He stared back. She broke first. "I just wish I was closer with you guys. You're my only friends at this school."

"You're my only other friend here, too," Jack admitted. "There's just complicated... family stuff. I'd like to talk about it, but I can't."

"I'm pretty familiar with complicated family stuff," Lavender chuckled.

"Unfortunately, Linda is pretty involved by now," he ventured. "It's really hard to explain, and my... parents make me be quiet about a lot of stuff. I got in a loooooot of trouble for telling Linda about some of it."

"Is your family part of the mafia or something?" Lavender asked.

"What's the mafia?" Jack asked.

"Are you serious?" Lavender snorted, but he looked genuinely confused. "It's an Italian crime group centered around family."

"Oh, um, I'd say that we are not part of the mafia," he said uncomfortably. "Also, I'm sorry for being so pushy about the Jasmine thing. That wasn't cool."

"It's okay," Lavender said. "It's also just... complicated. Don't tell anyone that."

"Not a spirit," he said.

Lavender giggled. "John, you're so weird." She shook her head.

"What? I thought people said that?" he said.

"People say, 'not a soul,'" Lavender corrected. "You sound like an alien sometimes."

"I think I just live under a rock," he said.

"I have another question," Lavender ventured.

"Shoot."

"Mr. London is helping me start a Gay Straight Alliance club, will you and Linda join?" Lavender forced the words out before she could change her mind even though her body trembled.

"Yeah, sure," he said. "Do I have to sign anything?"

"Lavender! You're not supposed to be helping him with his detention," the librarian exclaimed after she pushed open the door. Lavender and Jack jumped in surprise, nearly scattering the outdated library cards everywhere.

"Sorry, Ms. Scarlet," Lavender said sheepishly.

"She's helping from her own free will, Ms. Scarlet," Jack interjected.

Ms. Scarlet rolled her dark brown eyes as she pushed her braids over her shoulder. "Lavender, unless you're doing your homework or picking up a book, you need to go home," the librarian said.

"I'll go home," Lavender said.

"But then I'll be all alone," Jack whined.

"Yes, Mr. Mason, that's the point. It's detention, not social hour," Ms. Scarlet said, holding open the door for Lavender. "You only have two more days until Winter Break, anyway," she added as Lavender grabbed her backpack and fled the back room.

THIRTY-EIGHT

SNOWBALL EFFECT

The last day before Winter Break was a good day for everyone. Even Linda and Mr. London seemed to perk up. Although the walk to school was quiet because no birds were singing, Lavender felt weightless. She would have more time to hang out with Jasmine. The only bullying she would experience was from her stupid older brother Damien. She would have a break from studying for the SAT and could forget about her GPA for a few days.

But when she sat next to Linda in Art, Lavender noticed that her friend looked like she hadn't slept at all.

"Hi, Lavender," Linda said with a weak smile.

"Hey, Linda," Lavender said. "I'm so excited for Winter Break. What's the first thing you're going to do?"

Linda's smile deteriorated. "I'm not sure."

"That's okay, you don't have to do anything," Lavender said lightly. "I'm just looking forward to sleeping in."

"Yeah, me too," Linda said, not admitting that she had been having nothing but horrendous nightmares for days.

Then Mrs. Greene walked in, looking like a Christmas tree. "Happy Holidays!" she exclaimed. Little bells jingled on the somewhat realistic resin antlers that she wore on her head. "I'd like to remind you all that I am not celebrating Christmas, but rather Yule, the pagan holiday. But Happy Christmas, Happy Hanukkah, and Happy Kwanzaa to all who celebrate!" And then she proceeded to offer candy canes to the class. Linda and Lavender accepted.

Mr. London announced that there would be no homework over Winter Break. "I'll have your midterms graded by the time you get back though." Cheers erupted in the room.

When Jack stopped by the library after school, he found Ms. Scarlet packing her bag from behind the gigantic L-shaped desk. "What's my assignment?" he asked.

"John, forget about detention for today. It'll be our secret." Ms. Scarlet winked as she put on her vermillion scarf. He thanked her profusely and he ran out through the crowded hall until he found Linda outside and explained breathlessly. He found himself hollering with delight.

Lavender got to leave the school with Jasmine. Just with her, and it was amazing. She talked animatedly with her girlfriend all the way back to her home. But when she closed her bedroom door, instead of being greeted with a kiss, Jasmine's demeanor shifted.

"Is everything okay?" Lavender asked as she sat on her bed. Jasmine didn't join her.

"Lavender..." Jasmine started. She paused and took a deep breath. "I—I'm leaving."

"What?" Lavender asked, thinking it was some kind of joke. They just got there. "What do you mean?"

"I'm going back home. Like my real home. Not with Everett."

"Is it far away?"

"Yes."

"So..." Lavender started. But she quickly made up her mind. "We can be long distance. I've never done it before, but—"

"No, we can't," Jasmine interrupted.

Lavender felt like the floor crumbled beneath her. "What?" Her voice broke. "Wait. Are you... breaking up with me?" The words caught in her throat, like her body itself rejected the idea.

Jasmine nodded. Tears leaked down her pale cheeks, which were getting redder by the second.

"How long have you known you were going back home?" Lavender asked, scared to know the answer. Jasmine looked away. Lavender's heart raced.

"The whole time," Jasmine said quietly.

"You've been... using me?" Lavender asked, softly at first. Then her voice hardened. "Was this just *fun* for you?"

"No," Jasmine said sharply, surprising Lavender. "I didn't expect to fall for you. It wasn't part of the plan."

"What plan?" Lavender demanded. She couldn't read Jasmine's poker face, which made her even angrier. She wanted to yank out her own hair. "So, what, you're just giving up on us because it doesn't fit your *plan*?"

"I'm not giving up, it's a choice I already made."

Lavender felt like Jasmine just punched her in the gut. She imagined the shards of her life falling apart around her. *Again.* First Cody. Then leaving her life in Canada. *Now this.* Just when things were promising.

"I'm sorry," Jasmine said, reaching toward Lavender as if for a last embrace.

"Don't," Lavender said, recoiling and turning away. "Please, just... just leave," she whispered. She was trying so hard not to cry, but she felt her face growing hot from tears that threatened to spill over.

"I was going to leave without telling anyone, but I felt like I owed it to you," Jasmine said.

"Leave," Lavender said again, louder. The dam broke. "Just get out!" Lavender yelled at her. Jasmine flinched but turned and picked up her backpack by the strap and left. Lavender screamed in anguish and hurled her pillow at the closed door. She wanted to yell at Jasmine about how much she broke her heart, but she didn't want any of her family members to hear. As if they couldn't hear her stupid scream. Lavender turned and grabbed another pillow, but she screamed into it as hard as she could until she ran out of breath.

Someone knocked on the door. "Lavender, was that you? Are you okay?" Damien's voice floated through, his crackly but deep teenage voice sounding unconventionally worried.

"Go away!" Lavender shouted. "I'm fine!"

"Jasmine left."

"Good!" Lavender yelled as her voice broke again.

"Fine!"

"Fine!" Lavender shouted back. She collapsed back onto her bed, tears streaming down her face, before curling into a fetal position and ugly crying into her pillow.

It was all over.

All gone.

Just like that.

THIRTY-NINE

A GRAVE MATTER

"Jack?" Linda asked while they were lying side-by-side on her bed. "Yeah?" he asked, turning his head to face her, even though she was looking up at the ceiling.

"Do you ever visit graves?"

"Like… for fun?"

She giggled. He loved the sound. He realized he hadn't heard it since what happened with the tree spirit.

"No, I mean of people or spirits you knew," she said, returning to her solemn state.

Jack swallowed. His heart began to race. The image of the elf's frozen prison flashed through his mind. Would Linda think he's crazy for visiting the elf that he thought he killed? He ran his hand through his hair and down his face. "I sometimes do."

"Do you ever visit mortal graves?" she asked. "Have you been to a cemetery?"

"Sometimes, but I usually don't know the names of past mortals that I've befriended. I usually never got involved beyond playing in the snow or ice skating or something."

"Will you visit my grave?" she asked.

"Linda!" he exclaimed, sitting up. "Why would you ask that?"

"You're going to outlive me, assuming we're friends for the rest of my life," she answered, more pragmatically than he desired.

"I'm not even going to answer that," he said, lying back down next to her.

"I'll take that as a yes," she said.

He snorted. "You're impossible."

"I try my best."

They went quiet for a while, watching the occasional car lights that lit up the ceiling through the open blinds. "I have something to say, but I'm scared that you're going to hate me," he ventured.

"What is it?" she asked.

"What if you hate me?" he asked quietly.

"I mean," she said, taking his hand. She examined the remaining scabs from when he had punched Dan. "I already know you tried to kill an elf. Unless you killed someone else that I don't know about, it's hard to get much worse."

Part of him wanted to laugh, but the tangled knot of nerves in his stomach made it impossible. Before he could waste any more time thinking about it, he quickly said, "I used to visit the elf's resting place. Like when they were in the ice."

Linda was silent for a moment. He was terrified that she was in shock and that was the only reason she still held his hand. He held his breath.

"That's not as bad as I thought it would be," she finally said.

"And?"

"Geez, Jack, you made it sound like you were hiding some kind of bushwhacker massacre against the plant spirits from me," she responded. "That's actually kind of sweet and way less murderery knowing that you did that."

"I mean, that's how I found out that the elf escaped the ice prison. I went to go see them and they were gone."

"How long did it take you to start visiting them?" she asked.

"I'm not sure, at least a few centuries," he admitted. "It was really hard, but I figured I should at least commit to some form of penance."

"Lavender suggested that I go visit Kelsie," Linda said.

"How do you feel about that?"

"I'm not sure. That would be like admitting she's… not here. Which I know she's…" but her voice trailed off.

"Yeah, it would be a big step for you," Jack agreed. "There's nothing wrong with not going. Everyone has their own way of doing things. And there's no rush."

"What is the elf after?" Linda asked Jack, changing the subject.

He sighed. "Well, the first time was Mona's Amber. It's tied to her queenly power. This time… at the bare minimum, it's revenge."

Linda traced his fingers, which to Jack felt like she was shooting warm electricity through her fingertips into his hand. "At the maximum?"

Jack frowned. "I don't know. They weren't one to settle."

She took his hand and pressed it against her face. It felt like butterflies were going to explode through his stomach *Alien*-style. (Yes, he snuck into a theater to watch that.) "Do you ever make it snow in cemeteries?"

"They're hard to miss," he joked.

The lights were suddenly turned on, blinding both of them.

"Geez, guys, put a sock on the door," Emily said.

"Have you ever heard of knocking?" Linda retorted as she sat up. "We're literally just talking."

Emily snorted. "Sure, and my middle name is Naruto. Dinner is soon, don't get lost in each other's eyes and miss it."

Linda threw a pillow at her sister as she left the room, but Emily dodged it.

"Ugh, she's such a pain," Linda groaned, getting up to grab her pillow.

"I'm going to go wash up before dinner," Jack said as he pushed past her.

"What? Dinner's going to be in like fifteen minutes," she called over to him as he jumped into the bathroom down the hall. She couldn't see that he was blushing super hard.

FORTY

EVERETT AND JASMINE CLARI

"You've been crying," Everett Clari noted. "What have you been doing?"

Jasmine threw her big black coat down onto the old couch in his sad, dull living room. "Shut up, Everett, this isn't the time to get a conscience," Jasmine snapped.

"Jasmine, you've been staying out later and later..."

"I'll continue doing what I need to do. What are you so worried about?"

"I'm worried about you," he said.

Jasmine looked down at the pathetic red-faced man sitting in the worn brown corduroy chair. She laughed out loud. He flinched at the sound, his scotch sloshing in his glass and his tawny hair trembling. "Funny coming from the man who I caught burying a body."

"Jasmine!" he exclaimed. His face paled.

"You will do as I say, or I expose you to the authorities," Jasmine said coldly. "No one would believe you, anyway."

"I bought you a smartphone. I pretended that you are one of my own. I drive you around when I can, and I give you the food off my table. I let you do whatever you want, as if you were my own daughter—"

"Like the daughter that you killed?" Jasmine said dangerously. "Or maybe the other one, that Kelsie girl whose tragic death shook the town?"

Everett opened his mouth, and then closed it again. "Why did you choose me?" he asked hoarsely.

"What is it that your kind calls it? A 'crime of opportunity'?" she asked. "Maybe I just wanted to see you suffer, Everett," she said, walking closer to him. "Why let you rot in a broken prison system," she ran a finger up to his shoulder, and leaned in close to his ear before continuing, her voice low, "when I could watch you slowly lose your sanity, just like the people you broke with grief?"

He made a funny noise in his throat as she pulled away.

"Goodbye, Everett," she said, walking out of the room. "Get ready, I'll need you soon."

FORTY-ONE

LINDA DISCOVERS HER LEAST FAVORITE ELEMENT

The house was empty. Linda shuddered. She didn't like being alone anymore, and not just because there was an arson-inclined apocalypse-enthusiast on the loose. The thoughts about Kelsie that she was normally able to keep at bay with Jack and Lavender, and even with her siblings' hellish antics, would come crashing in. Linda wondered how long it would take before it would get easier like Lavender had said. Maybe it would never get better. She tried to shake away the depressing thought and ran her hand over her hair. She realized it was getting longer, reaching down past her shoulder blades from inattention. It was getting almost as long as Kelsie's when she— Linda tried to block out the memories, but they came anyway. The image of Kelsie lying in the open casket, her long brown hair fanned out around her face as if they caught her in the middle of sleep.

"Mom?" Linda called out into the house. No response. Which she expected—her parents were on a rare date, and her siblings out with friends. Linda inhaled deeply to try to hold back tears. She didn't want to have a lonely pity-party. She could handle this, she decided. *Maybe.* She marched into the kitchen and heaped a generous quantity of her mom's cookies onto a plate from the cooling rack and plopped herself on their faded light blue sofa in the living room. To distract herself, she put in family favorite cartoons. As the "Coming Soon to Theaters" reel began to play, Linda curled up in the chunky blanket that her mom knitted ages ago, taking a deep breath in the familiar, calming scent.

"Mrrowww!" Nicholas meowed a few minutes later as he padded into the room.

Linda nearly jumped. "Did you take your bell off again?" she sighed as he hopped onto the couch, right in front of her field of view. He head-butted her face in greeting, and she got a whiff of his cat food breath. He purred in response to her question and circled once before sitting in front of her to watch the animated rats run across the screen. Linda had to readjust her position to see past him.

Linda heard a knock on the door. She jolted upright to see that she was halfway into the movie and that her feline heater had disappeared. She groaned when she heard the knocking again. After hurriedly searching for the remote, which had evidently been knocked onto the floor, Linda paused the movie and ran to the door. It seemed a little too early for her parents to be back from their date, and she knew that Kris and Emily wouldn't be back until late. *Wouldn't they have their keys?* she wondered. She peeked through the curtain of one of the slim windows next to the door. When Linda saw red curls and pale skin, a trademark of Jasmine Clari, she removed the brass chain and opened the door.

"Jasmine? What are you doing here?" Linda asked.

The girl's eyes glimmered bright green like young clovers. She was bundled up in an absurdly large black coat, matching the one that Jack and Linda had seen on the person leaving Lavender's house that one time. But she was a little shorter... as if she somehow shrank a bit. Or she was being compressed under the weight of her gigantic coat. "Is anyone else home?" Jasmine asked, her voice sounding... different, like a creepy kind of different.

"Why?" Linda asked. "You're being weird. What's going on? Are you okay?"

Jasmine took a step forward as if she was going to enter the house, but instead slammed the freaking metal door into Linda's head. Her nose cracked. She reeled in excruciating pain. Stars and lights danced before her eyes as she grasped her forehead, pulling her hand away to see blood. She felt more hot blood stream from her throbbing nose. "What the fuck!"

Jasmine lunged toward her, taking advantage of Linda's disorientation. The level of evident calculation frightened Linda. Jasmine wrenched off Linda's communication ring, nearly breaking her finger, and Linda heard the ice smash underneath Jasmine's feet. Then it got even worse as Jasmine grabbed her by the hair and forced a folded cloth which smelled strongly of unfamiliar herbs over her mouth and nose. Linda's vision began to blur and blacken around her periphery. She tried to fight it, wrenching her head away from her captor. She swung her head and flailed her arms. But darkness took over.

FORTY-TWO

THE CHAPTER WHERE JACK DISCOVERS THE END IS NIGH

A bright blue light glowed, waking Jack up. He didn't realize that he had fallen asleep, but the windows were dark, and the only light came from the firefly lanterns humming overhead. He had face-planted in one of Time's books. Many more were haphazardly stacked before him. Jack groaned and sat back after being careful not to damage the page—he definitely didn't need any more apocalypse in his life right then. He exhaled with relief. He normally didn't fall asleep in Father Time's library, but he also normally didn't spend time in there.

A mouse squeaked in disapproval behind him. Jack groaned. He shook the sleep from his head and rubbed his face before he saw the blue light emanating from his ring again. His heart skipped a beat, sending icicles through his chest. *The distress signal.* As he was about to teleport, he heard the faint sound of ice cracking. A fissure appeared down the center of the ice gem. The attending mouse squeaked a slew of curses at him as the air swirled around Jack, rustling the book pages and papers before he disappeared.

As soon as he landed in front of Linda's house, he knew something was wrong. The Christmas lights twinkled in the eaves, the house lights were on, but the door was ajar. Nicholas stood on the porch in front of the door and hissed at Jack as he approached. "Easy, Nicholas," Jack said gently.

The cat sniffed the air and seemingly recognized him, allowing him to walk up the steps. "Mrrrp," Nicholas chirped before scampering into the house, his claws clicking slightly on the metallic threshold. Jack followed him and pushed open the door to find Linda's broken ring on the floor. Nicholas began smelling it, but Jack scooped it up in case the cat wanted to nibble on the broken ice gem. He didn't need the Waters family to return to a missing daughter and a frozen cat.

"Is Linda home?" Jack asked him desperately.

Nicholas blinked at him. Then he started to clean himself.

Jack groaned. "Why am I talking to a cat."

Nicholas stretched and padded toward the kitchen. Jack ran to Linda's bedroom, but it was empty and there were no signs of struggle. He ran to the bathroom, her parents' room, and then to the living room. Nicholas was chattering at the TV. A frozen image of a freaked-out rat glowed, and a half-eaten cookie sat on a plate. The sofa looked like someone had been sleeping on it and left the blanket in a hurry.

The cat brushed his head against the remote. Jack took a few seconds before figuring out where the "play" button was (mortal technology was unbelievably annoying), and the rat on the screen began moving and talking. Nicholas chattered excitedly as his tail flicked. Then it clicked. Linda was the one watching the deranged movie. "She was here! Thank you, Nicholas!" Jack exclaimed, scooping up his orange feline friend and giving him a hug.

"Mrrrrrowwww," Nicholas meowed in protest.

"Okay, I've got to run," Jack said, putting him down. He was about to teleport when he realized he had no idea where he needed to go next. "Oh no," he moaned, sinking to his feet. "Linda's not at home. Her ring is broken, which is something that she wouldn't do. Her family isn't home. Except for her cat." Jack looked at the orange furball. "Nicholas, what do I do? Do you know what happened to Linda?"

"Mrrp?" Nicholas chirped, staring up at Jack with his big jade-colored eyes.

"Why am I so useless?" Jack groaned. He took a deep breath. "Okay, Linda would tell me that I need to think from a different angle... Who else lives nearby? Lavender!" He teleported to his best approximation of Lavender's house.

"JESUS!" Lavender yelped. "John, what the hell? What the fuck just happened? Oh my God, where the hell did you come from?" Lavender demanded, scooting back to the edge of her bed. "Wo-oah!" she exclaimed as she ran out of space and fell off, pulling her quilt with her.

"Sorry, Lavender!" Jack said, rushing over to her side and helping her up. "I didn't mean to teleport directly into your room."

"Teleport? How the hell—what is happening?" Lavender groaned. "Did I ingest illicit drugs?"

"Were you crying?" Jack asked, noting her puffy eyes and the tissues on her bed.

"What? Um, yes, but—wait, wait, wait. *Teleporting?*" Lavender demanded.

"Long story short: I'm Jack Frost, I'm not John Mason, I'm the nature spirit that is in charge of ice and snow and I live with Mother Nature," Jack explained quickly, looking around for an item to freeze.

"John, are you high?" Lavender asked exasperatedly, rubbing her temples. "Am I high?"

He spotted a glass of water on her nightstand and grabbed it, letting it slosh slightly. "See? Look. It's water, right?"

"Yes?" Lavender said slowly, taking the glass from him.

He wrapped his hands around the glass and her hand, and before she could protest, he froze the water, frosted the glass, and chilled her hands.

"Holy fuck!"

"Yeah, so, Linda is in trouble. She's missing."

"Why didn't you start with that?" Lavender snapped. "What do you mean? Do we need to call the cops?"

Jack quickly explained all of the events and the broken ring and the distress signal. "So, that's why I didn't know what to do."

"Lavender!" Lavender's mom shouted from outside her bedroom. "Do you have a boy in there?"

"What? Um, no, *Maman!*" Lavender shouted back. "I'm just… on the phone with a friend from school!"

"Why are you talking to boys?" her mom demanded. Jack had to stifle a snicker when Lavender shot him a death glare.

"*Maman*, he's having… family issues," Lavender explained. "He's just a friend!"

"Okay, then," her mom responded, and Lavender imagined her mom shaking her head as she walked away down the hall.

Lavender turned back to Jack. "What am I supposed to do?"

"I don't know, that's why I came to you," Jack said.

"Oh my god, okay," Lavender sighed.

"How about you go look for clues or something nearby while I look at other places by teleporting?" Jack suggested.

"Fine. If neither of us find anything, we meet outside my house in fifteen?" Lavender asked.

"Okay, great. Bye!" Jack said. Then he disappeared in a whirl of light.

Lavender braced herself for a moment, and then slapped her own face. Yep, that stung. Maybe she wasn't dreaming. Regardless, Linda needed their help, and it was hard to go to the authorities about a missing person if magic might be involved. She hoped John—Jack— was wrong.

Lavender grabbed her phone from where it fell on the floor and raced down the stairs, straight to the coat rack by the front door.

"Lavender, where are you going?" her dad demanded as she threw on her coat and shoes.

"Linda is having an emergency, I need to go help her," Lavender said quickly.

"Is everything okay?" her dad asked.

"I don't know, but I need to be there for her, Dad," she said. "See you later! Love you!"

"Keep me updated!" he called after her as she ran out into the frigid night.

FORTY-THREE

LINDA'S REALITY GETS REMODELED.
AGAIN.

Linda woke up choking on blood. She rolled to her side and coughed violently, gasping for breath as frigid air stung the walls of her lungs. Her mouth tasted like copper. She looked up to see naked trees heavy with snow, their boughs hanging almost unnaturally around her. The stars arched across the black sky between the dark clouds. But the full moon remained uncovered, as if stationed to light the stage. She sat up and her head swam and ached. She shivered from the bitter cold robbing her under-clothed body of its heat. Her spasming muscles and throbbing nose did not help her focus her vision. She steeled herself to stand, but she fell back to her knees in the snow. The cold burned through her jeans.

"I felt this way before," someone said from behind Linda. She recognized the voice, but it sounded... deeper. More ancient. "It's called freezing to death."

The words sent more chills down Linda's spine, prickling like ice picks.

"If all goes to plan, your lover boy should come save you. If not, you'll die."

"Why?" Linda choked out. Fear, unlike anything she'd felt before, almost strangled her to silence.

"Ice is unforgiving, and I would delight in his horror when he realizes that his winter killed you." She chuckled menacingly.

Hot tears stung Linda's eyes before they cooled on her cheeks. "You're crazy," she said. "What did Jack do to *you?*"

"Look at me!" the woman commanded, wrenching Linda's arm so that she would look up into her captor's face. Linda shrieked as she looked up into wild eyes, their verdant green irises streaked painfully with a horrible white. A wave of nausea rolled through her, but she tried to force down the feeling. She figured she would surely be dead in an instant if she puked all over her captor. Red curly hair cascaded down the young woman's shoulders, untamed and giving off the effect of fraying.

"J-Jasmine?"

"I had to spend time among you mortal swine because I had nowhere else to go," Jasmine spat. Linda winced as her sinews screamed. Jasmine still gripped her arm, nails digging through Linda's sweater.

"You will not last much longer," Jasmine smiled, the whites of her teeth showing. Although her tone hinted at anger. "I expected more, maybe I misjudged the strength of a human's body. I survived for centuries in ice, but you may last only minutes." She let go of Linda, watching the shivering girl fall back to her knees. A vicious smile curled across her lips as Linda heaved. "Jack's fatal flaw is that he cares about specific people more than himself. It's quite useful once you get to know him."

"I'm insignificant," Linda said. But when she looked up slowly, since her head still ached from receiving a metal door, she noticed that Jasmine had disappeared. Linda looked back down in an effort to calm her head and saw a bloodroot flower blooming before her, unfurling from its leaves that sprouted through the snow. The intoxicating smell drew her closer, and despite grimacing with the effort, her mind went blank. She picked the flower.

Linda? Jack's voice carried to her ears as if far away. She heard the sound of a door creaking. *Where are you?*

Then the vision faded, and Linda found herself sprawled in the snow again. *Was Jasmine real?* she wondered. She felt her face, and, yep, her nose still felt terrible. She wiped the blood in the snow. Her sluggish brain struggled to cooperate. If Jasmine was gone, Linda could get up and just hurry home or ask for help from Lavender. Even Ruth. She sat back up again, sinking her hands into the freezing snow that bit into her skin, but unnatural vines suddenly tightened around her legs, forcing her to stay in the uncomfortable crouched position.

There was no escaping.

Jasmine was real.

And Linda was going to die.

FORTY-FOUR

RUTH'S PLAN

Lavender walked down the street, which was sparsely illuminated by the looming outdated lamps, looking for anything. (For what? She had no idea.) Jack had been right, of course, that Linda wasn't at home. Her whole family was gone, and all three cars were out of the driveway. It was chilling to see Linda's house empty and to think that her friend had been abducted. Lavender had to keep reminding herself that this was very different from what happened to Jane Clari, but she wasn't sure. This would be the second girl abducted from this town, and Lavender was only too aware of what could happen if she wasn't found. Lavender never told anyone, but she and her family strongly suspected that the Clari girl had been murdered. It had been over a year. The trail was cold. It happened a lot to indigenous people in both Canada and the U.S.: the cops take too long, don't prioritize the case, and later someone finds their remains if they find them at all.

"Lavender? Is that you?" a man's voice called from the other side of the street.

She looked up to see Mr. London. "Mr. London? What are you doing here?" Lavender asked, crossing the street to meet him. The streetlamp illuminated his hair like a halo.

"I could ask the same for you," he said. "I'm going to see my sister. I park at the school because her driveway is ridiculously small."

"Is your sister Ms. Leeds?" Lavender asked.

"I'm surprised that Linda and John didn't already tell you," he chuckled briefly. "Are you okay? You were just standing over there. It's not safe to be out alone like that."

"I actually live two houses away from Ms. Leeds. But…" Lavender hesitated. Should she bring Linda's teacher into this? She took the plunge anyway. John—Jack—would probably understand. "John and I can't find Linda. They were… supposed to meet but she sent him a message that worried him."

Mr. London's eyebrows creased in concern. "Did you already go to her house? Call her parents?"

"Yeah, Jack and I both did. No one is home. But we don't have her parents' numbers."

There it was again: John being called Jack. Mr. London knew that Linda claimed it was a nickname, but it always felt like a flimsy excuse to him. For what, he could not even begin to imagine. "That's alarming. Have you told your parents?"

"Not yet, I went out to check first, and then I found you," Lavender explained.

"I think it's a good idea for you to go back to your folks and call 911. I don't like the sound of this situation," Mr. London said, starting to walk down the street. Lavender didn't say anything, but she followed.

As they stopped in front of her house, they saw another person walking toward them from the dead-end side of the street. Mr. London and Lavender realized it was Ruth.

"I was almost there!" Mr. London called.

"I saw some flashes of light in the clearing over in the woods," Ruth said. "Maybe we should go investigate."

"Maybe we should call the police first," Mr. London suggested. Ruth and Lavender exchanged looks.

"What?" he demanded.

"Let's just go investigate first, George," Ruth said, turning around leading the way.

"There's something you're not telling me, Lavender," Mr. London said slowly as they followed Ruth.

Lavender looked away from him without uttering a word. But her heart pounded. Mr. London wouldn't believe her even if she tried to explain.

"It's usually not good if you're agreeing to one of my sister's plans," he sighed. Lavender stayed silent.

FORTY-FIVE

A BROKEN NOSE, A BOOK,
AND THE END OF THE WORLD

F inally, Jack landed in Linda's favorite forest. He had tried a couple other locations first, such as the place where the tree was burned and Ruth's house, but this was the only place he could imagine Linda *choosing* to go. Once he got his bearings, he saw Linda sitting in the center of the snow-covered clearing, the sacred text open in her lap.

"Linda, what's going on?" he asked carefully, walking toward her. But something was obviously wrong. Linda sat slumped over the book, barely holding it with her hands, which were bright red from the cold. She didn't respond to him. He began to think the worst and started running toward her almost soundlessly over the top of the snow. Jack stumbled when he saw a single bloodroot flower lying limp in front of her.

Then her head snapped up. "Jack!" she cried as he reached her.

He dropped to his knees and cupped her bloody face in his hands. "What happened to you? Who did this to you?"

"Jack, no," Linda wept, tears freezing on her face. She tried to push him away, but her hands were too weak to move him. "This is a trap. Take the book. *Now.*"

"What do you mean? You're freezing to death. You're going to get hypothermia."

"It's a trap," she said again. "Leave." Then she saw the vine tendrils tightening around his ankle. "Look out!"

But her warning was too late. The vines tore Jack from the spot and tossed him high into the air. Then he landed hard on the frozen ground a few feet away, knocking the wind out of him. His vision went dark.

Linda looked up. Jasmine stood over her, tilting her head while she smiled. "Oh, great, you came back," Linda said sarcastically.

Jack finally pushed himself up off the ground, mentally slapping himself, willing his body to cooperate. He shook with rage. When he stood up, his arms and legs were restrained by vines that exploded through the snow. He attempted to freeze them, but the frost immediately sloughed off. "*What?*"

Jasmine snickered while she watched him struggle. "You're not going to freeze my jasmine vines. They've been strengthened with the blood of a mortal, silly!"

He growled as he summoned his sword. A leafy tendril immediately snatched it from his hand with a simple gesture by Jasmine.

"You've never been the smart one, have you?" Jasmine smirked. She accepted the ice sword from her vine. "Even Linda realized I was different. But... you? You've always just listened to others."

"What the fuck did you do to her?" he demanded, straining against the vines.

She swung the longsword in her hands, slicing the air. Then she shrugged. "I did what was necessary, although I might've gotten a little carried away." She smirked and walked behind Linda, who shrunk away from her and clutched the sacred book more tightly. Blood dripped down her chin. Jasmine grabbed Linda's neck from behind, stroking her flesh. "Aw, the poor thing is getting cold, Jack Frost. But it's not something I would know about, right? It's not like my best friend froze me in a block of ice for countless human generations."

Jack leaned forward, straining against the vines to no avail. "Is this some sort of *sick* revenge?"

Jasmine laughed again, the sound chilling in the winter air before Linda slammed her head back into the elf's annoyingly pretty face.

Jasmine's grip tightened on Linda's neck, and she winced. "And you did your job. Now give me the book," Jasmine ordered.

"You're going to have to try harder to get me to obey you," Linda snapped.

Jasmine straightened, letting go of her. Linda exhaled a sigh of relief but froze when she felt the cold tip of the sword pressing into the back of her bare neck. "How about now?" Jasmine asked.

"Jasmine, stop it!" Jack shouted. "This isn't about her!"

Linda grasped the book more tightly to her chest. "I care more about the book," she said, although her voice trembled more than she wanted it to. She also knew that Jasmine could easily take the book from her dead body, but she hoped that it would at least buy time. For what? She had no idea. The sword lowered, although it nicked Linda's neck. It felt like ice shot through her veins.

"See, Jack? Smart," Jasmine laughed. Then she walked back in front of Linda and leveled a kick to her face. Linda screamed in agony as fresh blood began to flow from her damaged nose. The elf wrenched the book from her hands.

"I'm going to kill you," Jack snarled.

"Good luck with that," Jasmine snorted.

Then the vines fell empty in the snow with a flash of light. He appeared behind her, driving a dagger into her back. Jasmine made a choking sound before her mouth spread into a slow smile. Goosebumps ran down Linda's arms and back.

"Jack, you know nothing about blood magic, do you?" Jasmine chuckled. Then she flipped open the sacred text, making sure to overextend the binding and crack the spine. The trees around them flickered for a moment before fading into evergreens. The naked trees were gone. Linda watched the scene with horror, finally recovering from the ache of her face.

"I'll just stab you again," he threatened.

"Oh, yeah? And I'll just tear a page from the book," Jasmine said. As he withdrew the dagger, she turned and ran his sword through his abdomen. He cried out in pain as crimson blood trickled down the lengthy blade onto her hands and into the snow, dripping, dripping, dripping. Linda watched shell-shocked. She didn't move. She didn't know what to do.

"That—won't—kill—me," he gasped.

"I know," Jasmine said. "That's not the purpose."

Green light fulminated from the other side of the clearing. Mother Nature appeared. Her cloak rustled as if on its own. Then Linda saw an elf stick its head out from the cloak like a frightened child.

"Finally, Her Highness has made an appearance," Jasmine smiled with a welcoming gesture. "Care to take in the scene of the end of your reign?"

"Jasmine, what is the meaning of this?" Mona demanded.

"You remembered my name, how touching," Jasmine said as she put her hand on her heart. Then she considered the length of the shining sword in front of her, still embedded in Jack, who breathed hard. "I guess the Amber really does whisper to you."

"You're still holding onto the same fever dream from centuries ago? Pathetic," Mona spat.

"I know, Jack Frost really should've just killed me when he had the chance," Jasmine said. Then she picked up Jack's dagger and walked away, leaving him to sink to his knees while he gasped.

Linda crawled over to him, barely feeling the burning sensation of the snow. Part of her brain registered that this was a preliminary sign of frostbite, but she hoped that adrenaline would help her. At least for a few minutes longer.

Jasmine approached Mother Nature. Linda noticed that unnaturally thick vines of jasmine flowers began to ensnare Mother Nature's legs. But the vines slowly started to sprout leaves and flowers. *Is this a sign that she's getting stronger?* Linda wondered. *Or... is she losing control over her magic? How long does blood magic last?* Three elves began to hack and gnaw at Mona's vines, but their attempts were futile. Jasmine held up the book and opened it so that the spine creaked out loud. The little elves shrieked in horror. Mother Nature gasped and covered her mouth as her luminous skin paled.

Linda looked away to focus on Jack, who was making a very cringe-worthy attempt to pull out the sword himself. "Jack, stop," Linda said, "You're going to cut your hands."

He grimaced. "Yeah, I know. I'd just rather not be impaled."

As Linda grasped the hilt, a tremor ran through her. She could feel how deeply embedded the sword was in his body, and another wave of nausea ran over her.

"Linda, focus," he managed. "I'm not going to die, but I can go into shock."

She nodded and forced herself to pull. But the sword began to flicker in her hands. She looked up and saw Jasmine beginning to tear at a page in the sacred text. Mother Nature began to detach the Amber from her cloak. It glowed angrily as if in protest.

"Don't!" the elves begged, grasping her cloak tightly. "Don't give it to her!"

The dagger in Jasmine's hand flickered as well until it grew into a longsword. Linda looked back down and found that now the handle of a battleaxe was in her hands. Jack grunted. The wound was significantly bigger with an axe than a longsword. "Hurry," he said through gritted teeth.

Linda unsteadily stood up and yanked on the battleaxe with all of her strength until it budged. She fell flat on her butt while Jack cried out. The heavy axe fell to the ground with a loud thump, nearly pulling Linda to the side. She looked back up to the scene.

"I will destroy this book if you don't give me the Amber," Jasmine said evenly, which somehow was more terrifying than when she laughed. The elf placed the book on the ground and held the tip of the sword over the open pages.

"You will not. If you damage it then it will destroy you," Mona warned. Her typically regal tone wavered. Jasmine stared at her in silence. The Amber sat cupped in the queen's protective hands like a small flame that she was scared would be extinguished. Jack clutched at his bloody abdomen while he sprinted over with Linda. Jasmine shifted the sword so that it stuck into the binding of the book.

"Jack, stop," Mother Nature commanded. Jack and Linda froze a couple feet away from them.

"One…" the elf said, adjusting her grip.

Mona stood stoic, but the fear in her eyes was plain as day. "The power is a burden, the price of balance…"

"Two…" Jasmine continued. The entire forest flickered.

"Jasmine, please!" Jack begged. He was too frightened to move. If Jasmine damaged the book even more, anyone or anything could disappear.

"*You* had your chance," Jasmine snarled without looking at him. "You can watch your mortal die in front of you." She dragged the tip of her dagger under some lines. The scratching sound of the sharp metal against the fibers was agony. "Nature, I'm waiting."

Mother Nature extended her trembling hand. The Amber radiated brightly in her palm.

A branch snapped from behind them at the edge of the clearing.

"Linda!" Lavender cried.

Jasmine looked up, her face contorted with rage. Lavender drew back. "*Jasmine?* What are you doing?"

"Three!" the elf yelled, bringing down the sword.

FORTY-SIX

THE BLOOD OF LIFE

Linda dove for the book.

She had slightly misjudged the distance. She felt it slam against her ribcage and stomach, almost knocking the wind out of her. It definitely cracked underneath her. White-hot, searing pain arced from a single point in her back, slicing through her muscles and one of her lungs. With horrific certainty, Linda realized that Jasmine had driven the sword into her back. She was all that lay between reality and the apocalypse. She couldn't breathe. It felt like frost trickled into her veins. In her daze, she heard Jack screaming, "NO!" But it sounded far away.

Jasmine pulled out the sword.

Jack threw himself at Jasmine, tackling her to the ground. She hit her head, and he swung at her. The sword landed with a thump next to them, ringing against a hidden stone. Jasmine clawed at him, trying to wrap her hands around his neck, but he punched her in the throat.

Blood pooled in Linda's right lung. She heard screams and a sudden chill in the air, so cold that she felt the blood-soaked part of her shirt freeze. She coughed up hot, sticky blood into the snow in front of her, which she found had changed to grass. But even that began to get dark and blurry. Breathing was so difficult. Then, by some miracle, she felt strong arms pick her up off of the book. The familiar scent of balsam was comforting. She coughed up more blood, splattering Jack's chest. She heard his voice but couldn't make out anything. She was going into shock. *No. I'm dying,* Linda realized. She was losing a lot of blood, and she couldn't feel her limbs because of the frostbite.

Jasmine swung the sword down at them, but Jack held up his hand and a sheet of ice appeared. It shattered under the force of the blow, but it protected them. The three other elves jumped on Jasmine, knocking her over. Lavender, Ruth, and Mr. London sprinted to them.

"Lavender!" Jack yelled.

"I'm here!" Lavender said, falling to her knees next to them. "Oh my god, she's bleeding a lot."

"Take care of her," Jack said, pushing Linda into Lavender's lap.

"What?" Lavender demanded.

But he was already up, sword in hand, running to Mother Nature.

Linda coughed up more blood onto the ground as Ruth and Mr. London appeared. She heard Mr. London talking to her, but she couldn't understand the words.

"Linda, oh my God," he said. Ruth helped him and Lavender shift Linda back onto her stomach in an attempt to reduce her blood loss. His hands and his voice shook terribly. His student's dark ruby blood spilled everywhere, staining the grass, which had strangely replaced the snow, and their clothes and everything. He could feel her ragged breathing as he pressed his coat against her wound while Ruth hurried to pull off her layers.

Linda's eyes were still open. She numbly witnessed Jack hacking at Mother Nature's vine prison.

"She's losing some of her power," Jack told Mona once the vines sagged at her feet. They turned to face the elven melee. Jasmine had summoned bloodroot and jasmine plant spirits, and it was a raging storm of vines, dismembered plant spirits, and vicious assault. But the spirits were winning.

Mother Nature picked up the sacred book and she stroked the binding while she whispered a simple incantation. An ancient hand rose from the open tome and snapped its fingers. The elves and spirits began to move in slow motion. Jack ran over and began freezing and cutting down the disoriented plant spirits.

"Stay with us," Ruth begged Linda. She took off her coat and sweater before pressing the sweater into the wound. George hyperventilated. Lavender helped Ruth apply pressure to Linda's wound while Ruth took her brother's face into her hands. "George," she said. "Focus. Keep talking to Linda."

Linda coughed up more blood. "I feel..." she coughed again. "Terrible."

"It's going to be okay," George lied. He began to cry. He started telling Linda about what they were doing to help her and how Jack just pinned Jasmine to the ground with his sword. She looked worse for wear after the fight with the elves and animated plants. The little elves tied her up in vines. Mother Nature, or so he was told, did something magical to Jasmine with an amber stone. George told Linda how much he cared about her. And that he might be losing his mind. And then Mother Nature came over to stabilize her with the same stone.

Linda began to close her eyes. The warmth of the Amber against her wound felt so good, so comforting, like the warm blankets that her mom used to get out of the dryer on cold winter days in her childhood, the ones that she would share with Kelsie while they watched their favorite movies.

She heard Jack cry her name. But the wind rushed past her, and she tasted the blood in her mouth. "I love you," Linda forced out, only to end up in a coughing fit as hot blood pooled in her chest and throat.

FORTY-SEVEN

A VIEW FROM THE OTHER SIDE

All she could hear was heavy breathing, broken intermittently by stifled weeping. Linda followed the sound, stepping through the snowy forest. Her feet were numb. Her thin linen shoes were frozen to her skin. Her fingertips were blue. But she was alive.

The heavy breathing was louder, definitely that of a mortal man, a sound that she hadn't heard in hundreds of years. Suddenly, her ears pricked up as she heard something large and heavy being dragged through the snow. Her vision blurred for a moment, and she grabbed hold of a nearby tree to steady herself. When she looked down at her hands, Linda realized they were not her own. Her skin was disturbingly pale, almost like a corpse, and her fingers were long and thin. Suddenly, her head snapped up as if of its own accord as her vision cleared. She saw a man in the moonlight, pulling a large bag behind him through the thin layer of snow, leaving some fallen brown leaves exposed. The bag was disturbingly large.

"Who's there?" the man suddenly demanded. He looked up and dropped the bag at the sight of her. Linda felt a scream rise in her throat, but nothing came out. The black bag fell open, its cargo spilling into the snow: the body of the girl who had gone missing. Jane Clari.

"What have you done, mortal?" Linda's voice demanded, but again, it wasn't her own. It had a weird power that she wasn't used to, deeper and older. And it wasn't scared, not like Linda.

Her head turned to look beyond the man, who stood frozen in place, a vision of pure human fear on his face. On the road was a smoking car crash. A broadside collision. A drunk man struggled to get out of one car, while the other one held a family. The family's car had been struck at an angle by the drunk's, causing it to ram into a telephone pole. Linda could recognize that cobalt blue car anywhere. It was Kelsie's.

"Life for life," the unfamiliar voice said from Linda's mouth, as her head turned slowly back to the terrified man. "Protect mine, and I will protect yours."

The man gulped, then nodded. Linda's unfamiliar hand extended forward, although she wished with everything in her being that she could pull her arm back. He stepped forward so that his carmine face was illuminated in the moonlight. Her hand clasped with the man's plump, clammy one. "Everett Clari," he said weakly.

"Jasmine… Clari," the voice said. Suddenly, her arm was bound to his with jasmine vines, and in her periphery, she could see that the body of Jane Clari, wrapped in the same vines, disappeared into the ground, until only snow and dead leaves remained.

Then they ran through the forest, away from the car crash as sirens sounded through the trees, penetrating the frigid air. Linda wanted to sob and get away from the man, but her body moved on its own accord. Her chest hurt as the cold air stung the walls of her lungs, which slowly began to feel more mortal than elvish. Her bones ached from the chill. Then she followed Everett Clari through a dark door.

Linda felt herself falling, falling, falling through deep darkness, until nothing.

FORTY-EIGHT

GEORGE TELLS JACK TO SHUT UP;
OR, WAITING

Lavender sat in between Mr. London and Ruth while John—well, Jack Frost—paced in front of them. They were all covered in their friend's blood. It was streaked across their faces where they forgot it was on their hands and it was all over Mr. London's pants and Lavender's hands felt soaked with it. The four of them were kicked out of the room where Mother Nature and her elves were healing Linda. So, Lavender sat in a magical palace with her head reeling from a level of surrealness she had only ever seen in the 1980s BBC adaptation of *The Hitchhiker's Guide to the Galaxy*. She had also just seen one of her friends turn out to be Jack Frost, her ex-girlfriend turned out to be a homicidal elf that was leveraging the apocalypse for some bonkers revenge over some borderline omniscient piece of jewelry, all while her other friend was literally bleeding to death in her arms. It was all she could do to not have her sanity collapse in on itself. *How the hell has Linda handled it this whole time?* Lavender wondered. She voiced this to Jack.

"Hm? Oh, I don't know. She almost fainted when I first told her that I'm, you know," Jack said. "It was hard to convince her." He didn't stop pacing.

"How old are you?" Mr. London asked him incredulously.

"I don't know," Jack answered nonchalantly, as if it was a normal answer.

"Is science real?" Mr. London asked.

"Yes, for humans. It's just how they study the natural world."

Mr. London let out a sigh of relief. Jack continued to pace and run his hands through his hair, which made him look wild with how it stuck up, in conjunction with all of the blood smeared on his face and clothes. Mr. London expressed concern that they wouldn't have the right tools to heal Linda outside of the hospital, but Lavender and Ruth assured him that given the magical circumstances it would be okay.

"Mona and her elves are more powerful than any mortal doctor or surgeon," Jack interjected. Mr. London and Lavender exchanged looks. That wasn't the most reassuring given the wait time and his anxiety.

To distract herself, Lavender examined her surroundings. The inside of the palace was surprisingly warm and comforting despite how large and airy it was. She looked to her left, and past an incredibly long wooden table, tall arches stood open to a beautiful and lush forest.

"That's the summer season over there," Jack pointed.

"What do you mean?" Lavender asked. "It's winter."

"All four seasons are active at the palace at once," Jack explained. "If you look out other windows, you'll see."

"That sounds like a sinus nightmare," Mr. London said. Ruth rolled her eyes.

"You get used to it," Jack said.

"Am I allowed to look around?" Lavender asked.

"Yes," a child said, suddenly crawling out of the solid marble floor in front of them. The three mortals shouted in surprise.

"What the shit!" Mr. London exclaimed. The child giggled. Then George saw the pointed ears. He thought he was going to faint.

"Hyacinth, please don't scare them," Jack chided. "You know that mortals aren't used to the palace."

"But it's just so fun, Mr. Frost!" Hyacinth whined.

"Please don't call me that," Jack groaned. "I'm not that old."

"We've been having the same conversation for a hundred years," Hyacinth retorted. "You're old enough."

Jack groaned aggressively in a way that made Lavender chuckle.

"Well, miss, do you want to see the rest of the palace while you wait for your friend?" the elf asked Lavender.

"Can I?" she asked.

"Yes, of course, it's only the coolest thing ever!" Hyacinth proclaimed with joy. His little brown curls bounced. "Come on!" he grabbed her hand and pulled her from the bench. "You see, over here is the summer…"

"I'm coming, too!" Ruth said, hurrying after them.

Then it was just George and Jack.

"Do you know when we find out?" George asked quietly.

"No," Jack said, pacing again.

"Can you please stop pacing? You're stressing me out," George said.

"*You're* stressed?" Jack demanded. "*I'm* stressed!" He started biting his nails, which, given the circumstances, was way too gross for George.

"We're all stressed," George said. "Just take a deep breath and sit down."

"I can't. What if she dies?"

Watching Jack Frost trying not to hyperventilate made him start to hyperventilate. "Just shut up," George said angrily.

Jack lunged and grabbed his shirt. "The love of my life is up there and the only reason I won't break you in half is because she likes you," he warned darkly.

"I'm a high school teacher, it's going to take a lot more than that to scare me," George replied evenly. Then Jack crumpled into George's chest and started to cry.

"There, there," George said, patting Jack's back. "Let it out."

"What if we didn't bring her back in time?" Jack wept. "I didn't know she'd get… stabbed… it all happened so fast…"

"I know," George said quietly. "You did what you could."

"I'm sorry," Jack said after a while. "I made your shirt even more messed up."

"It's fine, John—er, Jack," George said as Jack straightened himself up and sat on the solid wood bench next to him. "I'm probably going to have to throw out these clothes, anyway. There's no way that I can show up to work with massive unexplained blood stains."

"Don't worry, the elves will help us get cleaned up soon. It's basic procedure," Jack said.

"Basic procedure? How often does this happen?" George demanded.

Jack chuckled darkly. "Often enough with nature spirits."

"Oh my god," George moaned, putting his face in his hands.

"Relax, I'm just messing with you," Jack laughed. Then he cleared his throat. "Well, sort of."

FORTY-NINE

OPENED EYES

A star shone in a pitch-black sky. Linda had difficulty separating the ground from the sky until she realized that she was floating. The star turned a painfully pure white and began to swell. Linda broke the surface of black water as the star kept growing until it was all she could see. She gasped for breath. Then the water faded away, leaving Linda lying on her back. Her eyes were already open. She realized she was looking up at a ceiling of marble and tree branches. She sat up slowly and looked down at her hands. They were hers and not the eerie pale, slim ones. She was still wearing the same clothes from when she died. Linda looked back up at the ceiling. It seemed impossible. The branches hugged exquisite carvings of flowers and leaves. She looked around feverishly. She sat up and realized she was on a bed with a faded soft quilt, which had a blue and white snowflake pattern. A few pieces of ornate, dark wooden furniture littered the room. On the wall across from the bed, dendritic tree branches acted like window frames between marble columns. The wall to her right seemed to be made entirely of deep blue glacier ice that glowed so faintly. Different images had been carved into it, including a life-sized one of her, standing and smiling like an idiot.

Linda suddenly pressed a hand to her chest and found it free of pain. Her heart beat steadily. Tears leaked down her cheeks. "Am I... dead?"

she asked the room. She heard a door creak behind her. Her head whipped around toward the sound.

Jack Frost stood in the entrance. "Linda?" he asked tentatively.

"Dear God, Jack, you look terrible," she said, taking in his positively wrecked appearance. Bloody fingerprints streaked down his face. His shirt was torn, frayed, and splattered with large splotches of blood.

But then she started to cry. Big, wracking sobs filled the room. She wailed into his solid, warm arms as everything rushed back to her. The vision. The pain. The sword. How far away everyone had sounded, how close she was to Kelsie yet so far away. Nothing would ever close that distance ever again.

"I'm so sorry, Linda," he said, but she barely heard him through her sobs.

"I saw her, Jack," she cried.

"Saw who?"

"Kelsie. The car accident. Jane Clari. The murderers," she wept, the words spilling out. "I had a vision. Jasmine was there. She saw everything."

Through her tears, Jack was eventually able to piece together Linda's vision. The story sent chills down his spine. His heart felt chilled just knowing the things that Jasmine did. *Who the hell sees a body and thinks of it as an opportunity?* he wondered uncomfortably. If it was up to Jack, he would've frozen the Everett guy to a tree and not minded if he caught hypothermia before he was found.

Eventually, Linda's breathing slowed. "I'm sorry," she said shakily.

"Oh my god, don't say sorry," Jack answered. "I think my sanity would implode if I had to live through all of that."

"What do I do?" she asked. "What do I do now?"

"I don't know," Jack said. "We can talk to Mother Nature and Father Time if you like. They're the wisest people I know. Mr. London, Ruth, and Lavender are also here—"

"Really?" Linda's head popped up. "Are they okay?"

"Yeah, they're worried sick about you, though. We all were," Jack said.

"Can I see them?" she asked.

"Yeah, of course! We can go there right now," he said.

Then Linda leaned forward, and her lips touched his, so lightly. Then she immediately pulled away. "OOPS, SORRY!" Linda exclaimed, her face boiling hot as she covered her mouth. "I misjudged the distance—I meant to stand up—sorry!"

Jack blinked in surprise before recovering. "Um, it's fine," he said awkwardly. "You're still in shock. It's fine. Um, yeah, it's fine. They're all downstairs." He stood up and started walking toward the door, but then he stopped to look back at her. "Will you be okay walking? How are you feeling?"

She slid off the bed unsteadily at first but regained her balance. "I feel fine, like I wasn't just stabbed," Linda said. "How long was I out?"

"An hour," Jack said. "Mona started healing you when we were still in the mortal land, but you were unstable and needed more medicine, so we brought you here." He reached out his hand and she accepted it. They walked down a cavernous marble hall arched with tree branches to the stairs, which seemed to be tree roots.

"How many trees are in here?" Linda asked. She counted at least fifteen steps on one flight.

"Oh, it's actually one big tree," Jack said.

"Like Pando the quaking aspen?" Linda asked in awe.

"Yes, exactly like them."

"Them?"

"Pando is agender," Jack explained. Then they reached the last step. After Jack made sure that Linda was still fine, he led her down another hall to a chamber with a clear brook running through it, as if the forest had its own room. Mr. London, Lavender, and Ruth were sitting on various stones, dressed in ivory-colored flax gowns like they were prepared to sing in some organic choir.

"Did I miss something else?" Linda asked, staring at their clothing.

"Linda!" they all cried in unison.

"Oh my god, I'm so glad you're okay!" Mr. London exclaimed, nearly in tears as he ran over, while Lavender practically teleported and began cracking Linda's ribs in a tight bear hug. Ruth joined them and patted Linda's back reassuringly.

"Don't ever do that again," Lavender said forcefully.

"What, get stabbed with a sword by a crazy person? I planned to do that again next Wednesday," Linda said.

"Don't joke like that!" Lavender scolded her, punching her arm.

"Lavender, give her a break," Mr. London chided, before giving Linda a tight squeeze.

"Ribs," Linda groaned.

"Oh, sorry!" he exclaimed as he let go.

"You guys are too strong," Linda tittered. Then she cleared her throat and glanced at Jack.

"Um, right," he said.

"What's going on?" Lavender asked. "Something else is up. Spill."

"Linda, do you want to say, or do you want me to—"

"You," Linda interrupted.

Jack snapped his fingers to summon an elf, who hopped out of the brook with a small splash, nearly giving everyone but him a heart attack. "Lily, can you please get Linda some food and water? Maybe some honey cakes?"

"Yessir!" her tinny voice answered, sounding just like tiny bells. Linda snorted.

"Don't call me that," Jack groaned.

"Okay... sir," the elf said, then grabbed Linda's hand and teleported her away before Jack could hurl a snowball. Lavender failed to hold in a giggle.

"Okay, so... Linda had a vision while she was unconscious," Jack said.

"Are you sure she wasn't just dreaming?" George suggested.

Jack ignored him and relayed everything he knew about Jane Clari, Everett Clari, and Kelsie. After he was done, Lavender looked like she was about to faint.

"Are you okay, sweetie?" Ruth asked, putting her arm around her and rubbing her shoulder.

"I mean, that was incredibly disturbing," George said. "John—I mean Jack, you called it a vision. Does that mean you think it's real?"

"I hope the fuck not," Jack said. "But she also had the dream while she was being healed with an extremely sacred artifact."

Lavender looked ready to puke. "I think it was real," she said uncomfortably.

"Are you okay?" George asked.

"What do you mean?" Jack asked.

"I... uh... Jasmine and I were secretly dating..." Lavender said shakily. "A lot of that stuff actually makes sense now that I know this." She leaned forward and covered her face with her hands. "Oh, God, I feel so terrible."

"Lavender, is that why you were crying when I found you? Did you and Jasmine break up?" Jack asked. Lavender nodded.

"Oh my god, I'm so sorry," he said before giving her a hug.

"It's fine, it's not like she turned out to be crazy or anything," Lavender said, laughing while she sniffled.

George sympathetically rubbed her back. "At least you know you're a lot better off without her," he pointed out.

"Yeah, true," she said.

"So, Jack... what do we do now?" Ruth asked. They all looked at him.

As if on cue, Mother Nature appeared before them. Ruth got on one knee and bowed, and Lavender followed suit. George looked at them with confusion until Ruth pulled him down with her.

"Thank you, mortals," Mona said with a smile. "You may rise." They rose. Mona turned to Jack. "How is she?"

"Linda had a vision," he said, and then he explained it for the second time.

Mother Nature looked stunned. "Well, that's disturbing," she said. "The only way to confirm it is for you to speak with our prisoner."

"Jasmine's here?" Lavender squeaked.

"Yes, but she is stripped of her power. She won't be bothering anyone," Mona explained. George noticed that Lavender, reasonably, didn't look very comforted by that. He realized it was probably a lot to see her ex try to murder her friend, even if it was for magical reasons.

"Why do *I* have to speak with her?" Jack demanded.

"You know her the best. And do you think it would be wise for me,

265

the Queen, to speak with someone who's targeted me twice?" Mona pointed out.

"Ugh, fine," Jack complained.

"That's settled. So, I came here to discuss an important matter. Your memories."

"Our memories?" George asked.

"It is standard procedure for mortals to receive a sleeping draught to clear their mind of traumatic events and for them to be returned home," Mother Nature explained.

"Is this why people wake up on the side of the road?" Ruth asked. George sighed and rubbed his temple.

"Occasionally, but mortals are usually given away to their own excess or crime," Mother Nature said.

"So... you're saying that we won't remember any of what's happened in the past couple hours?" George asked.

"Precisely."

"What about Linda?" he asked.

"Yeah, what about Linda?" Jack asked.

"It's up to her to decide. That level of trauma is quite unusual, but she also saved us all," Mother Nature said.

"Excuse me, Queen of Nature," George started.

"George!" Ruth scolded, but her brother ignored her.

"I don't like the idea of Linda being left alone with all of that if she does choose to keep her memory. She needs a support network with the mortal world. I can't speak for Ruth and Lavender, but I would like to support her."

"Yeah, Linda has a huge choice to make," Jack said with a gulp. Lavender looked up and realized he looked... scared. *Would Linda choose to remember him?*

FIFTY

LILY OF SLEEPING DEATH

"I ... could forget everything?" Linda asked.

"Yeah. If you want to," Jack answered, looking down at her. They were in Mona's throne room and Linda sat cross-legged on the marble floor where Lily had left her with an extra honey cake. Jack would've sat down with her, but he was too full of anxious energy to sit still. Mother Nature sat in her throne before them.

"The draught is called the Lily of Sleeping Death. The more you drink, the more you will forget of recent events. If you wish to forget about all of us, you can drink the entire draught. It is our gift to you," Mother Nature said. "Should you choose to decline, that is entirely for you to decide, and Jack will take you home."

Linda nodded. "Thank you." She glanced over at Jack, and she could tell that he was all nerves because of how he bounced on his toes. Even though he cleaned up, his hair still stuck up from the number of times he ran his fingers through it.

Mona snapped her fingers. An elf appeared out of a knotted branch in her throne. "Hyacinth, take Linda for a walk while she decides," Mona instructed.

"Actually, Mother Nature, I think I would like to take the lily draught," Linda said.

Jack felt like he couldn't breathe. He knew that this would happen, but part of him was hoping that it wouldn't. *How much would she want to forget?* His mind went immediately to the tree spirit that burned to ashes in front of them. How many times she cried and almost fainted. How she was stabbed. Knowing him only caused her more pain.

"Very well," Mona said. "Where would you like to take it?"

"Um… can Jack please be with me?" Linda asked.

"We will bring it to his room. We will meet you there soon," Mother Nature said, and then she faded into mist.

"W-what?" Linda asked. "What just happened?"

"She does that sometimes in the palace. One of the perks of being the queen," Jack explained half-heartedly. His voice was strained, and he couldn't hide it. He didn't want to influence Linda's decision one way or the other. Even still, he felt like his heart was about to break, like a delicate crystal hanging by a thread.

Linda raised the cup to her lips. The odor of the lilies flooded her nostrils, giving her a sense of peace and vacancy. But her hand stopped. "I don't think I can do this," she said as she lowered the cup.

"Are you sure?" Jack asked. He looked up at her from his seat in front of her on the grounding cold marble floor.

"I'm sure," she breathed. "I'd rather know the true story behind what happened to Kelsie… I feel like I owe it to her. She would want me to know."

"It will be a heavy burden," Jack said.

"I know," Linda admitted. Jack rested his head on her lap, exhaling.

Rosie came to collect them a few minutes later, gently pushing open Jack's door. "She's still awake? She didn't drink it yet?" she asked.

"Rosie, how many times do I have to ask you to knock on the door?" Jack demanded, getting to his feet. He heard Linda snicker behind him.

Rosie rolled her eyes. "There are more important things." She turned her attention to Linda, waiting expectantly.

"I changed my mind," Linda explained.

"Very well," Rosie said, looking at Linda with… respect? Linda couldn't tell, but Rosie stopped looking at her like she was some poor animal that Nicholas had dragged in after one of his rare outdoor adventures.

"Mother Nature will be expecting you downstairs with the other mortals. It's time to return home," Rosie said, gesturing for them to leave.

They walked quietly behind Rosie as she led them down to a huge marble staircase. At the bottom, massive tapestries that vividly depicted different seasons hung from each of the four walls. The arches between them opened to rooms that looked like they were overtaken by nature. Rosie, obviously proud of her queen, explained that the ground floor of the palace was divided into the North Room, the entrance; the South Room, which was the Great Hall; and the East and West Rooms. Mother Nature's throne room was in the main tower.

The South Room was alive with voices. Soft, vibrant music floated through the air. When Jack and Linda walked in, Rosie silently raced over to Mother Nature and whispered something in her ear, having to stand on her tiptoes. Linda squeezed Jack's hand when Mother Nature looked up at them. He squeezed it back.

Linda looked around while they waited and caught sight of Ruth and Mr. London, finally dressed in their normal clothes again, arguing over a purple bun of some kind while Lavender quietly sat next to them contemplating her life choices. Linda edged closer to Jack as the room quieted down. All of the elves and nature spirits (some loosely acquiring a humanoid appearance to sit at the table and drink from silver goblets) looked up at them, including her mortal friends, who waved and smiled. A man who Linda assumed to be Father Time, based on how ancient he looked in his grim black robe, looked up at them, too, from the opposite end of the table.

Mother Nature walked over. "How do you feel?" she asked quietly.

"As good as I can feel, I suppose," Linda said, glancing at Jack, who nodded in reassurance.

"You're one of the bravest mortals I've ever met," the Queen said, touching Linda's shoulder gently. Linda bowed her head. But then Mother Nature turned and addressed the room, which Linda realized was waiting expectantly for a verdict from their leader. "Bow before your hero, a mortal named Linda," Mother Nature said, her powerful voice booming through the open space. Everyone stood up from their chairs and bowed deeply, including Linda's friends. "Linda saved us all and risked her short life to do it!" Mother Nature continued. "Consider her a friend and aid her whenever she needs it. She protected us from the apocalypse for another day, a task worthy of an immortal."

Cheers erupted, bouncing off the walls in the great room and feeling big and loud. Linda blushed heavily, wishing she could run away from all of the attention. Thankfully, the musicians seemed to notice, and they began their jovial music again, slowly but surely building to a lovely song. Some elves began to sing in a language Linda didn't know, but it sounded merry as it mixed with the silver bells of the band.

Out of the corner of her eye, Linda saw Father Time nod at her. She stood in awe. Then he beckoned to her, and with gentle pressure from Jack at the small of her back, she walked forward. Once she stood in front of him, feeling nearly overwhelmed by his intense aura, Time placed a book in her hands. It was much like the sacred tome that Jasmine stole, but newer. The covers looked like it was freshly made from real, undying leaves. Linda opened the book. Silver characters curled, spelling out words and phrases that Linda could not hope to decipher. Time looked at down at her with his piercing dark gaze that contrasted his tan skin like ink on aging parchment.

"B-but I can't read the language," Linda stammered. "And this is yours!"

"Do not worry, Linda Estelle Waters. This is a copy. And time is on your side," Father Time smiled, his eyes crinkling with crow's feet, pushing the book further into her hands. She looked down to see a note tied to it, scrawled in what looked like what might've been real silver: *I know a student when I see one.* The letters curled in an unusual way, almost like… a different language entirely. She looked back up at him, but he had rejoined the merriment, sipping green liquid in a large ornate goblet that stood out from the others.

"Let's go, Linda," Jack said, lightly tugging on her arm.

"What? Oh, yeah, okay," Linda said, allowing herself to be pulled out of the trance and following him away from the table.

"I know Time can be a bit… mysterious," Jack commented as they waited for Mr. London, Ruth, and Lavender to join them at the edge of the hall. "You get used to it."

Mr. London made a point to say goodbye to Father Time, and although Linda and Jack couldn't hear what was being said, Mr. London started to blush furiously, and Ruth dragged him away.

"Do you have a crush on Father Time?" Jack asked when the group was together, his voice low. But the other mortals heard him, too.

"No, shut up," George said, blushing harder.

"It's never going to work," Jack said. "He's older than the planet."

"Shut up," George said again. Ruth snickered.

"You don't know that he's straight, Ruth. Homosexuality exists in the natural world. You don't have the advantage by being a woman."

"At least I know that nothing will ever happen," Ruth shot back. "I just know when a man is hot."

"Ew," Jack said, making a face with Lavender. Linda snickered.

They all walked slowly, following Jack to the probable location of the entrance. Hyacinth appeared next to Linda and offered her more honey cakes from hidden pockets in his purple robes. After she politely declined, he held her hand as he pointed out the snowdrops growing from mounds of moss along the walls in lieu of tables and vases, which were apparently mortal obsessions. Vines and branches stretched across the marble walls and floors. Tall arching glassless windows looked out onto a sort of magical spring-kissed forest that exploded with life. A clear stream bubbled and gurgled gaily a few feet from the windows.

"Doesn't the rain ever get inside?" Linda asked Jack.

"Aren't we allowed to have nice days?" he asked, his voice sonorous and deep, raising an eyebrow.

Linda felt warm inside at the sound. "Doesn't mean that there are always nice days," she commented, receiving a kiss on the cheek in return. Lavender saw this and noticed that they both looked surprised and started blushing. *Had something else happened beforehand in Jack's room?* she wondered. They seemed a lot closer and more comfortable, but still... not. Lavender decided she would interrogate one or both of them about it later.

The group walked further down the hall until they reached another spacious room, the domed ceilings hidden by leafy boughs that grew out of the walls. In the center of the room sat a granite boulder that sparkled faintly in the dusk pouring in. A fierce lioness statue sat on the boulder. It was almost larger than life, its sinews highlighted by the growing shadows. Suddenly, its tail flicked. The mortals jumped and yelped in surprise. Linda almost knocked Jack over while he laughed his head off.

"Meet Daybreak, Mother Nature's guard lion," Jack said to them.

"I thought Daybreak was a statue!" Lavender exclaimed.

"Me too," Linda lamented.

"I nearly had a heart attack. Jesus, Jack, you have to warn us about this stuff," George scolded as Ruth muttered in agreement.

Meanwhile, Daybreak turned to Linda and regarded her presence with interest. The lion's amber eyes flashed in the remaining rays of sunlight that came through the windows. She climbed down from her place on the boulder and brushed her head against Linda's shoulder, like Nicholas did to Linda's legs whenever she walked into the room.

"H-hi Daybreak," Linda said cautiously, and she gently pet the lion's immense head. Daybreak looked into her eyes before climbing back on the boulder and becoming still again. Linda realized that everyone was silent. She looked up and saw her friends staring at her with wide eyes. Linda turned to Jack and saw Mother Nature standing at the edge of the room, looking very pale.

"What's wrong?" Linda asked anxiously. "Doesn't everyone make friends with oversized housecats?"

Jack cleared his throat. "Um, no. Daybreak ignores everyone but Mother Nature."

"Oh," Linda said.

"I mean, I was staring because I was scared that the lion was going to eat you," George said.

"George!" Ruth scolded. She hit her brother's shoulder.

"Ow! Hey!" he said. "I was just being honest!"

FIFTY-ONE

STRONGER THAN SOJU

"I don't know if I could ever get used to that," George shuddered after Jack safely landed them all in front of Ruth's little house.

"I mean, it's not that bad. It's not like I dropped any of you," Jack commented.

"What?" George exclaimed. "*Dropped?*"

"Oh my God, Jack, don't scare him," Linda chided.

"That's it, I need soju," George said to Ruth as she started to unlock her periwinkle front door. "Do you still have that refrigerated bottle?"

"Of course, anything for my alcoholic *namdongsaeng*," Ruth said.

"I am not an alcoholic," George said.

"Can I have some?" Lavender asked as they all piled into Ruth's small kitchen, pulling back some of the chairs at the table.

"Of course," said Ruth.

"Absolutely not," said George.

"I'm fine with water," Linda interjected.

"Feel free to get out a glass," Ruth said as she pulled out the soju despite George's protests.

"Where are the glasses?" Linda asked.

"You two know where to find it," Ruth said to Jack and Linda, her eyes twinkling.

Jack and Linda glanced at each other. "No, we don't," they said hesitantly.

"I know you guys were here that one night," Ruth said. But she didn't sound mad. To Linda's shock, it sounded as if she was trying to hold back a chuckle.

"*You broke into my sister's house?*" Mr. London demanded. Lavender's jaw dropped.

"We thought Ruth was Jasmine!" Jack shot back defensively.

"Jack!" Linda exclaimed.

"Well, it's true," he retorted. "We knew that you had the sacred text at one point, Ruth."

"Ruth, what the hell?" George said.

Lavender took a shot of soju.

"Lavender!" George exclaimed, taking the bottle away from her.

"Can you blame me?" Lavender asked, barely able to mask her disgust at the burn of the alcohol. "Ew, how do you guys drink that all the time?"

"George, let the girl drink. Her ex turned out to be a homicidal maniac," Ruth said. "And *anyway*," she added quickly, cutting off her brother, "I didn't know it was *the* sacred book. Or that you guys were looking for one. I just found it, like I told Linda, and I felt like it was important, so I tried to transcribe it."

"How could you read the words?" Jack asked.

"I don't know, I just stared at it long enough," Ruth admitted.

"Okay, there will be no more underaged drinking in this house!" George said after Lavender snuck another sip of his soju.

Eventually, it was time for Lavender, Linda, and Jack to walk home. They said goodbye to Ruth and George and wished them a Merry Christmas (and Happy Yule for Ruth), and they made the short walk back to Lavender's house.

"Oh, fuck, I forgot to text them updates," Lavender groaned. "They're going to kill me."

"Maybe it's a good thing you weren't allowed to drink more," Linda commented.

"Hey, I think I earned the right to that shot," Lavender chuckled.

They each embraced before Jack and Linda said bye to Lavender, promising to hang out again soon, and watched her disappear inside. Just as they turned to walk away, the door burst open with a bang. Jack and Linda jumped as Lavender bounded out, tears streaming down her face. They could hear her parents yelling for her from inside.

"What's—" Linda started.

Lavender interrupted her. "M-my brother!"

"Damien? Is he okay?" Linda asked.

"No! It's Cody!" Lavender cried. "He's here! He's alive!" Lavender grabbed Linda's hand and pulled her into the house, Jack following close behind. Linda was scared to see a waterlogged little boy, but Cody was alive and well, and looked like nothing bad had ever happened to him. Although his face was flushed from Lavender's fussing and attention. Then Lavender's parents started to scold her for being out so long and smelling vaguely of alcohol, which they assumed was the reason she was obsessing over her little brother, as they had no memory of him ever being gone.

After they extricated themselves, Linda turned to Jack. "Take me to her house. Now."

They appeared in front of Kelsie's house. But the mourning drapes were still there. Linda ran around the corner of the aging grey abode to find Kelsie's room and looked in, praying that she would be there. The room was empty, but all of Kelsie's things remained, untouched. The lights were out. The family wasn't home.

"Take me to the cemetery," Linda demanded.

"Are you sure?" Jack asked. His eyes were soft with concern.

"Please," Linda begged, grabbing onto his waist.

"Okay," he said.

They landed in the cemetery. As soon as she got her bearings, Linda turned and ran, explaining through rushed breaths that she remembered where the grave was. Then suddenly, she stopped. And dropped to her knees. "I-I don't understand," Linda said as Jack approached her.

"I'm so sorry," he said as he knelt next to her in the snow and held her tightly. He knew her well enough by that point to know she was

275

about to cry, hard, in front of the grave covered with frozen and moldering flowers.

And Jack was right.

The carved name was clear, although etched with ice and frost: *Kelsie Robertson*.

FIFTY-TWO

THE BODY OF JANE CLARI

It was the next day. Jack steeled his nerves while he stood in front of the double marble doors that led to the prison beneath the palace. They were appropriately carved with scenes of imprisonment via thorns and brambles. He never liked that place. Ironically, it always gave him chills, and he always found a reason to be anywhere else. Especially when it meant that he had to interrogate the person that tried to kill his best friend. But no one else could do it, which meant he had to find a way to deal.

Twin water spirits stood guard in front of the doors, one on either side. Their natural forms distorted the carved marble. It was like staring at clear glass molded into the shape of very tall and heavyset people, but the glass was actually constant currents of running water. The angrier they got, the faster the water moved. The spirits were happy to serve Mother Nature, despite water spirits' natural inclination to flow freely in their original water source, because of her allowance for a certain number of drownings every year among other nature preservation efforts. *Sick bastards.*

"Hello, Jack Frost," the one on the left said. His name was a series of clicks and intonations that didn't directly translate into English from the Old Times (the language was still alive and well despite being nearly as ancient as Mother Nature). He and his brother shared the same name, so for informal situations, he liked to be called Edward.

"Here to see our prisoner?" the other twin, whose nickname was Ed, asked. He often liked to dye himself, and today he was tinted red from cochineal (it was his favorite color).

"Unfortunately," Jack sighed.

"You've got this," Ed smiled. "Just call Edward and I if you need anything." Edward nodded in agreement.

"Thanks," Jack answered. Ed gave him a fist bump before Edward opened one of the doors.

Jack walked slowly down the corridor between the barred prison cells, all of which were empty. Except the last one on the left. Every single part of his being wished that he was back at Linda's house, where he woke up on the couch that morning with Linda snuggled up against him after crying herself to sleep.

"Here to gloat?" Jasmine asked sourly as he approached her cell, bringing him back to the present.

A bitter taste rose in his mouth. "No," Jack answered. "You would know I'm not that kind of person."

Jasmine rolled her eyes. "You always were so boring. So, why are you here? To see if I regret my decisions so we can be friends and clear your conscience?"

"I mean, I hate you," Jack admitted to Jasmine. "I'm not here because I want to reconcile. I'm here because I care about Linda and her friends. Where is Jane Clari's body?"

Jasmine scoffed. "Everett Clari is being punished with the knowledge that he can't tell anyone about elves or magic or the end of the world."

"Everett Clari deserves to be in prison with other mortal murderers. Other humans deserve to know the truth about what happened to Jane."

"No."

"*No?*" Jack repeated with barely concealed indignation. A mental image of him ramming an icicle through her skull flashed through his mind, but he took a deep breath instead.

"I'm not doing anything for you," Jasmine said coolly. She stood up and moved to the back corner of her cell.

Jack inhaled sharply through his nose and crunched ice in his fist. "It's the *least* you can do."

She said nothing.

"Do it for Lavender," Jack said. Part of him worried that he would bust a blood vessel from all of the restraint he was practicing. *Jasmine will not get under my skin*, he told himself. *You are not the same person you used to be.*

In response, Jasmine called him a word that didn't have an English translation, and certainly didn't need one. She jerked her hand through the air in a sweeping motion. But nothing happened. She cursed again. "That hag stole my powers."

"You have nothing to lose, Jasmine. Just tell me."

"Thanks for the reminder," Jasmine sighed, resting her head against the surprisingly clean cell wall—Mother Nature felt it was more ethical. "*Fine*, I'll tell you where the body is buried."

After she grudgingly relayed all the details, Jack said, "Thank you, Jasmine." Then he turned on his heels and began to walk away.

"Jack!" Jasmine called after him.

"Yes?" he asked, stopping. But he didn't face her.

"Please tell Lavender that she wasn't part of the plan."

At first, he didn't say anything. Why should he do any favors for such a terrible being? He balled his hands into fists until his nails dug into his palms so much that he nearly drew blood. Jack closed his eyes and took a deep breath, letting it out slowly through his parted lips. "Alright," he said finally. Then he left, letting the heavy marble door echo through the silence.

After he said bye to the water spirits, Jack teleported back to his room and screamed into his pillow. And maybe created a crude ice effigy of Jasmine and punched her face off.

🍃

An elf, looking like a human child, toddled into the human police precinct in Maine.

"Can I help you?" the officer at the front desk asked.

"Wow, you look as beautiful as Mother Nature," the elf said, staring up at the officer in awe.

"Well, thank you, sweetheart," the officer smiled. "Now, how may I help you?"

"Can you give this note to the chief? It's important," the elf said, reaching up on his tiptoes to place the folded paper on the edge of the worn wooden desk.

"Um, sure, but what's your name?" the officer asked, examining the paper.

"Hyacinth," the elf answered sweetly, curling his mousey brown hair in his fingers. "Okay, I have to run! The paper is very important. Don't lose it!"

"Um, okay. Wait—!" the officer called. She finished reading the note and her eyes nearly popped out of her head. "Chief Rosenthal!"

❧

The next morning, Linda met her parents and her siblings at the kitchen counter. Kris and Emily fought over the blueberry muffins while Linda's mom looked like she wanted to pour a bottle of brandy into her French vanilla coffee. Linda's dad read the paper.

"Hey, kids, stop it!" their dad said without looking up. He snapped his fingers three times. "Listen to this! The Jane Clari case is closed!"

"What?" Linda asked. Even though she knew the answer.

"Jane's body was found. Everett Clari, the town's local attorney, is behind this mess. And his brother, Tim Clari, who's also Jane's father, it seems. Everett claimed that his niece's death was an accident during a big fight. And that some elves helped him bury the body because he promised to help prevent the end of the world. What a sicko," her dad said, closing the paper with disgust. "The police received an anonymous tip about him and where the body was buried. And when the detective brought Everett Clari to the location, he broke down and confessed to everything."

"Wasn't Tim Clari the drunk guy who wrecked the Robertsons'…" Emily started to ask, but her voice trailed off as their mom shook her head.

"Yeah, it was," Linda said. "I'm okay, Mom, it's just a fact."

"The paper speculates that Everett Clari's goddaughter, Jasmine, left because she found out the truth," her dad added. "That seems like shoddy journalism, but who knows."

"Most female victims are killed by men that they knew," Kris interjected solemnly.

"Well, that's unsettling," their mom said. "Where did you learn that?"

"In that women's studies class," Kris explained.

"Apparently, Everett Clari is trying to get off with an insanity claim, but it sounds like he had his mental break after the crime, so it won't work," their dad added. "Well, how about some morning brownies?"

"Mike! Those were for later!"

Linda shook her head, slipping off the stool and escaping back to her room. Nicholas was fast asleep on her bed in a pool of winter sunlight. Linda buried her face in his warm fur as he mewed sleepily in protest. She pulled back a moment later, catching her breath and spitting out some orange fur. The cat looked up at her as if thinking, "What did you expect?" Then he blinked slowly before closing his eyes again and stretching, extending his claws and showing his sharp white teeth while he yawned. Linda turned away to look out the window, wishing she was a cat whose only concern was which comfy place to sleep. She looked down and saw something sitting on the outside part of the windowsill. It was a honey cake.

FIFTY-THREE

CODY

Later that day, Linda's parents drove all five of them to the mall. Linda split off early after agreeing to meet back at the food court in an hour. As she wandered, she looked down at her hand. She had gotten so used to the ring that Jack had given her, but it was still gone after Jasmine had broken it. Linda rubbed her naked ring finger with her thumb. The events still felt so surreal, even though she knew they had happened. Jack was trying to keep Linda busy, and they were meeting that evening to hang out. He had suggested inviting Lavender, but Linda still wasn't ready for her to come to her home, which felt ridiculous after staring her own death in the face. How could she be scared of another girl friend coming to hang out with her? But it still bothered her. Somehow Kelsie's death was still more surreal and bizarre than being the only thing hanging in the balance between reality and the apocalypse while a deranged elf stabbed her.

Linda almost bumped into someone, which she realized after hearing some disgruntled muttering from a man carrying a few too many bags as he left the store. Linda looked up and saw that she made her way into a gift shop, which seemed appropriate. Other people milled about in the space, down through the packed shelves, exclaiming to each other things like, "this'll be perfect for so-and-so!" Almost every non-gift-related surface was decorated in faux pine garlands, red ribbons, pinecones, and shimmering gold and silver glitter. The over-the-top display was comforting to Linda, though. It reminded her of the best parts of her childhood even though Kris and Emily complained about how commercialized Christmas had become. Not that they were very Christian, just that another holiday was being consumed by the capitalist machine and no one seemed bothered by it. But for Linda, it was just one of the few consistent things in her life, like how no matter what, summer would become fall, fall became winter, and the snow would melt in the spring. Jack Frost would whine and complain. Beautiful consistencies like that.

"Can I help you, miss?" a friendly sales associate asked. Linda looked up. The associate was a young woman, barely older than her, but decked out in tinsel, jingle bells, and an antler headband.

"No, thank you, I'm just looking," Linda said, trying not to blush. Had she spaced out that much?

"Okay! Let me know if you need anything," she said cheerily, practically skipping away. A fake deer tail bobbed from one of her emerald-green belt loops. *That can't be comfortable to sit on,* Linda thought. Then she tried to refocus. *Gift shop. Gifts. Gifts for her friends. Right.* She pulled out the list that her mom helped her make earlier. It read:

Lavender: canvas

Mr. London: fancy red grading pen (to crush more dreams)

Ruth: new weird tea (metaphysical store?)

Emily: hot guy calendar

Kris: nerdy book

Nicholas: catnip

Jack: ???

Kelsie: flowers

Her mom barely hid her shock for the last entry. Linda ended up admitting that she was thinking about visiting Kelsie's grave. Her mom almost spit out her coffee, and her dad's coffee shot out of his nose.

"What?" Linda demanded.

"N-nothing, sweetie," her dad insisted as he patted her mom's back.

"It's great," her mom finally managed.

"Are you okay?"

"Totally," her mom said.

Linda still didn't know what to get for Jack. But before she got accosted by the Christmas princess again, she focused on looking through the aisles. She found the calendars and picked up a sexy firefighter calendar for Emily (an applicable gift but also a subtle way of calling her sister shallow). *What Christmas gift can a mortal even give to an immortal nature spirit?* Linda wondered with annoyance. She knew that gifts weren't everything, especially for a mortal festival that spirits didn't recognize, but she still wanted to give him something tangible when he visited on Christmas Day like they had planned. Maybe something to remind him of her in Pryddia. Although she felt silly for thinking like that.

As she was about to go to the cashier, Linda found the back of the store, which was filled with shining glassware and photo frames on glass shelves. She picked up one of the chrome frames and set it back down. It reminded her a lot of one of the framed photos Kelsie had given her one year with hearts glued onto it. Linda was about to turn away when a cornflower blue frame caught her eye. The color was like the shadows in deep snow. She remembered that her mom had insisted she take a photo of the only normal snowman that she and Jack made with its creators before it could melt. She made a quick decision.

After paying at a cash register that was so sparkly it nearly made her eyes bleed, Linda set out in search of the metaphysical store for Ruth's gift. Her mom had been surprised about Linda's sudden affinity for the weird woman down the street, but it was hard to explain the whole end-of-the-world thing without sounding like a lunatic. So, Linda just said that they became friends after the break-in.

"Hey Linda!" someone jeered. Linda looked around until she found the source: Beatrice. "What are you doing alone? I'm surprised you're not with John. I heard it's been getting hot and heavy. Did he take your virginity?"

"The dyke probably misses you, too," Heather sneered.

Linda's face grew hot with rage as she stared at them. Her hands shook. She wanted to yell at them that they didn't know what they were talking about. She wanted to say that their entire lives were being wasted on stupid shit that didn't even matter while their peers were murdered or while they narrowly missed the end of the world. That Jack and Lavender were amazing, unlike them, and that shitty people like them must sit alone in the dark and cry and deserve it.

But Linda didn't say any of that. She looked at Beatrice and Heather, into their stupid smirking faces coated with makeup to hide the pimples that everyone got and gloss to enhance their normal lips, and said, "I feel sorry for you."

They spluttered.

"Happy holidays," Linda said as she turned and walked away. She still shook and was so lost in her thoughts of ways to wish pain on her enemies that she nearly ran over her sister.

"Woah, Linda," Emily said, regaining her balance. "Didn't you hear me, Sunshine? I said I found that thing you wanted for Nicholas. Don't worry about paying me back, you're too dependent." Emily offered the shopping bag to Linda.

"T-thanks," Linda stammered as her brain refocused. She looked in the bag. "Thank you so much! I was looking everywhere for it."

"You're welcome," Emily said, softening momentarily. She looked past Linda. "Were those girls bothering you? Is that Emilia Colton's little sister?"

Linda looked back before nodding.

"Oh man, I'll be right back. I gotta catch up for… old time's sake," Emily said, shoving her armload of presents into Linda's hands. "Don't peek or I'll kill you."

Emily marched over to Beatrice and Heather. Linda couldn't catch everything her sister said but the two girls looked mortified. Heather yanked her cell phone out of her purse and began to screech to her mom.

"What did you say?" Linda demanded as she followed her sister down the escalators to the food court, trying hard to not look over the side and get vertigo.

"Oh, I just told her how much I missed her Adderall-dealing skank of a sister," Emily said nonchalantly. "Something tells me that Most-

Likely-to-Succeed Prom Queen Emilia didn't tell her parents about the Adderall she was stealing from her dad's pharmacy or getting caught giving—"

"Okay, I've heard enough," Linda said, whacking her sister with the bags to get her to shut up. "Anyway, thank you."

"Who said I did that for you? That girl had it coming," Emily said as they walked up to the chipping laminate food court table where Kris sipped coffee with their parents.

"Good Lord, Linda, what did you buy?" her mom asked.

"They're mostly Emily's," Linda said, putting them on the floor next to an open chair. "Can we print a copy of that photo you took of me and Jack with the snowman?"

"Jack!" Linda called into the hallway.

"What?" he asked, hurrying to the bathroom. "What's wrong?"

"Okay, this might sound crazy, but didn't I used to have freckles?" she asked. She turned to look back in the mirror, stretching and pulling at her skin. "My freckles are gone!" Linda whispered in disbelief.

"Let me see," Jack said, cupping her face in his hands and looking closely. "Huh. They are gone."

If she hadn't been so alarmed, she would've gone into shock from how close his face was to hers. She felt puffs of breath from his nose. His hands were warm and gentle. *Did immortals use shea butter to moisturize? Pull it together*, she thought, feeling her face burn. Her heart fluttered like it was about to take flight. She wished it wouldn't. "I remember feeling the book binding crack again when I landed on it." Then she grimaced. "I wish I wasn't reminded of that," she said quietly, feeling her back tingle.

"Wait," Jack exclaimed.

"What?" Linda asked. Then, "Oh my god."

"Lavender's brother."

"Oh God, that must be what happened," Linda said, suddenly

feeling sick. She leaned heavily against the sink counter. Jack sat down on the floor.

"I was hoping that there was some other anomaly that caused Lavender's brother to come back to life," Jack said.

"I'm so sorry—"

"Don't be sorry, Linda."

Emily walked up to the doorway. "What's wrong with you two?" she asked. "You're not pregnant, are you?"

"Get a life," Jack snapped at her. Emily's eyes went wide, and her cheeks went beet red. She didn't say anything as she walked away.

"Damn, Jack," Linda said, offering a hand to help him up.

He accepted. "Sorry, it slipped."

"You're not sorry," Linda chuckled. "I don't blame you."

They walked to a more private area of the house to talk out of earshot.

"So, some aspects of reality and time were altered after all," Linda said quietly.

"It's not your fault, Linda," Jack said adamantly.

"Yes, it is," Linda said sourly. "I was the one who damaged the book. I also bled all over it."

"Yeah, because you were protecting it from being destroyed by a sword," Jack pointed out. "Can you imagine what would've happened if Jasmine really did slash the book? Or shred the binding? It would've been an irreversible nightmare."

Then Linda's mom found them and requested that they cut out a gajillion snowflakes for the Christmas party in a few days.

"But Mom—" Linda started.

"We need things to be festive! Your father's parents will be coming!" her mom said, dropping a bunch of white paper and two pairs of scissors in Linda's hands.

"You know how to make snowflakes, don't you?" Linda asked Jack.

"Of course I do."

"But like with paper?"

"It is still a worthy art, like ice skating."

"You're hopeless."

"Wanna have a contest?"

"Sure."

"I'll make you eat your words," he said seriously.

"Oh my god, Jack," Linda said.

After he busted out three immaculately detailed snowflakes while she was still finishing her first, Linda commented slyly, "Wow, I've never seen you so focused."

Jack smirked without looking up. "Shut up, you know I'd ace a class about snowflakes."

Linda watched Jack working quietly, his profile softly outlined by the lights on the Christmas tree behind him. Jack looked beautiful. The thought startled Linda. Not because she never thought that before, but her heart fluttered at the memory of accidentally trying to kiss him in his bedroom. She remembered what Lavender had said to her—that Jack liked her.

He looked up, as if about to say something, but stopped when he noticed that she was already looking. "What?" he asked.

"Nothing," she said immediately, but she started blushing. He smiled at her. She folded her arms. "What?"

"You're cute when you blush," he said. Then he chuckled when her face grew even hotter.

"Shut up, Jack," Linda said. Her phone buzzed. Lavender sent Linda a text. *Is this real? My brother being back? We're the only ones who remember he died. He just said he had a bad dream that he drowned.*

Linda replied, *Jack said it's real.*

Not even five seconds later, Lavender said: *How???*

Linda typed back: *The book got a bit damaged between me and Jasmine. They said it's still better than what almost happened.*

Lavender didn't respond.

I'm so sorry, Linda messaged.

No response.

Lavender?

No response.

Lavender, Linda texted again. *I'm coming over.* Linda went and threw on her coat and crammed her feet into her boots, Jack following close behind.

"I had a dream that I died," Lavender's little brother said at the dinner table.

"It was just a nightmare," her dad said.

"It felt so real, like I drowned in that lake we used to go trout fishing at," Cody insisted.

Damien and Lavender exchanged looks. Cody never talked about dreams like that. But Lavender, unlike Damien, knew why.

"Cody, it was just a dream," their mom said. "You're awake now, it's over."

"But what if it happens again?" Cody asked.

"It'll be okay. You'll wake up again and it'll be all over," their dad said. "Besides, once you smell your mom's muffins in the morning, you'll feel better. Marie, those were divine. Wait! Lavender!" her father called after her as she fled the table.

Lavender ran up the stairs to her room and closed the door behind her despite her parents' protests. She didn't mean to be so dramatic, but she let out strangled sobs as she tried to push her pain back in. How could she explain to her parents that her brother wasn't dreaming, that she remembered years of her life without Cody?

She texted Linda angrily. *What had happened?* Lavender thought that they saved the book, and that was the end of that. She could've just taken the memory-wiping drug, but she didn't, and now she had to remember. Lavender had nightmares about seeing Linda's blood everywhere, of seeing her own ex-girlfriend running Linda through with a sword. The pure rage on Jasmine's face. Maybe she should've listened to Mother Nature and just forgotten everything.

"Lavender!" her mom yelled up the stairs.

"What?" Lavender called back.

"Your friends, Linda and Jack, are here!" her mom announced in her Québécois accent. "This had better be a fast visit!" Lavender wiped her face and bounded down the stairs as her mom continued, "You know how I don't like last-minute visits like this."

"Hi, Lavender," Linda said quietly, Jack standing right behind her.

"Come on, let's go to my room," Lavender said, pulling Linda upstairs after her. Once Jack closed the door behind them, Lavender dumped everything.

"That's okay, Lavender, it's a big adjustment," Linda said reassuringly.

"And I, as an expert in finding out people have come back to life, think you're actually handling it quite well," Jack interjected.

"Wait, has this happened before?" Lavender asked earnestly.

"Well, no, not exactly," Jack said, and he summed up Jasmine's dead-then-return arc.

"You killed Jasmine?" Lavender demanded, her mouth hanging open.

"Oh my god, I just thought I did, okay? Anyway, Jasmine tried to kill Linda—" Linda grimaced at his mention "—so you shouldn't feel bad for her."

"Wow, this is a lot to take in," Lavender said, rubbing her face.

"Yes, it is," Linda chuckled. "Knowledge can be a burden. Do you wish you still thought Jack and I were mysterious?"

"Well…" Lavender started. She took a deep breath then continued. "Sometimes I think about whether or not I made the wrong choice about taking the memory loss thing, but there are moments like this where I'm glad I didn't."

Jack made a face. "Like right now?"

"Well, yeah," Lavender laughed drily. "I like the truth. I feel like everyone is trying to hide it so much as it is. Maybe I'm… ready to face it."

"Are you still talking about the thing with Jasmine?" Linda asked, her eyes twinkling.

"I'm glad that I have my little brother back," Lavender smiled. "Do you want to go meet him for real this time? Cody loves Mario Kart."

FIFTY-FOUR

THE HOLIDAY OF BIRTH

T he next morning was Christmas, which Linda took as an opportunity to wake up her siblings at the crack of dawn, as per tradition. She started with Emily, an easy target since her sister's bed was across the room. Linda shook her awake and then ran to her brother's and jumped on him (oh, the joy of being the youngest). Eventually, after everyone was up, Linda waited with Nicholas at the Christmas tree while the elders grogged for caffeine with her parents. Then they unceremoniously opened the presents. Emily passed Linda a small dark blue box tied with a shimmery ice-blue ribbon. Tied around the ribbon was a white card that said, *To Linda*, in Jack's careful cursive. Linda set it aside for later.

After an hour, with everyone appropriately appreciating their gifts while Nicholas was high on catnip, there was a knock at the door. "I'll get it!" Linda yelled, running to the front of the house. For a moment, she paused, a shiver running through her as she remembered when Jasmine slammed the door into her face. But it wasn't Jasmine outside, she reminded herself, it was Jack. As planned.

Then Jack and Linda sat down in the hallway and exchanged presents. Jack tediously unstuck the tape while he unwrapped his, citing that this was his first-ever Christmas gift and wanted to savor the moment, but Linda felt like he was just trying to torture her. Linda pulled the end of the ribbon on her gift and the paper fell open in her lap, revealing a little box made of magical ice (it wouldn't melt without Jack's explicit instruction, she found out). She took the top off, and inside sat a small golden heart. Linda picked it up and realized it was a necklace from its trailing delicate gold chain. She looked closer at the pendant and saw that *For Linda* was carved carefully into the front. She turned it over and saw that *Love, Jack* was inscribed into the back. She ran her fingertips over the words.

"Jack, I love it!" Linda exclaimed, tackling him with a hug.

"Hey, hey, careful!" Jack said, falling back and holding up the framed photo. "Aren't these made of glass?"

For a moment, their noses were almost touching, but Linda pulled back and grabbed the necklace. "Can you put it on me?" she asked, handing it to him.

"Oh yeah, um, sure," he said, putting down the picture. She lifted her hair for him while he clasped the necklace around her neck. His fingers brushed against her skin, sending volts of warm electricity through her.

"Hey, kids, come on! Guests will be here in two hours!" Linda's mom yelled from the living room. "This place needs to be spotless!"

George found himself lingering at the Christmas punch bowl, as usual. The development of cell phones was certainly a necessary evil, and whenever he wasn't awkwardly watching the other people at the party, he awkwardly scrolled through social media. He could've already been at his parents' house, but he had agreed to go to his college friend, Steve Li's, party because they just had an adorable child who, for some unknown reason, they named Aphrodite. Clearly Steve and his wife, Hong, had never met teenagers. But they did make an adorable baby with a mop of spiky jet-black hair. George thought that Aphrodite was likely to be the future of punk rock if she kept it up.

George had forgotten how many people Steve and Hong knew and he reverted to his wallflower ways. Even on the rare occasion where he was forced to supervise a school dance (*God, the torture*), he found himself no longer attempting to be the commanding voice in the room while he clung to the edges of the bedecked gym, wishing he was elsewhere instead of breaking up the occasional hormone- and idiocy-fueled scuffle.

His mind drifted to Linda when he looked down at his drink. God, there was so much blood. The color of the spiced sangria was almost dark enough to be the color of blood, which wasn't helping him let it go. He had no idea how Linda was managing (Ruth promised to keep him updated) with remembering everything. It was disturbing enough to see and hear about everything, much less experience it. But he had a feeling that despite it all, she was going to be okay. And if she wasn't, she had them. His therapist was actually quite pleased with his progress, unless the topic of his ex-wife came up. Then Dr. Nathan's tight smile reappeared.

"Hey, you okay there?" a man asked.

George looked up, expecting to find Steve singling him out for being a loner just like during undergrad, but he found someone else. Even in the dimmed light ("for the ambience," according to Steve), George could tell that the man was gorgeous.

"H-hi," George stammered, wishing that he could hide his blush. "Yeah, just a bit tired. The holidays have been... a lot."

"I get what you mean," the man laughed. The sound was as warm as his deep brown skin.

"How do you know Steve?" George asked, clearing his throat.

"Oh, I know Hong. One of the gay best friends and all that," he said. "How do you know Steve?"

"We went to undergrad together," George said.

"Were you a wallflower then too?" the man asked.

"Yeah, the quiet bi one from the small town. Steve practically had to peel me off the wall," George chuckled. "What's your name, by the way?"

"My name's Carson. Yours?" Carson said, sticking out a hand.

"George. Nice to meet you," he answered as he accepted it.

Linda and Jack hovered by the adults-only punch bowl filled with spiked mulled wine. Since most of the people were her parent's friends and coworkers, middle-aged people she vaguely knew would stop her and say things like, "Oh my goodness! You've grown so much!" or "Wow! You're so tall!" or even better, "I can't believe it! You're in high school!" Somehow, Kris's and Emily's friends were even worse because Linda actually knew them.

Eventually, Linda dragged Jack down cellar to escape for a bit. "Adults are just so boring," Linda whined.

"I don't know why you guys ever want to grow up. It just seems to get worse," Jack agreed.

"It does!" Linda exclaimed.

"Is that mistletoe?" Jack asked, pointing to a sprig of dried leaves stuck between some of the ceiling panels.

"Oh, Emily must've put that there," Linda groaned.

"I honestly don't get the romantic significance. Mistletoe is a parasite," Jack commented. "Although…" he stopped for a moment, taking a breath as if he was mentally preparing himself. "Sometimes I feel like I'm a parasite to you."

"What? Why?" Linda demanded.

"I thought you were going to take the Lily of Sleeping Death when you woke up. I know it's selfish to be worried about you forgetting about me after all that I caused in your life, but—"

"Oh, Jack," Linda interrupted. She reached up and touched Jack's cheek. "I was never going to forget you." He grasped her hand and held it against his face, closing his eyes for a moment. Their foreheads bumped and so did their noses. A thrill shot down to Linda's toes like electricity, or like a ton of ravenous butterflies that made her insides feel like jelly. Jack's eyes were so soft as he looked down at her, and she felt his lips brush against hers. She stood on her tiptoes and kissed him. When he pulled away slightly, she grabbed onto his hoodie and pulled him back to her and kissed him again.

Jack giggled.

"Jack!" Linda exclaimed.

"I'm sorry! I just didn't expect you to do that," he said as she playfully swatted him.

"You're too tall."

"I know one way to fix that," he said, and before she could protest, he picked her up.

"Jack!" Linda shrieked before laughing. He kissed her cheek before putting her back down.

FIFTY-FIVE

HOLY SEPULCHER

"**A**re you sure you're ready?" Linda's mom asked as the car rolled into the cemetery parking lot. Her dad looked back at his youngest daughter for her answer.

"Yes, I think so," Linda said, although it came out more unsteady than she wanted. The pale lilies in her bouquet shook slightly from her trembling grip.

"No matter what, we're playing a board game after this, and I'm going to destroy you," Kris said helpfully from the backseat.

Linda rolled her eyes. "Thanks, Kris."

"Unless I destroy you first," Emily added.

"You guys are so annoying," Linda said as she unbuckled and opened the car door. A small breeze wafted into the car, filling her nostrils with the smell of clean winter air tinged with burning firewood from a nearby house. It was comforting.

Linda's feet crunched on the snow as she climbed out. She began walking into the cemetery after her family members joined her, clutching the bouquet for Kelsie tightly in her gloved hands. They had picked it up earlier that morning from the local flower shop, and unfortunately, the florist had recognized Linda from the funeral and decided to express condolences. It had tested Linda's resolve, but she was determined. Linda also held a framed laminated photo of her and Kelsie. She knew Kelsie probably wouldn't be able to see it, but it still felt meaningful anyway.

When she finally stopped in front of the same gravestone as the night of the end of the world, the same name was still chiseled into the rectangular slab: *Kelsie Robertson.* Part of Linda hoped that a different name would be on it this time, but of course, it was just wishful thinking. She knew now that what happened to Lavender's brother was random chance, just like Kelsie's car being the one that Everett and Tim Clari crashed into. Just like the snow and trees changing in the forest. Just like her freckles disappearing. Just like Jack Frost being her boyfriend. She didn't have to understand everything, and she knew that even Father Time didn't understand why certain timelines were more fragile than others.

Some things just are.

Linda bent forward and began to clear away the dead flowers that heaped at the base of Kelsie's granite headstone. She put them in the trash bag that she brought with her. Then she wiped the headstone with her glove, clearing off the two inches of snow piled neatly on top, and tried her best to wipe off the snow and ice from the carved letters.

Small snowflakes began to gently drift down through the air and land on the silent graves. Linda knew it was Jack's way of being there with her. She had just wanted to come alone, just to be with her late best friend. The only sounds were the nearby trees creaking in the breeze and the sound of her siblings walking through the rows of graves, looking for older ones.

Linda put down the bundle of white lilies against the headstone, along with the framed photo of the two of them making silly faces after being hyped up on sugar and Mario Kart.

"I'll see you again soon," Linda said quietly. "I love you."

And then she began to cry.

AFTERWORD

Thank you for spending time with *The Fall of Linda Waters*. If parts of this story stirred difficult emotions, please know that your experience matters.

This book includes themes of loss, grief, isolation, and identity struggles—woven with elements of supernatural peril and emotional ambiguity. These were explored through a lens of healing and connection, but they may have hit close to home.

If you found any part of this journey triggering, take what you need to recover—whether that's rest, reflection, or reaching out for support. You are not alone.

With care,

R.E. Kurz

ACKNOWLEDGEMENTS

A great deal of people helped make this novel possible. My mother, Amy Kurz—forever a teacher—encouraged me to keep writing when I first became interested in the craft in middle school. My father, Richard Kurz, introduced me to *The Lord of the Rings*, which inspired me to make up my own stories. My brother, Ian, always answered my technical questions about character injuries. Thank you to Dr. Thomas O'Donnell for making me see that writing could be a form of powerful self-expression when I really needed it (and for always supporting me and my antics). I also couldn't have completed this book without my friends and family who've read it over the years, especially Lucia Simova and Ayoush Srivastava. And thank you to Soncata Press for seeing something special in my first novel.

ABOUT THE AUTHOR

R.E. Kurz has been passionate about storytelling since starting to write *The Fall of Linda Waters* at age 12. Over the years, the project only continued to grow. R.E. holds a degree in Biological Sciences with a minor in Medieval Studies from Fordham University. R.E.'s writing has been published in *The Ampersand* and *Bricolage Journal*. When not writing, R.E. is passionate about advocating for social justice and reading more old books—the more ancient, the better.

Connect with R.E. Kurz on:
    Instagram: @re.kurz.author
    TikTok: @r.e.kurz.author
    X: @REKurz_author

Stay updated about upcoming events by visiting the author's website at www.rekurzauthor.com.

www.ingramcontent.com/pod-product-compliance
Lightning Source LLC
Chambersburg PA
CBHW030625110726
47901CB00002B/326